FORTUNE

ALSO BY AMANDA SMYTH

Black Rock
A Kind of Eden

AMANDA SMYTH

FORTUNE

PEEPAL TREE

First published in Great Britain in 2021
Peepal Tree Press Ltd
17 King's Avenue
Leeds LS6 1QS
England

ISBN13: 9781845235192

Supported using public funding by
ARTS COUNCIL
ENGLAND

In memory of Kim Robinson

ONE

Somewhere between Gasparillo and Chaguanas on the Southern Main Road, Eddie felt the engine slipping and gasping as if catching its breath and every now and then he heard a pop-pop and he hoped it would hold out, at least until he got to Strong Man. But there it was, broken down with smoke gushing out of it. He knew it wasn't gasoline and he knew he had water. The fan belt, maybe, or even the piston rings. No point looking under the bonnet until it cooled down.

He lit a cigarette, wondered how he could get a message to his uncle. A white sun punctured the sky, and there was a hard glare; some clouds low over the central hills. Not a good time to be stranded. No matter, somebody would come along at some point. He'd passed at least two cars heading this way, a buffalo cart full of coconuts and he'd almost stopped the old Indian man because his mouth was claggy, and then thought better of it. The cart would catch up eventually, unless the man had turned off the road already.

Glad of his hat, Eddie rolled down his sleeves and walked a little up the bank. A samaan tree offered some shade and from here he could see the direction he'd come from and think what to do. The land around was crispy and dry, hills scarred with black marks and drifts of pale smoke. He'd seen it too often, a bottle thrown, a careless cigarette, and next thing the whole hill was roasting like a side of meat. He spotted a brown dog with its belly bloated poking out of the grass. Just yesterday he'd hit a stray when it ran out into Coffee Street. He got out to check the bumper – surprised to find it there and hollering, its back leg jerking uncontrollably. Two children were playing marbles on the side of the road so he gave them each five cents for a soda and when they'd gone, not wanting it to suffer, he drove over the dog and crushed its head.

Eddie finished up his cigarette, and went back to the truck. He lifted up the bonnet and peered inside; nothing looked out of the ordinary. He checked the sky and saw vultures floating high like black stars. It occurred to him, it could actually be hours before anyone came by; he might as well set off on foot. He made his way down the other side and the road was blurred. From his hip flask he took a gulp of warm rum and it swooshed easily down his parched throat. He put his bag on his back, checked his watch and set out towards the capital. He'd be there by nightfall if he was lucky.

As he walked along the edge of the cane fields, his face poured with sweat, his feet were hot and swollen in his cracked boots. Cicadas were clacking and droning, a loud, unnatural, mechanical sound, as if something mighty was about to explode. And the thought came to him: none of this mattered, the heat, his thirst, the broken-down truck; what mattered was his meeting this morning with Sonny Chatterjee. He could hardly believe what he'd seen.

Over the years, rumours of black puddles appearing on the land had drawn oil men to Sonny Chatterjee's estate. Buried deep in South Trinidad, Kushi was a cocoa plantation of fifty acres; it had belonged in the Chatterjee family since 1905. Seen pooling at the foot of a tree, swirling on the skin of the Godineau river, there was talk of oil running free like honey along the path to Sonny's door. But Sonny Chatterjee had a reputation as a difficult and ignorant man. So far, no one had persuaded him to let them test the land, let alone drill on it.

Eddie had been watching it for a while now. The first time he turned up, Chatterjee shooed him away.

A week later, Eddie came back with a crate of pineapples.

'You again?'

Chatterjee's eyes were bleary from sleep.

'Yes sir, there are things to talk about.'

'I just wake up. You can't see that?'

'It won't take long. But if you'd prefer, I'll come back another time.' Eddie left the crate on the ground, and went back to his truck.

A couple weeks later he returned. 'I knew your father, Madoo,' Eddie said, as he walked towards Chatterjee, sitting outside the house in his white dhoti. It was late afternoon. 'My uncle owns Mon Repos.'

Chatterjee narrowed his eyes. 'Which Madoo?'

'Old man Madoo with the short foot.'

Eddie hadn't forgotten the sight of Madoo's crooked figure on horseback; one leg longer than the other, a birth defect. Some years ago, Eddie had heard that Madoo was electrocuted by a falling cable outside a pharmacy in San Fernando.

'Your uncle own Mon Repos?'

'I used to see your father when I was a boy, riding through fields of citrus shouting orders.'

'That's him,' Chatterjee said. 'He like to play boss,' and he told Eddie how his father sailed from Calcutta to Trinidad on the *Golden Fleece*, then after years of working at Mon Repos, traded his return passage to India for $5, and a piece of land. He planted cocoa trees. He'd offered loans to the villagers with high interest rates. He'd made a small fortune.

Chatterjee put out his arms, 'Bhap come here with nothing; he make all this.'

Eddie told Chatterjee how, like him, he'd lost his father; how it turned him quickly into a man.

'When your father pass, you can't stand in the shade.'

'Yes,' Chatterjee said. 'You must walk in the hot sun.'

Eddie called in to see Chatterjee every couple of weeks. He made the excuse that he was visiting his uncle nearby. He brought oranges, or mangoes, or bananas; whatever was falling off the trees. Chatterjee didn't thank him but he took what he brought. At first they stood by the truck and smoked a cigarette. Then after he had visited a few times, Eddie was invited to sit in the porch with the broken-down wall, where a warm breeze blew. They never ventured beyond here; the rest of the estate was out of bounds. Eddie was desperate to see it.

While they talked, Sita brought tea or juice, and she looked at Eddie from the sides of her eyes. She wore her hair in a plait, and her face was set, as if she had eaten something sour.

Eddie was sure that Chatterjee knew why he was there. Once

he said, 'If you come for oil, you may as well leave right now.'

Eddie kept quiet.

Chatterjee seemed exhausted; dark rings under his bloodshot eyes. He was only thirty-seven, but he looked twenty years older. Everything at Kushi looked tired. Walls needed paint, the yard was full of junk and there were buckets everywhere ready to catch rain when it fell.

Eddie asked, 'You have water?'

'We have tanks but no pump.'

Then Chatterjee told Eddie about the strange mushrooms he'd found clinging to the branches of his cocoa trees. He'd lopped off the diseased branches, cut away the rotten pods.

'From Brazil to these islands, millions of cocoa trees are dying. It's not just Kushi, Sonny. The whole of Trinidad is the same thing.'

'They say put oil, sprinkle flour. Scorch the trunk until it black and they fall off. I try all that. I get on my knees and pray.'

Eddie wanted to tell Chatterjee: forget cocoa, it's finished, but he figured Chatterjee wasn't ready to hear it. He'd wait.

Then the moment came when Chatterjee asked Eddie what was inside the bag he always carried. Eddie opened up the cowhide satchel. He brought out a folder with papers, documents, photographs.

'This, sir,' Eddie said, picking through them, 'is Beaumont, Texas. And this is where I once leased a piece of land, this land here with nothing on it.' The photograph showed about an acre of grass and a small shed. Eddie was standing next to it alongside another man, their eyes squinting in the sun. 'My partner, Michael Callaghan.' There was another photograph of this same land with a tall structure, and a metal pick.

'This cable tool, here, goes into the ground.' Then, 'This is what happened.' Eddie held up the photograph.

Chatterjee leaned in, pointed to the black mark on the image.

'That's oil coming out of the ground. It's called a gusher.'

Eddie had cuttings of newspapers showing pictures of cars, trucks.

'It's the future, Sonny.'

Chatterjee looked away at the early blue light sifting through the leaves of the immortelle. Mist hung in the bush giving the place a dreamy look.

'Cocoa's in serious trouble,' Eddie told him. 'You might save some of these trees, but chances are they'll take years to produce. You have something much more valuable and you're sitting right on it.'

'So they tell me,' Chatterjee said, lolling his head. 'Apex, Texaco, Leaseholds, all of them. They say I could make a few dollars.'

'I'm not talking about a few dollars. I'm talking plenty money.' Eddie held his hand high from the ground.

'Money to send your children abroad to study, buy yourself a new car; fix up your house. Buy your wife a diamond ring or a herd of cows. Pay a doctor when you need one. Apex won't tell you how much money is under your feet because they want it for themselves.'

All the while Chatterjee looked into the darkness.

'You understand? You're not dealing with a person; you're talking to a corporation. They don't care about the small man. Believe me, Sonny, they'll try to convince you that you're a small man.'

He didn't tell Chatterjee that just last week he'd been to see Charles Macleod – Apex's senior operations manager, to talk about employment. Macleod had spoken of oil on Chatterjee's estate. He'd called Chatterjee a 'coolie fool'.

The pay was as good as anything else Eddie might find in Trinidad, but there was something about Macleod that made his skin bristle, the strange force of the man, his bloodless complexion, eyes twitchy like fleas. Could you dislike someone because his eyes twitched? It would seem so.

And while Eddie kept quiet about Macleod, Chatterjee didn't tell Eddie that Charles Macleod had been to see him two days ago, and offered him a holding fee of $1000.

Eddie said, 'I've learned something, Sonny, we must set our sights on the future. There's no point looking back; we're not going that way. Sometimes you have to destroy the old to make way for the new. If you want me to help you I can.'

Then, this morning, after months of visiting, Chatterjee took Eddie by surprise.

'You have money to get started here at Kushi?'

Eddie looked at him. 'I need to speak to some people. But yes, there's money around. We can do some tests, take a look at what's there.'

'Why not see what you can do.'

Chatterjee walked Eddie back to his truck, where his boys were sitting in front, twisting the wheel, thin as sticks. He clapped his hands.

'Sons, show Mister Eddie what you find.'

They jumped down and ran off towards the forest. For the first time, Eddie was taken deeper into the estate. He followed the boys along a trail through semi darkness.

Eddie saw how the cocoa trees were bowed and wilted and rotting. He could see their spores, the marble patterning on their trunks; there was a smell of rot. Parts of the estate were overgrown, evidence that Chatterjee had long since given up. They climbed through ferns; high silver shrubs stalked up; dangling vines low like trip wires. They picked their way through until they found a clearing.

One of the boys found a thin pipe, and taking a heavy stone, hammered the pipe into the ground. Eddie watched a spurt of black liquid spit up and make a puddle right there at his boots.

He bent down, rubbed it between his fingers and held it to his nose: Mary, mother of God, he said to himself. The land was saturated. He wanted to jump in the air, wash his face with it, hold Chatterjee and shake him. Instead, Eddie said, and his voice was calm, 'Let me see what I can do. Give me a few days.'

'Doh take too long,' Chatterjee said, and for the first time in weeks, Eddie saw him smile, though there was a tightness around the man's mouth that made smiling look painful. 'I might change my mind.'

Eddie was thinking of all of this, and he pictured Chatterjee as he sat in his porch with his hands around his belly, looking out at the dark yard. And while fixing his eyes on the hazy road ahead, black and lumpy with new pitch, he felt in his bones and in his blood that his life was about to change. For months he'd been trying to figure out where he should be, looking for a direction. He'd found it this morning: yes, his fortune was no doubt buried right there in Siparia on Sonny Chatterjee's estate. This was what he had been waiting for, and he was so lost in this thought with the brutal sun hitting his face that he didn't hear Tito Fernandes' horn hooting until he was right there beside him, the Ford Model T car gleaming like a Christmas bauble.

'Hey,' Tito said. 'That was your truck?' He pointed behind him. 'They give a lot of trouble; I had one myself and got rid of it.' Then he said, 'Get in,' reached over and pushed open the door.

'Could be the belt,' Eddie said, 'I've felt it for a while, like a dog slipping a leash. If you could get me to a mechanic, I'll be grateful. This place is like a desert.'

Tito smiled. 'Everyone's in church and those who aren't probably should be.' Then he put out his hand and they introduced themselves.

Eddie climbed in, ran his eyes over the leather interior.

'Don't ask,' Tito rolled his eyes, ' If you made me choose right now – my dear wife or my car, I'm not sure which I'd pick. I know which is less trouble.'

Eddie stuck a cigarette in his mouth, cradled a small flame. He tried to figure out if he'd seen Tito before; his face was familiar.

'It's the future,' Eddie said. 'One day the roads will be full of them. And they probably won't look like this.'

'You've seen the Tourer?'

'Oh yes,' Tito nodded, 'in pictures. And the Bugatti. The Mercedes – a pretty, pretty car.'

On the left were rice fields and coconut trees. Tito accelerated along the Southern Main Road towards the Northern Range and the needle on the dial hit 46 miles an hour and it stayed and trembled there for five miles or so. The car rattled and shook; it felt like it was going fast because it was going fast. Eddie envied its thrust and power, especially after his slow drive that morning in Uncle Clyde's truck. Not bad at all. He could do with something like this. Yes, when he had some money, he'd buy himself a new car.

'Where you from, Eddie?'

Tito slowed down.

'I was born here. But I've been living in America a few years now. California, Houston. All over, in fact. You can make things happen there. Chances are they've been done before. In Trinidad you can be the first, a pioneer. It's hard to get things done. But you can make your mark.'

'Is that what you want to do? Be a pioneer? Make your mark?'

'Yes,' Eddie said, and glanced at Tito, 'in some ways. Don't we all?'

'Trinidad's changed. There's money, sure, but drive around at night, and people half-naked sleeping on the streets of Port of Spain. They say trouble coming again.'

'Strikes?'

'Push people down long enough and they come back harder. The British 'fraid the blacks, they 'fraid Indians, now, too. They tell the government, send troops! Send marines!' Tito put his fist in the air. 'People done with poor wages, long hours. You can't blame them. But Cipriani changing things.'

'You like him?'

'Yes, I like how he's a racehorse trainer, a Captain in the army *and* he's a champion of the barefoot man! They love him because he speaks for the poor. If they don't listen to him, there'll be much more radical leaders coming up. But who knows, he's a colonial, they might turn on him, too. Trinidad not easy.' Then Tito said, 'My wife talks about emigrating. I tell her yes, sure, let's go to America, give it a try. But Trinidad is home; I never leaving here.'

Tito winked at Eddie, and accelerated towards the south quay where the sun was low and yellow as a yolk. A cruise ship was sailing into the wharf, *Benediction*, in silver letters along the starboard, probably from New York, taking a tour of the islands. By the gate, a small crowd of locals waited. A young black woman posed with a macaw on each shoulder: something for the tourists. As the ship docked, passengers would drop dimes in the water and watch the local boys dive down to find them. Eddie had seen it time and time again – all up the islands, and he didn't much like it.

The sky was softening now above the new railway station with its arched windows and impressive pavilions. Trains ran regularly from here to San Fernando, out to Sangre Grande, too. He'd heard complaints – the building was a colossal waste of money, unnecessarily ostentatious, especially now trams and automobiles were proving more efficient and cost effective. Good news for oil; good news for Eddie.

'You have a wife, Eddie?'

'Not yet, I want to make my fortune first.'

'Don't wait 'til you're an old man like me. I was lucky to find Ada.'

'Love at first sight?'

'Yes, for one of us at least. We're a team. Mary Pickford and Douglas Fairbanks.'

'What's the secret?'

'Twice a week we go out for a candlelight dinner. Ada goes Tuesdays and I go on Fridays.'

Eddie grinned.

'You don't fight?'

'Yes we fight. About where we go on holiday. I say I want to go to Paris, and she says she wants to come with me.'

Tito was feeling better, thanks to his new companion.

Around the savannah horses were cantering, their bodies shining in the dipping sunlight; clouds of dust, red as cinnamon, puffed out behind their legs.

Eddie thought about his uncle. He should get a message to him.

Tito rolled into the driveway at the Queens Park Hotel.

'Let's get something to drink before we both pass out. Something strong. I've had a long day. Maybe I'll tell you about it some time.'

'You sure I'm dressed right? I have another shirt in my bag, though it's creased up.'

'Don't worry, you're with me. I have shares in this place.'

They parked and walked through the lobby to a long bar: wooden shutters leaned out into a garden, sprigs of bougainvillea on the tables; a woman in a long gown was playing the piano. Behind the bar, a young black man stood to attention in a bow tie and flashed his china-white teeth.

'Mister Fernandes. How are you?'

'Thirsty like a donkey in the desert, but apart from that I'm alive.'

'Glad to hear it,' the man said, and he nodded at Eddie.

Tito ordered a half bottle of gin and a jug of coconut water. 'Look,' he said, 'we'll drink a little, and then head back and sort out your vehicle. A man needs refreshments in this heat. I keep telling my wife, you worry about vitamins but you must never forget to hydrate. Especially in this hell hole.'

He smiled and his fleshy cheeks dimpled like doughnuts.

They found a table by the window and away from the bar. There was a kind of splendour here that Eddie had forgotten about – the polished wooden floor, modern overhead fans and starched tablecloths. This was a place for wealthy white Trinidadians, French Creoles, and American tourists. Eddie knew of the hotel, but he'd never had a reason to step inside. He should wash his hands.

Tito said, 'So what's your business?' Then, 'Let me guess, you're a planter.'

'Not quite,' Eddie said, 'I get bored; agriculture's not for me. Everything takes too long. I like to move around.'

'Construction?'

'Closer. I'm a driller.'

Tito cocked his head. 'Okay. That fits. You can't be short of work.'

'There's plenty to choose from.'

While the light changed and hotel guests came and went, Eddie and Tito emptied the bottle of gin and jug of coconut water and when it ran out, Tito called for more. The cook sent slices of pork and peppered shrimps, and hot bread. Eddie hadn't realised how hungry he was until he started eating. While they ate and drank, Eddie told Tito about his Uncle Clyde, and how he'd come back to Trinidad to help him up at Mon Repos Estate.

He spoke about his good friend Michael Callaghan and their search for oil in New Mexico. Their near success in Beaumont, and how they were scuppered by the owner of the land who turned out to be the biggest crook since Al Capone. He explained how he'd got caught up in the Teapot Dome in Wyoming, found the site on the edge of a football pitch and drilled down with a cable tool, and a pump. He and Callaghan had drilled the patch for five weeks. The well came in at 550 feet, one of the largest wells in history. Meanwhile, in New York, the owner was subpoenaed on four counts of bribery and corruption. He had no choice but to walk away without a cent. His nose was keen; he'd been unlucky. He'd learned his lessons. He wouldn't make the same mistake twice.

Eddie found himself telling Tito about his father, who had died in a volcano in St Vincent.

'They tell me he was on the mountainside when a stone fell next to him. Then the stones fell thicker, one or two were big, too big to be thrown by anyone's hands. Then he must have seen it was the mountain – pitching stones at him. He ran towards the sea bawling for help, ash and steam pouring out. Lava trickled down and buried the crops and houses. The volcano came like that, and no one knew. It spewed for days.'

He explained how his mother died soon after because her big heart was torn right out of her and there was nothing inside to keep her alive. At fifty-five years old, she fell asleep one evening and didn't wake up.

It occurred to Eddie that he was talking to Tito like he hadn't talked to anyone in years. It felt good, like putting down a heavy suitcase he'd been carrying.

'Mother was full of tears. Nothing worse than dying when you're alive. I'm glad in some ways she's gone.'

As he said it, Eddie knew it wasn't true. A day didn't pass when he didn't think about his mother.

Tito listened and nodded. 'Dying while you're alive is a terrible thing. A lot of people live like that.' He told Eddie he was brave. 'You're a fighter, you'll do okay. Most people live their lives like a sentence; you know what you want. I'm sure you'll get it.'

'I know what I want – I died twice.'

'You died how?'

'Malaria when I was eight. Then my plane crashed in Carcassonne. I saw angels come around.'

'Angels?'

'I don't know what they were but I figured they were angels by the light they brought. I thought that was the end. Everyone was dying. It was the war.'

'Were you afraid?'

'Of what, angels?' Eddie laughed. He took out another cigarette and lit it. 'I'm still here; there's no time to be afraid.'

'I like to think I have time.' Tito leaned back in his chair.

'There's nothing wrong with a little self-denial. I'd rather glance at things from the sidelines.'

'Sure, each to his own. It's just a different view.'

Tito raised his glass. 'To the angels.'

By now the air was thick and still. The waiter pushed back the shutters and there was a little breeze and Eddie saw that evening had come. Fireflies glittered in the darkness; he had never seen so many at once. His head was tight, and he felt good in himself. He felt a new charge and it wasn't just the liquor. He called through a message to his uncle; he would try to be there by lunchtime. He didn't mention the truck; he would pick that up tomorrow. Tonight he would stay in Rattan's hotel – it was cheap, familiar, a little on the rough side.

'I know Rattans. My low-life brother used to stay there; it's where all his friends hang out. He's another story altogether. I'll save that for next time.'

Tito apologised, he hadn't meant to keep him back. 'We could go and get my mechanic right now, he's there in Belmont.'

'No sir,' Eddie said, 'it can wait.'

Music started up. The song was a familiar, lively tune and a couple got up and started to dance, a slow, quick-quick step. They probably imagined they looked like film stars; their eyes never left each other.

'Love like dove,' Tito said.

Then, heady with liquor, Eddie was saying, 'There's a man called Chatterjee, he owns a big cocoa estate down in Siparia. It's full of oil.'

'All down there has oil – Fyzabad, Brighton, Point Fortin.'

'This is different. Chatterjee's place is floating on it. You can smell it in the air.'

'It's one thing to have it on your land; getting it out is another thing altogether.'

'No sir, not at all. Look at those twin brothers in Los Angeles – the Applegates; they drilled on the corner of Glendale Boulevard and Harman Drive using the sharp end of a eucalyptus tree. Two years later they have eighty wells and they're millionaires.' Eddie leaned in, 'Chatterjee's oil is so near the surface you could suck it up with a straw.'

'Then why doesn't he?'

'Because he doesn't know how. He only knows how to farm and his cocoa trees are dying.'

Eddie pulled on his cigarette, swirled the smoke around his mouth and blew it out.

'So how come Apex not in there?'

'Apex come and hassle Chatterjee to lease the land. Chatterjee says no.'

'Why?'

'Who knows? Macleod, the manager, has the charm of a cockroach. Maybe Chatterjee can't stand colonials. He doesn't want them on his land. Maybe he's honouring his father. He came on a boat from Calcutta fifty years ago and made something of himself. Chatterjee might not have any business sense, but he doesn't want foreigners. He prefers dealing with the ordinary man.'

'An ordinary man like you.'

'Yes, sir.'

'So you want him to let *you* drill?"

'Of course.'

'And why would he let you but not Apex?'

'Because I give a better rate. They only want to lease the land for a small fixed fee. I offer a percentage. I wouldn't need more than a dozen men. I'd treat his land with respect and keep costs low. I'll make money – money for me, money for him. I'll turn us into millionaires.'

Tito nodded. He looked impressed. 'Have you spoken to him?'

'When you picked me up, I was on my way back from his house.'

'In Siparia?'

'I drove down there last night and met with him.'

'And what did he say?'

'If I can get the money, he'll consider it.'

'Then you can buy your Bugatti.'

'And find me a wife.'

Eddie laughed and Tito laughed, a deep huwah-huwah that came from low in his belly. They drained their glasses and Tito called for brandy.

'I should go. I don't want to get you in trouble.'

'Yes,' Tito said, 'but I'm already in trouble. She knows where I am. I haven't laughed like this in a while. I've had a tough day, another time I might tell you about it.'

By now the girl on the piano had left, and the bar was filling up with a new crowd: visitors from the cruise ship, Americans, the beautiful people. They looked like they were enjoying themselves, as was Eddie. It had been a long time since he'd kicked back and spent time in a place like this. Not since he was in New York with Callaghan. He could get used to it.

'So how much do you need?' Tito leaned in, looked straight at Eddie. 'Name a figure.'

'Around ten thousand dollars, I guess, initially, to clear the forest, bring in water, build roads, equipment. It doesn't have to be new. I can make do.'

'Maybe I can help.' Tito's eyes held steady. 'Maybe I could find some money for you. Enough to get you started. We should talk.'

Tito got up and went to the bar to pay the bill; short and blocky from behind; a solid little man. Eddie wondered how drunk he was. They'd been here since after four and it was gone midnight. The last couple hours they'd slowed down, and Eddie was tired now, not drunk. But then he could take his liquor. He barely knew Tito Fernandes but he, too, seemed sober enough.

'Look,' Tito said, putting on his hat, feeling that he needed to lie down. 'We're having a party at my house on Saturday, why don't you come? You can meet my wife. There'll be music; the great and good will be there. We can talk some more if you wish.'

'Sure,' Eddie said. 'I'd like that.'

'Come as you are. You'll be a novelty with the ladies. Now, if you don't mind, you can drop me home and bring my car back on Saturday. In the meantime I can walk to the office.' He patted his chest. 'My wife tells me it's good for my ticker.'

Outside, the moon was low and full. Eddie drove Tito back to his home in Broom Street, and took in the pale, brightly lit house, with a curved driveway in front and on either side of the gateposts two large sculptures that reminded him of figures he had seen in the Tuileries, in Paris. The front door was open, and he watched Tito walk slowly up the steps to the entrance where a woman appeared in a white dressing gown, and put her arm around him.

The woman was striking, with dark hair pinned up, and in the strange moonlight her face took the shape of a locket, oval, shining. Her mouth was wide like a singer's, dark eyes reaching – trying to see who he was.

'See you Saturday!' Tito bellowed above the engine. '8 pm.'

Eddie caught himself, waved goodbye, and drove off into the night.

TWO

'Why is that man taking our car?'

'That man, my beloved, is Eddie Wade and we're going to do business together. You will like him.'

'Eddie who? Why does he have our car? How can you let him take it?'

They watched the car disappear into the night, then Tito and Ada went inside. They climbed the dark stairs to the top of the landing and a long corridor. She could now see that Tito was drunk. More stairs. He complained the house was full of stairs. Outside their bedroom, he caught his breath before a painting of his mother. Her collar was high around her throat, eyes like two holes.

'She looks sour, don't you think? I don't like sour women. I'm so glad you're not sour.'

'Not yet,' Ada said. 'I'm getting more sour by the day.'

Tito wasn't listening. He hummed to himself while he shuffled into the bedroom and started to unbutton his shirt; his fingers were too thick. A lamp threw soft light around the walls; the shutters were still open, the fan whirring and blowing out the lace drapes. Ada was wearing a white nightdress with embroidery on the cuffs and collar. Tito narrowed his eyes to bring her into focus. She looked young – a girl, with too much beauty.

'Don't break my heart, Ada.'

'What are you talking about?'

'Break my bones instead. I have 206 of them.'

Ada shook her head, knowing it was pointless to argue.

'You have all your years ahead of you. Not like me.'

Now he sat on the side of the bed and tugged at his shoes, apparently glued to his feet. He pulled at his tie until it came loose and then rolled back on the mattress. He patted the little hill of his stomach. It had been giving him trouble of late, and he had a sour taste in his mouth. He groaned like an old man.

'Help me, darling. This damn shirt.'

Irritable, Ada reached over and popped the buttons.

'How's my Flora?'

'Sleeping. Don't wake her.'

Tito got up and hefted himself out into the corridor, across the passageway into Flora's room where her light was still on. She had never liked the dark. Just last week, she said she'd seen a skeleton leaning over her, half covered by a cloak and carrying a cutlass. She had run to her parent's room and jumped in bed between them. She had seen death. Death was coming to them. It had taken them the best part of an hour to get her back to sleep.

Now she was curled up on her bed with her hair over her face. Tito plucked away the dark strands from her sticky mouth. She was breathing deeply, her cheek round and smooth like a gold peach.

'Tito, how much you drank?' Ada stood in the doorway, her face pale. 'I don't know what's happening to you.' She steered him back to their bedroom. 'These days you disappear into your own world. You don't care about anyone but yourself. You're drinking too much. You reek of liquor. It was rum you drank?'

He fell back on the bed.

'Gin. But not so much darling; not so much.'

'You were at the hotel? Who's this Eddie?'

'Our lucky star. All will be revealed.'

'My god, Tito! Why do you have to be so mysterious?'

She told him that she was not his mother, that she was tired of his late night gallivanting. If he thought he could wake her in the night like his father used to wake his mother at some ungodly hour, he could think again. Didn't he realise she was worried? Flora was worried; Aunt Bessie was worried.

'Remember how your father used to come home at all hours, wake your mother and tell her to find a chicken in the yard, slit its throat and cook it for him? You're turning into your father.'

Ada pulled at his trousers, eventually giving up and flopping down on the bed beside him with a loud, exasperated sigh.

Tito closed his eyes, relieved the day was over.

That same Sunday morning, after he'd said goodbye to Ada and Flora, he had driven out of town towards the east, passed the turning to St Joseph – where he'd told Ada he had urgent business. He'd made his way along the empty road feeling wretched. As the land rushed by – the cane fields and rice fields and the beautiful hills with their black scars and the lilac sky above them – he wondered how he was going to dig himself out of the hole he was in.

He had lost half of the family fortune in the New York stock market. He had more than $50,000 saved in a high interest account in the Bank of the United States, which, according to the press, was preparing to announce its closure. The Hoover administration and The Federal Reserve were doing nothing to slow the rate of bank failures all over America and Alfie Mendes, his accountant, had warned Tito not to invest any more. He'd never foreseen the fall of Caldwell. How could he? But worse, he had taken a loan against his business to invest in a bank in Tennessee that had collapsed last week. The family stores were in jeopardy. He couldn't face telling Ada.

Alfie told him he'd been lucky. There were men in New York who'd lost everything in one afternoon, hurling themselves from the tops of buildings.

'But what do I tell Ada?'

'Tell her the truth. Talk to her.'

'She'll be furious.'

'Not as furious as if she hears it from someone else.'

While Tito drove along the road lined with coconut trees, their branches tossing like hair in the wind, he wondered if he might have done better elsewhere? England? America? Europe? Perhaps. But with a lump in his throat, he thought of how much he loved this island. He could never have lived anywhere else.

He remembered with some sadness how at five years old he'd cried when he saw a skin of a tiger stretched out on the wooden floor of a house in Surrey, England. The lady of the house asked, 'Are you crying because of the tiger?'

Yes, he said, not because it was dead, but because it looked like a map of Trinidad. She took pity on him, went to the library and pulled down an atlas and she found the page featuring the British West Indies; the islands were scattered there in pastels against the blue of sea.

She said, 'I see what you mean. A tiger skin. Be glad that you love your country so.'

As he'd headed towards Manzanilla, Tito imagined himself driving along the tiger's belly, and as he felt the hot breeze blowing through the window he remembered how, in England, he'd never felt warm. No matter how many vests and sweaters he wore and how he positioned himself by the open fire in the great hall, his bones were always trembling. He traded baths with other boys, so he could soak in hot water three or four times a week. He lost weight. School meals made him sick; he survived on tins of mandarin oranges, slurps of condensed milk. Every morning, longing for the crabby hand of his mother's writing, he looked for letters from home, watched for a coral stamp showing Blue Basin and an airmail sticker. He waited for summer to come, not realising his mother had other plans for him: seven years at The Royal College of Surgeons in Dublin.

Tito hadn't cared for anatomical lectures, the minutiae of the human body and its illnesses. Clinical investigations and post mortems held no interest for him. He learned that to tug off the top of someone's skull you needed a bone saw and some force; tearing through the thin layers of tissue covering the muscles and internal organs wasn't always easy. He had learned how to make a button hole in the skin to hook your finger through and peel it away. The skin on the back peels beautifully, his lecturer said, because of glutinous fat beneath the surface.

Tito was mostly bored, his interest held only by the cardiology lectures. He'd found himself enthralled by the heart and its workings, its 100, 000 beats a day, the effortless pumping of blood around the body. He liked the idea of chambers, like rooms in a house and the blood's journey through capillaries, arteries, returning through veins and venules, like rivers, streams and roads and tracks. The heart was the centre of man, where his soul's fire burned. It needed to be tended. If its pathways were stretched and laid out, they would travel the earth twice. The enormous world of the heart! He'd asked his lecturer, was it possible the heart could actually be broken? Why yes, of course. Heartbreak could inflict damage like the blow of an axe. The heart can become diseased, rotten, an overworked thing of hardened muscle, a rock. He'd felt one in his hands – the enlarged grey heart of a woman brought from the psychiatric unit, who'd killed herself after more than fifty attempts.

Finally when he'd sailed home to Trinidad – his studies cut short by a bronchial infection in an appalling winter when Dublin's little houses on the outskirts vanished beneath drifts of snow – Tito was twenty-five years old. As the steamer approached the Dragon's Mouth, he watched the sea narrow itself between the four islands, like stepping stones along the twelve mile passage, and when he saw the tall black and copper cliffs and young palms along them blowing in the warm breeze, he felt his heart open. At Scotland Bay the sea was tourmaline and it seemed to him the pointed hills were awash with gold and he began to cry with joy.

His mother and father met him at the port, his father in his familiar white suit, his mother as tidy and neat as a new doll. At once, he saw the disappointment in his mother's face, and he knew that he had failed her. Long before they reached home she was asking what was he going to do? If he thought he could come home and lie around the place, he could think again.

It had been, Tito believed, the right time to come back. Recent trouble in Port of Spain over the installation of proposed water meters had caused unrest. Protesters had gathered outside the Red House and pelted it with stones and rioters poured inside and set fire to stacks of papers. The governor had to be rushed to safety at police headquarters. A young woman, Eva Carvalho, was shot at point-blank range by a policeman who was said to be her estranged lover, while twelve-year-old Eliza Bunting was bayo-neted through the chest. Victor Fernandes had been caught up in this fray on his way home. He was left badly shaken, a deep gash to his head from a broken bottle. Tito had told himself, now more than ever, his family needed him.

Victor Fernandes had given his son an apron and set him to work in the store. Fernandes Bazaar was 600 square feet with floor to ceiling windows, a room at the back where cocoa growers brought beans in exchange for goods. Tito was assigned to the storeroom upstairs to count stock. He took it upon himself to thoroughly clean the room and reorganise stock in a way that made it possible to see their quantities at once. He grouped goods by their type rather than use. He labelled every shelf and noted every item. He quickly understood how inefficient inventory led to financial loss; time spent looking for this or that was wasted time. All unusable items – out of date, or broken – were removed. Seasonal decorations were taken away and stored off site. Victor was astonished by his son's initiative.

Tito was popular with customers, his dark eyes warm and brown as brandy. He'd say, *Is there anything else I can do for you? Have a wonderful day*, *Do come back and see us soon*. He remembered names, 'Yes, Mrs Tibbits, can I put your bags behind the counter while you carry on shopping.' 'Hello Mrs Robinson, and how is your son today?' 'Red suits you very well, Mrs Davies.' He persuaded his father to offer refreshments to thirsty shoppers.

'We must make them feel cared for,' he said. 'Water the plants and watch them grow.'

He had filed, collated, and chased ledgers, often until late at night. In his lunch hour, he'd visited other department stores for ideas, or scoured the financial pages of the *Daily Star*. He encouraged his father to discount goods, and enable customers to purchase on high interest instalment plans. In those early days, Victor Fernandes imported goods mainly from Madeira – onions, the most succulent and nutritious beans, peas, garlic, wine, lace, tiles, biscuits. Tito persuaded his father to broaden their range. Why not bring in clothes? Or sell shoes? The same ladies who shopped for cookies needed to buy shoes and dresses and toys for their children. Don't send them to Bata or Millers. Couldn't his father see how Port of Spain was changing?

Tito found a supplier of fine leather ladies and gents shoes in New York. He told his father, 'The secret was that they must fit the shoe to the foot not the foot to the shoe.' He sought out fabrics through an old school friend in England, whose father and mother now lived in Bandra, Bombay. With their help, he imported silks and linens, silver and brass ornaments. Spices and herbs came from Europe, along with champagne and fine wines.

He'd brought ice machines into the city to sell to restaurants and bars. He'd purchased a stainless steel industrial pasta machine, and with Canadian flour, made the best spaghetti in Trinidad. He'd set up a five star hotel – right there in Marine Square. Now there was scarcely any important city in the world that Fernandes and Co did not import goods from.

Tito had located a large warehouse in the west of Port of Spain and refurbished the stockroom to make a second shop floor and installed a lift. His father complained when he saw the accounts: they were spending money as fast as it was coming in. But for all his complaining, it seemed to Tito that his father's protestations were half-hearted. The store was the busiest in Frederick Street: a new sign went up: Fernandes and Co – *Something for Everyone.*

Throughout these years, Tito had never grown tired of Trinidad, of the low skies, the dust or the choking heat, or rains when they came. Every morning, after he parked his car, he walked to his office in Frederick Street, stopped for coffee at the Hotel de Paris on Abercrombie, while puffing on his Anchor cigarettes. People would say, 'Good morning Mister Fernandes,' or 'Good day, Tito!' He'd watched friends emigrate to America or Europe. Tito would say, 'Where you running to? There's nowhere like Trinidad. You'll only go to come back.'

In the evenings, on his way home, he'd drive around the Savannah, looking out at the lights and it seemed the grassland was a lake and he could almost imagine boats upon it. He glanced at the hills behind, dense with trees and bush, and he felt a rightness about his life, as if where he had meant to go was exactly where he had been. And it often came upon him, like a fact, as it did now, that this was the country where he would live and where he would die. This dense green land with its woodland and rivers and mountains and sprawling beaches was his home.

That Sunday morning, after driving for more than two hours, Tito had pulled into the grassy lay-by, then swerved onto a narrow trail that he knew took him to the beach. He saw the tide was out and sand was pale as flour. There was no one there. It wasn't the time of year for holidaymakers. Just as well. He parked in the shade of an almond tree, turned off the engine, and found a driftwood log to sit on. He looked out at the foamy frills on the waves, and stared far out where the sea met the sky and found it difficult to see a separation between the two. Blue and more blue. The sun was not yet high. He loosened his tie, undid the top button of his shirt, and took a deep breath. He felt a little shudder in his body, as if he was letting go of something. There was a slight breeze and he could smell the sea's salty breath. He thought about Flora and Ada and felt his heart lift with love for them. They were a part of his heart walking around in the world. He loved them more than anything; he knew he had a tendency for heaviness, and Ada could always raise his spirits. But these days he couldn't find it in himself to make love to her. She deserved better; she deserved more.

He thought of the woman he'd almost married before Ada; she came to him like a photograph – Matilda Mendonca, daughter of a friend of his father's, a devoted Catholic. She had jilted him two weeks before their wedding for Carlos Acevedo, a younger man, an overseer on a sugar estate. He'd been beside himself. He'd known the cost of this emotional pain to the heart: a high risk of arterial fibrillation, erratic blood flow leading to an early, and often, sudden death.

For a year, Tito kept their wedding cake in an icebox and cut himself a slice every day to eat with his afternoon coffee. Some days he ate two wedges of the fruity, layered cake encrusted with marzipan and a delicious citrus icing. Eating the cake was a comfort. This was how he started putting on weight. It was because of Matilda and Carlos. Over that year, he convinced himself that Matilda Mendonca and Carlos Acevedo had ruined his life forever.

His brother told him he should do something, teach Carlos a little lesson, rough him up. It would make him feel better; help to quell the pain. Raul knew people who could help. Why should you suffer, he said. Let them suffer instead.

Eventually, Tito gave Raul $500 and told him to take care of it. Six weeks later, Carlos Acevedo was found beaten to death outside a rum shop on the road to Roseau, Dominica.

Then he'd met Ada – at the Country Club Old Year's ball – grown up and dazzling, dressed as the Queen of Diamonds. He had known her as a child but now she was different. He was struck by her brightness, her humour, all of the fifty-two moles he counted on her creamy skin. He courted her over a period of months. She swore to him that she would honour and cherish him; he knew that he could trust her. His beloved Ada.

To the beach, to the trees, to the vast sky, Tito had spoken her name aloud, 'Ada.' For the first time since his father died, Tito allowed himself to cry; big heaving sobs from his guts. He wondered in that moment if his financial loss was punishment from God for what he'd done to Carlos. Yes, perhaps, God was punishing him. He deserved it. He deserved to suffer. This thought made him cry more.

By then the sun was high, the sea a hard silver strip. He could fill his pockets with stones, and walk out into the water. Swim as far as he could. He would soon tire, hope for a rip tide to carry him out. The Atlantic was agitated at this time of year and it would quickly pull him down. What was he waiting for? He deserved to die; he had killed a man. Not with his own hands, but by his might.

Then he saw something. At first he couldn't figure it out. A buffalo? A cow? No, this was something else. A horse, as pale as a ghost was standing at the water's edge dipping its head. It was unusual to see a horse here on the beach. Still for a moment, it started to walk in his direction. Its mane was white, the pale legs lanky and young, a palomino. A palomino at Manzanilla. The horse had raised its nose as if smelling something in the air, smelling him, perhaps. Tito had always loved horses. He remembered from school: *The air of heaven is that which blows between a horse's ears.*

He walked towards it, sand falling over his leather shoes, the sun burning his watery eyes.

'Come,' he said, through his tears, and he put out his hand.

The horse approached him, moving quicker now, swishing its tail of white ribbons, flicking its long mane, its hooves quiet and quick on the soft beach. It stopped in front of him, shoved its soggy nose into his palm and he ran his fingers along its golden forehead; stroked the curve of cheek. Its dark eyes were shiny and seemed to hold the world inside them. Had it escaped from a nearby farm? To whom did it belong? It was well looked after. He remembered peppermints in his cotton jacket, and the horse crunched through them. 'You like that; you like sweets, eh.' After a few minutes, the horse glanced back alert to something further down the bay. Then it flicked its head and turned from him. Tito watched it trot back along the beach until it became small. Just before it disappeared into the hazy light, it glanced back at him, then carried on. He felt something inside him shift. What was the horse doing here? Had it come to tell him something? He wondered for a moment if it was real. A vision. A symbol of hope.

He looked up to the sky. 'God, if this is a sign, then help me climb out of the disaster I have made for myself.'

He'd got back in his car, and started for home, his mind strangely clear, blank as a fresh sheet of paper. He drove through the village of Mayaro, and through the streets of Princess Town and back along the Southern Main Road towards Port of Spain. About an hour later he saw a truck broken down on the side of the road next to a huge samaan tree. Further along this same road, a man was walking alone. That man was Eddie Wade.

THREE

Sonny Chatterjee remembered holding his father's calloused hand on the streets of Princes Town as they followed a procession, his small heart clattering to the rhythm of the tassa drums. Above the crowd, a young man sat on a wooden platform decorated with vines and flowers; a god. Dressed like Krishna, in turquoise and orange silks, the man smiled and threw pieces of coconut and lime and marigolds down to the crowd. Like something from a dream, Sonny watched as orange petals floated down through the sky. His father raised him up and he held out his hands. To catch a falling flower was a lucky omen.

Sonny had kept the marigold all his life, pressed between the pages of a book he couldn't read. But he didn't feel lucky. He had never felt lucky. Bad things had happened. His mother died of chronic dysentery when he was eight years old. He'd swiped off a toe when he was cutting paragrass for their cow. Along had come Sita, from Rio Claro, an attractive woman who'd brought into the marriage a small dowry and a gold necklace her mother had given her. She was an attractive women with a hurricane hidden inside her. Their first child, Hari, was afflicted by epileptic fits. Vikram came soon after – a whiny, underweight, screechy child. A daughter, Priya, followed but died at birth. Beyond what his father had achieved, but was now dying with disease, there had been nothing lucky about his life so far.

Kushi estate was situated halfway between Siparia and Barrackpore. Surrounded by crown lands, Old Man Madoo's property stopped this side of the old silk cotton tree. He'd built a modest wooden house, planted cocoa trees, little stalks that shot up quickly in the rich clay soil. He planted immortelles amongst the pine and cedar to protect the delicate cocoa. He planted pumpkins, baigan, bodi, bhaji and corn to feed his family while the cocoa trees grew. Madoo tended them, talked to them, he stroked their leaves. Women came from the village to harvest the pods and Madoo would ride a mule amongst them, making sure they picked well. Pods were carried in baskets from the fields, sorted and laid out to dry on the roof. Some were grated to make cocoa tea, the bulk were packed in sacks, sent on mules to La Brea, then shipped across the Atlantic to London and Paris where chocolatiers made use of them.

When Sonny was a boy, he liked to run between the cocoa trees, hide in their branches. The pods were gems of rubies and gold. He fished in the Oropouche River. He roamed to where the silk cotton tree stood, swung on vines that hung like thick green hair. The tree had roots like the folds of a long grey dress. The branches were thick and boughs were long, and from them dangled orchids and grey beards. He heard it said that between the buttress roots were doors to other spirit worlds, and this frightened him. His father said it was a magic tree. When, one day, Madoo caught Sonny throwing stones at a blackbird perched high in it, he took up a strap and beat him. Never throw stones at a silk cotton tree, it would bring sickness to the house, or some other misfortune.

Old man Madoo taught Sonny everything he needed to know. He ensured the cocoa trees were kept pruned, clean of parasites, ants, termites. By then the railway passed through Siparia and it was Sonny's job to see that bags were transported to Port of Spain, weighed and traded for store credit or cash. The cash Sonny earned, along with Sita's dowry, was kept inside the house, stashed inside the mattress on which they slept. They lived modestly. But Sonny made sure Sita had enough pretty saris to keep her happy, that the boys wore shoes and clothes without holes. There was always enough food to eat.

For all his hard work, Sonny lacked his father's drive, and though after he died, he did his best to run the estate as his father had done, it became more difficult. By then the markets and prices were starting to dwindle with a rise in surplus cocoa from West Africa. Sonny tightened his belt. Rumours were circling; more hardship lay ahead. A depression loomed in America. Sonny made enough to pay his labourers, feed his family and buy school books for his sons. But as the price of cocoa continued to fall, he found himself in debt. More and more he dipped into their savings.

Without telling her, Sonny used Sita's dowry (put aside for emergencies) to make urgent repairs to the property; he built a new high fence to keep out trespassers. He let go of the women who'd worked for years at Kushi. Sita and the boys were forced to help pick pods, polish and bag up the seeds. Sita moaned. The boys complained. She talked of returning to Rio Claro, to Ma and her sisters, Mira and Suniti. She grew to hate the estate and its lack of light. Sonny knew that Sita had always preferred the flatter lands, the sight of cane fields, open spaces and big skies. *Kushi too dark, the air too thick*. He asked her to be patient.

It was impossible for Sonny to manage the fields alone. The grass grew long; huge feathery ferns and vines now clambered over the forest floor. Trees and shrubs grew high and wild. Sonny was overwhelmed, exhausted. After the rainy season, parts of the estate were so dense that when he took his cutlass to chop at it, he saw above where fine leaves met, a strange cloud of green.

Then his worst fears came true: the cocoa trees started to die. Sonny didn't tell Sita he was frightened for their future. Was it possible he could lose everything? His father would tell him not to be defeated by a little fungus on the trees. *Hold on to Kushi, Sonny. What Sita know? This not woman business, is man business.* But maybe Sita was right? Should they go to Rio Claro? What if all the trees died? What if the estate was finished? He could start again, plant silk fig, plantains, or citrus. How long would it take to turn it around? They would have to plant afresh. Other estates were doing just that.

Sita tried to persuade Sonny to sell Kushi to one of the oil companies looking to drill.

'My father land, Sita. How you could tell me sell it? Is like asking me to cut off my foot or hand.'

Sita tried speaking softly to her husband at night; she put her head on his chest, and while they watched moonlight filter through the thin branches of the immortelle outside their window, she whispered to him, drew pictures with words of another life surrounded by those she loved. He knew what she was doing.

'Let we go, nuh, Sonny. Make life sweet. This life no good for we, especially the children.'

When he said no, she sulked, tightened her mouth. She told him, 'I never meet a man more stubborn than you. You shoulda take a wife from the deaf and dumb school.'

In the heart of the forest, Sonny sat down. What could he do?

In those days, he liked to smoke cigars. He took a match and lit a piece of wax paper so he could get a strong blaze to light it. That day, while the corn birds wheeled above him and he thought about his predicament, he threw down the lit wax paper and saw, to his surprise, the ground catch fire. A burst of orange flames. A sign of gas. A sign, he believed, from God.

For years Sonny had wondered if the black liquid seeping up from the ground was killing off the cocoa. But then he realised this same troublesome liquid was the very thing the Americans wanted to get their hands on. In Forest Reserve, Fyzabad, Point Cumana, big companies were setting up camp and drilling for oil. He'd heard the crashing of trees and terrible sounds of drilling and banging when he passed by those sites. Could oil be so much in demand? Why would he have it on his land? He'd thought it a nuisance. He wasn't interested in oil.

But then Eddie Wade had started visiting every couple of weeks.

'Oil is black gold,' Eddie said. 'We find it in unlikely places.'

Sonny hadn't much liked Eddie at first – his khaki clothes, his greased-back hair, his smooth way of talking – but Eddie's connection to his father counted for something. Over the last few months, he'd watched Eddie carefully. He listened to his stories of lucky strikes and fortunes made in Beaumont, Texas.

Sonny had also heard about explosions in Forest Reserve, La Brea. 'This oil business real dangerous.'

No, Eddie explained, pressure could be managed. There was a new piece of equipment that had changed everything. With a stick, he drew a picture of a blowout preventer in the dusty floor of Sonny's porch.

'It can flow and flow for years with no danger to anyone.' Eddie swept his hand up and away as if it was flowing, too.

Sonny had begun to look forward to Eddie's visits. He'd hear the truck in late afternoon, and shuffle himself outside. People joked that Sonny Chatterjee must know you forty years before he would let you in his house. Eddie not only sat in his house but also ate at his table. They shared rum, cigarettes, cigars.

Sonny told Sita some of the things Eddie said:

'If he telling the truth, our fortune right under our feet. We could stay here and make plenty money. Fix up the place; build a house next door to Ma. We could buy a automobile. I could take you out driving in the afternoons. I could drive you to Rio Claro.'

Sita's eyes were flickering.

'Better to lease the land, stay right here while drilling going on, and see how much oil we have. We take a percentage. We never make a good price if we sell it so. This way, we make more money.'

Sita said, 'How many cars it have in Trinidad? Who really need oil? Who want it? Not me, not you. You can eat oil?'

'Eddie say cars coming on the island every day. Look America. America is the future. What is there will come here. Even if in ten years it coming, it go come.'

Sonny knew he would soon have to make a decision. He didn't like Macleod; Eddie wouldn't hang around forever.

That Sunday morning, when Sita was stripping the bed, she saw the bottom of the mattress was wet. Rain was falling through a hole in the roof. While removing the sheet, she checked for the leather pouch in which their savings were hidden. She tipped the contents onto the floor. Assuming they had been robbed, Sita shouted for Sonny.

'Soneeeee! Soneeeee!'

'Yes, baby, I coming.'

He ran upstairs to see what was wrong.

The minute she saw his face, she knew.

As if she was holding a gun, Sonny put up his hands and slowly backed out of the room.

'Sita, listen nuh. Sita. Leh we talk. Come downstairs.'

She started to rage about her clothes, the ragged saris she lived in these days; about the state of this house – the peeling paint, lack of furniture. She raged about her difficult life. If she'd known she'd have to work like a labourer, she'd never have married him.

All these years living in the bush had come to this! Who coming here, no one! No one want to come here. How long since I see Ma? How long since we go Rio Claro? Ma not comin here. I glad no one come. Hari have no shirt or slippers that fit. We like blasted vagrants!

By now Sonny had fled outside, watching as Sita flung out every item of clothing she could find through the window.

Sonny stood shaking his head. 'Sita, come nuh. Sita. Enough now.'

But he knew it was pointless. When her temper started it burned like a wick; he braced himself for the explosion. And here it was.

Sita flew outside screaming and cursing with her hair loose. Hari and Vikram came running from the hill. They watched their mother pick up her cutlass and sharpen the blade on the rock. Sonny went to stop her, but she gave him a look that made him cower. He put up his hand, afraid she might chop him.

'Sita! Sita! Come, come. Enough! Leave the cutlass.'

He moved sideways like a crab.

She shrieked, 'Keep away! Keep away from me!'

Then she took off her long gold necklace, laid it on the ground. She raised the cutlass high, and hacked the chain into small pieces. She scooped up a handful of gold for each of their sons who were still as posts.

'Your father can't seem to make a cent, so all you better have something of mine.'

She looked at her husband as if she couldn't stand him, her cheeks streaked with tears. Then she picked up the skirt of her sari and ran inside.

Later that morning, Sonny stood amongst the cocoa trees. He took in the smell of the rotting leaves and heady scent of long white flowers. He glimpsed the blackened pods attached to white speckled, diseased branches. He shuddered at the clusters of pink wet fungus. It was everywhere. He loved this land, his father's land. They couldn't carry on as they were. He squatted down, pushed his fingers into the moist, dark earth and let the black oil seep up and trickle over his hands.

Let's see what Eddie Wade could do.

FOUR

His head tight as a clock, Tito made his way to his accountants' office on Charlotte Street. It was a hot, clear day. The grass was light brown and short trees were bony and leafless, the hills were black from burning. Bush fires on the weekend had destroyed a whole village; water supplies were low, and rains were not due for another two months. People had died. What to do? He'd promised to donate to an emergency fund. Ada was making cakes to raise money at a fete that same afternoon. He needed to check the water tanks at home; the pump had been giving trouble. His stomach was giving trouble. Everything was giving trouble. But today was a new day, and new hope had arrived.

Alfie Mendes sat behind a green leather-topped desk. A ceiling fan was slowly turning. Shelves were packed with files and folders, cabinets were loaded up with old books. Tito had known this office all his life. As a boy he had come here with his father, listened to his father talk about his finances, share his concerns. Alfie patted the pocket of his immaculate shirt, feeling for his pen. The man smelled the same, a lemony, leafy scent of Bay Rum. He didn't say hello or get up from his chair. Now in his mid seventies, his brown face was creased up like a paper bag. Under his shirt, Tito knew there was a bandage; a cancer from the sun had grown there. When the wound was healing, maggots crawled in and cleaned it out. A miracle of sorts.

'How's your chest, Uncle Alfie?'

'Don't worry about me, let's talk about you.' He waved his pen over a fan of papers on his desk. 'Who is this Wade guy? Right now, the store in Barbados is keeping you afloat, so to take money out and put it here? It's a mistake.' He shook his head. 'Oil business is risky business. Sure, if you have a conglomerate like American leaseholds or Apex, or Texaco behind you, and even then it's a risk. But this guy's a one-man band. If he says he needs ten thousand bucks, he probably needs twenty. These things always cost more. It becomes a never-ending investment.' He sighed. 'I can't believe you'd even consider it. You don't have ten thousand dollars to play with. You want to risk your home now, too?'

Alfie had always known this about Tito, that he loved nothing more than taking a punt on a risky new venture; he couldn't help himself. Sometimes it paid off; other times it didn't. Mostly Tito had been lucky; he'd had his father's business to fall back on. For all his easy-going charm, Tito Fernandes was as keen and determined as a bloodhound.

'I have a feeling about it, Alfie. I can't explain it. In my guts. If I don't take the risk, I'll lose the chance.'

'Chance to do what? Lose more money?' He threw up his hands. 'And who is this Sonny Chatterjee? How come he doesn't lease the land to one of the big companies? Why aren't they drilling the place dry all now. When there's a whiff of oil, these people come like piranha.'

Tito knew Alfie would react like this. Alfie was cautious, and he was also getting old. In the last few years, he'd grown more resistant to new ideas. When, five years ago, Tito suggested opening a cinema in Woodbrook, Alfie warned that the concept was wasted in Trinidad. *Who will pay to see these movies? It is a fad. Nothing more than that.* Alfie was wrong.

'Apparently, he has an uncle up in Mon Repos. But I can't find anything else, the guy is a mystery. His father was from St Vincent. His mother? Who knows? Who is Eddie Wade really?'

'He has lived in the States, he trained as a driller up there. His father died when he was young. He fought in the war, nearly died. He's hungry. I like that kind of hunger.'

'We're all hungry, Tito. In one way or another. Your parents never lived like you and Ada, you know. It was only in the last few years they had holidays; they did without so they could afford to send you away to school. Your father walked everywhere. He didn't need a car. It didn't do him any harm.

'Look at America. You know only too well what's happening there. We need to tighten our belts, brace ourselves for the trouble that's coming. Cocoa in trouble; sugar in trouble; the economy ready to take a downturn. Strikes and confusion.'

He pointed his finger at Tito, 'You, don't have money to invest. So if you really want my advice, it's no. It's obvious to me as daylight. But, tell me, how is Ada?'

'Ada is wonderful. Flora, too. Growing like a vine.'

'And your mother? I haven't seen her. She must be lonely. Tell her I will come see her.'

'I'm going there now. I will tell her.'

'Don't go asking her for money.' Alfie wagged his finger at Tito.

'Not a chance,' Tito said, and put on his hat.

Tito's mother was sitting in the veranda with her eyes closed, her thin legs crossed at the ankles, wearing her flowery house dress. Her mouth drooped a little, and she was breathing deeply. He put on the kettle, made a pot of tea and brought it to the table. He'd brought sweet buns from the bakery on the corner, a favourite. She could do with putting on some weight. Her tiny frame was bent up, and yet she had a paunch. He looked at her twiggy hands. Sun spots all over her arms and on her face. Frown lines cut into her forehead. She looked like his grandmother from Madeira, a lace-maker, a cook, and mother of ten; a woman with a terrible phobia of open water. Not unlike Ada.

Tito's bedroom hadn't changed in thirty years: his desk, thick medical books on the shelves, his old bed draped in the same white crocheted cover, pencil marks on the wall from when he was young and his mother had measured him and urged him to grow taller. 'You'll never go far if you're a little man.' The window looked out onto the garden – a cactus tree, a traveller's palm, a tall aloe tree with branches like great candelabra, two guava trees, and a chicken run. It could all do with a lick of paint, some modernisation. Apparently there were holes in the roof, but whenever he mentioned it she'd say, 'I can't afford all that. Where am I finding the money to do that?'

'You come from work?' His mother straightened herself up. 'I never heard you. I need a bell or something. Anyone could come in the damn house.'

He poured the tea, offered her a soft and squishy bun.

'Not that big thing. Cut it for me.'

Then she said, 'Any news? Raul?'

'All quiet. He's working, apparently. Irene said so.'

Since January, Raul, his brother, had been managing the store in Barbados. He was still working on a trial basis. Two years ago, in a flush of optimism, Tito had purchased new premises in Barbados: 900 square feet of a two-storey ex-showroom with shutters and wrought-iron awning in pale green. Opposite Weatherheads on the corner of Broad Street and Justice Street. The sign went up: *Fernandes: Something for Everyone*. It was a difficult arrangement. Raul dressed immaculately; he was easy with customers, but there were days when he disappeared without warning, and Irene, his assistant, had to telephone Tito. What to do? Should she go to the police? Could Tito come? Eventually Raul turned up, smelling of liquor. To keep his mother sweet, Tito tolerated it. The last few months he'd been going to Barbados regularly. He'd stay a couple days, go over the books, check stock.

'He has a woman there?'

'Who knows, mother. Raul is a mystery man. He has his friends. He's a big boy. As long as the store is running and there's no trouble, I don't care.'

She smoothed out her dress. 'You need to be kinder to your brother. I don't understand this resentment. I was never like that with my sisters.'

His mother would never admit that she had always favoured Raul. He looked like Rudolph Valentino, and spoke with a deep, crisp voice. He was full of compliments. He'd tell their mother she looked like a woman half her age. Was that a new dress? No one cooks like you. When he needed fifty dollars, he would go to his mother and she would give it to him. It was obvious to everyone but her.

His mother got up, fixed her dress, and tottered over to the steps and looked down at the garden. Tito thought how frail she was. They had buried all their pets in this garden – four dogs, three cats, two parrots.

'I never see Flora these days. She's boarding?'

It was hard persuading Flora to visit. Her grandmother was always telling her what she shouldn't do. Don't play the piano so loud; don't run outside in the hot sun; why you have to make such a mess in the kitchen when you bake? You should tie up your hair.

'Just Monday to Thursday. She has classes. So many studies. The nuns give her endless homework. Sometimes we struggle to do it ourselves. Ada worries over her algebra, conversational Spanish. She's too young to have so much. But there it is. The nuns must know what they are doing.'

Tito got up, stretched his arms. He wanted to talk to her about Kushi but he wasn't sure how to come at it.

His mother cocked her head. 'You reminding me of your father these days, Tito.'

'How so?' He fixed his trousers; they were feeling a little tight around the waist. He was doing less and eating more.

'I have to pull everything out of you. Your father was like that, he'd sit there and say nothing. Like a post.'

'I come to see you every day.'

'That's not what I mean. Everyone has their lives, you and Ada. Now Flora has her life, too. You understand? It's the nature of things.'

'Mother, you can come anytime to see us. You don't need an invitation.'

'But I do, Tito. You must know that. As much as I like Ada, I wouldn't want her to feel put upon.' He'd never heard her talk like this before.

'Well there is something I'd like to discuss with you at some point. An investment opportunity in Fyzabad.'

She waved her hand. 'I don't need investments.'

'But I do,' he said. 'You know what black gold is, mother? It could make us very rich.'

At last she was looking at him. Money: her weak spot.

'Oil is the future and we have a chance to get in early.' Then he said, 'I'll bring Flora to see you tomorrow. How about that? We can talk about it then.'

'If she wants to. Don't make the child come if she doesn't want to.'

'We're having a party on the weekend.'

'I thought you were cutting back on all that.' She shook her head, irritated.

'Well, we always said we'd have a party to celebrate Ada getting better.'

'You're always looking for an excuse to party. Ada getting better, the rains coming early, a new horse. Your father and I were never like that.'

She played with her earring, a solid green oblong that clipped onto her lobes. 'You see this catch, I need to get it fixed. Your father gave me these for our anniversary. Jade. Can you get it mended?' She dropped both earrings into his hand.

Tito put on his hat. 'See you tomorrow, I'll bring cake.' Then he said, 'Maybe we can take a drive down to Kushi Estate and see what you think.'

FIVE

For months Charles Macleod had been watching Kushi Estate. He'd heard the rumours of oil bubbling up, dribbling down the hill. He'd heard about oil on the surface of the Godineau River, puddling at the foot of cocoa trees.

Charles had arrived in Trinidad from Aberdeen in March 1923. Appointed manager of Apex Oil Services for the West Indies, he had more than proved himself. He foresaw the construction of a 26-mile 6-inch pipeline from Forest Reserve to the refinery at Pointe-à-Pierre, which included a pipeline from the fields to the refinery and its facilities. He'd initiated and supervised the construction of the jetty at La Brea. He'd found oil all over the southern terrain of Trinidad; despite enormous challenges, nothing had stopped him – not the high pressure sands in Parrylands which made it difficult to drill, nor the technical difficulties in Point Fortin. He had brought in heavy clays – the first to do so. He'd drilled a well in Forest Reserve producing more than 100,000 barrels, and there was talk of oil in Central, where work was due to begin. An island saturated in oil. Charles was determined to make use of it. He intended to leave Trinidad in a blaze of glory.

'I want a street named after me,' he told Elsie, his wife. 'Or a square. For Willie to walk down a road in Port of Spain and see his father's name: Charles Macleod Avenue, or Charles Macleod Boulevard.'

Charles had made his approach Sonny Chatterjee. Chatterjee was known to be difficult, so he'd turned up one afternoon with a bottle of fine Cutty Sark whisky. Chatterjee took the bottle then ordered him to leave. Charles was so taken aback by his lack of manners, he laughed. A few days later, he wrote Chatterjee a letter outlining his intentions. He hadn't realised that Chatterjee could neither read nor write.

When Charles heard that Eddie Wade had also been to see Chatterjee, that he had, in fact, befriended him, he felt no reason to be worried. What could Eddie Wade offer? A one-man band with no more than two pennies to rub together. But hearing of Eddie's interest had given Charles a jolt; it wouldn't be long before someone else came along with an attractive proposal. He needed to remind Chatterjee that he wasn't going away any time soon. Apex had resources. He wanted to get in first.

When Macleod pulled up that afternoon, Chatterjee was in the yard playing cricket with his sons. He saw the truck and he shook his head, irritated.

'Mister Chatterjee. I want to talk to you. You got my letter, I assume. We can discuss any concerns you might have. I'm here to answer those questions.'

Chatterjee put up his hand.

'Mister Chatterjee, you can't see I'm trying to help you? As I said in my letter, I can offer you a holding fee of $1000.'

Chatterjee carried on looking straight ahead.

'I'm on your side. We can help each other.'

'I already make arrangements.' His voice was terse.

'Oh? What arrangements are those?'

Chatterjee signalled for his son to throw the ball.

'You're going to work with a conman from Texas? Ask him how he will pay for it all.'

Chatterjee hit the ball high over the trees; his son ran off to fetch it.

'Eddie Wade is all talk.' Macleod made his hand into a clapping beak. 'He has nothing to offer. The sooner you realise the better.'

'Get 'way from here. You hear what I say? Go before I throw you off mih land.' He called to his wife, 'Sita! Sita!'

'You want to be a coolie peasant all your life? This isn't Calcutta. You should be grateful for opportunities. Eddie Wade is a swindler; his pockets are empty. He will likely blow you all up.'

'Sita, send for the police. Hear what I say. Send for them!'

Sita came outside, the boys went behind her. Macleod backed

away, got in his truck and drove up the hill. He felt the vein in his head start to throb, the thick blue line that stuck out whenever he lost his temper.

At home, Macleod found Elsie, his wife, crouched in a corner of the kitchen, her face in her hands. An African bee, black and as big she claimed as a rodent, was trapped behind the shutters; it sounded demented, loud as a machine. Elsie was screaming; she told him to get it out. At last, he opened the screen door and using a tea towel, he managed to whip it away into the yard. A tree had fallen and died nearby; inside its hollowed trunk, there was a nest. He'd suspected it when he saw a cloud of bees hovering above the broken roots. He must set it alight, get rid of them. A few stings could kill a man.

But it wasn't just the bee that had Elsie upset. She was more sensitive than usual. Six weeks pregnant, she was desperate to go back to Fife where her family lived, and to their five-bedroomed Georgian house in the town. The thought of giving birth in Trinidad terrified her. Trinidad was full of death. She felt that she would die, or they would lose the baby. She hated the insects, the heat, the rain when it came, the sea when it was rough and looked like it was boiling. Elsie Macleod had been trying to make the best of her life in Trinidad, but since she fell pregnant, she was unable to pretend. Whatever she'd had in place to keep her there, had fallen away.

'What is it,' he said, taking off his hat. 'The bee's gone. There's no need for all this.' He helped her to the table.

'In Scotland, bees are small and they make honey.' Then, 'In Scotland, you might get TB or pneumonia but you can't catch yellow fever or malaria. There's no mosquitoes. You don't get your head chopped off.'

A few weeks ago, while trimming their hibiscus hedge, their yard boy's neck had been severed by a flying sheet of galvanized iron in a high wind.

'Look at the English family who died up at Toco. People stood and watched. Five people dead. Didn't they know there was a whirlpool there? I don't understand this country. It's not my home. It's not yours. Why are you trying to make it our home?'

'There are whirlpools in Scotland. People die in storms. It's not just Trinidad. It's like anywhere else, only hot.' Then he said, 'We can get you to a private nursing home in Port of Spain; it doesn't have to be the government hospital. We'll find a British consultant; the company will pay for it. There's no reason to be so fearful.'

Elsie sat up straight, afraid with a new thought.

'I don't want any of them to touch me. They mustn't touch me.'

'You can't have a baby without being touched.' He laughed. 'You're just being silly now.'

'What if you're not there? What if I end up in the public hospital. What if they don't have the right facilities? What if I die?'

'What if, what if.' He got up from his chair, adjusted the belt on his khaki trousers. 'What if the door had a nose and could blow it.' His voice was stern.

Elsie put her hand up to her face, wiped at her tears. She'd caught polio when she was a child and her left hand looked as if it was clutching something, her fingers unable to open. A half claw. It had never bothered him; she was shy about it in public.

'Look, we will have a plan. A contingency plan. You're imagining the worst, fretting about something that hasn't happened, that won't happen. I won't let it happen. Do you understand?' He was getting used to talking to her like this. In Trinidad, she had lost faith in herself. 'We have Ruby. She's perfectly able.' Ruby, their housekeeper, had birthed most of the children in the village.

'Willie wants to go back. It's not just me.'

Charles knew this wasn't true. His son, as far as he could tell, was relishing the outdoor freedom here. Unlike his parents, he thrived in the heat, running barefoot about the place; he had made friends in the small Presbyterian kindergarten, and recently learned how to swim. Last weekend they had taken him to the north coast and he'd swum in the Marianne River. He liked to climb up high in the mango tree and hide from his mother. It was a fact; William was happy enough here. Happier than either of them.

'We'll talk about it later.'

Irritated, he left his wife sitting at the table. The day was turning out to be a disaster. He climbed into his truck and started it up. It was cooler now, the sun dipping behind the mahogany trees. The sky was pale, whitewashed. Mahogany pods were all over the yard, their seeds scattered. William liked to hurl them up in the air and watch them twizzle down. Macleod felt them crunch under the wheels as he reversed.

As he drove out onto the San Fernando Road, a new thought came to him; it made him feel calm. He wondered why he hadn't thought of it sooner. It was obvious and clear like a message sent from God: Chatterjee's land was saturated with oil; there was no reason it wouldn't extend beyond his fence, and the land surrounding Kushi belonged to the Crown. It stopped at the silk cotton tree. An anticline can be far reaching. If he couldn't drill on Chatterjee's land, then he would drill around it.

SIX

At Tito and Ada's house, two long tables were set up outside, doors pushed back and flambeaux positioned along the veranda wall. Women from the village had been working all day in the kitchen under Henrietta's supervision. Meaty cooking smells drifted in from a roasting hog outside.

Tito set up a bar with little lights shining all around it. His mother would think it excessive, but this party was planned long ago, and he'd made sure to keep costs down. He'd almost cancelled; now he was glad he hadn't. His feelings of hopelessness had gone. Something new was in the air. Ever since Manzanilla.

Upstairs, music played on the gramophone. Tito mouthed the words: 'Like Jack Horner, in the corner, Don't go nowhere, What do I care?'

'Tell me…' Ada held out the hem of her dress. 'I've had it taken in. I don't think it spoils the shape, or does it? Maybe it should be shorter.'

'Shorter yes, it can always be shorter. But it looks terrific. You look terrific.'

She made a face. 'I need you to be honest. My legs. My legs are okay?'

'They're perfect. I only tell you what I see, darling. I can't help myself.'

His mood was cheerful; she wasn't about to argue.

She'd spent most of the day making sure the tables were set right, brass polished, flowers cut and arranged, keeping an eye on the cook. There were days when she couldn't care less, but today she was glad enough to go along with Tito's excitement. It was a relief.

Guests started to arrive at 6.30. Junior drove the cars in and parked them at the back of the house. Twenty-five guests, people Tito had known for years. Faces he loved and who loved him.

Eddie arrived, dressed in a khaki shirt and pale trousers, freshly shaved, his hair combed back. He looked younger, boyish. He shook Tito's hand, gave him the keys to his car. He'd enjoyed driving it.

'And the truck?'

'Strong Man's taking care of it. I'll have it back in the morning.'

'Look, let me know when you want to buy a car. Just the other day I was looking at a Chevrolet. They're coming in all now, and in different colours. Red is pretty, a post-box red, not too bright. It has a different starter engine so you have an ignition – works like magic.' Tito clicked his fingers, 'I'm thinking of trading in mine and buying something else. We'll see. I'll introduce you to Macfarlane. He's the real deal. Brings in cars from Miami. Don't get me started, I could talk cars all night.' Tito handed him a martini, 'Come meet my wife.'

He found Ada talking to a woman he had never much liked. She had sloping eyes, as if she was disappointed in the world around her. Ada liked her. Apparently they met now and then for morning coffee.

'So you're the man who stole our car,' Ada said, taking Eddie in – about 5ft 11, a broad back, but fine boned.

She was friendly, as if she had known him all her life.

Eddie smiled, taken aback. 'It's a fine car.'

She looked different here, her face bright, a thick gash of lipstick on her mouth. Her eyes were shining, almost black. She was glamorous, made for the stage. A woman who could make people stop what they are doing to look at her.

'My husband loves cars. I can't understand it.' Then she said, 'Emily's father has more money than he knows what to do with. We've been trying to decide how to spend it.'

'I'm sure you'll have no trouble,' Tito said. 'Make up a shopping list.'

He steered Eddie away to meet his other guests and called to Henrietta to bring another tray of hors d'oeuvres. Tito liked nothing better than to see people enjoying his house, and his heart was bloated with pride. He'd drunk a couple of martinis and his head was already charged.

His mother was sitting by the steps, her small feet crossed, and she was talking to Ada's aunt Bessie, whom Tito had known since he was a young man.

'This is Eddie, mother. He's going to make us rich.'

She ran her eyes over Eddie, and he took up her hand. Tito knew that she would appreciate his good looks. Looks mattered to his mother. She never failed to notice if someone had put on weight or aged.

When the gong rang for dinner and the guests found their places, Tito took his position at the top of the table, his wife to his left and Eddie opposite her.

Ruth, Ada's cousin, spoke about her boys; she was tired of looking after babies. Her husband was an infant, too.

'I seem to have three children not four. Gerry behaves like an infant. Are all men babies in disguise?'

Tito said, 'I believe so. But they require your pity not condemnation. Are men infants, ladies and gentlemen? Let's see what people think.'

There was laughter.

'Well,' Ruth said, 'they want to be embraced and they like to suckle. I tried giving him a comforter but it didn't work too well.'

More laughter. Tito nodded at his wife. 'Here's to Ada, who gives me more than she could know. Here's to new beginnings.'

They clinked glasses.

Tito turned to Eddie, 'Six months ago, I thought I'd be a widow. My wife was at death's door.'

Ada smiled. 'He even called Father Anthony.'

Eddie said, 'Were you frightened, Ada?'

'Not really. I saw a strange shadow hovering near the jalousies, with gaps of light for eyes. It seemed to call me, pull me out of bed. I felt myself lifting up and travelling. I wasn't unhappy or scared.' She looked up at the chandelier and tried to recall the exact feeling. 'I felt like myself. I can't really explain it. Like when you're taking an exam and they tell you to put down your pencil. The exam was over and now I could go.'

Eddie said, 'What happened next?'

'I heard Flora scream from downstairs. Next thing, I was lying on the floor staring up at Tito.'

Tito said, 'Flora was busy with a jigsaw puzzle one minute, then on her feet and hysterical for no apparent reason.' Then he said, 'Ada believes our daughter saved her life.'

'Flora didn't talk until she was four years old. We thought she was an elective mute. We took her to Dr Shepherd, and then to a visiting paediatrician from London. One day, just after her fourth birthday, when I was putting her to bed, she said: 'Look at the moon; I wish I could touch it.'

Tito said, 'It turned out Flora's vocabulary was excellent. She described colours she saw floating around people's heads. Reds, oranges, blues and greens.'

Ada said, 'She's always known things; she has a gift. Once she told me she didn't like the red man in the yard cutting the hedge. Turns out our gardener had murdered his girlfriend. Stabbed her 37 times. 'A cut fuh every year she live.' She once saw my father holding up the avocado tree with his foot after a hurricane. She said he was white and see-through like a cloud. My father died when I was nine.'

Tito said, 'Flora tells me I am green, and Ada is blue.'

Ada looked straight at Eddie. 'I wonder what she'd make of you.'

Eddie said, 'You must both know the story of the king who meets death.'

'No,' Tito said, 'tell.'

'A king was walking in a garden when one of his servants came running in saying he'd seen death. He begged the king to give him his fastest horse so he could escape to Samarra. Later the king saw Death in his garden, and asked why he'd frightened his servant like that. Death said,' and Eddie leaned in, 'I was surprised to see him here when I was planning to take his soul tonight in Samarra.'

Ada said, 'So the servant thought he was running away from death but he was actually running towards it?'

'Yes.' Eddie reached for his cigarettes. 'There's an appointment, and one day we have to keep the appointment. There's no getting out of it. Until then we might as well live.'

Ada watched the tiny flame burst from Eddie's match.

Tito said. 'We should all have mottos, I think. That's a good one.'

'What's yours, Tito?'

'Love and be loved, and all will be well.'

'My husband is a romantic. He was going to be a heart surgeon.'

'Without love the heart will wither. I've seen its effects. It's actually the only thing that matters.'

'Here's to love and life,' Ada said, and raised her glass. Her head was feeling light. She was enjoying herself. 'Let's have more of it.'

When dinner was finished, tables were cleared and moved, and the band started up again. People got up to dance. Tito had never liked dancing and, in particular, he didn't like this new lively way of dancing. He'd foxtrot now and then, yes, but there was something about this solo dancing that looked too much like showing off. And where was the fun in dancing alone? Leave this to the young people. Ada knew how to Charleston, wag her arms, flick out her legs. Right now she was looking well practised – her feet tight and controlled. All eyes were on her.

'What do you make of this, Eddie?'

'It's not for everyone.'

'Have you heard about these dance derbies in America? People are going for ten or fifteen hours straight, winning big money in competitions. If you stop moving you're disqualified.'

'I tried it with a girlfriend. We lasted two hours. The winning couple walked away with $5000.'

'But these people are propping up each other or are they actually dancing?'

'They call it dancing. Couples have to dance, but they're really only picking up one foot and then the other. Usually the women last longest, men run out of steam.'

Ada said, 'Isn't that always the way?' She was patting her face with a handkerchief. 'It's why women have children.'

Tito gave Eddie a look. 'Since we had Flora, she's never let me forget it.'

Then Ada said, 'Maybe we should try a dance derby right here in Trinidad. I think I would win.'

Tito glimpsed her brightness, and he realised it had been

absent for a while. Ada could make people feel good. Her light turned a room full of heads. He'd been miserable and anxious for months. It had taken its toll; he must make it up to her.

He stood up, smoothed out his shirt.

'You're a little drunk, my darling. But no matter.'

He led Ada to where their guests were dancing. Put his hand on her waist and let her arm rest on his shoulder. Two steps forward, one step back, then to the side, close. And so on. He breathed in her citrus scent; felt the soft gleam of her dark hair, shiny as satin. He had always liked her legs: strong thighs, ankles turned slightly out. She complained her feet pointed out like a duck. She called them ten-to-two feet.

'You're having a good time?'

'I am,' Ada said, 'you know how to throw a party.'

'What do you think of my new business partner?'

Eddie was smoking a cigarette, looking out at the yard.

'Is he what you'd call a roughneck? He doesn't seem so rough to me.'

'He's a fortune hunter, darling. A fortune hunter.'

That night after everyone had left, Ada lay down with her husband drunk and cat-spraddled beside her, unable to sleep. Her heart thumped and her thoughts ran like ticker tape. She'd had too much to drink. It wouldn't help her insomnia. The more she tried to fall asleep, the more she stayed awake. Dr Shepherd told her to think of an event in detail, no matter how dull and before you know it will be morning. Often she stayed awake until the light of dawn crept through the shutters. It was a condition she'd had since Flora was born. It might send her to the madhouse. She'd heard of women like that.

How many martinis had she had? Five or six. She'd drunk wine, then brandy. She and Ruth smoked a cigarette in the garden away from Tito's eyes. Ruth could barely move in her tight, shimmery white dress made by Mr Robeiro in record time. She complained of her weight, she complained about living in San Fernando and her argumentative neighbour; the dog's distemper and the purple fat ticks she'd found sucking inside its ears. She complained about Gerry and his fishy breath. Both Emily and

Ruth were unhappily married, waiting for their husbands to die. It would be a long wait. Was that what happens when you're unhappy – you wait for your husband to die? Ada looked at Tito, the shadowy shape of his strong nose, the collapsed chin. She didn't want him to die.

For months, Tito had been preoccupied, agitated. He kept out of her way – leaving the house earlier and coming home late; he was drinking more. Not one drink in the evening, but three or four or more. Henrietta, first up in the morning, left out the bottle of scotch for Ada to see. Half or more was gone. It worried Ada.

Henrietta had come to work for her when she was first married. Heavy in frame, her strong African features made her look fierce; she didn't often smile. But she was as solid and trustworthy as the walls of Ada's house. Henrietta didn't care for men, especially men who drank, like her father, who, when she was a little girl, once made her kneel all day with her wrists tied together in the hot sun. She had never married, because she didn't want to marry someone as cruel as her father. She had a daughter through a chance encounter with a Grenadian skipper passing through the islands. Men were unreliable. Better she stay an old maid.

'Not all men are so,' Ada told her.

'Yes, Mister Tito different,' Henrietta said. 'A gentleman. When he say he going to do something he do it. You could set a clock by he.'

Tito could do no wrong, as far as Henrietta was concerned. But even Henrietta said, 'Mister Tito not himself.'

Most nights, after dinner, Tito sat in his study staring at papers and log books until late. He often spoke on the telephone in a hushed voice.

Ada started to probe.

'What's wrong, Tito? Is it something to do with me? Has something happened?'

'No, darling' he said, as if she was a child.

'Talk to me. You can tell me. Is it something I've done? You're worried about something. Is it your mother? Has something happened with Raul?'

She put her arms around his neck, kissed his dimply cheek.

'Stop fretting. All is well.'

Through his forced smile, she saw his face was long, his eyes dark.

Then last week he'd shouted at her.

'For Christsake, Ada, you can't leave me alone for once? You're like a mosquito whining in my ear. Find something to do. Go water the yard. Tend the orchids. Do something.'

The following day he was contrite. But once again, he stayed up late in his study. She found him asleep with his back slumped over the desk like a dead man.

They had stopped making love. He said the equipment wasn't working properly. When pressed he'd told her, 'It happens with age. I'm in need of new parts. The engine is seizing up.'

'But you're fifty-two not eighty-two.'

When she got sick, he'd moved himself into another bedroom. It took weeks to recover from the onslaught to her kidneys. Yellow fever was a killer; she was lucky to survive. Her skin was the colour of wax, and her body leaked a sour, acidic scent; she ached as if she'd been beaten. And even now there were days when Ada felt fatigued, and her skin was tinged with yellow, and she wanted to sleep and sleep. Tito was back sleeping in their room again, but his hands never came near her. Was he frightened to touch her? He had never been a zealous lover. When she heard Ruth complaining of how her husband tried to mount her daily like a dog, she was surprised. She couldn't imagine Tito doing that. Is that how some men were? She was naïve, slow to catch on.

She had started to wonder if Tito no longer desired her. The thought of this horrified her. At thirty-five, her body was softer and fuller than before. Were her thighs becoming spongy, her breasts less firm? She had noticed new lines around her eyes; a promise of future creases. She thought of the early days of their marriage, when Tito had made love to her; counted the moles on her body.

He hid his insecurities. When another man spoke to Ada for any length of time, or asked her to dance, she knew he didn't like it. He might say, 'Michael Jardine, he likes you, eh? I saw the way he looked at you.'

'Why wouldn't he? He knows you don't like to dance.'

Tito had talked of wanting another child. Ada wasn't so sure.

She'd hated being pregnant – the way her legs swelled, her breasts grew big as gourds.

On the night Flora was born, Ada buckled in her bed, certain she was dying. How could she feel this much pain and survive? The baby was breech, the doctor said. They were in for a long night. In the early hours, she begged Henrietta to send for Tito before it was too late. When he appeared, her forehead was wet, her body soaked, the sheet a tent over her legs.

'Goodbye, Tito. I'm sorry.'

'You're not going anywhere. Your life is with me, Ada. You, me and the baby.'

Ten minutes later, Henrietta held her shoulders while the doctor pulled at Flora's tiny feet. They dragged her out – and for a moment in that last volcanic rush, Ada saw herself from above and it seemed to her that the floor was pooled with blood like an abattoir in which a hundred cattle had been butchered. When Flora cried, Ada came back into her body; Henrietta placed her slippery daughter into Ada's arms.

'Lord have mercy – a girl!'

For all the pain and terror of her birth, since Flora started school, Ada had begun to wonder if Tito was right. Wasn't it better if Flora had a brother or sister?

To increase her chances of falling pregnant, Ada had followed instructions: she'd sipped grapefruit on waking, planted a bay tree in the yard, wore silk underwear, grated cinnamon on her evening meal. Dr Shepherd told her she must be intimate with her husband as often as possible. Nothing seemed to work.

Then Henrietta told Ada of a different kind of doctor who could help. An old woman bush practitioner living in the east. There were things she would need, a piece of Tito's hair, a thread from her wedding gown, a note of agreement and ten candles, one for every year of marriage. Ada thought about it, but then she'd fallen ill and was forced to put the idea of another child to one side. Now Ada was stronger and more than anything she wanted her husband's touch. How would she fall pregnant if not by an immaculate conception?

The last few days, to her relief, she'd seen a change in Tito. He was more like himself. When he arrived home from work, she heard his familiar whistle in the hall. He was excited about the party; about his new friend Eddie Wade.

She saw at once that Eddie had something about him – a confidence or purpose. It was in his walk and his voice. She hadn't expected him to be so young. He must be mid-thirties. He was good-looking, his hair slicked back, his green eyes set deep.

He wore cheap, sweet cologne, Limacol. His clothes were cheap; the khaki fabric coarse, poorly stitched. His battered boots were more suited to the forest than the polished, mahogany floors of their house. She wondered why he hadn't made more of an effort. He could have borrowed slacks, a dinner shirt and decent shoes. He looked like he'd come straight from the field. He ran his fingers through his hair when he talked.

She saw the women looking at Eddie. Emily whispered, 'Who's the cute roughneck?'

Before she left the party, Ruth made a point of going over to him. She leaned in, "Goodbye Eddie, good luck. I'm sure we'll see you again."

He was not like the laid-back Trinidadian men Ada knew. When he spoke, he fastened his eyes on her as if she was the only person in the room. But it wasn't only her. She saw him do the same with others. Perhaps it was his French and Portuguese blood. She hadn't realised he was born in San Fernando, then emigrated to America when he was fifteen. Freshwater Yankee. Why come back to Trinidad? Most people liked to get out – apart from her husband for whom Trinidad would always be paradise.

'I'm here to find oil,' Eddie said, and there was something in his expression that made her certain he would.

'You believe in yourself, Eddie.'

'Of course. Don't you?' Then he said, 'You remind me of someone but I can't think who.'

'Well, you don't remind me of anyone. No one at all.'

It was true. Eddie was like no one she'd met. It seemed to Ada he could have fallen out of the sky.

SEVEN

Tito and Eddie drove down to Siparia together in the darkness. At dawn, Kushi was still filled with dark blue light; trees were black and dense. Eddie said the air was cool as Canada; he was glad of his jacket, his shoes and socks. Chatterjee came out to meet them; hair combed, barefoot, wearing a dhoti. He stood aside to let them into the dark kitchen at the back of the house, where chickens came in from the yard and pecked around their feet.

Eddie was relieved to find Chatterjee in a cheerful mood. He'd warned Tito that he could be difficult; today was not going to be easy. They might leave with nothing. It was a possibility.

Eddie sat at the table while Tito opened his brief case. Chatterjee nodded at $2000 laid crisp and flat, as promised.

Sita went to the fire and took down the coffee pot. She brought cups and condensed milk to the table. Then she laid out paratha, a bowl of curried chataigne, baigan.

'Eat,' Chatterjee said, 'nothing good does come from a empty belly.'

While the sun broke through the trees and seeped into the room, Tito read aloud the lease drawn up by Alfie Mendes. Chatterjee listened and followed Tito's eyes on the page. Every now and then he interrupted.

'No, Mister Fernandes, you not understanding me at all.' Or 'No, Eddie, you know better than that.' At one point he got up, and went outside; they heard him cursing in Hindi. Tito looked startled.

'Christ,' Tito said, and went to the doorway. Chatterjee had his arms raised to the sky.

'Leave him,' Eddie said. 'He'll come back.'

Sonny Chatterjee made himself clear: a year was all he could offer. He was troubled by rumours of American oil companies hacking up agricultural estates with little compensation. He wanted something in the contract to protect against damage to the land. Sita was fretting about the boys, the noise, the chaos. One of his sons suffered with fits. He was worse when unsettled. If they found nothing, then what? A year was plenty. He had agreed a year and no more with his wife. That was final.

'We not used to people here. Sita like a quiet house. You understand?'

'You can't lease land for a year,' Tito said, looking at Eddie. 'What's the point? By the time the trees are cleared it will be June. You only have to do the math. A year will pass like that.' He clicked his fingers.

Chatterjee shook his head.

'A year and no more,' he said.

Eddie, knowing this was likely their best offer, said, 'Look, a lot could happen in a year. We can agree to no drilling after the year is up. It would be foolish to stop production because of a twelve month lease. If we find oil, it could flow for many years.' Then Eddie said, 'How about we stop drilling after twelve months, but we take commission on the oil from those same wells for five years.'

'Two,' Chatterjee said. 'Two years and no more.'

Chatterjee wanted a higher rate of royalties. He waved his hand at ten percent. 'Ten is too little. Thirty better. Plenty better.'

Eddie said, 'It's more than Apex offered. Didn't Macleod offer you 3%?'

'Yes, and I tell them no. I'll say no to you, too.'

When Tito Fernandes and Sonny Chatterjee eventually signed a 12-month contract for the mineral mining of Kushi estate, Siparia, in exchange of 25% royalties, Eddie felt mostly relief.

After papers were signed, the men emerged sweltering and parched into the porch, surprised to find the sun was high in the sky. They looked each other in the eye, shook hands. Chatterjee in his dhoti; Tito in his tailored crumpled linen suit, black hair flopping in his glistening face; Eddie in his rolled-up shirt sleeves, as if ready to start drilling at once.

'Here's to us,' Tito said, blotting his brow. 'Let's make it happen.'

Chatterjee's grip was firm; for the moment his uncertainty gone.

'You know the word fortuitous, Sonny? When things happen by chance for good reason. It's what happened here with all of us.'

They sat in the porch; drank champagne from tin cans – inscribed *Bordo Evaporado*, sweet condensed milk – with soldered-on handles. It was the first time Chatterjee had tasted champagne. He'd expected it to be sweet. It was bitter and he liked it.

'Get used to it,' Eddie said, 'You'll be drinking a lot more from now on.'

The men were hungry, and when Sita appeared with a tray of banana leaves, they were grateful for curried channa, curried fowl, fistfuls of rice. They didn't say much but the stillness in the air made them feel certain they were on the edge of something momentous. Eddie thought how long he had waited for this, and how suddenly, in this last week, it had materialised, as if the hands of angels had put it all together.

'God is good,' Chatterjee said. 'Praise God.'

Eddie raised his cup. 'To the angels.'

EIGHT

It took thirty-five days to clear away the forest on the north side of Chatterjee's estate, the patch where oil first came up and dribbled around the stick like a miracle. Twenty-two men and women came from the villages around with axes, picks and saws. These people, known as the Tattoo Gang, knew the forest and they hacked and chopped through hundreds of diseased cocoa trees, the immortelles above them, and the cedar and pine around them. Branches were dragged away and the trunks of smaller trees were lifted onto carts and pulled away by buffalo. Women cut and tore at the undergrowth, culled the knotted and tangled bush seething with bachac ants and termite nests big like heads, stuck to the pale immortelles. These wilder parts hadn't been touched for some time. Eddie came upon an armadillo, a howler monkey and a quenk. Unafraid, the creatures squatted on rocks and stared at him.

'Look,' Eddie said, to the others, 'we have company.'

He clapped his hands and the animals scuttled away.

Tendrils hung like thick ropes, tangled and knotted; it often took days to clear a few yards. The workers were paid according to the number of felled trees and by the amount of earth they'd shifted. Eddie assured Tito, although slower, it was cheaper than bulldozers and trucks. He reminded him of his own words: 'We're here to make money not spend it.' Though Eddie agreed with Tito's suggestion that they install a telephone in Chatterjee's house. That way they could keep him informed of progress.

They worked from first light, stopped for lunch at 11 am. There was rice, bread, beans, oranges. Sometimes Sita made cake or cut up fruits. They carried on until nightfall.

The sun was a bully, hot enough to make you feel to die. The air was thick with mosquitoes and sandflies; then there were the Jack Spaniards. They caught in the hair of a young woman called Mercy who had come from the village looking for work. Eddie had employed her to cook for the workmen and keep them refreshed with water. That day, Jack Spaniards flew inside the tiny caves of her ears and when she opened her mouth to scream, dived into her windpipe. Mercy was carried choking to the house where Sita soaked her head with vinegar and tipped aloe juice down her burning throat. Eddie drove her howling to Point Fortin where a doctor quickly injected her with a high dose of epinephrine. Her body puffed up, and then went down.

There were snakes: macajuel, anaconda, even deadly mapepire, but the men and women were too quick for them. A swipe of the cutlass and their pointed heads were off – livers extracted and spread onto the workers' skins to stave off mosquitoes. Eddie himself found a 12-foot boa at the back of the outhouse, curled up in the shade like a small child. He shot it first between the eyes, then decided to skin it without cutting. 'Look,' he said, holding up the mottled body, 'like taking a sock off a leg.' With this peeling and rolling came the birth of some ten small snakes, small and thin as bangles and half of them dead. 'You ever see anything like that?' he said, tipping the babies into a bucket. 'Delicious fried up like whitebait.'

Once the trees were gone, they started to level out the incline and the men dug hard into the dry earth and the women carried trays of this earth on their heads to the place where they would build a dam, which Eddie said they'd need for overflow. Chatterjee couldn't imagine an overflow of any kind but Eddie told him it would come.

'As sure as I'm standing here, make no bones, the oil is right underneath me like a lake.'

Chatterjee admired Eddie's self-belief. It was something he had never had; his nature was cautious, mistrustful. But he wanted to believe Eddie.

Chatterjee was up at 4.30am most mornings; he put on a shirt, took his coffee outside and sat on the bench his father had made. It was cool; sometimes a dense white mist swirled and thickened around him. He liked to watch the sky change from blue-black to palest blue; see the sun peep through the trees, climb into the yard and light-up his body. He breathed in the ripe smell of damp earth, mixed with the perfume of angel trumpets that grew outside his porch. Dead leaves made a mat under his feet. He sipped his coffee, sweetened heavily with condensed milk, and listened to the forest waking, the high trill of corn birds, parakeets chattering; the occasional cry of howler monkeys. These sounds were the familiar songs of his life.

Since Eddie's arrival there were new sounds, shouts from down inside the heart of the estate, disturbances, machinery, terrific banging, sawing, chopping. He'd hear the deep thud of a large crashing tree – big immortelles of fifty or sixty feet – and feel his soul flinch. Then there was the hum of the generator. It started at dawn and carried on all day and into the night. Meanwhile Eddie's trucks trundled up and down the track, carrying equipment, people, supplies.

Sonny pictured old man Madoo sitting bent over amongst a heap of crimson and yellow pods, picking them apart and laying out seeds to dry. He saw himself, a young barefoot child with curly hair, and his father offering a pod from which to scrape and eat the sweet sour pulp. *Sonny, what really going on here? Sonny, what all you do? Sonny, be careful. A thousand trees gone in two days?*

As he expected, Sita complained about it all; about the roar of the trucks as they made their way down the track. She hated the dust. She didn't like Mercy, especially now that she was in and out of her house all day. She didn't like these people on their land. She tried to keep their sons away from the site. She shouted at them until her voice was hoarse. She told Chatterjee it better be worth it – this chaos – to their lives, to their children's lives. He reassured her, and in doing so he tried to reassure himself.

It was hotter once the big trees were gone and the land became scorched and cracked like burnt skin. In fact, the whole place crackled with the heat of a furnace. But as Chatterjee said, at least it was dry, and it wouldn't be so for long. *Rain go come.* Discarded tree trunks were split in four and once the ground was clear, laid down in a row like the dead, covered over with clay and gravel. This was how the road into Chatterjee's estate was made.

Eddie worked alongside and helped where he could. He liked to take a spade and dig down deep, rub the damp earth in his hands, put it to his nose, lick it from his finger. He was no geologist, but he had an idea of what to look for; and he was more than hopeful. For the first time in his life Eddie felt like he was in charge. A far cry from his early days in Texas.

He'd seen his first well come in when he was nineteen-years-old, shaking peanuts in a field in Texas. The oil fountain shot up, and turned green and then gold, and he thought the earth was turning inside out. He had never seen anything more beautiful. In that moment, he knew what he would do with his life.

In Beaumont, as a young man, Eddie learned all he could from the boiler-workers, the drillers, and mostly from boomers who swooped in, worked for a while, then moved on when they heard of somewhere better. He'd worked for a businessman who owned most of the town. Walter Well told him, *You're going places, and by that I don't mean jail.*

Eddie shared a shack with a Puerto Rican toolie. Walls were so thin; when a dust storm blew in, the place rattled like a tin bucket. People got sick a lot. Beaumont water was soupy and tasted of frogs. It started with stomach cramps, high fever. If you caught 'the Beaumonts' you had to take a few days off.

Eddie was happy to stack pipe, feed the boilers, wash down the derrick, dig holes. For a time he was a roustabout, looking after the neatness of the field, picking up broken rods, junk pipe. He dug ditches to manage waste water; he took care of repairs, made sure the tubes on boilers were swabbed. He looked after the steam engine, monitored the oil pumped from each well. When a whistle blew in Beaumont, you knew a well had come in. Everyone came to see and cheer. It was good manners to do so.

It was here in Beaumont that Eddie met Michael Callaghan. One night, after Eddie had just been paid, two men jumped him and stole his monthly earnings: $150. Callaghan saw the whole thing from his truck. He held up the men with a .45, marched them back to where Eddie was lying in the road, his face globbed up with blood. He told the bandits, 'The only talking I'll be doing is with my gun. So hand the damn money back to this poor sucker.'

A more experienced cable-driller than Eddie, Callaghan was a bendy, scrawny man with red hair. A man for detail. Eddie might come with the big plan; Callaghan knew how to make it happen.

Once, after they'd got together, they followed a lead of Eddie's that took them five thousand miles south, along narrow trails into the dark heart of Santa Maria de Vitoria, El Salvador, where they found a skin of oily iridescence on the surface of San Francisco River. They set up camp. After two months of dry, sizzling weather, rains arrived early and suddenly. For ten days they were trapped in their camp, unable to move; sure they would die. They returned to Texas, poorer, thinner, their chests bubbling with phlegm.

Still determined, Eddie drove with Callaghan far across the rocky land, as far as Corsicana. South of the 'Cotton Belt' railroad track they drilled for oil and they drilled for water. If a supply of hot artesian water came through, people came in hundreds believing it would cure all kinds of ailments. Old men with long beards got down on their stomachs and drank it. When they eventually found oil, they were scuppered by a crook now serving time for corruption in Auburn State prison.

By the time he left Texas, Eddie had felt defeated. 'It can do that to you; this oil business,' Callaghan told him. 'It's not a game for pussies.'

The telephone line was faint and crackling; Eddie shouted into the mouthpiece.

'Kushi Estate – this is gonna be big, Callie. I mean real big. I can see the stuff bubbling.'

'Remember the preacher in Beaumont? He said the same thing; said he could see through the ground, and if you paid him fifty dollars, he'd hold his hands up to the sky like he was touching God.'

'He found that seepage up at the creek.'

'A fluke.'

Callaghan liked to tease.

'Those were the days of oil-smellers and witches. Those days are done. You don't need special powers here.'

'The soil has sand? There must be clay, shale? What about gas?

Is there a landing jetty? Without that we risk seawater damage. Where are the nearest facilities? Can we pump it out to a port? What about fresh water? You have a water supply? We can't do anything without water. What about this guy who owns the estate? He's not a crook?'

Eddie checked that he could not be overheard. 'He's no crook. He's stubborn, but he's no crook.'

'It's not going to be like Salvador? Tell me that much.'

'Forget Salvador. Forget Beaumont. I know what you're thinking. This is Trinidad. You hear me, Trinidad.'

Other men came from the villages: Tripe, Mister Long, Gelliseau, Mete and Horatio. Then Larry and Richard Gaskill were brought in from Apex in Forest Reserve, after they jumped ship. He warned them, he couldn't pay Apex rates. Right now, Eddie knew, labourers all over Trinidad were becoming aware of their rights, and fighting for higher wages; the Workers Association had made sure of that. He didn't have a problem with it. He had his terms and he laid them out – stay with him and work hard, and they'd be rewarded further down the road. The oil business was a fickle business. He told them, look out for one another, rest when you can; no alcohol on his watch. Especially once they started drilling. 'We'll need our wits about us.'

Gelliseau was strong, his arms ballooned with muscle, his back shaped in a V. He didn't say much but, like Mete, he knew about construction and had worked at La Brea on the jetty. Long was stringy and agile, he had laboured for years on a sugar estate and that estate had now closed. Long had six hungry mouths to feed, from two-years-old up to fifteen. Then there was Horatio Sanchez. Eddie trusted Horatio at once; he had a steadiness about him, a sense of duty. He was quick to smile, showing gaps between his front teeth. He lived in Claxton Bay with his mother; his father died in a cane fire when he was five. He'd worked on rigs in Barrackpore, Los Bajos, and trained as a technician. When Horatio realised Blacks weren't paid the same as Americans or Europeans, he left Trinidad for Venezuela where salaries were equal and where oil was booming. Then one night Motilones attacked the camp and fired a poisoned blow-pipe arrow into the back of his friend who later died. Horatio came home. He said he was glad to be at Kushi, and Eddie was glad to have him.

More men would come when Eddie needed them from Danny village, down towards the coast. He agreed a daily rate, and he was sorry it wasn't more. For now this was his team.

Grace Montano arrived from the village. Tall and heavy, with ample breasts, born right there in Fyzabad, she told Eddie how her parents had come to Trinidad from St Kitts looking for work. Her father, known as Bridgeman, had helped build the Red Bridge at Plaisance Park, the Silver Caroni Bridge and Spring Bridge in Moruga. Now she needed this job; Bridgeman was ill, his skin flaking off like old paint, a consequence, she was sure, of years working with cast iron in the hot sun. His medicine was expensive and came from America. Grace was shy with strangers, and kept her eyes down. She had heard about Eddie Wade, how he'd come to make his fortune. When Mercy told her that Eddie Wade was looking for someone, after months of praying she would find work, she felt sure this was a sign from God.

Eddie showed Grace what to do – where to wash and hang his clothes, where to prepare food and how to work the stove.

'You can cook?' Yes, she could cook, she said.

The first night, Eddie said he'd never tasted pork so chewy – like a bicycle tyre. Grace put her hands up to her hot face. 'Nobody ever say that about my cooking.'

Eddie laughed. 'Grace, that was the best stew pork I ever had,' he said, and he meant it. 'Make that every day, I'll be a happy man.'

He knew how people treated their workers, but it never made sense to him. If you treat someone kindly, then all will be well. Why make things hard for yourself?

'You don't want to get married?'

'Yes, sir – so I could put on a white dress and walk down the aisle.'

'You could do that anyway,' Eddie said, 'you don't have to be married to do that.'

'True, sir.' She laughed.

'You have children?'

'No sir.'

Eddie had heard she'd had a son when she was sixteen, but he knew why, in her position, she wouldn't tell him.

'How old are you Grace?'

'I have forty-five years, sir.'

'You ever steal anything?'

She shook her head. 'Only plum, when I was a girl. They didn't taste good.'

'I've stolen all kinds of things, Grace. Money from my father; I stole from a pawnshop in Phoenix when I had nothing. I stole food from a diner when I was hungry and desperate. You might be shocked to hear a white man like me did all this. But I did. It wasn't a good time.'

'Yes, sir.'

'Have you done bad things?'

'No sir.'

'I have. I almost killed a man, and I slept once with the wife of a dear friend of mine. I have a daughter I never met. She doesn't even know her father's name.'

Grace looked him in the eye. She hadn't expected him to talk so openly.

'So you see, Grace, I want to be honest with you. And you need to be honest with me. That way we can work well together. I can't pay much, but if the wells come in, as I think they will, everyone will get a little extra. That's the deal.'

'Yes sir.'

Every morning, Grace walked the two-mile road in the dark from the village to the site. The bush was high, and trees were tall and shadowy. She carried a lamp of coconut oil and the flame lit up her way. Bats dashed above her; she kept an eye out for mapepire. She took her time; she was not afraid. Grace had faith, and she believed God walked before her to clear the path of danger. She arrived each dawn when the mist was still thick in the bushes and on the silk cotton tree with its head of wild hair.

She put on coffee to boil and bakes to rise; she fried the eggs with their sunny sides down just as Eddie liked them. She cooked enough for the men who ate together. She tidied around the place, washed out Eddie's clothes. Then she walked up to Chatterjee's house to help out there, returning before 10 to cook lunch with vegetables brought by Mercy from the market. The men ate at 11 am, then along with Mercy, Grace cleared away their dishes. Late afternoon she carried drinks down to the barracks. The men were always glad to see her and though they sometimes made jokes, mostly they were respectful, especially when Eddie was around. She left after Eddie had eaten dinner and she had cleared up after him. She worked slowly, as if she had until the end of the world. Eddie was grateful to have her there.

The estate was full of bats and they hung in the trees like rags. For a couple weeks, Eddie slept in the truck and often woke to a bat lapping blood from his toes. He tried sleeping in the cabin with the windows up, but it was too hot and his legs cramped. Chatterjee never offered a room in his house. He knew that Sita wouldn't like it. She seemed uncomfortable around Eddie. She never smiled or spoke directly to him. Eddie didn't care.

He was glad when his workers chopped down the 70ft cedar tree and used the wood to build him a cabin. At last he had somewhere to sleep, to prepare food, and a place out the back for washing. A tank fed the shower, a biscuit tin lid with some holes punched in. It was basic, but it was his. Its musky smell reminded him of his mother, and her carved jewellery box embellished with elephants and hibiscus flowers that he had kept with him. Inside was a piece of his hair, from when he was a child and also a long dark lock. He often missed her, and her words of encouragement. 'Keep going,' she'd say. 'It takes years to make an overnight success.' At the front of the cabin, he put out a couple planters' chairs brought down from his uncle's estate, with wooden slats he could rest a drink on. When Grace saw him there, she said, 'Eh-eh, *Mister* Eddie.'

At night the yard was nothing but blackness, so Eddie bought hurricane lamps and dotted them around. Otherwise you moved like a blind man feeling your way around the place. Twerk-twerk said the crickets, pong di-di, the frogs, and while he sat in the porch with his flask of rum and his cigarettes, he listened to the hiss and crackle and rustle of the bush, and it seemed to him to be alive with its own heartbeat. Bu-dahh, bu-dahh, bu-dahh. When he looked up the stars seemed far away and tiny as pins.

That first night, he felt something on his chest, a soft heavy

70

object. Sure someone was in his room, he shouted, and flung out his hands. Big and thick-legged, the spider hit the wall like a tennis ball. When Eddie woke, he saw the outline of the brown shape like a man's hand spread against the mesh. Another night he felt the house swaying and he wondered if there was an earthquake. He'd felt earthquakes up at Mon Repos – heard the roar like a truck coming and the tremble of the ground as it shook under his feet. But it wasn't an earthquake. Wild hogs were butting against the stilts of his house, scratching off mud, rubbing at their skin.

Eddie wasn't lonely; he had enough things in his mind to occupy him; plans and hopes for making this happen, logistical hoops to figure out, costs to work on. And when he'd done some of this work, he had memories he liked to conjure. He thought about his little girl in Oklahoma. Was he was doing all this for her? Maybe. He would find his way to her one day, give her all the things he wished he could give her. Not just material things, but his heart, which he felt was half carved-up with her name hot branded upon it. He didn't know too much about love, but he was certain that he loved her by the longing he felt to know her better. Was that what love is, a certain kind of longing? He thought about Kathryn, her mother, and her long red hair that looked like it was coated in light. When he looked at the night skies, he recalled the meteor shower he'd seen with Kathryn in Palo Duro Canyon. She knew about stars. She said the darkest skies make the brightest stars. *It's not the star you see but a glow that left the star light-years ago.*

Ten years older and a widow, Kathryn wasn't a beauty. She carried a pistol in her belt, and nothing seemed to frighten her, only her own loneliness. In those early days she was tough in a way that people who are hurting can sometimes be.

'You won't find better food in the whole of Beaumont,' she'd say, of her travelling cafe. 'Or a better cook. That goes for the whole of Texas.'

She always gave Eddie extra, even baked him lemon meringue pie because, she said, he reminded her of her husband who'd died in a railroad accident in Mississippi. The train driver had swallowed too many kidney pills, fell asleep at the throttle and collided into the rear end of a freight train. Jack was standing up, helping someone get their luggage, and he was pitched through the window so hard he split in two. She told Eddie, 'I've thought about tracking that driver someday and shooting him in the head.'

Her breasts were small and peeped out now and then from her blouse. She liked to tease, but as far as he knew she never went with anyone.

Then one evening, she invited Eddie back to her hotel. They drank whiskey together at the bar, then she took him up to her room. After they'd made love, she told Eddie, 'There's nothing you can do to bring them back. When they're dead they're dead. I'd do anything to see Jack come through that door.' She cried a little; Eddie held her close.

She was free in her pursuit of pleasure in a way that he hadn't experienced with younger women. She guided his hands and slowed him down, cooed with pleasure. He hadn't realised how much pleasure a woman could feel. She told him that she pleasured herself most days. She showed him how she did it.

"All women do this?'

'Who knows. If they don't, then they should.'

Lying there in the small hotel room under the patchwork quilt, they listened to the icy wind rushing through the eaves. Kathryn asked him about his life. It was good to hear about the tropics, she said. Snow was coming; they could keep each other warm. Tell me again about the warm sea; tell me about the poui trees.

Kathryn taught Eddie how to dance. Once a week there was a live band playing in town and she showed him how to listen for the rhythm, use his feet, how to hold her, how to stay straight and tall while supporting her; how to be loose in himself. She showed him how to waltz. She seemed to be happier dancing than at any other time. She seemed to forget her grief.

They spent five months together.

'Don't worry,' Kathryn told him. 'I won't fall in love with you and you won't fall in love with me. This is good for us both. Everybody needs a little affection.' She told him that she liked his skin, the shape of his back. She liked his way of talking. 'You talk like you're singing.' Maybe one day she could go to Trinidad with him, see where he'd come from.

One afternoon, he told her to close up the café early. They caught the train into Houston, took a tram to L'Escargot, a high class restaurant in the theatre district. Eddie tried not to show that he was intimidated by the immaculate table cloths, the politeness of the softly spoken waiters, the candlelight, the piano playing in the bar, the French menu. When the check came, he paid without flinching. He'd never before blown his monthly earnings on a meal. Kathryn was grateful, he could see that, but she made sure to tell him that she could have had just as much fun with him if they'd gone to a bar in downtown Beaumont. He didn't need to spend that kind of money on her.

They took the train back to Batson, and the sky was black and endless. They were quiet, and there was an awkwardness in the silence, and it seemed to come from Kathryn. Eddie suspected that she was thinking about her dead husband. He wanted to fix it for her, to make her better, but he knew he couldn't. No matter how many dances, or how you made love, how you talked through the night, you couldn't change the lean of somebody's heart. Truth was, he felt lucky to know her, a woman of the world, a woman who understood things, who knew what she liked, and what she didn't like. He wanted to tell her all this that night but something held him back.

Then without saying anything, two days later, Kathryn packed up her travelling café and left. Eddie asked around Batson, then he caught a ride into Beaumont to ask there, but no one knew where she'd gone. Someone said they'd heard she'd gone east to the salt mines. She'd never mentioned salt mines or anything about going east. Eddie was baffled. When he realised there was no way of finding her, he tried not to think about her. He tried to forget her face. For many weeks he avoided walking by her hotel. He got on with his life. Callaghan asked him what was wrong. He didn't know what to say; he barely understood it himself. He felt bruised, but he knew the bruising would pass.

A year later, a letter arrived.

Dear Eddie,
Edith Ella Wade Franklin was born September 14ᵗʰ 1925.
She looks like you. Same eyes as far as I can tell.

I don't see any merit in farewells. I thought about you a lot. You are a good man. Maybe that's why I left, because you deserve more. She is the best gift you could've given me. I am more grateful than you will ever know. One day maybe you'll come to meet her.
Yours, Kathryn

She included the post office box address and a photograph of a round-faced pale child, her head done up in a bonnet and wearing a long dress, a christening outfit, no doubt. When Eddie saw the photograph – Clifton Studio, Oklahoma, marked on the back – something happened inside him. Her eyes reminded him of his own mother, and he was aware of the distance between them, and not just in miles. It reminded him that the things he had loved were somehow always out of his reach. If we knew what was coming, would we do things differently? Perhaps, so.

Every month Eddie made sure to send money to the post box address in Oklahoma. Before he left Texas, he thought about going east to find them. He knew what it was like to be without a father, told himself that a girl's father is the standard by which she'd judge all men. But right now he had nothing to offer, no home of his own, no money to speak of. He figured if he could make enough money, he could go to Oklahoma and persuade Kathryn to marry him. They could start to build a good life together. For now, he let Kathryn know where he was going; she could write to him at his uncle's estate up at Mon Repos.

Two months before, Kathryn had sent a picture of Edith sitting by a fir tree with baubles hanging from it, with snow around the picture frame; it wasn't real, a trick by the photographer to make it look like it was Christmas. This picture was stuck on the wall of his cabin here on Chatterjee's estate. Every day, when he poured himself a cup of coffee in the ceramic cup with the painted-on flag he'd brought from Texas, he told his little girl good morning.

NINE

Tito's investment in Fernandes/Wade/Chatterjee Limited came mostly from a $8000 loan guaranteed by Fernandes Holdings Ltd, from the National Bank of Canada. Mrs Fernandes agreed to invest $5000. To cover any shortfall and contingency, he sold $1500 shares in the Queen's Park Hotel. He was sentimental about the shares given to him by his father. One day he'd buy them back.

More and more Tito understood the enormous potential of oil; not just for automobiles and motorcycles. Sometime soon, tractors would replace buffaloes in the fields. Aviation was becoming more popular. Lindberg had made his first transatlantic flight. There was talk of a new oil-water emulsion used in road construction in America; rumours of an English company setting up a bitumen refinery right there in Trinidad with a jetty made from greenheart timber and reaching over a mile into the sea.

While Eddie and his men cleared the land, Tito spoke to conglomerates in Texas and Miami. He made contacts in Atlanta, Georgia. He approached refineries in Houston. He was keeping an eye on the markets. Trinidad was on the edge of a new era: cocoa was struggling, sugar estates all over Trinidad were closing down, but oil was headlining the finance pages of British newspapers. If sugar was sweet gold, oil was black gold. The British wanted it, the Americans wanted it. He'd never thought about investing in oil; his fingers were stuck in enough pies. It was risky, dangerous, with too many unknowns. He'd been frightened off by stories of blowouts, explosions and fires. But Eddie assured him the risks these days were minimal; and he'd seen for himself the iridescent puddles of oil on Chatterjee's estate. Success, Eddie said, was only a matter of time.

Tito didn't tell Ada that if Kushi didn't work out, they'd have to sell up and buy a smaller home in a less desirable neighbourhood. He felt he had to keep this from her. It would all work out.

After meeting with Eddie, he was puppylike in his excitement.

'This kid has determination like I've never seen,' he told Ada. 'It's what good luck's all about – you work hard, you get lucky. Not many people understand that.'

'What does Alfie say?'

'What Alfie Mendes knows about oil you could write on the back of a postage stamp.'

Tito had persuaded himself that if Alfie was wrong about cinemas making money, he could be wrong about oil, too.

In those early days, Eddie parked his truck outside Tito's house in the shade of the African tulip tree and Henrietta would lead him inside. She took him to where Tito was waiting and they shook hands like old friends. On a good day, the journey from Kushi to Port of Spain took just under three hours. Eddie was thirsty for a cold beer, and Henrietta was glad to fetch it for him. She liked Eddie. He was polite; he looked her in the eyes. Some visitors barely looked at her at all. Once when Henrietta brought her baby daughter to the house, Ada's cousin Ruth was visiting. When the baby started to cry, Ruth said, with genuine surprise, 'Look, Ada! It cries real tears.'

Eddie asked Henrietta how she was; what was on the menu today. If he slipped her a dollar would she make him her famous macaroni pie? What was the sermon about in church, Henrietta? Can you pray for all of us?

Eddie wore his khaki shirtsleeves rolled up, light canvas trousers, steel-capped boots. He had the habit of running his fingers through his thick brown hair – the confidence of a man who knew he was good looking. For all that, Eddie wasn't vain. He couldn't care less about clothes or about how he appeared to others; he gave his full attention to whomever he spoke and made them feel as if they mattered. When Ada knew Eddie was visiting, she made sure to be at home.

While Tito and Eddie looked over figures, maps, contracts spread upon the dining table, Ada wandered in and out. When she asked Eddie to explain how the site would work, he drew a picture of a derrick, described the banging action of the drill pipe. He showed her how oil came out of the ground; *sucked up like Coca-Cola through a straw*; he explained how it could be turned into kerosene. He told Ada of a three-hundred-feet circle around each well, and how they'd have to spread themselves out. The formation of sand, silt and rock sat like layers in a cake. Ada liked the way he spoke; his accent was a mix of Trinidadian and American. Some words were drawled out as if he'd just arrived from Texas. He used his hands a lot. His passion and hunger shone off him like sweat. She could tell Eddie liked an audience. He wanted to share his ideas, and she was glad to listen.

'How does it sound to you, Ada?'

'Highly impossible and entirely possible.'

She laughed, then Eddie laughed, too.

'The world's about to change,' Eddie told them, his palms turned up as if presenting a gift. 'Hundreds of cars are coming into Trinidad. They all need kerosene. A big wave is coming and we've got a chance to ride it.'

Flora called him Uncle Eddie. He taught her to play rummy. He shuffled and flipped the playing cards, slapping them on top of one another, riffling the deck with a cascade finish like a croupier. Things he'd learned on the field when a shift was over and there was little else to do.

He took a coin and made it vanish between his fingers. Flora tried to prize his hand open and saw it was empty.

'How you did that?'

He plucked the coin from behind her ear.

'Uncle Eddie,' she said, giggling. 'Tell me how you did it.'

He dropped the coin into her hand.

Tito said, 'A good magician will never share his tricks.'

Flora said Uncle Eddie was lilac with a little bit of blue.

Ada said, 'What does that mean?'

'I've never seen anyone lilac before.'

Eddie said, 'Just as well it's one of my favourite colours.' He told them about the lavender fields he saw when he flew over Carcassonne.

If it was too late to drive back to Siparia, Eddie stayed for dinner. He talked about his days in Beaumont, sudden lucky strikes that blew a hole in the ground as big as a house and spewed for days. He told Ada and Tito of the ride he took in Howard Hughes's car that shone like a lollypop. He spoke of a baby daughter in the Midwest whom he'd never met. He had a photograph in his wallet. Ada and Tito listened while Henrietta carried plates and dishes in and out, topped up their glasses with wine.

'She's a doll,' Tito said, looking at Edith's photograph. 'Her mother must be a beauty.'

Ada imagined Eddie must've had his fair share of women.

'Maybe one day, you'll go back there and marry her mama,' Ada said. 'Little girls need their daddies.'

'Maybe,' Eddie said. He noticed Ada's lashes were black, thick, fluttery.

Tito said, 'There's a saying: what's meant for you will find you even if it's beneath two mountains. What isn't meant for you won't reach you even if it's between your two lips.'

TEN

From his office, 300 yards from Chatterjee's fence, Charles Macleod watched Eddie and his men at work. He watched them lay out pieces of wood like an apron on the ground. He had been waiting to see their first derrick, and here it was.

Every morning, at sunrise, he sipped his tea and watched as the dark green mass became lit as morning broke and the sun gilded the silk cotton tree. Taller than his Scottish home, he had never seen a tree like it. Beyond, he could spot a clearing in the land. It was like watching ants. He screwed his binoculars up to his eyes; he could make out the women walking from the main house to the barracks. He knew Eddie by his forward leaning gait; Chatterjee by his bell-shaped torso. As far as he could tell, and from all he heard, Eddie was scrimping on machinery, fixing up bits of old equipment and employing inexperienced crew who knew nothing about the business. Eddie would get tired, worn down, disenchanted. He might turn to them for assistance. It was still early days. Charles told his foreman, 'They are clowns, running out of time. The rains will soon be here. We can pull up a chair and watch this disaster.'

Meanwhile, Macleod brought in drillers and toolies from Barbados, South Africa and England. He had extra men from San Fernando. Rumour was he worked them hard. He imported a bulldozer, four brand-new trucks; sophisticated drilling equipment from a factory in Liverpool. There was a fire engine, comfortable accommodation for the team which included an on-site doctor; table tennis facilities, a bar, a laundry room where local women washed and hung clothes out to dry. Charles Macleod could drill wherever he wished on the hundred and ten-acre site. He was optimistic. There was sure to be oil somewhere.

He told Elsie they had to give it six months. Distraught, she had sobbed into her hands, rocked herself in the chair. He reassured her; this was the last operation for him in Trinidad. Once they struck oil, she, Willie and him, would leave on the first tanker out, headed for Hound Point. He tried to convince Elsie that it wouldn't take long; the land was saturated. It was like turning on a tap. They just had to find out where the taps were. It was possible they would find oil almost immediately. He spoke breezily, encouragingly; her support meant everything to him. He needed to know she was behind him.

Feeling smaller than herself, and frightened of his wrath, Elsie agreed, though everything in her felt this new venture was a terrible mistake. Scotland was calling them – couldn't he hear the cries of his homeland?

When Macleod arrived that afternoon on Kushi estate, clean in white gabardine, Eddie was irritated.

'You've no business here, Macleod. This is private land.'

'Good morning. Just a courtesy call,' he said. He'd come to show Eddie a map with the spot marked where they'd start drilling in the next couple of weeks. He stood on the bank. Eddie noticed his leather belt and silver buckle: the letters CM. His boots were shiny and new.

'We've measured it out exactly. Chatterjee knows and if he says he doesn't, then he's lying. You know how these Indians lie.' His eyes darted around the place, as if he expected someone to spring out from somewhere.

'Okay,' Eddie said, looking at the map. 'Any closer and we'll be having a different kind of conversation.'

Macleod took off his hat, ran his finger around the inside rim.

'You know we got these new barytes coming in from Arran. It's fine, like stuff used for making paint and it works. Much better than the old stuff we've been using up until now. It will save us time, cut out the number of blowouts.'

Eddie looked out at the field, his face giving nothing away. He was hot; sweat soaked through his shirt.

'We have more equipment coming down from Scotland at the end of the month. We have facilities, Eddie. You hear me. A fire truck, a doctor on site. Everything you need, and medical supplies. You know what I'm saying.'

'No, what are you saying?'

Macleod brushed the air with his hand, a theatrical gesture.

'Well, we could still do this together. It's not too late. With your experience and my backing from Apex, we can make it happen quicker. We can make our money and get out. The rains will soon be here.'

'I hear you, Charles, but it wasn't my decision. Chatterjee has a mind of his own. He's smart enough to figure out he'd get a better deal here with me.'

Across the site a hawk flew with something hanging in its talons and it looked like it was alive and flailing. They watched it for a moment until the hawk dropped into the trees and disappeared.

Then Eddie said, 'You know as well as I do, cocoa is finished. He wouldn't make anywhere near the same amount of money with your people. He wants money. He's been poor for years. You can't blame him for that. You'd be the same.'

'Maybe so. But we have reliable equipment, reliable men. No offence meant but we're not some back-yard banana business. You understand that. As far as I can tell, you have only one guy here with any real experience. The rest are green, barely out of nappies. What do they know?'

'We have the two guys you fired from Central. They seem alright to me.'

Macleod knew about Larry McGuinness and Richard Edgehill, who'd jumped ship. He had caught them running out in the yard, drunk, naked, fooling with a pistol. The pistol went off and fired through the roof a few times.

'I have a child at home. I don't need more to mind when I'm at work. You're welcome to them.' Then he caught himself. 'Look, all I'm saying is, why not think it over. We could still come to some arrangement. Speak to Fernandes.'

'I don't think so, Charles. But thanks for asking.'

Macleod put on his hat. Eddie looked up at the sky. It was soon going to be sunset, the light was fading quickly now.

'We have a responsibility to these people, Eddie. We need to run things properly.'

Eddie started to walk away. 'I know all I need to get this oil out of the ground. That's what matters here.'

'You don't know your bible, son? The parable of the house built on sand?'

'Don't preach to me, Charles. I'm done with all that. Seems to me you're in the wrong business.'

Macleod cleared his throat.

'He who builds his house on rock, I will liken to a wise man. But he who builds his house on sand: the rain, the floods come, winds blow, and beat on that same house.' Macleod put his finger in the air. 'You hear what I'm saying, Eddie.'

'So long, Charles.'

Eddie left Macleod standing on the steps and he walked down towards the field, stepping over bits of cut bush left over, and red brown puddles from last night's unexpected rain. Macleod walked back over the pathway, hoops of sweat under his arms, and climbed over the fence that took him back onto Apex land.

ELEVEN

Eddie had heard of abandoned drill sites left to rot in Palo Seco and San Francique. It was cheaper for companies to leave behind their heavy tools than ship them back to America. It seemed disrespectful to him, and he knew this kind of dumping was exactly what troubled Chatterjee, but he could make it work in their favour. He took Horatio with him, who knew the routes better than he did. Some of the roads were rough and they took turns to drive. The heat was terrific, like driving through a fire they couldn't see.

During those early days, he and Horatio tramped through overgrown oil fields, hacking at long grass with their cutlasses. In decaying lodgings they found crockery, bunks, glass bottles, a family of boa constrictors curled up in a storage cupboard. Apparently there were many around. They'd escaped from a snake farm in Mayaro, hitched rides with travelling trucks and bred quickly. Horatio drove through villages of mud huts, wild and full of cane; places Eddie had never been before. It was a new world for him.

Mostly the equipment was disappointing. Skeletons of derricks half taken down were surrounded by tall grass; the wood wasn't good for anything but burning. Horatio found the carcass of a cow, flesh half pecked away, with pale ribs exposed, legs erect; like a table turned on its side. Underneath the cow was a bed of good-looking tools, so they tied it to the truck and dragged it over the wasteland watched by circling corbeaux.

They hauled chains, bundles of wire; they stacked a 30-foot length of pipe into the trailer and tied it all down with old ropes – it would always come in use. An old blowout preventer was half-buried in the ground. The size of a torso. Eddie wondered if it had been in an explosion. They would have to come back, bring more men, break it down, a bigger truck. For now they covered it over, out of sight from anyone with the same idea. Save themselves a couple hundred bucks. 'Risky when they're rusty,' said Horatio. 'One leak and we're finished.' Eddie said no, not to rule it out; fixed up, it could work as good as new.

Whatever they found, they took to Two-Weeks, a well known blacksmith in Point Fortin. A small, Indian man, who, according to Horatio, could take a piece of old pipe and turn it into a flute.

'Why do they call him Two-Weeks? Because he takes two weeks to finish a job?'

'No sir!' Horatio grinned. 'When he was a baby, his mother leave him with a friend. She say she go come back for him in two weeks, but she never come back. She gone Venezuela. He never see his mother again. So, after, they call him Two-Weeks.'

Horatio was concerned that they were stealing. Would the police come looking for them? Perhaps they should notify them. He didn't want to find himself in trouble.

'Think of it as scavenging,' Eddie said. 'No one wants leftovers, we're doing them a favour. Clearing up the mess.'

Horatio wasn't convinced. The equipment belonged to someone else. They might believe Eddie, Horatio said, but him? A black man? Horatio sucked his teeth. They'd pitch him in a cell and throw away the key.

Eddie put up his hand. 'No, they'd have to prove it. Let me tell you, Horatio, there was a guy called Pete in Batson, Texas, accused of stealing an eighty-inch cable tool bit. An eighty-inch cable tool bit. You hear me? Now, those things are heavy, too heavy for your average man to carry.'

'Yes, sir. I know how they heavy.'

'Evidence showed that he never drove to the rig, so if he'd stolen this bit, he'd have had to carry it.'

'How do they know he didn't drive?'

'No tyre marks; grass grew all around and none of it flattened by wheels.' Then Eddie said, 'So in court, they had the bit there. The jury looked at it. They figured there was no way any man could carry that alone. It was just too big. So they cleared him of any charges. At the end, as everyone got up to leave, he said to the judge, 'This my bit, now?' Yes, said the judge. Pete walked over, got it into his arms and walked right out.'

'So he had take it all along?'

'That's right.'

'But he was real strong.'

'Stronger than they knew. Like all of us.'

Ahead the sky was darkening and cracked with gold. The end of the day.

'You must take opportunities, Horatio. We get one chance. Be like Pete. Don't let anyone put you off.'

Along the roadside, a woman walked with a basket balanced on her head, her narrow hips wrapped with yellow fabric. She stared as they passed.

'You have someone in the village, Horatio? Someone to lay down with.'

'Me?' Horatio glanced out of the window. 'I done with all that. I have my mother, sir. She is a good person. She does cook for me and keep the house clean. And she does wash my clothes. I not looking for trouble.' He waved his hand. 'Women carry you, but they never bring you back.'

It occurred to Eddie that, yes, perhaps, he was done with 'all that' too.

On the way home, they often stopped off in a Chinese food parlour. They took a few glugs of rum and filled up on meat buns. Gloria and her husband Kip ran the little establishment. They'd heard about Eddie and they were glad of the business he brought.

Gloria spoke quickly. She had thick black hair cut at the neck. She made buns, crispy pies, usually deep fried, heavily seasoned and full of flavour; stews and soups, heavy breads. Out the back, Kip roasted wild meat – deer, manicou, agouti.

When she saw the truck, Gloria would say, 'Look Mister Eddie come to eat! Bring a chair, bring a table. Make him welcome. Let him fill his belly.'

Tito sent three miles of pipe by steamer from Port of Spain, and this was carried along the train tracks from Cedros by carts. Eddie brought in men from Danny Village, Pepper Village and Fyzabad. The ground was dug four-feet deep to make the long tunnel. A digger would have been quicker. When Tito suggested Eddie rent one from Charles Macleod, Eddie said he'd rather claw it out with his own hands.

They lowered each piece by pulley into the ground; three men to lower it in, one to line it up and then another to hammer it in place. Then followed the lead machine, which poured molten lead around the pipe joints. They worked best at first light and in the late afternoon until it was dark, cooler and then another shift took over while men stood by with lamps. Eddie was there the whole time – cheering them along, while orchestrating the delicate job of lining up the pipe correctly.

Towards the river, the earth was hard with coral and the men broke their tools easily, as if they were sticks. Eddie ordered more tools. He made sure the men were fed and watered. Sita baked biscuits, and boiled peppermint sticks for them to suck. Mercy brought them down. They made jokes. Mercy never smiled; had the wasps left their stingers in her? Why was she so? Eddie liked her, her way of walking, saying little. She was pretty, with slanted eyes, and he wondered if she might be part Chinese. He told her, 'Don't mind the boys, they only want your attention.'

After three weeks of digging, three hundred and eighty feet of pipes were laid and fixed and a steam pump was constructed and installed at the mouth of the river. When at last water trickled in from the Guapo River to the estate, everyone was glad to see it. They stood around the pipe and cheered, the men from the village, Horatio, Tripe, Mister Long and Mercy, Sita, Chatterjee and his two sons. Tito drove from Port of Spain and brought a trunk full of cold beers for everyone. Chatterjee was pleased. He had never known running water on his land; it seemed to him a kind of miracle.

He told Eddie he knew he'd come to shake up the place. 'Make we rich.'

That night, while he lay beside his sleeping wife, and listened to her deep breathing, Chatterjee realised his feeling of doom had lifted enough to see beyond a future of disaster he'd envisioned for himself and his family. What if, through meeting Eddie, his luck had changed? What if he could prove to Sita that this was so?

What if he could show her it was her good fortune to be married to him: Sonny Chatterjee, son of Madoo with the short foot, heir to Kushi cocoa Estate, father of two sons; oil entrepreneur and shareholder of Fernandes/Wade/Chatterjee Limited?

TWELVE

A steamer from America had landed at La Brea. On board was Michael Callaghan and barrels full of equipment and tools. The water was calm that day, and the dawn sky was streaked as if a dye ran through it. Eddie waited on the jetty with Horatio, Long, and Gelliseau. By the time the ship had docked, the light was up and so was the heat. Callaghan was one of the first off, and he spotted Eddie at once.

'You made it,' Eddie said, hitting him on the back. 'I always said I'd get you here somehow.'

He could see at once that Callaghan was unwell. His face beaded up with sweat, the whites of his eyes were pink. He told Eddie how in Jamaica he'd picked up something. He'd left a trail of yellow shit in the sea.

'Jesus!' Eddie saw the lines of sweat running down his neck.

'God knows how many fish I've killed. There were others. Two dead bodies thrown overboard north of Curaçao.'

Eddie offered his flask and Callaghan tipped back the rum into his throat.

'Remember the Hopi? I keep thinking of the Hopi.'

One day, in Sedona, Arizona, they'd seen a man on a mule and thought he was a mirage. The Hopi man called to Eddie and Callaghan with some urgency, and drew a prophecy of the doomed earth with a stick in the sand. He said there was no oil where they were drilling. He also said they'd die before they were 30 years old, which both frightened them and made them laugh.

Eddie tried to hide his disappointment. He'd have to keep an eye on Callaghan, something he hadn't planned on. He wondered if it was contagious.

'Forget the Hopi. We made it past 30. You look like hell. We'll get you a doctor at the other end. Why not ride on the truck up to the estate; I can let them know you're coming. You can rest up.'

'You think I came all the way from Texas to rest?'

Callaghan lit a cigarette, tied a red bandana around his forehead. He signalled to the men, to where crates were being dispatched, then towed onto land. There were hundreds of barrels. Horatio started to count them. Callaghan carried a checklist and a leather bag Eddie recognised.

The men lifted pipes onto the back of the truck, tied them on with ropes. When the next truck came, they loaded the barrels by rolling them up the wooden plank into the tray. It would take all day.

At the river's mouth, King and Mister Long held onto the mud hose and between them carried it up to the barge. 'Watch the sides,' Eddie yelled, as the barge almost toppled like a toy boat in a bucket. The men were stripped off to their waists by now, their bodies gleaming with sweat. It was early, the sun's eye still far from the sky's centre. It was going to be a long day. By the time they reached upriver, the place was sizzling; the air so still the bamboo barely twitched its bright leaves.

At St John's estate, more men waited and the equipment was unloaded onto carts and led by oxen up the hill to the flatter grassy land. From here, they could journey on more easily to Chatterjee's estate. The oxen were strong and white with curled horns and they walked slowly and with power. Eddie didn't want them over worked; they were essential, apparently sacred. He could believe it. Some men followed on foot, while others took the return ride back along the Godineau River to start over. Callaghan went with them. Eddie said he should go to the house and Chatterjee could call the doctor.

'You're no good to me dead. Let's get someone to check you over.'

But Callaghan insisted on working alongside the men. He stopped only to drink water or to empty his bowels in the bush. Twice, he threw up in the river while the men sat on the bank and ate chicken cooked up with rice.

That night Eddie stayed at the bay with Horatio, Long, King and Gelliseau. They smoked cigarettes, drank rum from a large bottle

Eddie had carried from Mon Repos. They boiled blue crabs they'd caught in the roots of the mangrove and sucked on the purple claws; the meat was brown and sweet.

Eddie told the men, 'Let me tell you something about crabs. You know why they walk sideways? Because they have knees on the sides of their legs. It makes them run that way.'

Holding up a pincer he said, 'To extricate your finger from a crab's claw, all you have to do is squeeze the eye.' Then he told them the story of Henry, the black Englishman.

'Young Henry came home to Tobago after seven years in England. He spoke like an Englishman, all his Trini accent was gone. One morning he sees a barrel of crabs at his mother's home. He says' – and here Eddie changed his voice – '"Mother what are these crawling crustaceous creatures?" And his mother says, "You nu know they ah crab boy?" Henry tells her, "Oh, let me assist you to extricate them from their humble position at the bottom of the barrel." Then it happened, a big blue crab held on to him and pinched him hard.

'Hear Henry, "Mumma, Mumma, oh Gawd Mumma help me. Squeeze de eye, squeeze de eye!"'

The men laughed and Horatio laughed so much he had to get up and walk around the fire to catch his breath.

'Mister Eddie know how to make joke.'

Horatio dropped on his knees and tears streaked his face. Stars glittered like crumbs of silver and some fell and sprinkled themselves over the sky. Eddie counted nine in all, and it made him think of Kathryn and Edith, and wonder where they were right now. Then King, Gelliseau and Horatio sang songs Eddie had never heard before. They taught him their ballad of longing, a version of an old Welsh hymn.

Lord, I long to see that morning,
When thy gospel shall abound,
And thy grace get full possession
Of the happy promised ground
And all the borders, all the soil
All the forests, all the oil
Of the great Immanuel's land!

They sang and they sang. Then they linked arms and walked around the dying fire until they were exhausted and glad to lie down. Eddie slept that night with his back against a container, his legs stretched out, and his Panama hat over his face. The air was full of mosquitoes, and he felt them chewing at him while firing off their high-pitched sirens.

When dawn came, he woke with the sound of a ship's foghorn hooting over the bay. He got to his feet. 'Come, come,' he said, clapping his hands. The men lit the fire and heated coffee, emptied their bladders in the dark sea. It was cool like Christmas and the grass was wet with dew.

The second shipment arrived intact, more lengths of pipe, the diamond bit he'd ordered from Houston, a brand new swivel. Once again, the men came from the estate; Chatterjee drove the truck and they piled in the back.

The sky was dark that morning, clouds thick and dirty looking. Eddie was glad the sun was hid and hoped it would stay that way. But then around 10 am, rain started. Drip, drip, a dotting here and there, and then it came in a sudden rush. Thousands of jabbing needles broke the river's skin, and then more arrived in white thick sheets and they could barely see and soon they were soaked through, the noise tremendous like a waterfall.

By the time they reached the bank, Eddie told the men to halt and they looked for shelter. But there was nowhere to shelter. They managed to carry the last crates onto the wagons, but the oxen were reluctant, pulling back, straining against the new weather. Long refused to climb onto the cart because, he said, the rain would make him sick. So Eddie took hold of the whip and, furious, lashed first at the man and then at the oxen until they moved, slowly at first, then they picked up pace, their heads downwards. When he arrived at the estate, he yelled at the men through the rain, 'Not long now!' He knew the path would soon be impassable. If they stopped they could wave goodbye to their equipment.

Thunder broke. Eddie put his face to the sky, let the rain fall into his mouth, while the men scrambled to the house and took refuge under the eaves. At Chatterjee's, Eddie bellowed at the men to finish the job and to carry the damn equipment, which they eventually did. They dragged it inside the vast and empty cocoa shed. Here they used sheets to dry off what they could. Eddie told the workers to go home and rest.

'You all did good,' he said, exhausted. 'Go sleep.'

By now it was dark, the sky still thick with cloud.

Chatterjee stood in the doorway, his hands on his narrow hips, a blanket wrapped around his shoulders. 'That is it?' he said, 'No more? You carry everything?'

'That's right. It's all here. We have everything.'

'You alright? You don't look so good. Sita made dhal; we can bring it up to the house. Grace went home. I tell she to go. Mercy, too.'

'Where's Callaghan?'

'Last I saw him, he was going by you.'

Eddie made his way down to the cabin where water was starting to rush and collect underneath it. He unpeeled his clothes and dropped them on the floor. The rain was so loud he could barely think.

Callaghan was lying on the table. His fever was high and he'd stripped off his shirt. He sat up when he saw Eddie. A rash of red welts studded his back. He begged for ice.

'I don't have ice, Callaghan.'

'Tell my wife I love her.'

'But you have no wife.'

'This is Salvador, Eddie? Salvador?'

'No, we are in Trinidad. You are here in Trinidad.'

Eddie stayed with Callaghan through the night. At some hour of the morning, when the rains had stopped, he heard a strange gurgling sound. Callaghan's eyes were rolling back in his head. His body was soaked with sweat. Eddie carried him out to the truck and put him in the tray. It occurred to him that Callaghan might die.

'You saved me once, Callie, I won't let you go.'

The road was dark and falling away. Landslides were common after heavy rain, and this had been the heaviest he'd known it in months. The road was alive with shadows, and they bothered Eddie. An elephant wandered in front of the truck and he braked hard, afraid he was going to hit it. But when he flashed his lights there was no elephant there, just a samaan bending over in the road. Then a man appeared as tall as a house, waving his giant gloved hands at Eddie. Then he saw it was a coconut tree. Eddie pulled over, rubbed his face, took a glug of rum. In the back, Callaghan was bleating. The road was empty, the bushes tall on either side.

At the hospital, Eddie parked outside, wandered into the entrance and yelled for help. Two orderlies took Callaghan onto the emergency ward; a nurse saw him into a bed. Eddie told him goodbye, wondered if he'd see him alive again.

'Callaghan, the Hopi don't know shit. You get yourself better.'

Eddie headed back to the estate, sweating, his eyes sore and tired. The sky was beginning to grow light like silver. He couldn't remember if this was the start of the day or the end of the day.

At noon, Eddie woke to sunlight in his room and covered his eyes at once. They were on fire. His whole body ached as if he had been beaten. He wanted to stand but his legs were weak. He was cold; cold as if he was in Beaumont in the middle of winter. He wrapped his blanket around him and wandered outside barefoot. He remembered ice on the River Eden as solid as a floor; he recalled fishing for salmon in spring. Salmon. He had loved salmon. He saw the herring in his hand and pierced it with a hook, then he sat on the lumpy bank, hauled out the line into bubbling water where the salmon were jumping and thick and plenty. He'd catch a ten pounder if he was lucky. There seemed to be none there now, just brown water, brown from mud and rain. At first, he didn't see Grace appear on the steps. Then she was there like a vision.

'You okay, Mister Eddie.'

She helped him up, felt his body quaking with fever. He looked flushed. He shielded his eyes, grinned at her.

'Grace,' he said. 'What are you doing here?' Then, 'It's been snowing,' he said. 'Keep me away from the damn river, Grace. I might fall in.'

By now he was shivering so much he had to lie on the floor. He asked Grace to find blankets.

'You sick,' she said. She gave him water from a tin cup and he drank it. 'There's no snow here. This is Trinidad.'

'Mister Callaghan bring sickness to everybody,' she said. 'Rain yesterday don't help.'

'Callaghan,' he said. 'Where Callaghan? Callaghan is dead, Grace?'

When Tito heard both Callaghan and Eddie were sick, he started to fret. If Eddie should die, what would happen to his investment? The agreement between himself and Chatterjee was based on Eddie's expertise.

'He won't die,' Ada said. 'I feel it in my bones.'

'You're sounding like Flora,' Tito said, puffing on his cigar while walking up and down the passageway. 'You can't know. We can't know. No one knows what's going to happen.'

But it was true. That morning, out in the garden, Ada had felt so strongly a sense of Eddie's situation and of all things being well. She couldn't easily explain it.

'He's come here to do something and he's going to do it. Mosquitoes won't stop him.'

'Let's hope you're right.'

What Tito couldn't say, couldn't let Ada know, was that if Eddie died and their plans failed, they would lose everything.

He spoke briefly to Chatterjee by telephone. What was happening? Was Eddie showing any signs of recovery? Who was taking care of him? Was he eating? Was it definitely malaria? Could it be something else? A virus? Tito had worried about mosquitoes but this was the first he'd heard of malaria in South Trinidad.

'These damned creatures lay eggs in flower heads and coffee cups, buckets around the place; they kill more men than war. They nearly killed my wife.'

He offered to send his own doctor, Dr Shepherd.

'He cured Ada of yellow fever,' Tito said, though he wasn't sure it was true. 'I could ask him to come first thing. He could at least take a look at him.'

Chatterjee told Tito, send him, yes, but remember the roads were flooded and more rain coming. Callaghan was in the hospital and Grace was taking good care of Eddie.

Chatterjee was jittery, too; his stomach unsettled. His land was stripped bare, equipment was stacked in the cocoa sheds; workers awaited instruction. What if Eddie died? How would he recoup? To save himself from worry, Chatterjee decided they must be vigilant: do away with open water containers; steer clear of the river; wear long sleeves, long pants, veils, hats. Cover exposed skin with a paste concocted by Mercy from lime and thyme. With Horatio and Gelliseau, Chatterjee fitted fine wire mesh over windows and doors.

Sita was fretting. She stayed indoors, her body and head covered in cloth. There was malaria in the village, and down in Pala Seco. Chatterjee was foolish, she said, they should have sold to the Scotsman.

'All-ah-we get sick. All-ah-we go dead.'

Eddie woke with shooting pains licking around his skull. Grace cooked rice but Eddie shook so much he couldn't sit up or put a fork inside his mouth. Pain was lightning through his body; sudden, terrific pain – in his joints, his head, the bottom of his foot, his gut. He wrapped the blanket around him while his body jerked and twitched on the hard floor, and he begged Grace to help him.

She took his head and held it steady in her strong hands and she put water in his mouth, a little rice. Eddie threw it up, the rice flew out of him, the water everywhere. He lay down and crawled on his knees to the wall where he could lie pressed up against it.

'Mister Chatterjee say three men have it. He send for the doctor.'

'Tell Mister Tito it means nothing. Tell him. Tomorrow we start to build the derrick.'

Across the fence, Macleod waited to hear news of Eddie. With any luck, he and his men would all be too weak to start drilling any time soon.

Eddie slept and slept and when he woke, Grace gave him sugar water from a pipette and wiped him down with a cool rag. When the doctor eventually came, he looked to Eddie like his own late father and Eddie started to weep. 'The volcano didn't kill you?' He put out his arms, his eyes moist with joy.

Grace told him, 'He not your daddy, Mister Eddie.'

At one point Chatterjee arrived with coconuts for Eddie to drink; he said the scooped-out meat, the jelly, would be good for him. He wouldn't stay long just in case it was catching.

'Yes, Mister Chatterjee,' she said, 'I will give him. Go, go.'

That night Eddie shouted for his mother. He sat up and looked into the far corner of the room and said, 'Thank you, Mother.' Grace said, 'You see your mummy, Mister Eddie? Your mummy not here. You are here and I am with you. I won't leave you.'

'If anything happen to me, send everything to Oklahoma. Thirty-one Park Street, Cleveland County 2198. Tell Edith I love her. You know my daughter is called Edith. I love her. She doesn't know I love her. I wonder if her mother called her that because it sounds like Eddie. You think so Grace?' Eddie was crying now, and Grace sat on the floor beside him, and she took up his hand and patted it until he fell asleep.

Grace slept on the floor beside Eddie. She told him she wouldn't let him die. She came when he called out; she changed his blankets when they were wet. She wiped his forehead. When his body was shaking, he rattled on the floor and cried out for her to lie on him. Instead, she unscrewed the door, hefted it down and she lay it on top of Eddie and this gave him some relief as his body went quiet, his legs stopped jerking.

She sang to him because this seemed to give him some relief – hymns from her childhood and songs her father taught her from St Kitts. She sang about God and His Angels, she sang about hope, the love of your neighbour; she sang about the sea, the birds; she sang of loss and love.

Eddie said he'd seen angels before. Were they coming for him again?

'No, Mister Eddie.' No angels coming yet.'

Grace was troubled to see someone as strong as Eddie thrown to the floor by a mosquito. She didn't want him to die. She understood there was a quiet she could find within herself. And in this quiet she could, at times, feel the pulse of God. That night, while the wind blew hard against the cabin's thin walls, and the rain fell heavy, she sat with her hands on her lap, palms up, her face tilted to the ceiling. And while Eddie lay at her feet, his body contorting in pain, she turned her eyes inward. She slowly breathed in and out. She felt herself lift into another place. It was both dark and comforting, like love. Into this nameless place she whispered, 'Eddie, Eddie.' She felt a peace descend upon her, and in that moment she knew Eddie would survive. She knew it as surely as she knew her father was called Bridgeman. She smiled a broad, joyous smile and tasted the tears that ran down her face.

Next morning Eddie was sitting up, thin as the stray dog under the house, his stomach bloated, but he was able to eat rice and drink tea without throwing it back up. She didn't tell Eddie about the things he'd said. She didn't know if they were true things. She didn't tell him how long she'd been there. She didn't tell him that she had prayed for him. She told him only that Callaghan was better. After he was discharged from the hospital, he came back to camp. Mercy took soup to him three times a day; soup of cock-foot, calf-tongue, pigtail, cilantro, hot pepper and peas. It had cured him! Horatio was now sick. Mercy would make soup for him too, and send it by his mother. This fever was everywhere. But God was on his side. Nobody dead. There was work to do. He must get strong.

THIRTEEN

It would take them the whole morning, leaving Port of Spain as the sun was rising over the Gulf of Paria where the sea was still and shining. According to Tito, Sonny Chatterjee's estate was past San Fernando, somewhere behind God's back.

'Why do they call it Kushi? Ada asked. 'It sounds like a name for a pet.'

'It means happy living,' said Tito. 'In Hindi.'

As Tito drove towards the east, the sky grew from dark blue to gold. They were going fast.

'Tito, slow down. Or my hair will come loose and frizz up.'

Ada's hair was curled and pinned and set against her head in the new fashionable Errol waves – and only God knew what it would look like after a whole morning of travelling by motorcar. Mrs Fernandes sat in the back staring out, her eyes like two coins in her sunken face. Through the breeze Ada said, 'Isn't this wonderful?' But Mrs Fernandes didn't answer. Ada was sorry her mother-in-law had come. According to Tito, she'd invested money in the well; she wanted to see where it had gone. He'd warned them both, it was likely to be hot and dusty as hell.

Beyond Caroni Swamp they passed through fields of sugar cane twice the height of men, crowds of bright-green floppy leaves. The road seemed so straight to Ada, like a road you'd take if you died, straight to the hills, to God. The sky ahead, by then a lighter blue, had strips of low cloud like cotton torn off and thrown there. It struck Ada how big and sprawling this land was, and how little she knew of it. She barely left her neighbourhood except to visit shops, Flora's school, restaurants, or the beauty parlour. If Trinidad was a person, she had seen, perhaps, only its face – not its torso, or hands, or feet.

By the time they approached the Paramount Hotel, the sun was on top of their heads; Ada's hat was not nearly enough at this time of day. They needed to get inside to the cool. Tito swung the car into the palm tree lined driveway and pulled up next to the broad steps where a boy in uniform was waiting. They could leave the car here, the boy said; someone would take it to the back and wash it, check oil and water levels.

Ada lifted her arms to the sky. It felt good to feel her blocky new heels on the ground. From here she could make out the sea, a spread of dazzling blue, the sunburnt land rising toward her, the narrow hilly streets, and just below, a big flamboyant tree with its pale trunk and dangling black pods. She must pick a couple and take them home for Flora; they could make dolls – paint them, glue on lace, buttons.

Mrs Fernandes said, 'Somebody get me some water,' and started up the steps. 'Don't worry to bring me here again. I'm too old for all this. This is for young people like you.'

Behind his mother's little head, Tito raised his fist.

'At least she called you young,' Ada whispered into his ear.

From their table, they could see San Fernando Hill, thick with green forest but for a chunk of white, like a cheek bitten out. Ada saw how the hill rose alone out of the ground – there was no range.

Mrs Fernandes said, 'What have they done?'

'They're using the stone for construction,' Tito said. 'Roads, houses, the new hospital.'

'They going to destroy this country,' she piped.

'Who are *they*?' Tito said, while looking at the menu.

'Barbarians ruining this island.'

'Your son is a barbarian, too, mother. You realise that.'

Ada rolled her eyes, knowing what was coming.

Tito said, 'It's not greed and wanting that's the problem, it's meanness.'

Mrs Fernandes carried on, 'We should put these people to work the fields in the hot sun until they can't stand up; give them enough food and water to keep them alive and when they ready to die, bring a doctor. Pitch them out in the field again.'

They were sitting under the ceiling fan, which Mrs Fernandes said wasn't such a good idea after all because the food would soon get cold. It was already not quite hot enough: overcooked fried fish, a soggy potato pie, christophene au gratin, blackened plantain fritters.

Ada stared out into the garden of fruit trees – orange, lime, star-apple. Beyond, a trail of purple bougainvillea fell over the hotel's high wall. She would ignore her mother-in-law, wouldn't let her ruin the day.

Mrs Fernandes said, 'I don't know what young people want anymore. When we were young we had simple lives – not all this.'

'What is all this, mother? You mean a car? Lunch? Some cold water to drink?'

Tito untucked his tie from his shirt; a silk tie embroidered with tiny lotus flowers – Ada's anniversary gift.

'No.' Mrs Fernandes said, wiping the corners of her tight mouth. 'I'm talking about things. Since when did we need so much? The more you have, the more you want.'

A huge butterfly floated past, its patterned wings like yellow and black cloth.

'Look,' Ada said, pointing. 'Don't you love butterflies. Sometimes I just want to follow them.'

The waiter came and took away their plates, and offered dessert. There was lemon meringue pie, pineapple upside-down cake. Coffee. Crème de cacao?

'Have you never wanted things, mother?'

'I needed things and I got them because your father gave them to me. But I didn't want for the sake of having them. There's a difference. We live in an excessive society.'

'Excessive or aspiring?'

'People are greedy. They don't know when they have enough.'

Tito took out a cigar and lit it. 'Greedy or hungry'

'It's the same. One leads to the other. Like an animal feeding on its own tail.'

'Look, when we make money, you won't complain.'

Ada excused herself and went to the bathroom. In the glass, her face was glistening, and she flattened down her puffy hair with a little water. She reapplied her lipstick and patted her cheeks and nose with powder. She would have liked to take off her clothes and run down the hill to the sea and splash her hot legs.

It had been months since they last took the little boat and sailed to the holiday house in Scotland Bay. Why had they left it so long? It invigorated her. She must tell Tito. All this talk of money made her feel gloomy. Her mother-in-law was particularly bad tempered today.

Outside, against the glare, she saw her husband slumped back in his chair and the pointy profile of Mrs Fernandes – all bone and skin, her bent body weighing no more than 80 pounds these days. Her cheeks had gone, just the jaw was strong – overshot, holding up a cluster of sharp teeth like a little manicou.

But she wasn't always like this. Apparently, when Victor Fernandes first saw her walking on the savannah in a long white dress with her black umbrella, a tiny sausage dog under her arm, he was struck as if by the finger of God. Philomena De Silva was everything he had ever dreamed of in a woman: a beauty. She was out of his league, people joked; he was reaching too high.

Ada thought, as she stood in the cool corridor of the Paramount Hotel, Wasn't it better to reach than not to reach? To pluck the shiny apple from the highest branch of the tree? It was for Philomena De Silva that Victor worked so hard and, most likely, because of her that he died of a coronary aged 72. Right there in Marine Square next to the fountain. A full life well lived. Wasn't that all you could hope for?

They crossed the Oropouche Lagoon and from there to Oropouche itself. Tito drove through cocoa plantations and coffee estates. The road was covered with pitch from the pitch lake at Brighton. The pitch had softened and wrinkled in the sun. There was a smell of coconut oil; huts of mud with palm-leaf roofs.

They twisted through the dusty town of Point Fortin where a street market was busy; stalls with bundles of bright green bodi, piles of sweet potato, cassava sticks, breadfruit, oranges, and yams propped up on wooden crates. People were walking in the road and did not move out of the way until Tito sounded his horn; they stared after the car.

Who were these people, these country folk? Some stood and watched and Ada waved at them: Indian women in saris with their children; a barebacked man tugging a goat; skinny boys racing alongside the car, laughing. They wore short pants, no shoes; their skin dark and gleaming in the bright sun.

'I wish I had money to give them,' Ada said. 'They have nothing.'

'Are you crazy?' Mrs Fernandes said, shifting in her seat. 'These people are ignorant. They poison their wives; they set them on fire. Next thing they hunt you down for more money.' Her voice was higher now.

'Your wife is insane, Alberto.' Mrs Fernandes gave a strange laugh, a breathy huh–huh sound. 'My son married a crazy woman. How about that.'

Tito stared ahead at the road. He looked older than his years; he looked old enough to be her father. Ada wanted to shout at him. In all the years she had known Tito, he had never stood up to his mother. Like a little boy, he was always trying to win her approval – something Mrs Fernandes would never give. Right now Ada hated him for it.

Tito honked his horn, and helped his mother climb out of the car. Two men in overalls and hard hats were standing on the derrick platform. There was a great deal of banging behind them; more men pulling and tugging at something Ada couldn't quite see. In the still air she breathed in the stench of dirt and machinery and sweat. The derrick towered above; its pointy triangular shape reaching high into the sky, the skeleton criss-cross frame like the mast of a ship.

Ada saw Eddie straddled on the platform, his hand raised in a kind of salute. His face was filthy; he wore a hat, shirtsleeves rolled up, a broad smile.

'Sir,' Eddie shouted. 'Come!'

Behind him a wheel was slowly turning. 'Mind your feet.' The ground was rough and stony, leftover trunks of chopped trees, broken pieces of wood. On the far side, a skinny dog lay under the platform sleeping. The dog started to bark.

'Trinket!' Eddie yelled.

The three made their way up the steps, Ada walking behind Tito and her mother-in-law. The derrick floor was higher than she'd thought; planks were missing.

'It's safe?' Tito said, guiding his mother's little white shoes.

'Yes sir, just about safe enough for your ladies; walk this side.'

Eddie came around the top of the steps and steered them away from the broken planks.

He shouted above the din. 'We just started on here yesterday. There's been a delay on cement. In Trinidad, if you wait long enough, everything comes.'

Mrs Fernandes screwed up her face, put her hands over her ears.

'Yes, ma'am, I apologise. Don't worry; we won't keep you here long. The pistons are giving trouble. I'll get them switched off for a while.' Eddie called up to two men standing on the platform.

Ada said, 'I didn't expect it to be so big.'

Tito started walking away slowly, back down the steps with his mother. Mrs Fernandes had seen enough. They'd head over to Eddie's place, and wait there. Tito signalled to his wife to follow them. She ignored him and looked away. She hadn't come all this way to sit in someone's porch.

Eddie said, 'You don't want to go with them?'

'No,' she said, and she took out a handkerchief to dab her face. She pointed at two men straddling the rotary table platform, hands around a thick pipe. The platform was vibrating.

'What are they doing?'

'The pipe runs into the hole. When we start drilling the lever goes down, it twists into the ground to make the hole deeper. Then mud flushes down to clear it, plasters the sides.'

'This is Horatio,' Eddie said, and the man waved at Ada. 'That's Callaghan up at the top.' Ada looked up to see a red-haired man. 'He likes it up there – you can see the mountains of Venezuela.'

Another man jumped onto the platform. Callaghan swung down from a short ladder and said, 'Howdy.'

His face was friendly, freckly.

'Boilers behind us.'

It was hot enough to die.

'How deep does it go?'

'Deep as we need; sometimes oil is near the surface, other times you might be 1500 feet or more before there's a whiff of it. We reckon its pretty close to the top. But you never know.'

'My father looked for oil in La Brea. He took a couple men

down there and they tried to get it out. When he sent it to England, it was so fine they said it couldn't be real.'

'He sent it to a chemist?'

'Yes. He said it was artificial.'

'A chemist who knew nothing. I'm sorry to hear it. Your father was ahead of his time.'

Aware that Tito might disapprove of Ada here with him, Eddie started down the crooked steps. Horatio quickly put out his hand to help her.

'We don't get many ladies around here,' Eddie said. 'You've made their day.'

For the first time that afternoon, Ada smiled. She realised how battered she'd felt – the journey, the heat, jibes from her mother-in-law. She was tired of her vicious little comments.

The skinny dog followed them to Eddie's cabin where Tito and Mrs Fernandes were waiting in the veranda.

'My brave wife wanted to go up the top, no doubt.'

'Brave or foolish?' Mrs Fernandes smiled, her eyes tiny and black as seeds.

'She seems brave to me,' Eddie said. 'Sita refuses to come anywhere near the drill.'

Ada glanced at her mother-in-law, then at Tito, who seemed oblivious. Did he choose not to see? Ada took off her shoes and drew her knees up to her chest.

Tito said, 'It's looking good, Eddie. A tight ship.'

'Yes, sir.' Eddie lit a cigarette.

Mrs Fernandes said, 'How long does it take to know if you'll find something?'

'It's not a question of if, mother, it's a matter of when.' Tito stretched out his legs, short and thick like logs. 'The oil is there. It's not like sugar or rice. You get one crop and that's it. We find where the crop is and get it out. Isn't that right, Eddie?'

'Yes, sir. The oil is waiting for us. All the signs are there. Trinidad's on the map. People are arriving everyday from America, South Africa. We couldn't be in a better place.'

Tito said, 'It happened in Texas, too, right? I read about it. People came in thousands. Then they started breaking the law, stealing and trying to get by.'

'Prisons were full so they tied them to the trees. Put a hoop around their necks. They got wet in the rain. No one cared because they figured they'd done bad things.'

Mrs Fernandes clapped her hands; mosquitoes were starting to show themselves.

'We could try it here.'

'What's that, mother?'

'Barbarians. Tie them to the trees.'

'There was no real infrastructure,' Eddie said, 'they never saw it coming.'

Ada took out a small jar of citronella from her purse; she had a few bites already. She started to rub the cream into her arms.

'They're out early tonight.' Eddie slapped his hand on his arm.

'You were sick, Eddie? You're better now.'

'Yes,' he said. 'Sick as a dog. Another life gone.'

'You put in mosquito screens,' she said; 'that's good.' She tapped on the gauze covering the window. 'It's hard to believe something so small can kill you.' Then she said, 'Cedar?'

'Yes, we cut down the tree,' he pointed over to the flattened out land behind them.

'I love the smell of cedar.'

The door to his cabin was open and she glanced inside.

'May I?'

She felt Mrs Fernandes's eyes firing into the back of her head.

Tito said, 'As you may already realise, Ada is curious as a cat. I apologise.'

She wandered into Eddie's cabin. The walls were thin, and the floor was rough. His clothes hung on nail hooks; his camp bed was made up neatly.

Eddie followed, unsure as to how he'd left it.

Ada looked out of place: her heels, her white dress, as if she had stepped from the pages of a magazine. He caught her familiar citrus scent. She belonged in another country, not here in this hot place. She deserved seasons and the clothes that went with them.

She was looking at photographs and newspaper clippings he'd stuck on the wall.

'Texas. A piece of land I tried to buy. Someone else got hold of it and made a mint. It's there to remind me.'

'You have good instincts, Eddie.'

'Maybe with some things.'

'And who is this?'

'That's Monty, my dog in Beaumont. Do you like dogs, Ada?'

'Some more than others. Like people I guess.'

She scooped up her hair, and made a knot, a habit he'd noticed. He saw damp strands stuck to her pale neck. Her ears were small, the lobes tiny and pierced with gold studs. Her pretty chin was prominent.

'Edith. Taken at Christmas. In Oklahoma.'

Ada wanted to ask him if he had a photograph of her mother. Was she beautiful? Was she blond or dark? Did she look like a girl or a woman? – but Tito was calling. She could hear his irritation.

'Adaaah!'

'You should come to town more often. We can introduce you to some people. You must go crazy here alone.'

'I like my own company.'

For a second or two their eyes locked; her cheeks flushed.

Then Ada said, 'That's good. Most people can't stand to be alone.'

Tito called again, more loudly, 'Ada!'

Eddie started outside to where Tito was on his feet and looking out at the site. A warm breeze was blowing.

A whistle came from the derrick.

'I don't want to drive back in the dark. It's already late.'

The light was dimming, and the sun's glow stained the wall orange.

Ada said, 'I was telling Eddie, he should come to town more. We could find someone for him. Don't you think so, Tito?'

'Yes, we just need to know what he's looking for.'

'There's a river a couple miles away. Next time, you all should take a swim. Mrs Fernandes, too.'

Mrs Fernandes, said, 'Ada doesn't know how to swim.'

Eddie said, 'An island girl who doesn't know how to swim?'

Easter, 1905, and Ada was staying with her cousin Ruth, Aunt Bessie and her father at the holiday house in Bacolet, Tobago. She was eight years old. Ada had loved the blue beach house; its living-room doors opened out to a veranda where a moonflower vine ran along the wall. Here, black and yellow caterpillars crawled; thick and long as her fingers. The house and its easy big rooms made Ada feel calm; she enjoyed meals around the mahogany table; the golden glow of hurricane lamps at night. She loved the sapphire sea; its gentle rush.

Two years older and ahead in everything she did, Ruth said it was time Ada learned to swim. All week Ruth taught Ada to kick her legs, using a rubber ring and she floated on it near the shore, leaning her upper body, allowing her legs to pummel her up and down the bay. She learned to tilt her head to the side and take in air. 'Keep your head on your opposite arm,' Ruth would say; 'use it like a pillow.' The water was so clear Ada could see below tiny transparent fish, coral chunks and broken shells amongst the gritty sand. She loved to walk along the floor of the sea. Every day they got up, ate breakfast and went straight into the water to practice their swimming.

Rosetta, the housekeeper, sat on the terrace and watched the girls all day. Her hair was braided and pulled back into a bun. She had children of her own, now grown up. Though she said little, she had a way of looking at Ada that made her feel she must behave herself.

Ada's father liked swimming around the rocks to the other bay. The water was rougher there, its suck was hard. Waves were often high. They were high that day and beaded with foam.

Ruth and Ada had been in the sea all morning. Ada had finally learned how to swim without using the float. She liked the feeling of power, of cutting through the water. Ruth said one day soon they could race, and no doubt Ada would beat her.

Rosetta said it was time to come out or they'd look like two prunes. Lunch would soon be ready. When last Ada saw her father he was sitting on the beach reading a newspaper, his legs splayed, his back tanned to mahogany. He said he might go for a dip to cool off before lunch.

Ruth and Ada tramped up the sand, and started skipping on the terrace to dry off. The sun was hot on their heads.

Banana split
Banana split

What did you get for arithmetic.
Banana, banana, banana for free
What did you get in geometry.

The skipping rope was wet, its weight was slowing Ada down.

'Daddy, you could find another rope for me? This one too heavy.'

She looked around and realised he had gone. He was swimming out. His head was getting smaller and smaller.

'Daaady,' she yelled, but he didn't look back.

After lunch, Aunt Bessie said, 'He'll be here just now.'

By late afternoon, Rosetta had a strange look on her face. Ada had a feeling in her stomach as if she had eaten a lot of air. She and Ruth went to collect chip chips from the far end of the beach. Ada kept looking out, hoping to see him. They filled a bucket, then walked back home and put them inside the sink for washing and boiling. No one washed or boiled them. The table was laid for dinner; they picked at fried bakes and salt fish.

Eventually, Aunt Bessie called the police. The police marine boat went out into the dark sea, its searchlight bright as a moonbeam. Aunt Bessie put her arm around Ada. 'Don't worry child. He'll be back; and let me tell you, when he come, he'll hear my mouth.' Her voice quivered at the end, and Ada knew what she was thinking. He wasn't there that evening, and she knew he didn't come back that night because she stayed up waiting. Next day, marine guards searched the coastline further up the island.

Without involving her in any discussion, Ada was taken back to Trinidad by steamer. The boat had three levels; cabins were below the deck. The sea was calm as glass and it was clear. When they reached half way, Ada waited until her aunt was asleep; Ruth was absorbed in her book. She left the cabin quietly and found her way onto the upper deck. She climbed a little ladder up to where the British flag blew; no one saw her. At the front of the boat, Ada stood on the narrow ledge and looked out. She wondered where her father could be. He was out there somewhere.

She hit the water hard; it took her down. The deeper water was darker blue and she felt herself sinking further. She could see the underbelly of the boat, and she saw it chugging away. She could hear the terrible roar of its engine. Above, the sun cast its light.

She tried to push herself up to it. Water filled her mouth, and she could feel her heart drumming.

Then, a white explosion. Someone had dived in. The lifeguard was pushing through the water to get to her. He looked straight at Ada and dragged her up. She felt the force of his kicking legs as they burst through the surface. She unclamped her mouth and gasped for air.

Aunt Bessie was concerned that she had jumped on purpose. Ada told her she had slipped. If she didn't believe her it was too bad.

Ada wanted to tell Eddie all of this that day she came to Kushi, when Mrs Fernandes cut her down as if she was nothing, and Eddie said, 'An island girl who doesn't know how to swim?'

FOURTEEN

They started drilling on the 1st July, and Eddie knew he would never forget because it was the same day Edith was born. To the morning sky, he said, 'This is all for you, baby girl, make no bones about it.'

The air was hot and clouds hung like grey sheets threatening to come down. Like breathing in an oven, Callaghan said. At least they weren't in Beaumont or Alberta, where they'd have to thaw out the ground with coal and straw, scoop out snow before they could start.

'You don't remember the snow drifts. We lost days.'

'I'd take the cold any day,' Callaghan said.

'Not me,' Eddie said. 'You can keep your winters.'

'You can keep your mosquitoes.'

Callaghan ran his hand through his red hair, wiry as a thistle. 'I lost two weeks of my life.'

'Tell me about it,' Eddie said. 'I shook hands with my maker.'

They stood over the rotary table and fed the drill pipe into the hole, let the engine take it down into the earth, twisting quickly to start with. While it turned, the table cranked around and Eddie remembered its whistly song; it felt good to hear it again. He looked around at his team, glad to see Callaghan, his face flushed with heat, eager as a young dog. Mete was up the top, his hat tied on with a piece of cloth. Eddie told Long and Gelliseau to pay attention. When they weren't in the steam room, they were all eyes on the derrick floor.

Eddie checked on the mud as it spurted back out into the slush pit, where its chips and cuts were filtered before it was sucked out and cleaned. He scrutinized the sand, the clippings of clay. It was as he'd thought: some water, sand, thin traces of oil.

Callaghan felt it between his fingers. 'Sweet Jesus. This is beautiful.'

The skies stayed dry, and they were grateful, though Eddie figured it wouldn't be long before rain came again. The season was soon upon them. They'd been lucky so far.

Once they'd drilled to the height of the derrick, Callaghan saw to it that more pipe was attached, and this took some time; it was careful and precise work with Larry and Horatio on hand. Callaghan and Eddie made sure the pipe was aligned, and they attached more pipe to the upper end. The string went down again, deeper, deeper, and the men worked well together. The bit chewed through the ground, through coral, stone, rock, earth, before it was worn through from grinding like an old tooth, and they removed it. Eddie brought another bit – brand new, and this was attached, and the string was lowered again.

'Money well spent,' Callaghan told Eddie. 'You buy a quality piece like this and in the long run it saves time. We'll need to order a couple more as back up.'

Callaghan knew how Eddie had scrimped. He knew how it could backfire. He didn't agree with fixing up old equipment. It was how accidents happened. He'd warned Eddie, but they had little choice on this first well. Tito wouldn't spend another cent. It was true Two-Weeks had some magic about him; the rotary table that Eddie had found down in El Paco worked like new. For now it was good enough.

'As soon as some money comes in, we buy new tools,' Callaghan said. 'Or I'm back on that boat to Texas.'

Callaghan worried about gas. Eddie figured the pockets were deep in the ground, below 2000 feet. They didn't need to drill that far. The oil here at Kushi was close to the surface. 'Any sign, and we get the hell out.'

When they hit rock, the whole derrick shuddered. Some of the men were afraid, quick to scamper up the bank. They'd wait there to see if anything else happened. Grace came running outside. There was enough talk around the place of accidents. Just last week, a gas explosion in Forest Reserve had killed a 25-year-old driller from South Africa. He flew burning in the air like a comet. Callaghan said in America, on average, each site lost two men.

'It's just how it is.'

'Not here,' Eddie said, 'I won't let that happen. Not at Kushi.'

At night they took turns to sleep – a few hours here and there, and then it began again and the sun rose and the world seemed new. It was at this early hour that Chatterjee's estate was beautiful to Eddie. The white light in the forest hung like ghosts, and the sounds of the forest waking – the high call of the birds, frogs, howler monkeys – announced to him that with a new day came new hope. Eddie knew it was only a matter of time. The oil was waiting for him.

From across the fence, Charles Macleod heard the spudding and clank of the pipe, the hammering of the Kelly; he saw puffs of white smoke appear through the trees as the steam room fired up. With binoculars, he watched Eddie on the derrick floor, overseeing the drill pipe as it fed through the rotary table, and he wondered how long it would take before they saw signs of the black stuff. He hoped with all his heart that they would never find it.

His own men had drilled three separate wells, and none so far had seen a drop of oil. Early days. There was nothing to be concerned about. If anyone should worry it was Eddie, with his hotchpotch kit and his band of stragglers. Macleod did wonder if he was wrong to think like this; to wish a man to fail. When Eddie was ill, Macleod had found himself hoping he wouldn't pull through. If Eddie had died, he would have gone straight to Tito Fernandes with an offer.

As the sky grew dim, he saw Eddie's men sitting on the bank, and when the wind was right, he heard them singing songs, and he couldn't help give way to the contempt he felt. There was something about the way Eddie had swooped in and taken Kushi for himself that had riled Macleod. He had never felt this way about anyone.

Every morning, after his coffee, Chatterjee wandered down through the estate. Where the land was shaved and stripped bare, he told himself, one day he would grow it all back, the cocoa, the grass, the immortelles. He checked the skies to the east, a good indicator of weather to come. He often saw Apex trucks passing by on the new road Macleod had built around the estate. A private road with a guard. He was aware of the silk cotton tree looking on – its branches wide as many open arms; leaves frilly and green from recent rain.

On the site, Chatterjee stood below the trembling derrick floor, hands on his waist. It made him twitchy, the clanging and twisting of the drill, the sliding of the metal into the hole, the force with which it penetrated. Horatio sat at the top of the tower while those on the floor kept alert. It was too loud to think. Chatterjee looked for Eddie, Callaghan. He offered his predictions, warned of rain or high winds, clear skies, Sahara dust. He asked for news. He asked about Macleod. He worried that Macleod could suck out the oil before Eddie had chance to reach it. It made sense to him that this could happen.

Callaghan told him, 'Don't go concerning yourself with Apex. It looks to me like oil stops right by your fence.'

He took a cup from the shaker filled with mud and slush, dipped in his finger and licked it.

'Two or three days and we'll be seeing oil. A week at most. I'd put my mother's life on it.'

Chatterjee's eyes narrowed, then he smiled. There was a goodness about Callaghan; he was someone you could trust. It was obvious to everyone after a time. It had taken Chatterjee a while to see it.

Part of Chatterjee's disquiet came from Sita. She bombarded him with questions every day. Why so many men? When they go shut off that blasted noise? How was she supposed to rest? Where they put the oil when it come out? It could start a fire? Who manning the steam room? Why smoke pouring out the roof? When the oil coming? And so it went.

Before sunset, Eddie put a daily call through to Tito.

If Tito wasn't there Eddie spoke to Ada.

'Did it come? Any sign at all?'

'Nothing yet,' he'd say. 'But get ready. It's coming any day now. We're getting closer. Pray for us.'

On the fifth day of drilling, Eddie hit something hard – rock or coral, and the drill stalled and then it stopped. The whole derrick creaked and groaned with pressure. Horatio jumped down and headed for the verge. Then the derrick was still again. Eddie suspected that the bit had broken. Callaghan told him they should pull it up and look at it. This would take a couple hours, at least.

'Let's make a whip, divert the thing.'

'And if it doesn't work? Pushes the bit in the wrong direction?'

Eddie was sure it was a block. They didn't need to pull it up. A decision like this could cost them money, slow them down.

'Let's keep going while we can.'

While they were deciding what to do, Long was letting in the casing when the lever on the brake, a club of iron about five feet long, swung from behind and struck him. He staggered forwards with his hands in the air, then clattered onto the muddy floor. Blood poured out of a slit in his head. He was bawling, 'I go dead, I go dead.' His eyes were bulging with fright. Callaghan said something about a first-aid box but there was no first-aid box. Grace brought a towel, a pail of water. Everyone stood around while she tended to him.

Eddie wanted to yell at someone, but he didn't know who to blame. He wondered if this was their first death. He hoped not. Not yet. They had barely begun. They sat Long up, carried him out to the truck.

By the time they reached the hospital the towel was crimson, Long was shaking, and the back of the tray was pooled with his thrown up lunch.

'Don't let him sleep,' the doctor said, after he'd stitched up the cut. 'It can be worse than it looks or better than it looks. Keep an eye on any swelling.'

It was late afternoon when Eddie drove Long to his home near Los Bajos. This was a small village of ten or eleven houses and a single parlour.

Long asked Eddie to pull up by the coconut tree. His house was built on stilts, a patched-up galvanize roof, blue curtains flapping in the breeze. There were potted plants either side of concrete steps; an old bicycle was propped up. At the sound of the truck, Long's wife came out, a trail of half-naked children behind her.

She wore a white dress, falling off one shoulder. When she saw her husband, she looked afraid. She checked his bandaged head, his lanky body, looking for wounds. The children herded around. One child was screaming, pulling at her mother's hem.

'Mister Wade?'

She looked straight at Eddie, not shy as he'd thought she would be.

'I'm sorry,' Eddie said, and he felt uncomfortable. 'He'll be okay. We came straight from the doctor's office.'

She was thin apart from her protruding stomach. Long hadn't said anything about another baby on the way; she must be almost nine months.

'You don't think you should buy your men hard hat?'

Eddie heard the anger in her voice.

'Every day he come home, I say, "They ent give all you hard hat? Where your overalls? Still no boots?"'

Long tried to hush her, draw her close. But she kept on.

'You pay your men pittance, Mister Wade. Is all of us to feed here. You feel is okay if they die? Who is Long anyway? Who is he? Nobody. Some nigger from Los Bajos.'

Eddie put up his hand and turned to walk away.

'God don't sleep, Mister Wade.' She spat on the ground in front of her.

Later, Callaghan sat on the step outside Eddie's cabin. It had been a difficult day, though they'd managed to retrieve the bit – a relief to them both. Some of the men were concerned, asking about the safety of the structure. Why had this happened? Could it happen again? Callaghan had reassured them. Long was unlucky, perhaps a little too keen. It was a warning for everyone to be diligent.

Eddie had turned off the engines and for the first time in days, apart from the noises of the forest, there was silence. He was glad of it. The men were in their barracks, and some had gone home. Grace was cooking dinner. She brought two beers and the men drank them quickly.

'These things happen,' Eddie said. 'The men aren't experienced.'

'He should never have been letting out the brake on his own.'

Callaghan looked down at his filthy boots, kicked away dried mud.

'Maybe we should have a doctor. You know, like they did in Beaumont. Companies who could afford it.' He shook his head, as if he didn't know what to say. 'They're our responsibility, Eddie. It's not just you and me. Some of them have families.'

This wasn't America – there was no trade union for oil workers yet. If something happened, employees couldn't claim compensation from Fernandes/Wade/Chatterjee Limited. It was true, these men were vulnerable. But Eddie had explained his terms and they'd agreed to them.

Callaghan's kept his voice low. 'We don't know the land. You said it yourself. It's unpredictable. They have a doctor over at Apex. We don't even have a first-aid box.'

Eddie knew Callaghan was right. Macleod had a doctor, strict procedures to follow in case of an accident. He'd heard Apex's alarm in practice ring out across Chatterjee's estate. A honk like a ship's horn could be heard for miles around. Apex men wore overalls, hard hats, knee caps, special reinforced leather boots. They took breaks for lunch and dinner. They had showers, a place to wash their clothes.

Today was difficult, but no one was dead. He didn't like the way Long's wife had made him feel. It reminded him, as if it was yesterday, of a 27-year-old floor-man hit by a hook and travelling block in Peace River district. Ralph Winchester was from Surrey, England. Enthusiastic, fine looking. By chance his wife and son were on site when it happened. There was talk that the well would come in that day. While spudding the pipe, sheaves broke loose and fell with some force. When the block hit Ralph's upper body, his wife thought quickly enough to cover her son's eyes. They had to scrape Ralph from the wood, fold him back into the man he was. Eddie had picked out his wedding ring, washed it clean. The next day he gave it to Ralph's wife whose face was creased with pain and rage, not unlike Long's wife, today. But Ralph's wife had some money, she had compensation. These people would get nothing.

It was easy enough to pick up bandages, plasters, iodine. He would do that tomorrow, and when they'd made some money, he, too, would put safety precautions in place. For now, they must get the oil out of the ground. There was no money to spare. Tito had warned him, they must keep their belts tight. They were one man down, but they could make do.

Two days later, as dawn broke, Grace arrived with Malaki. The boy was 27, he was heavy in himself, his legs turned out at the knees. His hair was silky, tied back. She asked Eddie if, perhaps, Malaki could help out in some way. He was hard working.

'Sure,' Eddie told her, and shook the boy's hand. He knew this was Grace's son; bringing him here was a sign she trusted Eddie.

Fair-skinned, Malaki's eyes were green, and like his mother's eyes, they were big and sad. He had a gentle, easy way about him. Eddie was glad to give him a chance.

'You can look after the neatness of the field. Everybody starts there.'

Eddie imagined the young man might have been teased; he hadn't seen many who were as big as Malaki.

'Follow me, Malaki,' Eddie told him, and started down the track. 'Take your time. You'll learn these ropes soon enough. We're one big family here.'

FIFTEEN

Every day Ada asked Tito for news of the well. He was surprised by her interest. She explained that she had seen the operation with her own eyes. People were talking about oil – in the store, at the hairdressers, in the bank, the country club. Oil was on everyone's lips. There were rumours of corporations destroying the land. Was it true? Tito said, yes, maybe, but not Eddie, not on Chatterjee's land. They were careful. They would only drill where he said they could. This was different. They were not like Apex; they were not Trinidad Leasholds.

That morning, as she read the newspaper in bed with her coffee, Ada found an editorial feature on the future of kerosene. The article mentioned aeroplanes. She had seen an aeroplane once fly over the savannah when she was Flora's age. The little plane twisted and dived and she was sure it was going to crash. The crowd were screaming, some covered their heads. But then it lifted back up, as if blown by the breath of God, and floated over the hills. Now a Venezuelan airline was flying in to Trinidad once a week. People were talking of a runway in the east. She knew from Eddie that aeroplanes ran on gasoline. Eddie was right, the world was about to change. The wave was coming.

Ada thought of all this as she dressed, buttoned her linen blouse, shorts, and fixed her hair. Flora was singing outside. It sounded like a sea shanty. Since when had her daughter become so musical? Flora, her beloved Flora. Over the last year Flora had made friends with two girls from San Fernando who boarded at her school. She had begged her mother and father to allow her to board, too. She would share a dormitory from Monday to Thursday. When Ada took ill they had decided she could try it for a while.

On those boarding days, Ada missed her sleepy face at breakfast, the sight of her playing in the yard, her quick feet climbing the wooden stairs, the high call of 'Ma-mah!' Yes, their days together were now more precious.

Outside, Flora was looking for mole crickets and fallen fruit shaken from the branches by the strong winds of the rainy season. At night they'd hear them thud as they fell and hit the ground. Mangoes, avocados, five-fingers, guavas. Flora liked to collect the fruit before squirrels or bats or rats got to them. Last night the wind was gusty; there'd no doubt be plenty.

From the landing Ada looked down at her daughter standing under the trees: barefoot, and still wearing her lilac nightie, her skin nutmeg brown. She looked small – all of her years, but small. One day she would be grown and gone. Ada hoped she'd have freedom, copious opportunities and voyages. To know another life, a life beyond marriage, childbirth and making a home. Sometimes Ada wondered if her life, the kind of life that all women were taught to want, was not the life she should have let herself fall into. Did women have hunger like men? She was certain they did; domesticity made them forget. Perhaps hunger appeared as restlessness, irritability; the remedy was a sedative, sea air, a shot of rum. A night in the madhouse. Young women were encouraged to find a man to build a cage in which they could be kept. She had done just that. Tito had built a golden cage for her filled with material comforts. It was best not to think about it. She would encourage Flora to seek another path, even if it took her away from Trinidad. The thought of this made her sad. Flora was her life, her heart.

Ada called through the window.

'Flora! What did I tell you?'

'Look, Ma-mah!'

She'd found two avocados already; they had little teeth marks, and were bruised. She held up the bright green fruit.

'You should be wearing shoes. Go and put them on.'

Just yesterday Junior had caught sight of a scorpion, its belly large with babies. It ran inside the ferns before he could kill it. One sting and Flora could be dead.

Ignoring her mother, Flora carried on searching under the

tree. She found two more avocados. Now she came to where Tito was sitting, drinking his coffee and where Ada was coming to join them. Flora laid the pears out in a line.

'Daddy, what does oil look like?'

'A bit like syrup or treacle. Why, darling?'

'Last night I dreamed of black water. All over the floor and out in the road and things were floating on it. I wondered if it could be oil.'

'Well, yes,' he said. 'It can look like black water.'

'It's coming then,' Flora said, with certainty. 'There'll be a lot of it.'

Tito got up and kissed the top of his daughter's head. 'You're a clever cookie, my Flora. If you're right, I'll buy you a horse.'

SIXTEEN

Just as Eddie said, and how Flora saw it in her dream, oil soon arrived. Three weeks of drilling and Eddie heard Callaghan shouting, saw the rush of men to the derrick floor and figured something must be wrong. A deep groan from below ground, and as he ran along the ridge and up the steps to the platform, the earth started to shake. Next came a fizzy hissing sound. Eddie was up there at the mouth of the hole in time to feel the loud pop like a ball from a canon and see a burst of black liquid shoot some hundred feet high beyond the crown and into the blue sky.

His men ran for cover, fleeing up the bank to the safety of the steam room. Then they started yelping, ran down the bank again and jumped up in the air, throwing off their hats, and letting the fountain fall back on their upturned faces and splatter like black rain – a dispensation from God – on their skin, in their hair, over their clothes. Eddie took off his hat, too, and let the oil pour down on him. He rubbed it into his face, into his scalp, he felt it splatter on his chest. Long, Tripe, Horatio were staring up at the column of oil. On the bank, Grace held onto Mercy. Mercy's hands were up in her face. She was yelping. 'Look it come! It come!'

Eddie shouted, 'Call Chatterjee, call him!'

Horatio started for the house, but Chatterjee was suddenly there. Eddie took his arm and raised it above his head. 'Sonny, what did I tell you. What did we tell you?' Then he yelled into the air, 'Hallelujah! Halle-fucking-lujah!'

'Fetch your wife,' Eddie said to Chatterjee, 'she should see this. It doesn't happen everyday. You hear what I'm saying!' But she was already on her way, running down the hill with their boys. 'Come, get up here!'

Eddie looked around at the black dripping men, the tower of

oil, the derrick floor awash with it. He wanted to hold it in his mind like a photograph. Along the fence, he saw Macleod's men standing and watching. When a well came in, it was good manners to cheer or clap, even if the well belonged to somebody else. Macleod was there, too; Eddie could see the outline of his hat.

Meanwhile the oil gushed. From above, Callaghan shouted down to him to close the well off. They had run the drill pipe in too far. 'We hit a spark and the whole thing goes.'

Eddie called for timbers and clamps, and he sent Malaki to fetch them. 'Get the irons stacked up at the house.'

Mister Long and Gelliseau carried them. They fastened them onto the derrick while oil rained down.

'Check the pump, Horatio. We need to siphon it off.'

The oil sprayed hard like it came out of a giant hose; thick, blasting in their faces. Eddie was coated in the stuff; it was in his mouth, his ears. He strapped on goggles, sealed them onto his eyes with tape. He put on a slicker hat and a cape. Then he straddled the pipe with a hack saw and worked at it. Mete and Callaghan stayed close, their clothes and faces black with oil. At one point Eddie looked up at them both and laughed.

'Who is who,' he yelled.

On the bank, Chatterjee stood with his wife and their sons. Sita had her arms around the boys, one on each side. Her eyes were fastened on the workings of the derrick. Eddie waved at her, and she nodded at him.

Eddie cut the pipe in two, and it sprung apart enough so that, together, they could pull it off. Callaghan and Mete held onto each side and wrenched the valve free. Mete pitched it down on to the ground. Then Eddie dressed the threads all around. 'See, Callie, this isn't so bad.'

There were two hours of managing the fizzing pressure on the blowout preventer. 'See what I tell you, Horatio! See this, see how this will save us?' They fixed the stuffing box on the casing connections, and they worked at it and worked at it.

Grace brought chicken stew and rice and laid out the plates on the wooden fold-up table, and they took turns to eat; never leaving the well unattended. And when the sun was gone they switched on the generator Eddie had found in a heap in San Francique. It was temperamental but tonight it worked, and he was grateful that they were able to see what they were doing.

'Let there be light,' Eddie said, and he put his hands out to the sky. He felt alive. He'd seen enough wells come in, and he knew what to expect. But this had been early, much earlier than expected. At 600 feet!

They were still bringing in the well in the early hours, and it flowed easily into the newly constructed wooden tanks. The sound of the flow was sweet to his ears, and Eddie felt certain they had hit something big. Callaghan, Mete, Eddie, Gelliseau, Horatio, Long and Malaki put their arms around each other and made a circle. They were exhausted, giddy as drunks. Eddie showed the men how to control the flow of oil; it was strong, and it seemed to Eddie they were lucky.

'Remember this,' Eddie said, looking at each of them. 'This is the beginning. Don't forget it. You made this happen. We made this happen.'

He walked up to the house in the dark, sticky with oil, his hair full of it, his face streaked like he had crawled out of a swamp. Chatterjee let him inside the house to use the telephone. Tito's voice was thick with sleep.

'Did we strike big? Is that how you say it, strike big? Was it a gusher? Tell me, tell me. Ada is awake now. She's desperate to know. I'm desperate to know.'

Eddie laughed.

'I can't tell yet, but it looks good. It looks very good. It will pay, I'm pretty sure of that. This well will pay. In fact, I'd put my life on it.' Eddie realised his eyes were blurred with tears. It wasn't joy, so much as relief: his instincts were right.

'Thank God,' Tito said. 'We'll throw a party.'

While spirits were high at Kushi, the mood at Apex was not. When the well came in, Charles Macleod had stood by the fence watching the rush of crew to the derrick floor to stare at the black tower. He watched Eddie jump in the air, fling up his hat; saw Chatterjee goggling up as if he'd seen a chariot clatter down from heaven. Their excitement was palpable, galling; boiling up Macleod's blood. After ten minutes, he rallied his men. 'You think this is a fucking show? You want to stay gawping all afternoon like apes?'

In the office, he tore down the map of Siparia and pored over its contours, rivers and points of elevation. He marked the spot where the oil had arrived. He scoured his geological papers to seek out patterns of anticlines; he rubbed his head, paced the floor of his office while looking out of the window at Eddie's site where the pump kept pumping, and steam puffed up into the sky.

For the first time, Macleod ordered his men to drill all night; take turns to nap, he didn't want to hear of tiredness. He saw them looking at him as if he had lost his mind. He'd known this would happen, but not quite so soon. There was nothing he could do. He left the site early, told his foreman to keep watch.

When Elsie saw him arrive mid afternoon, she knew what had happened. She tried to make light of it; said something about how his day would come. 'Failin' means you're playin'. It could be worse.' As soon as she said it, she was sorry.

He sat until nightfall outside in the porch with his bible, where there was a little breeze, and where Elsie, tiptoeing, brought him a tray with half of a roasted chicken, mashed potatoes, boiled green beans. His favourite supper. She was frightened of him when he was like this. He had never raised his hand to her, but more than once, in a rage, he had pitched his dinner plate across the room. There were stains on the walls of their dining room in Fife: gravy, meat, soup, liquor.

That evening, Macleod turned to the psalms, and when he found the lines he needed, he whispered them to himself over and over.

'Show me the way I should go, for to you I entrust my life. Rescue me from my enemies, LORD, for I hide myself in you.'

Chatterjee got up later the next day, rubbed his head with coconut oil, put on his shirt. Sita was already making roti over the fire, her hair neatly plaited. Silver bangles up to her elbow jangled as she flipped the disc of dough from hand to hand. It was all familiar to him, this scene, the sound of her bracelets, a smell of fire, the fierce crow of the cockerel in the yard outside. And yet, for all its familiarity, everything was different.

He recalled the feeling yesterday in his body when he saw the oil blast over the top of the derrick. He wasn't prepared for the roar, or the shuddering earth. He hadn't expected to feel excited; to be afraid. When he saw Sita and the boys come running towards him, he'd felt an urge to protect them, send them back up to the house. Yet the thrill was something he wanted for them, too. He couldn't deny them that.

Along the wall outside, he spotted a row of soda bottles. Vikram had already been down to the site to fill them from the pools of oil on the ground. Like molasses, the oil was dark and gloopy.

'He want to sell it out on the road.'

Sita gave Chatterjee a look, and he realised it had been a long time since she had been anything but miserable. Her eyes were muddy brown, the whites had grown yellowish; her mouth was tight, thin-lipped. She was not a beautiful woman, but she had something long forgotten – a kind of mischief, and today he was reminded of it. She gave him his coffee and rather than sit on the bench, he started down the hill, his heart lighter than it had been in years. He began to whistle a tune that he remembered from his father. It had been a long time since he heard it.

The sun was coming up; the glow of the forest was misty and bluish; already heat was rising. Corn birds shrieked as they flapped slowly and then up to higher ground where they nested in the silk cotton tree. The disruption had affected them, too.

Eddie was coming out of his room, dressed, his face puffy. Trinket followed him; tail upright like a post. Eddie shook Chatterjee's hand.

'Nothing like honey to get the bees excited.'

He was about to start the pump; let the oil out through the pipes, start flushing it into the large tank. He was giving the men an extra hour. Yesterday, they'd worked like dogs. Malaki was already cleaning the floor, collecting tools; laying out broken pieces of pipe.

'Sita want to know if we rich.'

'Tell her, this one will cover our costs. We pay Tito, Two-Weeks, the men. The next oil well will pay us something. The one after will fill our pockets. As sure as I'm standing here.'

SEVENTEEN

They headed out of town, following the coastline. Ahead the hills were blue-black; Eddie could make out their pointed tops. He could hear the thrum of cars behind, a convoy of five or six, bright car-lights illuminating the tall grass. Ada sat in the back, her scarf a white flag blowing behind her. Her dress was white satin; her lips the colour of ripe cherries.

They drove through the quiet suburbs of Port of Spain, and out towards the west. They came to a village – wooden shacks rising up the hillside; three or four rum shops, a couple of parlours. Tito slowed down to avoid a pack of stray dogs wandering in the middle of the road. Music poured out from somewhere; a spoon beat on a bottle – clah-cluh-clac cluh-cla-cluh. A smell of salt fish and onions frying. People were walking in the road. Young girls crouched in conversation by the drain. On the corner, men played dominoes. They stared at the passing cars.

'Hold onto your hats,' Tito said, and pushed his foot hard on the accelerator. The wind whooshed through Ada's hair and they left the village behind.

Now the sea was visible on the left; specks of light from a faraway boat were blinking. Eddie saw the moon above, small and neat as a spit curl.

The hotel shimmered: threads of lights dripped over the entrance, leading along the pathway to the foyer, and the shining chequered marble floor. A band – musicians in white – played a chirpy string song that Eddie recognised. Waiters welcomed guests with cocktails; carried trays of canapés of crab and shrimp, little hot bread rolls. Tito and Ada greeted their guests, and introduced Eddie. Eddie drank quickly, and his head soon felt light.

Tito said, 'You know what I say, Eddie? Let the gods know you are grateful and they will smile on you again.'

Ada said, 'Remember Emily, Eddie, you met her at our place?' Then, 'Eddie, come see my cousin, Ruth. Remember her? She came to our dinner that night.'

He wasn't sure who was who, but he nodded, and spoke when he needed to. He tried to make a good impression. He shook hands; he was polite.

'So you're the man who brought in the oil.'

'Let me shake your hand, rub off some of that good luck.'

'Mister Wade, entrepreneur, oil man.'

'We hear you have the Midas touch.'

At the bar, Tito said, 'They'll be coming down to Siparia with their tools.'

Eddie lit a cigarette.

'I guess this is what happened in Texas.'

'Thirty-five thousand in a single month. Buggies, trains, wagons and horses. Madness.'

'Well, it's a ticket out of poverty, and a lot of those folk must've been desperate. Most people live and die desperate, Eddie. They never get a chance to sing their song. You and me are lucky; we get to sing our song. A lot of people here tonight are lucky.'

Eddie took in the room – the high ceilings, the chandeliers.

'I know it isn't quite your scene, but maybe you should tell yourself it is. There are worse things in life to get used to.' Then Tito said, 'Next time a well comes in, we must come down there and see it. Give me some warning.'

'Hard to know for sure.' Eddie said. 'There are signs but they don't always mean a thing.'

Eddie thought about the drinking holes he frequented in Texas, the rundown hotel bars, the grimy saloons. He remembered the honky-tonk; an old house with fifteen or twenty girls, putting on a little show and how they'd try to hole you up in a booth and get you to buy keys to their room. Eddie never wasted money that way. But he knew plenty who did and he wished some of those people he knew then could see him now. He thought how different things look when you've come through them.

Later, Ada found him sitting at a table with two sisters. The sisters looked alike – blond and long-limbed like mannequins. They had been asking Eddie about California.

Eddie excused himself, followed Ada to the terrace.

'I'm desperate for a cigarette.'

'Sure,' he said.

He was feeling pleasantly drunk. Flambeaux burned, their yellow flames shifting in the wind and lighting the broad steps below that led to the bay. He could hear the water's soft rush, its wet lap.

Ada slipped off her shoes, and hooked them on her fingers; she felt the cool sand underneath her feet. Here the air was cooler and quiet.

They found a place to sit, and Eddie felt for his cigarettes. She bent forward to let him light it; her dark hair fell on his fingers.

She could smell him, his leftover aftershave, faint sweat.

'You're a popular man, Mister Wade. Don't tell me you didn't notice.'

He laughed. 'Can't say I did.'

'Emily said you look like an American actor.'

'People see what they want to see.'

A little breeze blew and carried the music on it. He was glad to be here with Ada away from it all. He wondered if they could be seen from the terrace.

Ada saw the sky was alive with stars, and she blew her smoke up to them – a long straight plume.

'Stars are mortal, did you know? We're looking at the glow left after they've long gone.'

'I like that,' she said, her eyes glittery.

'Do you like it here, Ada?'

'It reminds me of my father. We swam here when I was young.'

'You miss him.'

She glanced at Eddie.

'We all miss someone. You must miss Edith.'

'I'll see her again some day.'

The air was still, and the black sea rushed up spilling beads of foam. Eddie looked at Ada, her thrilling red mouth, the line of her pale throat. She could feel his eyes.

'Do you feel as if your life has a plan, Eddie?'

'If I hadn't met Tito on the side of the road we wouldn't be here now.'

'Yes, everything changed in that minute.'

The idea of a plan, a shape to her life, was exciting. 'Maybe we won't know until the end. Maybe we all become stars when we die.'

He leaned back, and she felt his arm brush against her. He unbuttoned his cuffs, rolled up his sleeves.

Ada knew she shouldn't be here alone with Eddie; if anyone saw, they would have something to say and the bacchanal would start. For now she'd had enough champagne not to care.

'That's Gasparee.' She pointed out to sea. 'Can you see? Then there's Scotland Bay. We have a house we rent there.'

He looked out at its stretch, the dark mass.

'We're going soon, a little crowd of us. You should come.' She looked at him. 'Tito would like it; you've cheered him up.'

It hadn't occurred to Eddie that Tito might be anything but contented with his lot.

'Since he met you, he's like a new man.'

'I'm sorry. He never said.'

'No, he wouldn't.' She stubbed out her cigarette, her head spinning a little. She wanted to say, Trinidad can suck the life out of you.

From a nearby road came the faint tooting of car horns. Taxis were arriving to take people home.

Eddie checked his watch. 'We should head back.'

'Yes, Tito likes to know where I am.'

Early morning light sliced through the shutters in bright thin strips. Eddie looked around the guest room at its white walls with framed sepia photographs of people he didn't know. Ada and Tito's family. A marble washstand was draped in his dinner suit.

He could hear noises downstairs. It was just before eight and the room was hot. He ran his mind quickly over last night: the party, whisky highballs, young blond women. In the early hours, his head swimming with liquor, he laid here and thought of Ada; he thought of her in ways he knew he shouldn't. He'd emerged from sleep slowly, reluctantly, hoping he hadn't stepped out of line. Only in his mind, perhaps.

He washed his face in the basin and checked himself in the mirror, combed back his hair. He put on his work clothes, found his hat. Downstairs, Henrietta was carrying a pot of coffee. She gestured to the immaculate table fully laid with silver. In the centre was a tower of fruit; there was bread and cheese, sliced meat. It reminded him of a hotel dining room; the kind he rarely stayed in.

'Coffee, Mister Eddie? English tea?' Then she said, 'Eggs, ham, and bacon. Cook made bakes. Whatever you want.' She straightened his napkin, pulled out his chair. 'Madam took Flora to school. She come back just now.'

In the kitchen he could hear someone singing. Eddie thought how different this was to his own morning ritual. His head hurt and he wanted to get back to the site. He thought about waiting to see Ada. But it was better that he go.

He thanked Henrietta and told her he'd pick up something to eat on the road, said goodbye and made his way out.

The world was quiet and unfamiliar to him.

On the Savannah, horses were grazing in the gold, pale light. The burnt grass of a few weeks ago was now a vivid green. After a month of heavy rain everything was growing at a rate. He was thirsty as a sailor and bleary from lack of sleep, but mostly Eddie felt good in himself, as if the world and all its glorious beauty was offering itself up to him this morning. He pulled over, bought coconut water and doubles from a vendor shading by the broad samaan. The vendor had one leg. He said his name was Mister Hoppalong; he came every day from his mother's house in Dry River. His mother got up to make doubles at 3 o'clock this morning.

'You don't have a wife?'

'I nearly marry once,' the vendor said, raising his stump. 'The lady broke it off.'

Eddie laughed, and the vendor laughed, too – a loud cyak, cyak.

His head clanging like a door in the wind, Eddie drove through the lower part of the city now, past the barrack yards, boxlike dwellings nailed together where poor families lived. Filthy, flimsy shacks sleeping up to ten; rooms cut in half with a curtain or two. He wouldn't wish it on anybody. Tourists would avoid this part of town and rightly so. He was reminded of a brochure in a travel store in Houston advertising Trinidad as a holiday destination, a paradise. It was no paradise. There was tension in Port of Spain, especially in an area like this packed with immigrants from other islands, and young folk from rural parts of Trinidad coming here to make money. At night these streets came alive with music, gambling, prostitution. Men played whe whe, drank rum and chased after women. Dogs barked and howled and you could hear the high cries of sex. Eddie had heard it himself. For now it was quiet. On the corner, a young boy was naked, washing himself under a standpipe, while outside Rattans Hotel, a woman in a tight crimson dress stood in the doorway; she looked like she was waiting for someone. She blew her cigarette smoke his way.

On Frederick Street, pedlars laid out their wares: haberdashery, toys, birds; destitute men and women queued at the Salvation Army for hot food. He drove through Marine Square where trams were running and ringing their bells; people were walking in the hot sun, well dressed, going about their day, and he slowed down by Tito's store – struck by its beautiful frontage, colourful bunting and contemporary signage – **Fernandes: Something for Everyone**. He'd witnessed Tito's popularity last night. A man who liked people and whom people liked. Eddie had been struck by the excess of the evening – champagne, fine foods, chandeliers, evening wear. White people. French Creoles. The crème de la crème of Trinidad society. A smell of money. Yes, money had a smell and it hung in the air all night. His mind drifted to Ada at the end of the evening, back at the house, the sight of her as she made her way upstairs; Tito's eyes, big and following her like a puppy. Her neck bare, her back exposed by the long V in her white satin gown.

'Good night,' she'd said, a little drunk. 'Don't feel you have to shoot out early. Stay and have breakfast. Don't you think so, Tito?'

'Yes, my darling. Eddie can stay as long as he wants. But I suspect he'll want to get back to work. Now we've found the oil we have to get it out. Isn't that so, Eddie?'

'Yessiree,' he said. 'I'll be heading off early.'

It was already 10.00 am; half the day was almost gone. What was he thinking? Eddie was glad to hit the Southern Main Road and head back towards Siparia.

After her father died, Ada was sent away to boarding school in Newbury, Berkshire. The tree-lined drive ran for a mile, and was home to young deer that ran between the horse chestnut trees. There was an orchard filled with apple and pear trees. The apples were gold and their flesh was sweet. The school was sprawling, gothic.

It was a relief to be away from Trinidad. She didn't have to talk about her father, about what had happened. Ada didn't know that she was sad. She followed instructions, studied. Some of the girls teased her because of the way she spoke.

She made friends with Jennifer Cowes, a freckly blond girl with a pudgy face. Whenever there was revision to be done, Jennifer would say, 'Always eat your frogs first. Then we can do whatever we like.' This made Ada laugh. Jennifer's mother and father lived in Kensington, London; her father was a conservative politician. One day Jennifer told Ada that she was glad she went to the toilet like white people did, that she felt the cold like white people. She could never be friends with a native. Natives were disgusting.

Ada felt her cheeks burn. 'What do you mean by native? You mean, someone who belongs to a place? Because if that's so, then I'm a native too. I'm a native of Trinidad and Tobago.'

Jennifer made a strange noise with her throat.

'No, you're not like that. You're like me. You could easily come from England.' She put out her arm – white and squidgy as a piece of dough – alongside Ada's.

'Look, see what I mean. We're almost the same colour.'

That afternoon, the Cowes' driver took Ada back to school. She asked to be dropped off at the gates so she could walk the long driveway alone to the house. The rain came in a fine mist and it was cold enough for dragon's breath. As Ada walked between the chestnut trees, their branches grew claws and they seemed to be trying to get at her. Ada started to cry. She cried for her father, for herself, for the home she'd left behind and the people who understood her.

Two weeks later, Ada returned home to Trinidad. She was seventeen years old. She wasn't sure what she would do with herself. Ruth was engaged to be married to Gerry Fitzwilliam, a geologist working at the oil refinery. She would soon be leaving her mother's house to start a life with him. Ruth told Ada, 'You must come out with us, we can introduce you to someone.' When Ada pulled a face, she said, 'You don't want to be left on the shelf. It can happen to anyone. Even someone like you.'

Then in his forties when she met him, Tito's hair was still black. Though he had put on weight, Ada liked his face and she found him attractive. He was short but he was authoritative. She liked his deep clear voice. He understood what it was like to be sent away to school. He told Ada that she would settle back soon enough.

He talked about her father; told Ada how her father had set up a school for the blind in Guyana. 'Your father was brave. Don't forget that; you are him and he is you.'

He brought Ada orchids, candies from America, fashion magazines. He smelled of cologne. They sat in the veranda, and talked about many things until night fell. Sometimes he stayed for dinner. Aunt Bessie warned Ada, 'Tito is falling in love with you. Unless you want that to happen, I suggest you tell him you have a boyfriend in England. Make it up. No one has to know.' She told her that Tito had been jilted by a woman, who had run away to Dominica with an overseer with the looks of a movie star.

'Who would do that?'

'Matilda Mendonca, that's who.'

One day Tito took Ada to the beach at Macqueripe. They walked together down the steps. It was his favourite beach, he said. He liked the curve of the bay, its soft, low waves. At night he had seen phosphorescence. It was perfect for swimming in the afternoon.

'I don't swim,' Ada said, 'not since Daddy.'

Tito said, 'Well, I rather like swimming but I don't much like getting wet.'

They sat on the striped chairs outside the hotel terrace, and he talked about his plans for the store – a lift, an ice cream bar. He talked of his upcoming trip to New York. He was looking for jewels to import – opals, rubies, sapphires.

'You ever went to Manhattan, Ada? I would like to take you there. You'd see some things. You will like America. It's a big place.'

The sun was coming down, the sky was blue and peachy.

'Is it true you were going to be a cardiologist?'

'Yes. Once I saw an operation to take out a bullet from the heart of a soldier. When the surgeon tried to remove it with a pair of forceps, the heart contracted and sucked it back through the wall into another chamber.'

Ada pictured the soldier, lying on the operating table, under a fountain of blood.

Then Tito said, 'Did you know, you can live with a bullet in your heart, Ada? There are soldiers all over the world who live like this.'

'You can live with a bullet in your heart?'

'Yes. The heart is a mysterious and wonderful thing.' Then he said, 'And to answer your question, I could've been many things. Just as you can be many things. But yes, a cardiologist. My mother's plan.'

'Maybe you can answer something for me. Is it possible my heart could have a hole in it? From when Daddy died.'

Tito took up her hand, and patted it.

'My dear, Ada. Your heart is complete. I know when a heart has badness or loneliness. There is nothing wrong with yours. I can promise you that. Your heart is perfect.'

He had dreams, he said. Big plans. He knew the exact house he wished to buy on Broom street, the countries he wanted to visit before he died.

'Did you know your dreams can keep growing, Ada? I must remind you to dream.' Perhaps she would like to be a part of his dreams. He had been hurt once before, but now he was ready to love again. Unlike this other woman, he knew he could trust Ada.

'We have known each other for years,' he said. 'I've loved you for a long time.' He kissed her; his lips were soft, his breath smelled of peppermints.

On January 21st 1922, Ada and Tito were married in Greyfriars church on Frederick Street.

EIGHTEEN

No one predicted the worst rains in the history of Trinidad. Roads out of Siparia grew thick and muddy, tyres glued themselves into it. When a truck was stuck, wheels spun and sprayed red mud. Men from the village brought wood, and slid the planks beneath the tyres, allowing the trucks to crawl a few more yards. Chatterjee said he had never seen a rainy season like it. Sita complained. If they were in Rio Claro where her mother lived in a house on stilts, the rain wouldn't reach.

Kushi estate soon flooded with soupy brown water, the men wading up to their ankles. Rain never seemed to stop for long; it thrashed the land and trees and filled the river. They covered the rotary table with a tarpaulin of sorts and tried to keep going. The river grew swollen and full, the same colour of shit, Callaghan said, that trailed out of him in Jamaica.

Monkeys called out their sad songs; beetles with horns appeared from nowhere; clouds of mosquitoes, centipedes as long as Eddie's foot showed up inside the barracks. Mercy screamed when a centipede slid out of a cup towards her lips. Callaghan, nearby, saw the creature – its body long and thick with brown rings and strong red feet. He flung it into the bush. Then he carried Mercy, too terrified to walk, up the hill to the house.

Later, Eddie said, 'There's easier ways to have a girl put her arms around you. If you like her, you should ask her out.'

'Maybe I will,' Callaghan said. 'When we're done here.'

For twenty-four hours, they were stuck while the rain held them captive. Some of the camp had to relocate to the top of the hill. Chatterjee and his family moved into one room, Callaghan and Eddie shared the vacated room together. Mercy and Grace were downstairs next to the kitchen. Grace sent Malaki home to her father. Callaghan taught Mercy to play cards; they stayed up late playing poker for matchsticks by the light of candles.

Mercy had a way of looking at Callaghan that made Eddie take notice. Her eyes were the colour of dried grass – a dirty burnt green, and her hair was piled on top of her head. She was skinny, her limbs long and rangy. She didn't know who her father was, but her mother worked for a wealthy family in San Fernando.

'Mister Callaghan,' she'd say, tucking her hair behind her delicate ears. 'Show me how to win.' Then, in between games, 'Tell me about America. What you all did Christmas time. Tell me how snow does feel.'

Grace saw something growing between them, and warned Mercy to be careful.

'But Mister Callaghan nice.'

'Men like Mister Callaghan doh marry girl like you.'

Grace told Mercy about Mr Wilkinson; how she worked for the family in Forest Reserve from thirteen years of age, and how, in that house, the English woman, Mrs Wilkinson, clapped her hands when she wanted something.

'She talk to me like I crawl out the lagoon. If I outside picking washing from the line, or sweeping the veranda, Mrs Wilkinson shout so loud her face turn purple.'

Mercy listened while stitching the hem on her cotton dress. Outside the rain made a stream by the door, and the heat was thick and sweet with flowers.

Grace told Mercy how she was forbidden to eat the meals she was ordered to cook. She slept on the floor in the washroom. Then one day, Mrs Wilkinson accused Grace of stealing money from her purse. When Grace denied it, Mrs Wilkinson hurled a cup of hot tea at her, scalding her neck, her chest. She showed Mercy the patches of pink scars like a trail of tiny islands above her collarbone.

'I put my belongings in a paper bag and leave. Mister Wilkinson come looking for me in his fancy automobile. He beg me come back. They give me somewhere to hang my clothes, a bed. He visit me every night in that bed.'

Mercy knew the rest, and she knew Malaki. She also knew that

Grace worked for the Wilkinsons until they left Trinidad for England five years ago.

Grace said. 'Forget Callaghan. Any fool can make baby.'

The river kept rising each day. Trees floated in the brown water, broken branches, stumps. Eddie found an ocelot in his kitchen one night, its patterned coat shimmering like sequins; it was finishing up a plate of stew. Grace took a chicken bone and threw it far out in the yard, and watched the cat disappear into the night. She had never seen an ocelot up so close. A sign, she said, of other worlds. Or maybe, like Noah, they would have to build an ark.

Eddie reminded Grace that Noah had used oil to seal the ark.

'Two coats to keep it watertight. Like the walls of Jericho – sealed with oil and tar.

'The animals were in the right place, and so are we. It will pass, Grace. The rains will pass and all shall be well.'

Where the hillside had fallen away, some of the roads collapsed entirely. The land was soft and crumbling like cake. Tito sent sandbags, and these helped prevent the roads from turning into a swamp, but there weren't enough men to distribute them. In Trinidad, when rain was heavy, people stayed at home. Bed weather, they said. There was talk of dengue fever. Eddie praised Long and Horatio for their steadfastness, told them it would all come good. Callaghan said, if it isn't one thing it's another in this godforsaken place, and Eddie knew the phrase had come from Mercy.

They lost a truck down a ravine. Mister Long threw open the cabin and leapt out just before it flipped. Catching himself in the rocky fall, he gripped onto a clump of bush and managed to save himself.

'Another life gone,' Eddie joked. 'Watch yourself, Long. Like me, it seems you're marked.'

Eddie admitted to Callaghan that he was sorry they hadn't started in the dry season. All this would slow them down. The oil was there but they couldn't get at it. They must wait. Chatterjee said it would be another few days, and then the rains would stop for a while.

'How do you know?' Eddie asked.

'This breeze comes from behind us, from the east. It never carry rain. You'll see.'

Macleod watched the weather from his office. His men were still drilling; they wore waterproofs and they built a cover over the derrick floor. The land here was higher. There was little flooding. He was lucky.

Macleod came to see Eddie that morning. Wearing rubber boots, a protective Mac that looked fresh out of a department store, he told Eddie, he had a truck there for him to borrow if he wanted; a pump to suck out the water filling up the site.

'My bulldozer could clear those tracks in half a day.'

'We can't pay you for it.'

Macleod looked at the river of mud falling down the hill.

'You know what I want Eddie. There's plenty in the pot to share. We can come to an arrangement.'

'I admire your persistence. It's how you get places, I guess.' Eddie walked on to the steps. 'But it doesn't work with me. We'll manage. Thanks all the same.'

Macleod was driving home that evening when he saw Mister Long and Grace, standing by the side of the road in the half light, watching water rush over it, ankle deep. There were rumours of caimans swimming along these roads; they could pull a man down. It was difficult to see where the road ended and the hillside began. Macleod slowed and Grace thought he was going to offer them a ride, but he drove on, spraying a fountain of water alongside them.

In the morning Eddie heard that the sandbags he'd used on the main road had burst. With Callaghan, and the rest of his men, he spent the next two days shovelling sand away while the water sloshed around their ankles and sweat poured down their faces.

As Chatterjee said, the rains soon stopped. With its dry lips, the easterly wind sucked out the damp and everything quickly grew again. The place was bursting out of itself, exploding with life. The rising sun brought mist; it looked like smoke around the forest. The air was thick with moisture; it smelled of earth, oil and rotten fruit. To give them a chance to catch up, Callaghan turned off the well pump.

'It's crazy,' Eddie said. 'We need to lay some pipes from here to La Brea so we don't have to use the roads. Not right now, but soon. When the floods have cleared. When we've made some money.'

He had notice from Tito. New equipment had arrived at the docks in Port of Spain. A storage tank – to store oil, a crate of drill bits, extra pipeline. It was impossible to bring it all down it to Siparia. The roads couldn't hold the weighted trucks. Customs officers were becoming impatient.

'They'll just have to wait. There's nothing we can do.'

Tito had an idea; they could use his warehouse out near Macqueripe. Why hadn't he thought of it before. It's there and it's empty.

'You can fill it to the roof. Let's keep production going. I'll take you there myself. There's no time to be lost.'

NINETEEN

'Tito said you were a boxer in the army.'

'Yes I was. You fall down, get back up again.'

Eddie took his hands off the steering wheel to light a cigarette. 'You have to believe you can win.'

'Is that what you want, Eddie, to win?'

Eddie glanced at Ada, shifted the gear stick.

'Maybe. We all like to feel we can achieve something. That we have a choice in the way our lives turn out.'

He drove away from the city, following the coastline to Bayshore. A hot breeze poured through the window. The sky was white with glare over the grey sea.

An hour ago, Ada was closing the shutters in her bedroom when Tito telephoned, exasperated. Electricity in the store had gone and he was supposed to drive Eddie to the warehouse that afternoon. Now he had to stay behind and operate the old generator – everything was melting. His manager had gone home sick with gastroenteritis. A day of small disasters.

'I can take Eddie,' Ada said. 'I know where it is.'

'No, darling. It's hot as hell out there. Weren't you going to rest? He'll just have to come back another day.'

'He's coming from South?'

'He's on his way as we speak.'

'Haven't you lost time already with the rain?'

'We're two weeks behind.'

'So why waste another day?'

Though the idea made sense, Tito didn't like the thought of it. She wanted to go.

'It won't take long. We'll be back before sunset.'

Henrietta had been inside when she heard Eddie arrive. She

came out in time to see Ada getting into the truck. Her hair was up, her lipstick bright, bare legs.

Eddie called out. 'Good afternoon, Henrietta.'

He apologised for the filth, the dust, the smell of gas.

Henrietta was confused. Was something wrong? Had something happened? Why was Ada going out alone with Eddie Wade in the afternoon?

Ada didn't have time to explain.

'Did you like Texas?' Ada asked.

'No one likes Texas. People go there to find their fortune, not to make a life. It's full of crooks. California's another story. The houses, homes of the big stars and fancy restaurants.'

'Did you want to stay?'

'Yes, in San Luis Obispo, right between San Francisco and Los Angeles. I set my heart on it. There was a big well, a tank farm for storing oil. A storm blew up and lightning hit the tank. Two men lost their lives.'

'Terrible,' Ada said.

'Yes, it changed the place. People couldn't stop talking about it.'

At the crossroads, the engine spluttered and the truck slowed. It was about to stall. Eddie changed gear, worked the pedal.

'You need a new truck,' Ada said.

It occurred to him that things came easily to her, that Tito must give her whatever she wanted. She didn't know how privileged she was.

Ahead Ada saw a hut where Tito often bought pineapples, watermelon.

'The turning's somewhere here.'

The fruit lady was sitting behind a display of avocados. High cheekbones gave her face the shape of a diamond.

'She'll be telling Tito she saw his wife with another man. You know how these people talk.' Ada waved at the woman. 'Trinidad is full of eyes. Thousands of eyes everywhere.'

'Small island,' Eddie said. 'It has its drawbacks.'

'Sometimes it makes me want to scream.'

Now the land flattened out, and Eddie got up some speed. His shirt sleeves rolled up exposed his brown forearms. One hand was on the steering wheel, the other rested on the window.

Ada could feel the warm breeze. She'd forgotten how she had always loved it here, the giant samaan trees, branches thick with bromeliad, leaves like black net, then the flat lands – pastures of green fields and meadows gently rising to the pointed forest hills. She suddenly felt free of something; perhaps it was this place, its openness.

'Have you ever seen the bamboo tunnel, Eddie?'

'No, I've heard of it.'

It's not far. I can show you.'

He checked his watch.

She said, 'It'll take ten minutes. Maybe less.'

What would Tito say? It was one thing to go with Ada to the warehouse, but another to visit a remote beauty spot.

She gave him instructions to follow the road as far as the church, then take the trail on the left. The small houses, the golf club, the long thin road were all familiar. She clipped up her hair, fanned herself with a folded-up map.

'Can I ask you something?'

'Sure,' he said.

'How do I seem to you? Happy or sad? Somewhere in between?'

He looked at her and then back at the road.

'Hard to say. I haven't quite worked you out.'

She laughed.

'You make me sound mysterious. I'm not.'

The bamboo tunnel reached some 70 feet high; its poles of yellow came together like long fingers clutching a mass of tiny green leaves. Eddie turned off the engine and they got out of the truck. Ada took off her shoes and walked barefoot along the path, feeling the soft dead leaves, staring up at the bamboo roof. It looked to her like the vaulted ceiling of a church. The green light reminded her of a picture book she'd known as a child; magic lamps and genies, Arabia.

She called out to him, 'Isn't it incredible?'

The air was thick with moisture; a clacking of crickets; leaves flitted in the hot breeze. Eddie watched Ada step slowly and ceremoniously along the dark path as if it was leading her somewhere. She wasn't tall, her waist was narrow, hips wide; shaped like a coca cola bottle.

A parakeet shrieked, burst from above flapping its wings, then another, then another and they rushed out of the tunnel towards the open skies. Ada glanced back at Eddie leaning against the truck door, smoking a cigarette. She was aware of her sticky dress, her damp skin, this unlikely scene. She stepped into the light, saw something in his eyes. She wasn't sure what it was.

'We should leave,' Eddie said, and he started up the engine. 'Tito will think I've kidnapped you.'

They headed onto the main road. Eddie accelerated to make up for lost time and the green world rushed by. A cloud hid the sun and more clouds were gathering over the sea. More rain to come. In the wing-mirror, the wind blew back Ada's dark hair like a banner. She looked young and beautiful. He would have liked to tell her this. He wanted to say that Tito Fernandes was a lucky man.

At home, Ada explained to Tito how the wrought-iron security gate was rusted up, shutters stiff to open, that Eddie had to prang it open with a tool she didn't know the name of. She told Tito about the two tarantulas sleeping in the broken basin; a nest of Jack Spaniards hanging from the rafters. When he asked what they'd talked about, Ada said, the usual. Politics, the King's visit in July; the rising price of cocoa; how to make a Gin Rickey cocktail. She didn't tell him about the detour to the bamboo tunnel.

Next morning, after Tito left for the store, Ada lay in bed, caught in a memory that arrived from nowhere. She recalled sailing back on the boat from Southampton when she was just seventeen years old and a man whom she had glimpsed during the journey. He wore a uniform. He had dark hair, tanned skin. Stripes were on his epaulettes. His boots were polished. A lieutenant, he said, when they finally spoke, and she asked what kind of officer he was. He was heading back to Boston. Lieutenant Michael Darwent; he was thirty-two years old and his family came from Milwaukee.

For three nights, after dinner, the lieutenant danced with Ada in the grand ballroom. The shiny pine floor was slippery; he held her close. On the upper deck they watched the dark sea and he pointed out the Great Bear, Orion, Andromeda. He told her she was a girl of great beauty. He kissed her with his tongue.

It was the first time she had a sensation of desire, of wanting to be touched in other places. Away from the crowds, he had felt her breasts, pushed a hand between her legs. Ada went with it, feeling herself carried along while knowing she ought to stop. But then he took her hand and she realised his trousers were open, his zipper undone. She was startled and pushed him off, told him he had read her wrong. She ran back along the galley, hurried down the narrow steps. Back in her cabin, she was shaken. She wept, shocked by what had happened, shocked by her own longing. Next day, the ship docked in New York, and Michael Darwent disembarked. She never saw him again.

TWENTY

Callaghan tested the land, looking for the usual signs – shale, sand, the colour and smell of the dirt. He was astonished by this place, by the strange formation of the earth here at Kushi. He wandered slowly with his red head down, carrying his leather bag with his testing kit – flask, pippet, his small metal tools, Petri dish. He dug a pit of eight feet or so, climbed inside and scraped away samples of the soil. While testing for clay, sand, shale, he found mud, fragments and lumps of dark coloured oil-stained sandstone, a jumble of fossil mud volcano parts. He marked up the map with crosses, question marks.

'We can't just go by a feeling,' Callaghan said. 'It's as good as throwing your money away. We need to be sure.'

It was late afternoon; the light was softening, the sky a pale unbroken blue. Eddie and Callaghan could see Macleod's camp beyond the fence. The silk cotton tree, 100 feet or more, looked like a tall woman, her head twisted to one side; its roots were the frills of her long grey dress. Callaghan looked up at the boughs, the dripping wooden vines. 'They grow in South America, too. The wood's soft, easily hollowed out. They use it to build canoes.'

'Chatterjee says it's full of jumbies. People brought offerings here for centuries. If we cut it down we'll have bad luck.' Eddie looked up at the tallest branches. 'They believe it.'

'Shame,' Callaghan said, and combed back the elephant grass. 'Just look at this.'

He pushed a long metal syringe into the ground and slowly sucked up the soil. A quarter of the tube quickly filled with dark liquid, like black blood.

'Never seen anything like it.' Callaghan held it up to the light. 'This spot right here is swimming in it.'

Eddie was distracted; he was looking over at Macleod's bunga-low. He could see the road Macleod had built and the long window of the office where a light shone until late. He'd heard Macleod owned a fridge to keep his drinks cool – and also that he was getting twitchy – each drilled well dry as powder. They'd drilled down to 2000 feet, which was expensive and hazardous. Apex would soon be asking questions.

When Eddie last saw Macleod in Port of Spain, he'd crossed the street to talk to him. They stopped outside the bank; the sun burned down. Macleod was keen to talk.

'Your lucky strike could've been random. I saw something similar in Argentina. A sudden flurry of oil in a place no bigger than a hopscotch court. We brought in crew and equipment. But that was it. Not a drop more.' He smiled. 'Hopefully that won't be the case for you.'

Macleod looked pleased with himself, glad to hand over a bad memory.

'How about yourself, Charles?'

Macleod took off his hat, ran his fingers around the inside rim. 'No reason not to be optimistic. You know how these things are. Luck can change like that.' He clicked his fingers and smiled. 'Don't worry about us. You've enough on your plate.'

Macleod didn't tell Eddie there were concerns from Apex in London about the amount of spend, the lack of oil so far. He didn't tell Eddie that his wife was unable to hold down food; while her belly grew into a small dome, her bones pressed up to her skin. The doctor had warned that if she didn't improve they would take her into hospital. Elsie was afraid. She said if she died it would be his fault. If they lost the baby, she would never forgive him. She lay all day beneath a mosquito net, while Ruby kept close watch.

Elsie had started having nose bleeds; no one knew why. One morning, Macleod came in to find her pillow saturated crimson. A halo of blood. He didn't know her for a moment; her face was pale as a saint. He shouted for Ruby, his heart jumping with terror. He barked her name, Elsie! Elsie! Then he took up her withered hand and begged the angels to save her. When Elsie opened her eyes, he felt that he had only just managed to pull her back from the edge of death.

146

That day, in Charlotte street, Macleod didn't tell Eddie any of this. He wanted Eddie to know that he would keep drilling next door to Kushi for as long as he could. He would find oil. He was sure of it. Even if it killed him.

They settled on a spot 500 feet south of the original well, away from the river. Callaghan said it was possible this configuration was gassy; he'd heard Macleod's men talk of gas on this side. But it was irresistible to Eddie; there was already smatterings of oil in the top clods of earth. Not quite as much as where the cotton tree stood. But it was something else, he said. A gift. As long as they didn't drill too deep, they should keep away from danger.

Like another miracle, in three days, at a depth of 300 feet, mud started to boil up through the rotary. There wasn't time to call Tito to let him know. The mud came higher and higher, then with more force, firing up through the top of the derrick and with such pressure that the drill pipe started to move up. A piece snapped off and then another, whipping away the travelling block, and clipping the elevators, knocking over the smokestack of the boiler. Gelliseau and Long scattered from the erupting derrick, watching as the pipes broke off. Rocks shot up and fell upon the land. Eddie had seen this happen before, and he knew it should calm down after a while. He and Callaghan took cover near the steam room. They waited and watched. Eddie saw Macleod's men appear at the fence. He looked for Macleod but he couldn't see him.

After fifteen minutes, it slowed right down. Eddie jumped back onto the derrick floor, where mud was thick and deep. He called Long to bring shovels and together they slopped it away. At one point, a large chunk of mud burst out of the hole and exploded, spraying them with shattered pieces. A little blue gas followed it, then it all quietened down. The gas was gone, the air was still. There was the sound of corn birds fretting somewhere. The men were silent, waiting for something else to happen.

Eddie stared down into the hole, sure it had finished spitting. Frothing up was the bubbling oil, a greenish black, and lovely to his eyes. Like it was breathing, coming up and sinking back with the gas pressure.

'Look at this, he said, 'look at this coming now.'

The oil kept coming up and over the rotary table and with each flow it came a little higher and a little higher and finally, it fired up clear through the top of the derrick with a roar.

'Woah!' Callaghan pitched off his hat and leaped down to the bank.

The men ran down onto the ground, watched the oil rush out, blackening everything it fell on. Eddie turned his face to the sky. Thank you, God! This was the moment; here it came like a promise. 'Look,' he shouted. 'Watch it come, here it comes!' Second time in two months. The first one was no fluke. The flow pressure was strong, as if they'd cut into an artery. Callaghan slapped him on the back. 'You were right, I give you that. You were damn well right. This is something else.'

Grace ran down the hill, and stood by the steps where the oil had pooled. She took off her shoes and put her feet in it. The oil was all over Mercy – splattered in her hair and on her dress; she'd been caught in it as she was crossing the camp. She turned her face to the top of the derrick where the oil was shooting, her mouth gaping.

Callaghan called out, 'Ever see anything like that?' Mercy shook her head, still staring up at the tower of oil. He kissed her dirty cheek, put his arm around her waist. She didn't seem to mind.

Chatterjee was grinning, staring up at the column. Sita stood behind him with the boys. They kept well back, no doubt afraid of what could go wrong. Yet despite her trepidation, Eddie saw that Sita's face was lit with awe.

'Boy!' Chatterjee shouted. 'Three days! God is good. God is good.'

Eddie said, 'You've been living on a gold mine and you never knew it. It's been waiting for us, Sonny. All these years. Waiting for us to come and get it out.'

It felt that way to Eddie: the oil was meant for him. That night he fell asleep counting barrels in his mind, and the thousands of dollars they would make.

Crude oil was taken to a central station at Fyzabad, and onto

Pointe-à-Pierre. There it was treated and changed into kerosene, run off by pipeline to a tanker in the bay.

Tito found a plant in Texas, another in Minnesota, both willing to pay more than $8 a barrel. It was a fact, Tito said – and he held up the front page of the newspaper to prove it. Right now Trinidad was the largest oil-producing country in the British Empire. Kushi estate was part of that statistic. The quality of oil was high, and so was demand. Cars were popping up, so motor gasoline was in huge demand. The new cracker plant on the refinery in Point-à-Pierre was capable of turning the crude into kerosene, gasoline. There had never been a better time for Eddie and Tito to sell their oil to America. All over Trinidad, people were talking about Kushi.

Money came slowly at first – a few cheques to cover costs, to pay Chatterjee; then there were repairs; Two-Weeks' fees. The days they lost in the rains. Some extra for the men, bonus cheques he had promised. The cost of the fallen truck; Callaghan. But for all these expenses, for the first time in his life, Eddie had money in his pocket. And more cheques were starting to arrive.

Chatterjee said, 'At last, money come.' That day, when Eddie gave him an envelope thick with cash, he put it to his lips and kissed it.

Eddie opened a bank account at the National Canadian Bank in Marine Square with his first $5,000. The young clerk ushered him to a side room where the manager appeared and shook his hand and presented Eddie with a silver pen, engraved with NCB, and a shiny pin for a tie. He had heard all about the oil.

'We look forward to working with you. I always tell my clients, go out on a limb; that's where the fruit is.'

Afterwards, over lunch in the Queen's Park Hotel, Eddie told Tito how he'd only ever scraped by – rent, food, a few beers at night. Sometimes, the company of a good woman.

'Look, we all want money. Banks like to give you money when they know you have it, but when you haven't, they treat you like a leper. You were broke but not broken. Get used to the idea of having it. Buy yourself a decent car. Put some away. You'll want somewhere to live. Send some to your daughter; start a college fund.'

He looked down at Eddie's khaki trousers, his battered boots.

'Buy yourself some new clothes. I'll send you to my tailor, Robeiro. Come by the store, we have Italian leather shoes, tanned boots.'

'You know me, Tito. I don't care about all that.'

That afternoon, they ordered Portuguese wine and stayed drinking in the restaurant until evening. They ate from a special Portuguese menu of shark soup, bacalhau, little potatoes and crème caramel.

'Ada tells me to watch my waistline, but today we're celebrating. And by the way,' Tito said, 'my wife thinks you're terrific. If I was a jealous man, I'd say she was infatuated. Eddie this, Eddie that.'

Eddie took a glug of wine. 'You're a lucky man, Tito.'

'I am.'

Tito kicked back in his chair. 'Look, I'll give you a piece of advice for nothing. Find a woman with fire in her. Ada has fire in her. A woman who has fire, if you love her, she'll warm up your heart.'

'If you don't, she'll burn down your house.'

Tito laughed, a deep laugh that Eddie had come to recognise.

'That's exactly right, Eddie. She'll burn down your damn house.'

TWENTY-ONE

Robeiro's shop was above Woo Fung's Chinese restaurant. A long, dusty room with shutters that were mostly closed. A ceiling fan was spinning, pushing around a smell of grease from downstairs. The cutting table was stacked with bolts of cloth, while on the wooden shelves more reams of cloth were piled up. Two sewing machines stood near the grubby windows. On the wall were faded pictures torn from magazines and newspaper clippings.

A Portuguese man with a wispy moustache that looked as if someone had drawn it on, Mr Robeiro was short and scrawny. Tito had warned Eddie that he liked to talk.

'You're an oil man, Mister Wade? You make plenty money in Fyzabad.'

'We're not counting our chickens. It might take time before they hatch.'

'We need to smarten him up for when they do,' Tito said, rocking back on his heels.

Mr Robeiro gave Eddie a dress shirt to put on in the little cubicle at the top of the staircase.

'Prepare for the best. Expect the worst.'

Tito sat down, looked through a catalogue of patterns, flipping the pages quickly.

'I lost my uncle down there,' Robeiro said. 'Big explosion; you hear about that? Two years ago now. They say the pipe popped out like a piece of macaroni. Three men dead.'

'There's always bad news,' Eddie said, buttoning himself up. 'If you listen to it, you'll never do anything.'

Mr Robeiro measured him – chest, arms, back, neck. Then he measured his legs, the outer leg, waist. He moved quickly. Tito said Robeiro was always in a hurry – a hurry to make money. If you're measured on a Monday, by Friday you're wearing a brand new suit. For all his chat, he was the best tailor in Port of Spain.

Tito got up and looked at the shelves of fabric, felt some of the material between his fingers, held it to the light.

'Something pale, something fresh. Keep away from the damn khaki. This,' he said, pulling at a ream of cream gabardine. 'One in cream and one in white. You can never go wrong with a white suit. White suits everybody.'

'Khaki has its merits,' Mr Robeiro said. 'Doesn't show dust, or dirt.'

He checked over the measurements. Then he said, looking Eddie in the eye. 'But Mister Fernandes is right. If you're after a wife, you need to set out your stall. Right now your stall needs an overhaul, Mister Wade. A white suit is a good place to start.'

'So they tell me. But I'm not looking for a wife.'

Mr Robeiro noted the cloth that Tito had liked. He pulled out a wide drawer filled with small compartments. He fished out thread, buttons, zips, binding cloth. He didn't look to Eddie like a man of seventy.

Tito said, 'Robeiro, tell Eddie how you keep so well.'

'Sardines, salt fish; a spoon of peanut butter before bed. The usual.'

Eddie felt out of place; he would rather be on the site. He could hear people out in the street, someone calling. 'Boy! Boy!' It was early afternoon; there were many other things he could be doing.

Tito showed him a suit with wide lapels, and a boxy jacket. The slacks were wide in the legs; Eddie had seen Tito wearing something similar.

'You see this, Eddie? This is very fashionable; you should have this kind of style. It's perfect.' Then he said, 'Don't you think so, Robeiro? This will suit him very well.'

'Sure' Eddie said, keen to leave. 'That will do. Two of those – one in white and one in cream. Whatever you think.'

'And a tie. We have an assortment of ties at the store. In every imaginable style, colour, texture. I can show you. Shoes?'

'Don't even look at his shoes,' Tito said, shaking his head, staring down at Eddie's battered Derby boots. 'We have new stock of Italian leather shoes in the store; high grade, black patent. We'll find you something.'

When they left, stepping out into the glare of the street, Tito said, 'Come by, now. We might as well get it over with. I can see you're suffering.'

He laughed, and then Eddie laughed, too.

TWENTY-TWO

They took Tito's boat from the yacht club and set off from the mainland, late afternoon. The boat chugged through the calm, glossy water and streamed out by Carrera Island, through the first Bocas. They passed the rocky corner of Gasparee, and then round again to the next bay. The sky was blue and clear, as if you could take a piece of chalk and write on it. A pod of small dolphins were jumping ahead. They followed them into the next bay, and here they slowed and turned, putt-putted towards a white house with purple bougainvillea growing above the door.

There was a small jetty and Tito moored up alongside it. Henrietta climbed out first; Tito helped Ada out of the boat, and Flora followed her mother up the steps. Eddie carried a crate of provisions, felt the sun on his back and it felt good. They climbed more steps to the veranda. Tito flung open the veranda doors and the sun spilled in.

'We have food, we have champagne. Everything we could possibly want.'

He kissed his wife on her cheek. She would change and go with Flora to see the mule on the hill. The last time they were here it was sick. Ada had a bag of leaves, some old fruit. They might visit Ruth and Gerry further down the bay. They'd be back in a while.

'If I died here, I'd be a happy man,' Tito said, lifting the covers from the veranda chairs. 'You have your version, Eddie. Where would that be?'

'Out on the field. Doing what I do best. You can scatter my ashes from the top of the derrick.'

'Dedicated to the end.'

He showed Eddie his room across the hallway. Take a rest, or check out the beach. They'd meet for drinks in an hour or so.

There was no rush. Nothing much happened there.

Alone, Tito stepped out on to the terrace. After the rain, the water looked dark green and its movement was gentle. Now the hills were darker too, the shape of the island a black cut-out against the light. A boat was coming, but then it scooted around the top of the bay and went out again. He liked the sound of the sea, the sloop-sloop of water on the rocks below. His whole body readjusted when he came here. Something to do with the sea's rhythms and his heart.

He went to the kitchen where Henrietta was wiping down the wooden surface with soapy water, rinsing off the cutlery. The place was dusty; drawers were full of ants. They hadn't been here for a while. Later, she would sweep the outside; wash away the sea blast.

He went back outside, watched the banana trees with bright green figs fluttering their floppy leaves. He listened to the song of blue birds. And it occurred to Tito, for no particular reason, that Ada might occasionally be bored with her life. Was it possible we shrunk ourselves to fit our lives? Ada was still young; was there still growing to be done?

Eddie glimpsed the fish from the terrace; it appeared above the water like a dream.

'Did you see that?' He stood up.

Tito came to the edge and looked out. Flora shielded her eyes; she had seen it, too.

'Ma-maah! Come see!'

It came again, higher now, glittered for a moment in the light. The tail was long, its body fat and shimmering.

'Jesus,' Eddie said. 'What is it? Grouper?'

'Could be.'

Eddie said, 'You have a line?'

Tito laughed. 'These fish are fast. We've no chance.'

But Eddie was already putting on his shoes.

Flora was on her feet. 'Can I go?'

'No, darling. You'll stay here with me.'

'You have something we can use for bait?'

Inside Henrietta was seasoning meat. She put scraps in a tin cup for Eddie.

'Be careful you don't capsize the boat,' Ada said. 'We won't be coming to look for you when it's dark.'

Inside the boat house, Tito found a box of hooks, a couple of fishing rods he'd kept over the years. He rowed the small boat around the front of the house. The calm water was silky, a deep green. Ada was sitting on the lounger, her legs stretched out. Flora sat on the wall looking out at them. They putted away and she became smaller.

It was a while before the fish came again. Eddie glimpsed it by the rocks, its arrow fin slitting the water.

'Saw it? Like a piece of jewellery.'

He jabbed the hook into the meat, raised the rod.

It came again, this time closer; it jumped high in the air – all three feet of it, glistening, its silver back tinged with yellow.

'Whoa!' Tito clapped his hands. 'Look at that!'

Eddie cast the line out over the water.

A minute later, the fish was there, tugging. Then it was gone. Eddie reeled in the hook and saw the bait had disappeared.

Tito said, 'See how quick it is.'

'It's hungry. Let's try again.'

Tito laughed. 'Eddie, in all my years of coming here, I've rarely caught a thing. The odd snapper. Cat fish. Crapaud.'

'In Texas, you to talk to the salmon. It comes.' He fingered the water. 'Let's see.'

Tito held the oars while Eddie attached another piece of bait. He cast the line further behind the boat where he imagined the fish might be.

The fish quickly reappeared, its mouth open for the bigger bait. This time, it caught itself. Eddie pulled at the line, tugged hard, standing up now in the boat. He raised the rod high, kept his finger on the spool. Tito leaned in, to steady the weight.

'I got him. I got him. He's damn strong.'

Eddie hauled the line high out of the water, the fish wrestling like a young child.

He quickly wrapped the line around the spool. He wound it round and round while trying to stay upright, the weight and force of the fish pulling him towards the water.

'Christ,' Eddie said, thumping it down into the belly of the boat.

'Hit it, Tito! Hit it with the oar.'

Tito picked up the oar and clubbed the fish on its head. He bashed at the fish. Eddie stood back, watched it flip up and spring out of the boat and splosh back into the sea.

Then he yanked the line and the fish jumped back up. He slapped it down hard into the boat now, and held it there while the head twisted and its tail beat against the floor of the boat. Eddie picked up the other oar and he hit it. Together, they beat it until its tail twitched and flicked. It shivered one last time. It was dead.

By the time they got back to the house, guests had arrived.

Eddie and Tito carried the fish up the steps to where they were waiting. Ada moved aside, gathering up the hem of her long cream dress. Flora stood on tiptoes trying to see.

'Dear God,' Ruth said, standing back. 'It's huge.'

They laid the fish on the ground, and they all stood around. Tito was a little breathless. Sweat poured down his face; his heart was working hard.

At least three and half feet and thirty pounds; shiny as sequins, its thick mouth open, it stared at them with its silver marble eye. The yellow markings on its back were smeared, as though someone had taken a brush and painted it. Blue under the throat; blood around the head made a burgundy rose.

Flora squatted down on her haunches.

'Is it actually dead?'

'Yes, darling,' Tito said. 'Dead it is.'

Eddie said they should pack it in ice, take it back home tomorrow.

'It's a beauty.' Ruth stared down at its glistening face.

Gerald shook Eddie's hand. 'Congratulations.'

'Well, if it hadn't opened its mouth, it wouldn't have got caught.'

Then Flora said, 'It's a waste.' She started to cry.

Ada reassured her. 'The fish has had its life. We'll turn it into food; it's not wasted.'

Tito opened a bottle of champagne. By now the sun had almost gone and the water was dark as ink. Ada pulled Flora onto her lap, nuzzled into her warm head.

Tito said, 'Eddie, I had a good feeling about you the moment I met you. I'm never wrong about these things. It's been a long time since I caught anything. Years in fact.'

He puffed on a cigar, swirled the smoke in his mouth. 'You should have put money in the well, Gerry. We told you.'

Henrietta finished laying out the table with crockery, cutlery, napkins and glasses. Ruth had brought meat, cooked and still warm. There was rice, potatoes, fresh peaches. Tito opened two bottles of Portuguese red wine. They perched on loungers and ate around the circular table. The night was still; the sky a forest of stars.

Flora wanted to go to bed; she was bored, tired. She wanted to read her book. She wanted her mother to go with her.

She tugged on her mother's hand.

'No darling, we have guests.'

'I want you, Mama.'

'I'll come see you in a minute. Go put on your nightdress.'

She ran off, sulky, her feet heavy on the stone floor. Usually Ada would follow. Was there no end to her motherly duties? Couldn't Tito go and see about his daughter? There was no point in asking him.

She called out, 'Henriettaah!'

Tito said, 'Our daughter is very sensitive. Unfortunately Ada's made a rod for her back.'

Ada felt like saying something mean. Instead she said, 'Tito, why don't you make one of your deadly Alexanders.'

He got up, sighed, and went to the bar. He poured cognac and crème de cacao into the shaker, threw in some ice and shook hard. He sloshed it into the triangular glasses, then grated nutmeg on the top.

Ada changed the record to something more lively.

'Who'd like to dance?'

Tito was exhausted. The champagne, the wine, and fish had tired him out.

'My young and restless wife.'

The song reminded Eddie of Kathryn and their dancing days in Beaumont.

Ada looked at him.

'Is it true you took part in dance competitions?'

'Yes,' he said. 'But I'm no Fred Astaire.'

Eddie got up, asked for Tito's permission.

'Go right ahead,' Tito said.

Eddie rested his hand on Ada's narrow waist, and she tilted her face to him. He was heady with wine and the wine allowed him to forget himself. He remembered the steps: sway left, step left – sway right, step right; step back, left foot, step forward, right – travelling, advancing, pivoting, and gliding. He could smell Ada's hair, and he liked the way it smelled, and he liked the feel of her dress, the press of her hips. It had been a long time since he'd held a woman; he was sorry when the song ended.

Tito said, 'He has an unfair advantage.'

Gerry said, 'Where did you compete, Eddie?'

'In Texas.'

Ruth said, 'I love Texas. The Lone Star state. I love America full stop.'

Then Ada said, 'Well, today my husband said he's never leaving Trinidad.' She took up her milky cocktail.

'My wife is forgetful. I've taken her to many places.'

Ruth said, drawing up her knees, 'She hasn't forgotten; she just wants to see more. Isn't that right, Ada?'

Ada walked towards the edge of the veranda. 'A happy wife makes for a happy life.'

'And a poor husband makes for an obscure husband.'

Then Ruth said, 'Did you hear about the Browns?'

Gerry shook his head in disapproval.

'Emily Brown suspected that Arthur was having an affair. Last week, she came home early from tennis and saw his car there, but she couldn't find him. In the veranda, her parrot was shouting. She has an African parrot called Delilah. Well, she stood by the cage. She thought it was telling her hello, hello. But it was saying Ella, Ella.

Ada said, 'Ella?'

'Yes. She went into the shed, and there was Ella Singh and Arthur.'

Ada said, 'What were they doing?'

'You know.' Ruth raised her eyebrows.

'Ah,' Tito said. 'What did she do?'

'She told them both to get out. Then she fell on her knees and cried. Arthur picked her up and put her to bed.'

'He didn't explain himself.'

'No,' Ruth said. 'He carried on as if it never happened. There was nothing to do but call the doctor, which he did.'

Gerry got up. 'Look, no one knows what goes on.'

Around midnight, Ruth and Gerry got up to leave.

Ada said, 'You're going already?'

Ruth said, 'We all need our beauty sleep. Even you. Especially after all that dancing.'

Ada listened to the sound of Tito breathing like the engine of a truck. She rolled on her side, and looked through the shutters at the creamy moonlight. The world was still awake; she could hear the lapping sea. She got up and wandered into the passageway. The air was still and hot. She checked on Flora, tucked in the mosquito net, her face swollen with sleep. She felt guilty for letting Flora go to bed alone. She'd never done it before; she would make it up to her.

Eddie's door was open. She could make out the shape of his back in the faint light. She had watched him that evening: when he smoked, he pinched the butt of the cigarette between his finger and thumb as he sucked hard. He held her waist tightly when they danced. A man of the world, he'd brought something different to their lives. She hadn't wanted the evening to end. Had Tito noticed?

Just then, Eddie turned onto his back. In full view – his chest, his narrow stomach, a shocking patch of groin.

Tito's footsteps in the passageway; always a light sleeper. She quickly went into the kitchen and poured a glass of water, her heart thudding.

'The water in the jug is boiled,' he said, naked, squinting in the light.

'Go back to bed. I'm coming now.'

'What were you doing? Are you alright?'

'I heard something. A bat or a lizard.'

To make a point she looked outside. There was nothing there.

In the morning, Eddie dived from the rocks. While Ada drank coffee on the terrace, her head heavy from lack of sleep, she watched him swim to the other side of the bay. He swam like it belonged to him. Apparently, Tito said, Eddie was once a competitive swimmer.

'In Texas, he raced in regional events. He lost speed after the plane crash in France. When he broke his arm, it added on a couple seconds.'

Flora said, 'Is there anything Uncle Eddie can't do?'

'No, I don't think there is.'

They watched him get out of the water, stand on the jetty and look out at the hillside behind him, at the trees full of pale blossom. Then, after a few minutes, he swam back towards the house. The sea was green and shiny, and he chopped through it.

When Eddie reappeared, dripping and exhilarated, Ada said, 'How was it?'

'Like a bath.' He wrapped a towel around his waist, climbed down the steps. 'Does the thought of swimming frighten you?'

'Yes. It terrifies me.'

'If it terrifies you, then you must do it.'

Ada saw his legs and feet were whiter than the rest of him.

'Why on earth would I do something that terrifies me?'

'To remind yourself you're alive.'

They sailed back to Port of Spain. Eddie said goodbye, got into his truck. Tito followed him for a while along the road towards town. Bronze glinted off the trees and shimmered on the water. Everyone was quiet; the return after a weekend away was always like this. The sea air and hot sun was tiring. But Ada wasn't tired. She watched the back of the truck, the shape of Eddie's head, cigarette smoke funnelling out.

They reached St Clair. On the wind, she breathed in ylang ylang. A scent she loved.

'Tito, where's the ylang ylang tree? Stop the car.'

He said, 'What are you talking about?'

On the corner of Gray and Alcazar, she reached up and took a handful of the curly yellow flowers from the lowest branches, crushed them in her fingers. They smelled exquisite.

TWENTY-THREE

Once a week, Eddie drove into town for a meeting at Fernandes Holdings, in the office at the back of the store. He and Tito looked over figures, rates of production; they calculated expenses; they discussed US markets. They talked about Chatterjee; the price of equipment they needed to replace; they talked about Eddie's truck and when he could afford to buy himself a car.

'MacFarlane's bringing in some new models. That truck you're driving is like a covered-over wagon.'

'It gets me from here to there.'

'Sure, but there's nothing like staring off in the distance while pumping gas in your new motorcar. Let's see what MacFarlane delivers.'

One day, Tito said, 'Sometimes, Eddie, I think the world we live in is benign. Other times, I think the opposite. This country is full of desperate people, crabs climbing on top of one another. You'd never know it by the way we live. Ada is clueless.' He clipped the end of his cigar, and walked over to the window.

'I like to think people are as honest as you make them believe. If they think you trust them, they'll never lie or double-cross you, never steal from you. That's actually been my experience.' He sucked hard on his cigar; little clouds of smoke puffed out.

'What do you say, Eddie?'

'I'm not so sure.'

'Let's try something.' Tito looked out across the street. A barefoot child was selling newspapers under the awning. 'See that kid – his family probably live in those barracks. They might be from one of the other islands. They send the little boy out to work because they have to. He should be in school. Let's call him over.'

Eddie leaned out and whistled loudly.

The boy came at once. Six or seven years old, his dark hair was matted, and his cotton shirt flapped where buttons were missing. He stood at the window, gazing in at the two men; he cast his eyes around the office.

Tito handed the boy a twenty-dollar note.

'Son, take this down to the bank. I want ten dollars in one dollar bills and ten dollars in fifty cent pieces. Now go down there and get it changed and bring it back. Then I'll buy all of your newspapers.'

They watched the boy scamper down the road.

'Now what do you think, Eddie? Will he come back?'

'I don't know. I doubt it.'

'I never saw him before, but I know he's coming back because I expect him to come back. He knows I expect him to come back. So he'll be back.'

Ten minutes later the boy came back, and with the right order of change. Tito gave the boy the money and sent him on his way.

'What does this say, Eddie?'

'I'm not sure. Tell me.'

'Believe in somebody and they'll do the right thing. Take my brother – he has your spirit of adventure, but he's a crook. Some of the most poisonous people come disguised as family. I wouldn't trust him as far as I can throw him. I've known you a few months, and I'd trust you with my life. How's that?'

They talked about exploring other sites in different parts of Trinidad or going next door to Venezuela. Tito had heard of new wells just outside Caracas. He could bring in geologists, scout for oil further south in Costa Rica.

He always invited Eddie to take lunch somewhere, or later for cocktails and an early dinner at the Queen's Park Hotel. Eddie enjoyed these outings into Port of Spain. Tito was showing him another world. At the Portuguese club in Richmond Street, Tito was especially popular. 'Tito! You have cigars?' 'Come let me buy you a drink.' 'Tito, where's your beautiful wife? Tell her hello.' These business men were people Tito had known most of his life; they shook his hand, or slapped him on the back.

'Meet Eddie Wade,' he'd say, 'this fellow is going places. He's one of us.'

They drank Gin Rickeys at the Ice House Hotel. Mary Pickford's in the Tennis Club. There were young women around, dressed up, accompanied by their chaperones, and Tito noticed, despite his work clothes, how Eddie's good looks caught their attention.

'Let me introduce you,' Tito would say. 'You can take your pick.'

Eddie wasn't interested. Hadn't Tito heard about the man on Besson Street who smoked a stick of dynamite and blew off his head to prove his love for a woman. 'Yes,' Tito said, 'love can send you mad. There's no doubt about it. But if you wait too long, you'll be old like me. By the time you get the nuts you won't have the teeth.'

Tito drove Eddie to his favourite hotel in Macqueripe. It was busy; young people sitting around the pool. They sat on striped beach chairs and drank champagne. It was another world, a world Eddie had circled around, but it had never been his.

'Champagne is good for the heart. You knew that Eddie? When my doctor tells me to watch my diet, I drink more champagne. I instantly feel better.'

Tito told Eddie about the things he saw in medical school. 'A man came in with a three-quarter-inch wound in his left ventricle caused by a stiletto heel. You wonder how you'd survive that. But the surgeon showed us how to sew it up in three little silk stitches.'

'He lived?'

'No, two days later he died of an infection. He was Italian. He'd run away to Dublin from a mad woman.'

They smoked cigars, and Eddie told Tito about the house he went to as a child, on the east coast; how he learned from his father to skim stones along the stretch of river.

'Let me see,' Tito said, and sat up.

Eddie looked around for a pebble the size of his palm.

'Use your thumb and forefinger to spin it. Aim to hit the water at between 10 to 20 degrees.'

Keeping his aim as horizontal as he could, Eddie threw the stone towards the sea. Sure enough it skipped over the water, bouncing off the surface more than eight times.

'You can get right up to 15, or 20. You just have to find the right stone.'

No matter how Tito tried, after one or two bounces, the stone disappeared.

Eddie also took to calling in to see Tito at home. He'd take a drive out to the warehouse in the early afternoon, and call in on his way back to town. Ada looked glad to see him. She played the gramophone, and sometimes Tito complained it was too loud. She clopped in and out of the veranda where they talked, leaving a trail of her orange scent; if she sat with them, she glanced through a magazine or darned something; she practised the piano. She'd played as a child and recently started to play again; there were tunes she played well, Mozart's *A Little Night Music*, Chopin's *Preludes*, and when Eddie was there she made sure to play them.

'That again,' Tito would say. 'Play something else! Don't you think so, Eddie? She must learn some new songs. What about Beethoven? Debussy?'

If Flora was there, Ada took out dominoes or cards and played with her daughter on the table in the veranda – within close proximity to Tito and Eddie. She'd looked radiant these last weeks; everyone was telling her. The intermittent fatigue she'd suffered for months had disappeared. Her complexion was re-stored, her cheeks aglow. She looked forward to Eddie's visits, she wanted to hear news of Kushi.

Flora teased. 'Ma-maah,' she called when she heard the truck arrive. 'Uncle Eddie is here!'

Now and then, Eddie saw Ada looking at him and he wondered what she was thinking. He looked at her, too – at her legs, her ankles, her breasts. She was a thing of beauty; out of his range. He felt a strong current running between them.

TWENTY-FOUR

When Eddie saw Ada by chance in Frederick Street, he was taken aback as if he had somehow conjured her there. A truck had toppled its load; wooden crates filled with clucking chickens lay in the road. A tram line had stopped; passengers were disembarking onto the sidewalk. Other cars were trying to get through. In Memorial Park, people were protesting; a trade unionist on a megaphone was calling for a strike. It was chaos. Motor car horns were loud; people were shouting. In the crowd, Ada looked flustered.

Eddie called out, 'Hey! Ada!'

He explained that he was on his way back to Siparia. He'd met with Tito earlier.

'I was on my way to Lapeyrouse. The road is blocked. I thought I might as well go home.' She looked up at the steely clouds and felt the first few drops of rain.

'It won't last. Come, let's get something to drink.'

The bar at Rattans Hotel was busy and brawly. It was a large room with windows at the front, circular tables, and a long horseshoe bar around which were mostly men. A veranda stretched on either side. It was filling up. Ada in her cream dress, white shoes and new leather purse, felt out of place. Eddie ordered highballs, found them a quiet spot in the corner. It wouldn't be quiet for long; more people were hurrying in, sheltering from the rain.

Someone nearby was speaking loudly with an American drawl.

Ada hadn't realised how thirsty she was.

'Have you been to America, Ada?'

'We went to New York as part of our honeymoon.'

'City of Dreams.'

'Do you know Manhattan?

'Sure.'

'It snowed and it was only October. I thought I'd die of cold.'

Eddie offered her a cigarette.

'You liked it?'

'Oh yes. The department stores, the fancy restaurants; hotel bars. Blue martinis in the Four Seasons in downtown Manhattan.' She sighed. 'I could live there tomorrow.'

'You've heard of a New York minute? It's as long as it takes for the lights to turn green and taxis to blow their horns.'

The American was shouting now, complaining about a lack of ice. They watched him leave.

Then Ada said, 'That day we drove to the warehouse, I asked if you thought I was happy or sad. You never answered.'

He hadn't forgotten.

'You're neither. You're someone who has a lot of life inside. But you pretend you don't.'

He took out a cigarette and lit it.

'Why would I pretend?'

'It's how a lot of people live. They make a life for themselves and hold on to it. Underneath, they wonder if there's more. It's a hunger. We all have it.'

Ada didn't know whether to be annoyed or amused. She was curious; he was guessing, but he'd guessed right.

'Hunger?'

'Yes. People bury it. There's nothing wrong with it. It's how most people live.'

He noticed her collarbone was dotted with sweat.

'You don't live that way, Eddie?'

'No. I never have.'

She thought how quickly they began to talk of real things. Conversations with Eddie were never about the weather.

Eddie said, 'I'll settle some day, I expect.'

'I can't imagine it. You're a free spirit.'

He laughed.

'So are you, Ada. You just don't admit it.'

Men's voices in the bar were louder now. They sounded drunk. Ada felt her head airy and light. The scotch had gone straight there.

Two women dressed up like it was night time and they were going to a party – breasts high, tall heels, their hair curled and big – were standing by the bar. It was obvious to Ada they were prostitutes.

Ada said, leaning in, 'Is it always like this in here?'

'Sometimes it's much worse.'

'I wonder what Tito would say if he could see me now.'

For a moment, she held his eyes – river green with amber flecks. She felt a rush of heat.

'What do you think he'd say?'

'He'd tell me to come home at once.'

'And what would you say?'

He was looking at her mouth, the cupid's bow.

Ada's heart beat quickly, pushing blood into her cheeks. 'I'm not sure.'

Eddie was forgetting himself; Ada belonged to someone else.

'Do you do it on purpose? Look at people in this way.'

'I'm not doing anything. I wouldn't do anything you didn't want me to do.'

She put down her drink. 'I should go.'

'Don't.'

He put his hand on hers.

'Christ, Eddie.'

She looked around. Had anyone seen? Did anyone in here recognise her?

He was staring at her, burning holes in her clothes with his eyes.

'What are we doing?'

She stood, and her bag clattered to the floor. Eddie picked it up and she started for the lobby. Outside the rain was a thick, white, impenetrable curtain. It occurred to Ada that she could speak to the concierge about a taxi, wait for the rain to slow down. She could call Tito and ask him to come, fetch her. But while standing now by the desk of the concierge, she realised she didn't want to go home.

His bed was unmade, the shutters closed. Ada stood near the door, looked around and saw where he'd left his shoes, shirt, comb, papers. A thousand thoughts. What was she doing here? Who had seen her? Did anyone recognise her as she walked along the corridor? Could she leave now?

Eddie touched her cheek; put his other hand on the back of her hot neck. He smelled of sweat, machinery.

'Eddie,' she said, shaking her head.

He took her face in his hands and kissed her; she could taste cigarettes on his tongue, inside the cave of his mouth.

When he lifted her dress to find her flesh, she let out a cry as if hurt. She felt under the cloth of his shirt; started to open the buttons. They fell together onto the balled-up sheets. He gently pushed her back, undid her zip. He slid his fingers along her legs, then up inside her underwear. She gasped. Her eyes half closed, she said his name. Her dress was twisted up beneath her; her dark hair spread out on the pillow.

He was astonished by his immediate rush of pleasure. They were strangers to one another. He groaned as he fucked her; her legs were high around his back. He pressed himself into her, feeling now her little breaths, her eyes on his mouth. He held himself for as long as he could. It was over quickly.

After, he cried a little; he was unsure why. Guilt, or a memory of happiness. Astonishment, perhaps. Yes, he was astonished. He had forgotten what it was like to be touched.

'I'm sorry,' he said. 'It's been a while.'

Ada licked his tears, she kissed his whole head, his ears, the back of his skull, the top of his crown.

She said, half smiling, 'What have we done?'

He sat up, his mind strangely quiet; he reached for a cigarette.

Eddie saw himself from above. The scene here, the two of them laid out on his bed. His penis was soft now, curled away. Her fullness was not what he expected; the weight of her breasts, their roundness when loose. Dark moles all over her skin. 'Yes,' she said. 'I have 52 moles.'

She was embarrassed by her legs, the thickness of her thighs, some scattered blue veins. 'I have my mother's figure,' she said. 'My mother was heavier than me, and two inches shorter. Can you imagine?'

She looked down at her hands.

'You see here,' she said. 'A dog bit my finger when I was three, took the tip right off. Father stuck it back on with iodine, held it with a strip of cloth. I don't like to draw attention to my hands. It looks ugly, don't you think?' The finger was crooked.

Ada touched the lump of scar like a ribbon on Eddie's neck. 'Who did this to you?'

'Bandits, when I lived in Texas.'

'Did they take anything from you?'

'Yes. They took my wages, but Callaghan got it back.' He lit a cigarette, took a sharp pull in.

'Do you have someone like that, Ada? Someone who fights your corner?'

'I used to think so. But Tito's different when his mother's there. His mother hates me. Only Flora. I have Flora.'

Then she said, 'Flora has a bend in her finger in the same place. Sometimes I think it's connected, but how can it be?'

Outside, a corn bird rang out a shrill tune like an alarm.

'It can't happen again,' she said, holding the sheet as she stepped from the bed. 'No one must know. Tito will kill you. He will kill me. You've no idea.'

Ada wandered out into the light. The rain had stopped; drains were full of brown water. She found a taxi, pressed herself into the seat and told the driver to hurry. At home, she ran upstairs, avoiding Henrietta, who, she suspected, would see something in her eyes. Everything was as she had left it. Comb, powder-puff, a sprinkling of talc on the bathroom floor. The window open; a dress she'd decided not to wear tossed on the chair. She studied her face in the mirror – without make up, a younger face. She unclipped her hair, gathered it around her shoulders, wondering what he had seen. She examined her profile, her long neck with its hoopy lines.

Ada washed, tied her dressing gown around her waist. Then she lay on her bed, and stared at the ceiling where the fan was spinning and she tried to calm herself. What if someone saw her leave the hotel looking dishevelled? Had a friend of Tito's seen her in the bar? Glimpsed her in the corridor. Would Tito know what she had done by looking at her? Would he see it in her eyes? She had done something very wrong; like Ella Singh.

TWENTY-FIVE

There were two ways to reach Rattan's Hotel. The obvious route was along Frederick Street, 100 yards from the store. But there was another way in via Knox street, a small alleyway, easily missed. Narrow and shadowy, detergent smells from a laundry wafted here. Opposite to the laundry, a side door led to the services entrance and the dark stairwell of Rattans. This was the route Ada took.

Rooms were mostly the same. A view of the yard and the olive tree. The walls, once white, were now yellow and a stale smell reminded Ada of sweat and bleach. There was a lamp, a portrait of a girl who stared with sad brown eyes. Shutters were open just enough to let the air in, and Ada could hear the sound of vendors in the street. She heard dogs barking. Now and then she heard the cries of lovers and it frightened her. It was hot and the ceiling fan never seemed to work. There was a washroom where two or three cockroaches clung to the ceiling, or clattered along the floor; their waving antennae made her shudder.

Their time was limited. Eddie never knew when he was coming to town until the day before, then he'd telephone the house, hope to find Ada at home, and let her know when he was arriving. He stayed the night in Rattans; as soon as Tito had gone to work, she would come to the hotel. They'd have an hour or two at most.

At first their lovemaking was urgent, desperate. Ada's shyness didn't last long. Eddie couldn't wait to undress her, to touch her skin; its moistness and scent – neroli she said, worn by the Empress Bonaparte – reminded him of fruit. Her beauty was pronounced: pointed chin, soft, dark eyes; skin smooth like the inside of a queen conch shell. Her small nails, square cut, the high arch of her foot, the curve of her soft white calf. He worked his mouth all the way up her leg and stayed between her legs until she trembled. He loved her breasts, firm pots of flesh, the tiny hard brown nipples; he put his head on her stomach, cupped his hand between her legs, slid his fingers inside her. She raised her hips, watched the back of his head, the thick brown hair, wanting to claw at it. He searched her body like a thief, looking for something; he wanted to enter her everywhere.

Afterwards they lay side by side; they smoked a cigarette. They stared at one another. There was never enough time.

When Ada left, Eddie felt as if he had been disassembled, parts of himself discovered and rearranged. He walked over to the store to meet with Tito, through the hot street, collecting himself, gathering his thoughts. He pushed away thoughts of wrongdoing. Ada had assured him, just because she desired him, it didn't mean she had stopped loving her husband.

'The heart is like a country; it can hold more than one person. It's as big as America. I knew the moment we met. I just didn't tell myself. What could I do about that? Nothing. It was as if you'd fallen out of the sky.'

'You say it like you didn't have a choice.'

'I didn't. And neither did you. It's just how it is. We knew it all along.'

She talked of borders, immigration. She had let him in, and he had let her in. They had set up residency in one another.

He begged Ada to be careful; cover her tracks, be consistent.

'If ever he asks you about me, deny it.'

'Like Peter, in the bible.'

'Yes,' Eddie said, 'like Peter.'

Once Tito had discussed any urgent matters, Eddie tried to get away. Lying didn't come easily. His list of commitments grew long: customs, shipments, Callaghan, a business meeting somewhere. Some were lies, excuses, to free himself, but he was also busier now than ever before – and it worked in his favour. To keep away suspicion, Eddie still took up Tito's offers of afternoon drinks at the Queen's Park Hotel.

When Eddie left Port of Spain and drove back towards San

Fernando, he carried Ada with him, exhilarated, charged, along the Southern Main Road, passing fields of rice and cane and wild bush beneath open, changing skies.

He was frightened by what he'd started to feel for her. It wasn't what he had wanted, what he came here for. He wanted to make his fortune, nothing more. He felt consumed, enraptured. Like a fire-eater – each moment together, a mist of fuel followed by a rush of flames.

For the first time in his life, he studied his own face; the thick eyebrows; his deep-set eyes that Kathryn had said were like looking down two wells. What did Ada see? His teeth were white but uneven, a slight gap between his two front teeth; his chin was dimpled, his face thin, tanned, his cheekbones prominent.

When Grace saw him staring into the biscuit tin lid he used as a mirror, she said, 'Mister Eddie, you alright?'

One day, Ada asked, 'What is this?'

They lay side by side, looking up at the ceiling.

'What's this thing we're making here?'

Eddie said, 'I don't know. I don't need to know.'

'Perhaps if we name it, it will die.'

'Yes.'

'But it is *something*. Isn't it? It's not nothing.'

'It's not nothing.'

That was the same day Eddie left through the front door of the hotel, and caught Ada departing from the alley, and he called out to her as though surprised to see her there. They spoke on the sidewalk as friends might; glad of a few minutes more. It was a privilege to see her outside like this, to gaze at her lit face!

He didn't expect to see Charles MacLeod crossing the street, headed towards the Royal Bank of Canada. Eddie recognised his hat, his long shape and stride. A few seconds earlier, and Charles would have seen them.

TWENTY-SIX

One day, Tito came home unexpectedly to find Ada out. When she came in, he asked where she'd been.

She said, 'To the library.'

'So where are your books?'

Ada thought quickly, 'There was nothing I liked. The usual.'

'Nothing?'

'They need to change their supplier. The stock is old.'

She was hot and smelled of Eddie, and she ran upstairs to the bathroom. If Tito came near her he would know at once.

He called after her, 'Where are you running to, my Ada?'

Another day, when he smelled cigarettes on her clothes, he asked if she had been smoking. She told him no.

'Well someone has and if it's not you, then who,' he said. 'Flora?'

Then Ada said, in a voice she used when she wanted something, 'Sometimes in my room when you're out, I take a puff or two. You know I like smoking. We all have our bad habits.'

He shook his head. 'Well, I suppose there are worse things.'

'Yes,' Ada said, 'there are. There really are much worse things.'

Tito's thoughts were mostly taken up by Kushi. It was his job to ensure shipments were properly orchestrated and the transfer of oil to the waiting ships that left once a week for America was a logistical headache, especially in the rainy season. The store in Frederick Street was being refurbished – a new lift installed, floors stripped and varnished. New stock from Southampton had been delayed by a storm off the Scilly Isles which threw over the tanker. He was talking to his insurance broker about compensation.

He was distracted, too, by concern over his mother, who had

176

fallen on the stairs – a labral tear to the hip – no bones broken, but sore and more irritable than usual. Her skin was thin like tissue paper; the purple bruises down her left side looked like a truck had run her over. And there were renovations to be done to her leaking roof. The place was full of buckets: one positioned under the eaves, another by the laundry room, which she couldn't possibly heft, another in the veranda. The plink plink of dripping, she told Tito, would send her to the madhouse. Every day he left work early to go to her, and see what he could do to help.

Aside from this, he was due another visit to Barbados – he'd been putting it off. Would Ada like to come? It seemed unfair to leave her behind.

'What about your mother, what if something happens. One of us should be here.'

His taxi had barely pulled out of the driveway when Ada went looking for Henrietta. She was clearing dishes from the dining table. Ada started to help, carrying the jug of orange juice, dirty plates. She took up the vase to trim the anthurium stems.

'I've been thinking, you haven't had a break in months. Why don't you visit your mother and daughter? Take the day off.'

Ada knew that Henrietta's mother and her daughter lived in a tiny wooden house on stilts in a south-eastern suburb. She had visited once when Henrietta was sick. The simple home had shocked her. They had nothing: a dress or two, cloth hanging in the windows, mattresses on the floor, a few pots, tin plates, a couple wooden chairs.

Henrietta looked surprised. 'Mister Tito wouldn't want me to leave you.'

'Don't worry about me.' Ada smiled, pouring the water away. 'In some ways it's easier when he's not here.' Then she said, 'Wouldn't you like to see your mother?'

Henrietta nodded; the thought of it softened her face.

'Well that's that,' Ada said, and she wouldn't take no for an answer. She called her driver and asked him to take Henrietta up to John John at noon. She packed a box of food – biscuits, rice, jam, smoked meat, dried fruits, rum, flour, sardines, peas, a tablecloth. In the doorway, she pushed the box into Henrietta's arms.

'Take this and give it to them with my blessing.'

Henrietta frowned.

Ada's heart was galloping, her blood rushing around her body. Could Henrietta sense her excitement? She was sharp as a tack.

'Sometimes it's good to be alone. You know that feeling, Henrietta. Time to pray, gather yourself.'

Eddie parked two blocks away. He came through the side entrance, the entrance used by Henrietta, the gardener, delivery boys. As soon as he was inside, Ada closed the shutters and locked up the veranda. She was wearing her dressing gown, feet bare, her hair pinned up. Her heart was on fire.

He made love to her in the hallway against the console. He carried her upstairs and when they reached the bedroom – the bedroom for guests – he turned her around on the mattress and pushed his cock so deep she felt him in her spleen, his pubic hair rubbed into her flesh. She groaned, and then came little breaths until she felt the rush of currents and her pleasure reached and tipped over itself. They slept for a couple hours. When she woke she felt teary; in the mirror her face was full with love. She smelled of it. Her fingers, her hair, her mouth, her breath.

She ran him a bath. The cast-iron tub from England had feet like the paws of a lion. While Eddie lay in the water fragranced with bay leaves, she prepared dinner. It had been a long time since she'd cooked anything. She'd smothered a leg of lamb with molasses and roasted it slowly for hours. This was all they ate – slow-roasted lamb and some tomatoes from the market, a bowl of olives, half of a peach. She opened a bottle of Bordeaux, and they drank some of this, then lay on the bright kashan rug, a wedding present from Tito's mother.

When the telephone rang, Ada let it ring and ring. Then it started up again, and she knew it was Tito. She answered, glad of the poor line. She shouted into the mouthpiece. She couldn't hear him and he couldn't hear her. She was relieved.

When Eddie was naked, quiet, his penis bent and soft, she closed her eyes and traced his nipples, his ribs, put her hand on the place where his heart beat, felt the dip of his stomach, his boyish hip bones. If she was blind, she could find him in a crowd.

'When we were in the beach house, I saw you sleeping and your sheet had fallen away. I saw everything. Tito almost caught me.'

Eddie put her hair away from her face, hooked it behind her ears.

'I pictured you when I was here in this room.'

They compared the length of their arms; the span of hands, the width of their wrists. They slept with their arms around one another like children.

Next day, the rains came. They spent the morning inside listening to its clatter on the roof. The garden was a blur; pools of brown water collected over the grass and it looked like a swamp. They watched from the veranda, knowing they were safe from visitors. The arrival of the downpour couldn't be more perfectly timed.

While lying across his chest, Ada described to Eddie the journey she and Tito took from New York to Trinidad. How the water was unusually calm, how dolphins followed the boat – a pod of ten or more – and how she'd felt truly blessed, that her life was exactly how she wanted it to be. The sky was pink and white like candyfloss.

'You know when it's like that, you feel you could float up into it. Maybe because you notice the sky even more when you're at sea. But then a woman screamed. She'd gone inside her cabin and found her husband hanging. A note on her pillow. It said, 'Tired of it all.' That's what it said. 'Tired of it all.' Can you imagine? They were newlyweds on their honeymoon. How could he be tired so soon?'

'People hide things.'

'But it felt like a sign to me. The whole trip was soured. Someone died. And he was a honeymooner like us. It made me think our marriage was doomed.'

Eddie kissed her head. He didn't want her to be melancholy. Then he said, 'Where else did you go?'

'Paris. We stayed in a hotel next to Notre Dame. There were a lot of Americans; I don't know why. Summer maybe. I never expected to see them.'

'Did you like Paris?'

'In a way. I'd like to go again, someday.'

Then she said, 'We went to the menagerie. Well, there were all kinds of animals, seals and snakes, monkeys. There was a lion and he came right up to where I was standing at the cage, and he stared at me. He opened his mouth and I was afraid, like he might be able to rip through the bars and pull me inside. All through lunch we could hear the lion roaring, I felt like he was calling me. Like I was prey.'

Then Ada said, 'When you were out in the fields, did you get lonely?'

'There were ladies around. They'd hang around the local bars.'

'Did you get to know any of them?'

'There was a woman called Lila, she had a kindness about her. Everybody liked her. One of the drillers, Lenny, married her. Just like that.'

'He married a prostitute?'

'Lenny said it's one thing to marry a girl who's been waiting for a suitor to come along, but to be chosen by a woman who's known a lot of sweethearts is another thing altogether. I admired him for that. They settled out in Montana on a farm. They were happy as lambs.'

'I could never be happy on a farm.'

'No, I imagine you couldn't.'

He told Ada about the wells in California. The fires he saw, the men who burned up. He talked about the trip he took with Callaghan down to Salvador.

'You've had a lot of people die on you.'

'We have one life,' he said. 'It's briefer than you think.'

Then she asked, 'If you hadn't been an oil man, what would you have done?'

'I saw a travelling circus in Texas when I was sixteen. The owner lost a tiger when it escaped down the street, and a police officer shot it. The man who ran it was French. I thought about it for a while – joining a circus. You're always packing up, always moving on somewhere.'

Ada climbed on top of Eddie, and held him down with her knees. Her hair was a veil, her lips pillows of blood. In the rush of pleasure, he felt something dislodge, a piece of himself break off and fly away, a piece of his calcified soul, perhaps; he didn't know for sure, but whatever it was it made him weep. He wept as he had when he lost his father more than twenty years before in a river of lava.

'You've doing something to me. I'm coming apart.'

'Maybe we're coming together. Maybe that's what this is for. We've found the other side of ourselves.'

Before he left, Ada said, 'Do you want me, Eddie? Are you scared of wanting me?'

'Not scared,' he said. 'If I was, I'd want you just the same.'

'What are we going to do?'

'Put one foot in front of the other until we get somewhere.'

'What if we end up somewhere we don't want to be?'

Ada was confused. They had reached up and touched something startling and rare. But when she tried to imagine a future with Eddie, she struggled to picture a life together. Where would they go? What about Flora? Could she really leave Trinidad and all she had known? Her life with Tito was a good life; her love for Tito was not lessened by what she felt for Eddie. There were rumours about Tito's ex fiancée's lover found dead in Dominica. What if the same thing happened to Eddie?

By lunchtime he was gone. She drifted around the house hating its emptiness. She stripped the bed, put the sheets downstairs to wash. She checked every room for evidence, a hair, a thread, a coin. All the while, her body roared with longing.

She went outside in the heavy rain and let it soak her down; she waded ankle-deep in the brown water. The sky was tin grey and it was coming down on her. She didn't expect to see Henrietta, standing in the passageway behind a veil of rain. She'd returned earlier than expected. She brought a towel and wrapped it around Ada's shoulders.

'Madam, you saw something? What happen? Something happen' to Mister Fernandes?'

When Tito returned that evening, Ada was glad to see him. She was wearing her dressing gown and lying on her bed. She allowed herself to be comforted. She told him that she had stayed at home all day. Fatigue, sickness, the old yellow fever symptoms. She didn't want to lie; his concern intensified her guilt.

'Henrietta wasn't here to look after you? You should've waited, sent her home another day. What were you thinking?'

He was sorry that he left her. Next time she must come with him. He brought black cake; a pashmina shawl imported from Bombay. He couldn't decide on the rose or the sapphire. He was glad he bought the rose. He wrapped it around her shoulders.

'Look at you,' he said, 'when you cry you are more lovely.' Then, 'I've been thinking, we must have Eddie to dinner. He insists on that hotel. He should come here. We can feed him up a bit. The man never eats. We should find someone pretty for him. Yes, it's time we found Eddie a woman. Don't you think so?'

He asked if she had been to see his mother.

'Rain kept me here. See how the yard is flooded.'

Ada stayed in her room. Tito said he would be up soon. There were invoices to sort. The house was quiet and tidy, her life folded away in cupboards, hidden in drawers, in pictures on walls; her mother and father looked on from the dressing table. She was heavy with secrets. The walls of this house, the breathing wooden floors of her home, the mattress where she lay flat – she let them all hold her.

TWENTY-SEVEN

Mercy spotted rainbows on the rocks at the Godineau River. Iridescence from the oil had seeped through and left its mark. Callaghan said they should drill nearby. Right now, men from the village were clearing away long grass. There were other signs: oil on the upper cruse sands, soft shale, high levels of salt. It looked ideal. But there were things they needed to do before drilling began. He came to Eddie with a list.

There was work to be done on the rig; they'd need new pipe from the last drill when the pipe was jammed and part of it snapped off. The travelling block was also damaged from the blowout; its repair would delay assembly of the derrick for a few days. The blowout preventer was showing signs of wear – they should buy another. The rusted-up blowout preventer Eddie had found in a field down in Palo Seco was almost defunct. Perhaps they could ask around. Or import a new one from New Jersey; he had a good supplier there. It shouldn't cost more than a few hundred dollars.

Callaghan had heard about a new mechanism to control the casing, drill pipe and sheaves together, a Triplex, developed in America, all the rage in Texas. Macleod had brought one in to speed up the entire operation and allow them to drill deeper. Callaghan told Eddie they should invest in a product like this; they could always sell it on. But Eddie said no, not this time.

'We don't need to go deep. Look how close to the top we've found oil. Let's stay with what we have. Two-Weeks can fix up the travelling block. The blowout preventer can go another round or two.'

There were rumours that Macleod might be heading back to Scotland. So far Apex had drilled eight wells and none showed traces of oil. Eddie guessed he'd hold out until their lease was up, then try to negotiate a new deal for himself with Chatterjee. He had heard, too, that Charles's pregnant wife was staying in the hospital, and she hated Trinidad. She was threatening to leave if he didn't make a plan to return to their homeland.

Over the next few weeks, two more derricks went up. Both site number three and site number four came in within days of one another; at 400 feet and 550 feet. The oil shot out like champagne from a shook-up bottle. It was astonishing to Callaghan, who had never seen so much oil in such a concentrated area. He told Eddie, 'It's a driller's paradise; we'll make the history books. This whole estate is sitting on a glacier of oil.'

By now everyone knew what to do. Horatio and Mete were confident enough in closing off the well, while Long managed the pressure, and King kept his eye on the engine room. Eddie and Callaghan were there to oversee it all; making sure the oil ran into storage tanks, then off to the pipeline and straight out to the plant. Malaki kept count of tools and equipment and those that needed fixing.

The sun shone down, and the new pipelines running from Kushi meant they no longer had to carry the oil in trucks out to the refinery. Ten-inch pipes running for eight miles carried crude out to La Brea and Point-à-Pierre. The pipes, though costly, saved time, complications with the poor roads and bad weather. Tito told Eddie that real money was starting to come in now. Five producing wells and all of them fully operating. For the first time, Tito said, there was money to burn. How about that!

Eddie thought of Ada when he was out in the hot field; while watching clouds above the forest and wondering if rain might fall. He thought about her when he lay down on his camp bed at night. He imagined her above him. He touched himself; he called out her name in the dark. He conjured her in the early hours of morning. Where he'd once thought of Kathryn, it was now Ada. He'd want to tell her things, suddenly, in the middle of the day: a tender exchange he'd witnessed with Callaghan and Mercy; or news of Trinket heavy with puppies; the delicious goat stew Grace had made – he wanted her to taste it; tell her about a fresh puddle of oil he'd spotted at the foot of a dying cocoa tree.

Callaghan noticed. 'That grin on your face, Eddie. Something tells me it's not only about oil.'

Eddie brushed him off. 'Look around, everyone's happy.'

It was true. Long, Horatio, Gelliseau, Tripe, and King. Even Chatterjee was cheery; he was smiling more often these days – the slit of his mouth lifted at each end, and he spoke to the workers in a friendly way. Sometimes Eddie heard big bawdy laughter coming from where Chatterjee was standing, one leg on the step, telling jokes to the men.

He bought bicycles for the boys and they rumbled along the road outside, clattered down the hill knocking over the little fence that kept chickens inside. Sita wore new saris; her face was less stern, her fingers crammed with gold rings. Chatterjee painted his house orange, like a marigold flower, hung a wooden door with a knocker. He fixed the wall at the back of the kitchen; bought chairs and a matching table for the porch. He installed a water tank at the rear of the house.

When Chatterjee purchased a second-hand black Ford Model T car for $300, Sita joked, 'Never see-come see-go crazy.' He took Sita out driving in the late afternoon. If there was time, he drove into San Fernando, idled by Happy Corner bar in the hope of seeing old drinking buddies. He chugged up Coffee Street and tooted his horn, swung around into Rushforth. Sita dressed up for these occasions; her plaits were two shining ropes, knees clamped together. Chatterjee told her to relax. It was safer than a horse and cart.

'I doh like horse, neither.'

Chatterjee wasn't about to dress up for anybody, but he slicked back his hair and wore long pants and a clean shirt.

One day, they made it all the way to Rio Clara. By the time they reached, the sun was going down; they were thirsty and hungry. Meena heard the noise and came outside; a line of children of varying heights ran around the car yelling.

'Ma! Ma! Look Sita and Sonny! Look Sita hair! Look she clothes!'

Sunaree stroked the car bonnet, swung her legs inside; the children climbed into the trunk, honked the horn. Sita looked out at the dark green fields, cane soon ready for cutting. She remembered how she loved this land.

'Kushi never have breeze.'

Chatterjee rolled his eyes. 'My wife never happy.'

It wasn't true and he knew it. Sita was happier now than since the early days of their marriage. She felt better about herself, better about her life with him. Things – money, possessions, belongings – mattered to Sita. At last he was able to provide.

While curry goat bubbled in the black pot, Chatterjee drank rum, pulled a cigar from his pocket, and puffed on it, and watched as the women sat on the dusty ground and talked, and admired Sita's jewellery, and slipped on her shoes. They dabbed their faces with cosmetic powder, kholed their eyes. She'd brought cloth, ribbon, silver, a purse for each of them. They told Sita they were sad; she would never likely come back to Rio Clara. Her mother asked how long the oil men were staying.

'Me eh know how long they staying. But it noisy – trucks and wagons come and go all day. Sonny say we go come here when they finish. Build a house by all you. I waiting to see.'

Ma told her to be careful, to stay away from the drilling.

'Oil not meant to come out, Sita. It bury in the ground for reasons. People die in Fyzabad. In Forest, too. They should leave the land just so. What old man Madoo would say?'

Chatterjee shook his head. 'All you frighten. You frighten progress. What you think the car running on? It need oil. Everything need oil. You talk like them coolies from Calcutta.'

Ma gave him a look, her eyes big like a frog's. 'Maybe we talk like coolies from Calcutta because we *is* coolies from Calcutta. Just like you.'

Sita burst out laughing, and she looked at her husband affectionately. Then everyone was laughing, including Chatterjee.

Eddie gathered his workers together one night to share a crate of cold beers, open some bottles of rum. In front of the barracks, he roasted a hog on a spit. They strung up some lights, and the men pulled the tables outside, threw white sheets over them. Mercy and Grace joined them at the table.

Eddie handed out their little rolls of notes, crisp from the bank.

'Don't blow it on rum, or women; it's called a bonus 'cause it's extra. Like my bank manager says, save your money and it will save you.'

He gave Grace extra wages, for helping him when he was sick. 'Buy yourself a wedding dress, or something for your father.'

There were new work clothes for the men, blue canvas boiler suits, hard hats, and steel toe-capped boots. Long showed Eddie the scar where his hair refused to grow.

The night was warm, and all was calm; everything was as it should be. Under the bright moon, steam pumps nearby called, shush-pah, shush-pah.

At one point Long said, 'Tonight feel just like Christmas.'

Horatio raised his glass. 'By Christmas, Mister Wade and Mister Fernandes will be millionaires.'

It seemed to Eddie that it was possible. If things carried on in the same direction, by the end of the year they might well have enough money to buy their own tanker, collaborate with another oil company, such as Regent Oil, in London. They could scope out other parts of South Trinidad, explore minor oil pools in the Central Range, or in the deeper south eastern region where sediments came from the Orinoco. Over thousands of years, these sediments were squeezed from muds into good sands, over and over to make oil in neat little patches of concentrated land. This land was blessed, Callaghan said. Yet, less than a mile away, Macleod wasn't having much luck. It was a game of chance. A mystery.

Eddie didn't like to leave the men alone, but if all was running smoothly, he and Callaghan took off for a couple hours. They drove to the Paramount Hotel; they drank at the Tennis Club bar. Eddie indulged his love of highballs, and gin martinis. Discovered Lobster Thermidor, pheasant, smoked salmon. They stopped by at the Union Club to catch horses racing on a Saturday afternoon. The high society of San Fernando was there, along with folk from poorer parts, risking monthly earnings on the races.

Horse owners doubled up as jockeys and grooms. Eddie knew how to ride, and when he was invited to race, he was quick to say yes. He donned a hat and gripped the whip; his boots were too big for stirrups. People started to recognise him; they knew who he was, wanted to shake his hand. In his khaki trousers and shirts, he was easy to recognise.

Eddie and Callaghan drove down to the quayside, parked up, ate oysters and looked out at traders arriving from Venezuela in their dugout canoes selling hammocks, parrots and raw sugar. The market place buzzed with vendors, snake charmers, fortune tellers.

At the back of Eddie's mind was little Edith, and close beside her was Ada. He had never felt more alive than now. He had a sense that all of life was rushing easily through him – a force of love he hadn't experienced until now. He longed for Ada – her smell, her fingers, her teeth, her little ribcage, the arch of her feet, the back of her damp neck, the sound of her laugh like a hundred bells ringing at dawn. He wanted to say, Callaghan, man, I'm in love. I love this woman. Let me tell you about her. Callaghan would think him foolish, jeopardising his future. He'd remind Eddie of all he was working towards, the huge success now within his reach. He wouldn't want to hear it.

Eddie didn't like to think about the future. As far as he could tell there was hurt ahead; decisions to make. It couldn't carry on forever. Tito deserved more; he was part of a triangle he didn't know about. It was cruel. There were days when Eddie felt like the King of Trinidad and others when he felt grubby as a cockroach crawling in a drain. When he looked at Tito he felt ashamed, as if he'd killed somebody. Eddie told himself he deserved to suffer and he would suffer. There were no winners here. He veered between despair and euphoria, hope and hopelessness.

Grace was outside early that morning. She had rice to pick through and wash, and she sat on the wooden steps as she separated out the dirty-coloured grains, balancing a tray between her legs. Beyond the clearing where the derrick stood, trees were full and tall, and some were thick with vines and these vines made a green canopy. The forest creaked, hissed and birds cried out; frogs sang their sirens. All this stopped once the steam room started up and drilling began.

She wondered what it was all for – why suck out the oil to make kerosene and put it in an automobile, to drive around and get some place fast. Grace might ride in an automobile but she'd never own one, neither would Malaki. When she saw roads busy in San Fernando, she wondered who was in such a hurry and where were they rushing to. They should slow down. People must learn to sit with themselves.

Eddie appeared from inside, sipping coffee. His hair was wet and slicked back; he was dressed for Port of Spain.

'You going town today, Mister Eddie?'

'Yes, Grace. Just for the night.'

She would make sure he had a clean shirt.

'Long time since I gone there.'

'How many times you been?'

'One time.'

'It's not all it's cracked up to be. But it would do you good, Grace. Bars, parlours, plenty places to dance. I'm sure you like to dance.'

He smiled, showed his white teeth. He took out a cigarette and lit it.

She was certain Eddie had a woman. He was taking better care of himself; she'd smelled perfume on his clothes, and there was something about his manner, a part of him taken up, elsewhere. Eddie was the kind of man a girl would easily fall for. A local girl would suffer, like Mercy with Callaghan. Grace had told Mercy she should go to school, study hard. Forget Callaghan. Mercy didn't want to know. *Ah does love he. Yuh cyah help who you does love.*

Eddie looked out. 'How's Bridgeman these days?'

'Plenty better. He growing pumpkins in the yard and they real big.' She put out her hands. 'Pumpkins shy; they always hiding behind vine leaf.'

'That's good to hear. You must bring one. I'll pay him for it.'

She told Eddie of trouble in the village.

'Chin – they call him Chin because his chin does stick out – went behind a woman from Point Fortin. The gyul win a beauty competition and feel she something special. A light-skin gyul with hair to her waist. He leave his wife, his four children and gone Tobago with she.'

'Things don't always follow a straight line.'

Grace shook her head. 'In a few years, you will see. Everybody will see. They go cry blood.'

'Is that how it works, Grace? People get their comeuppance?

'Maybe.'

'If that was so, bad people in the world would suffer more.'

'Maybe. God doh sleep.'

'People fall in love. Married or not. They don't always have a choice.'

He looked at Grace in a way that made her know she'd guessed right.

'Everybody have a choice.'

Eddie threw the dregs of his coffee in the bush.

'I'm not so sure.'

Grace stood up slowly, and fixed her dress at the back, creased after sitting. The rice was done.

'Me eh know, Mister Eddie. Yuh cyah build happiness on somebody else pain.'

TWENTY-EIGHT

A few days later, Tito called on Eddie to invite him for dinner, a party in town. Beautiful girls, excellent food, the *haut monde* of Port of Spain. People he should meet.

'These days you're too busy. I hardly see you. What can I do to persuade you. You can't work all the time.'

Eddie agreed to go. He put on the white suit made by Robeiro, a pair of new shoes. He drove down to Port of Spain early that evening and parked his truck at Tito's house.

Ada wore black; Eddie had never seen her in black. The lace around her neck was delicate, sleeves fitted to the elbow. Her eyes were alive; her hair pinned up with a red hibiscus in it. Eddie tried not to look at her.

She put her face up to the sky, breathed in the air, full of rain. 'Can you hear the frogs? They're all out tonight.' Then she said, 'You must always eat your frogs first.'

'What are you talking about,' Tito said. 'Frogs? Who eats frogs?'

'It's an expression I learned from a girl at school. You do the thing you don't want to do first. Then you can get on with doing what you really want.'

It didn't occur to Tito that Ada might be talking about herself.

They joined the line of people outside, and Eddie saw some familiar faces. A crowd he was starting to recognise, sophisticated, moneyed, French Creole.

Over dinner, Eddie avoided Ada. Instead he spoke to the daughter of the manager of the Royal Bank of Canada, Delores Gray. Raised in Vancouver, she wore her hair in flat curls, had wholesome good looks, a square jaw, even white teeth. She spoke of black bears; glimpsing the Northern lights from their log house in Squamish. She had been to Texas with her parents, and she knew of the restaurant in Houston where he'd taken Kathryn. Eddie told her about his days in Beaumont, years of looking for oil.

'You've had quite a life,' she said, her blue eyes running over him. He could ask her out; she was giving him the right signals.

When dinner was over, Eddie saw Ada at the bar. He kept his expression neutral. It was impossible to know if anyone was watching.

She was feeling unwell.

'What is it?'

'I don't know, dizziness. Something.'

She put her hand to her head.

Behind them the crowd was thick. Tito was standing in a circle of men, smoking.

'Follow me,' Eddie said, and led Ada to the passageway.

The maître d' unlocked the door to the deputy manager's office, and let them inside. Did the lady need water? Or anything else? Should he call a doctor?

'No' Eddie said, 'just a few minutes.' He'd wait with her.

When Eddie closed the door, Ada smiled. She admitted that she was jealous. She'd seen the way Delores Gray was looking at him. Wasn't she Canadian? Canadian women had a bad reputation.

'Reputation for what?'

'You know.'

Eddie shook his head.

'Christ, Ada.'

He kissed her hard; she felt the swell of him, and she undid the button on her dress to let his hand inside. He pinioned her against the door, covered her mouth. With small quick movements, he started to fuck her. Someone knocked on the door. Then went away.

'Too risky,' Eddie said, doing himself up. 'This is madness.'

Outside, they heard voices.

Ada fixed her dress, adjusted her stockings. She prodded her hair.

Eddie found Tito in the passageway, coming out of the gents.

'Just the man I was after,' Eddie said, and took him to the office where Ada was now sitting in front of a portable electric fan.

Tito rushed to his wife. 'What is it, Ada? You're ill?'

'I'm fine now.' She wiped her head with a handkerchief. 'The music was getting to me. Maybe something I ate. I don't know.'

'Let's take you home, darling,' Tito said. 'The music is getting to me, too.'

He asked Eddie to help him get her to the car.

As they left, the maître d' caught up with Eddie. He gave him the red flower dropped on the office floor, looking at Eddie with narrow eyes, as if to say, I know exactly what you were doing.

When they reached the house, Eddie asked Tito if he would like him to help get Ada inside. 'No, go back to the party, have some fun with Dolores.'

Another day, Ada was leaving through the side entrance of Rattan's Hotel when she bumped into Alfie Mendes coming straight out of the laundry store, holding a tall brown package.

'Ada,' he said. 'What are you doing here?'

'Frederick Street is crazy.' She waved her hand, pretending to be bothered by the heat. 'I was desperate for a glass of water.' She pointed inside the hotel. 'That place is a hell hole.'

'Yes, I should expect so. Not a place for someone like you.' Then he said, 'Are you well? You want me to call Tito? We could go to my office and telephone him from there.'

'No, I'm fine. I'm just keen to get home. Don't mention to Tito; he'll only worry. You know how he frets. Next thing he's sending me out with a chaperone.'

She laughed awkwardly.

Ada wondered if Alfie noticed that she was wearing little make up, her hair was not styled under her floppy hat and her cheeks were hot. She was desperate to get away from him. If he took her hand he would know. Her breath was thick with Eddie.

When Alfie offered to hail a taxi, she said the walk would do her good. He looked surprised, curious. As she crossed the street, she felt his eyes on her back.

TWENTY-NINE

Tito called Eddie to tell him about the new delivery coming into MacFarlane's. He'd caught sight of new cars in the forecourt this morning.

Eddie left Callaghan in charge and headed into Port of Spain.

Now he walked around the side of a brand new Ford Model T, the very latest version, to look at it from the front. 'Reliable, economical, good speed. Take a look at the finish.'

The salesman, Mr MacFarlane, in his mid-forties, flung open the door and pointed to the dash. The wheel was elegant and made of walnut, the circular dials were neat and clear, there were little glass containers on either side of the windows which held sprigs of flowers.

'See the pedals, easy to use. Check the silver handles, the leather pocket. You can keep your wallet safe in here.' He flipped open the glove compartment, swished his hand inside then locked it back.

It smelled of leather, of newness. McFarlane showed how quickly the windows wound down, and closed the door with a solid clunk.

'Nice,' Eddie said, and leaned back in the seat, his legs too long for the pedals.

MacFarlane showed him how to push back the seat, to give him more space. 'Look, with this car, you can't make a mistake.'

This wasn't just salesman patter. MacFarlane believed in these cars. Eddie knew the car was pricey, more than he wanted to spend. As Tito said, look at it, try it out, get your taste buds fired up, and you'll know which one to buy.

McFarlane crossed the showroom to another Ford Model T, red and shiny as a cherry.

'This is a model from last year. Same as Mister Fernandes. See how the starter is at the front, just like with your truck I expect.'

Mr MacFarlane went to the cabin, flipped up the lever, then cranked the front three times. It started up, a deep energetic growl. 'Not as sweet as the new Model T; you can hear the difference? It sounds kind of rough. But it's a good, reliable car. Reliability is everything. You wouldn't want to get stuck somewhere between here and Siparia.'

'Yes,' Eddie said, 'it needs to be reliable.'

'But a car isn't something you buy every day. I climb into my car and I feel like it's my birthday. Isn't that how we want to feel?'

He called Eddie to follow him. 'We live once, Mister Wade. And if we live well, it's plenty good enough.'

Mr MacFarlane spoke to the receptionist, asked her to bring them refreshments in the office. He had one more car to show Eddie.

They stepped into the dark back room where the air was noticeably cooler. MacFarlane switched on the overhead lights and opened the shutters in the large glass window.

'They call it the Mighty Mercedes. It roars like the trumpets of Jericho.'

In the centre of the showroom was a long, cream automobile. It was lower to the ground, with big, silver, shining lamps. The hood line cleared the engine by only inches, the rims over the slender wheels were smooth and curved like ribbons, and the silver fender made the car look like it was smiling. On the bonnet, was a three-pointed silver star.

'Now this has a starter ignition. First one of this type. You don't have to crank it up, just turn the key, press the button here.'

The engine started, a lovely, strong rumble.

Eddie ran his finger along the chassis, his heart thumping now. He peered inside, opened the door and climbed in. The inside was cream leather, a double steering wheel – silver and wood; the several small dials were set in a tortoiseshell panel. Like a cockpit. The seating in the back was cream and immaculate. He tugged at the canvas hood.

'It can come up. Let me show you.' Macfarlane pulled up one side of the hood, and Eddie took the other and they set it in place.

The back stretched out to make a long, perfect nose. Eddie looked down at the engine, pristine and simple looking.

'7.1 litre engine producing 225 horsepower. Nothing here can touch it. We can take it out on the road, and you can see how it runs. Believe it or not it can hit up to 100 mph. About 150 of these in the world right now. It even has a radio. And a car key to start it up.' He sliced the air with his hands. 'No other car in Trinidad has this starter mechanism.'

'How much is it?'

'Well, put it this way, you could buy four of the other cars for this. But why would you want four Model T cars. Today we'd need only a deposit, 10 percent. Someone to guarantee the loan. Is there someone who could vouch for you?'

Within half an hour, Tito was in the office signing papers for Eddie's loan. Then Eddie drove his new car out of the forecourt into bright sunshine. Startled by the loud roar of the engine people on the sidewalks turned to look.

Eddie cruised by Queen's Royal College, Whitehall and Roomor, which locals called the wedding cake house with its wrought-iron decorations. It was late afternoon; people walked in the sun, some with parasols. A line of boy scouts stood, open-mouthed, and watched the car glide by. Eddie tooted the horn and waved. Around the Savannah, down Queen's Park East, and left along the stretch into downtown, past Robeiro's, Fernandes's store, then round the back street, Rattans, the Portuguese club.

Tito leaned back in the seat, his face glistening in the heat.

'Something said to me, that car has Eddie's name on it.'

'I couldn't have bought it without you.'

Eddie drove fast along the familiar main road towards the east. But the route felt different, the way the cane fields and the trees rushed by, and the bright blue sky came at him as if he was flying right into it.

On this straight road, he kept up the speed, and with the hood down, Eddie and Tito felt the power of its engine as it raced alongside the hills. Eddie raised the lever on the wheel further; his stomach lifted with the surge of extra power and he watched the dial hit 80 then 90 mph. His face was stretched, blown wide in the wind. Tito was pressed back into his seat, hair flat.

'San Fernando in under two hours,' Eddie shouted through the breeze, 'and if the roads were better, even quicker.'

'You can race her in competitions, Eddie,' Tito yelled. 'Leave them all standing. She's a goddam beauty.'

'Hear this,' Eddie said, slowing down as he clicked on the radio. It was crackly at first, but then the song came through. He turned up the volume and dropped right down to a slow speed so they could listen.

Tito shook his head, and smiled, his cheeks dimpled. He moved his hands like a conductor. 'I know for certain, the one I love… I'm done with flirtin… just you my love.'

'Remember that day I picked you up. Who'd have thought – nine months later and look where we are.'

Eddie drove at terrific speed along the stretch of rice fields and canefields, and he took the turning up towards Chaguanas. The few cars on the road honked their horns as he overtook and he felt as if the road belonged to him. He saw the samaan tree where his truck had broken down that day and banged his hand on the horn as he passed.

When they arrived back in town, it was almost dusk. They swerved into Tito's driveway, and pulled up outside the steps of the house. Eddie tooted the horn.

Ada appeared like a vision. When she saw the car, she put her hands up to her face. Tito made his way up the steps to his wife, slipped his arm around her waist. She was fresh from a bath, her hair still damp.

Flora appeared from inside, holding her skipping rope. Home for the weekend. Tito was glad to have her here. She had grown; her legs stretched out of her shorts.

Eddie said, 'Hello Flora.'

'Hi, Uncle Eddie.'

Ada followed her daughter to the car.

Flora ran her finger around the silver leaf. 'Does it go really fast?'

'Yes, it does.'

'As fast as this?'

She jumped quickly through the hoop of rope:

'Banana split, banana split,

What did you get for arithmetic,
Banana banana banana for tea,
What did you get for geo-ma-tree'
She caught her foot.

'Like that? As fast as that?'

'Not quite. But ask your father. He drove us home.'

Ada peered inside, inspected the back.

'Can I go for a drive, Tito?'

Tito watched from the steps.

'I could whizz her round the savannah, and bring her straight back.'

Tito wanted to tell his wife to come inside; another day, another time.

'Sure.' Then Tito said, 'Maybe Flora would like to go, too?'

Flora made a face.

Ada climbed in front before Tito changed his mind. She could tell he'd rather she did not go alone with Eddie.

She told Eddie, 'As long as you don't go too fast.'

'But you have to go fast, darling,' Tito said, irritated. 'That's the whole point. It's a racing car.'

Flora and Tito watched them go, heard the tyres catch on the corner. They gave each other a look.

'What do you make of Uncle Eddie?'

'He's okay.'

'I thought you liked him.'

'I do.'

'Not so much? Is it ever since he caught the fish?'

Flora shrugged. If she had anything else to say, she wasn't going to say it now.

Then Tito said, 'How's my colour looking these days?'

'You're always green, Daddy. Like an emerald with a little bit of sea mixed in.'

They sat in the veranda and Tito took out a packet of playing cards. He shuffled the deck, flipped them onto the glass table and cut the pack.

'Rummy. Best of three?'

Henrietta brought a jug of fresh lime juice.

'Bring scotch,' he said; 'it's been a long day.'

He felt tired. Today, for the first time in a while, he'd been a little breathless. He wondered if he should take a few days off. Spend some time with Ada, Flora. They could go to the house in Scotland Bay.

'How's school?'

'Did you know Christopher Columbus was buried in Seville? They took him to Santo Domingo and then to Cuba. Then they took him back to Seville. He was a pioneer... Are you a pioneer?'

'I'm something but I'm not that.'

'Is Uncle Eddie?'

'No, he's an oilman, not a pioneer.'

'Mama says he is.'

Flora pushed back her hair; she was looking more and more like Ada. Her figure was more like his own mother's – athletic, bony. She was a natural athlete, excellent at scaling a wall, climbing trees, sprinting.

They played a few games, then Flora got up to look out at the road. There was no sign of them. Tito checked his watch. They'd only been gone fifteen minutes.

When they arrived, the sun was setting. Tito saw something in Ada's face that made him take note, a new kind of brightness. His whole body was alerted to something he couldn't articulate. He told himself to be sensible: any woman would be the same. It was no ordinary car. It was the stuff of dreams.

'I told Eddie he should join us for dinner.'

'I have to get back,' Eddie said. 'See how she'll do on the roads at night.'

Tito was relieved; he didn't want company. He wanted to be alone with his wife and daughter.

'Good luck,' Tito said, 'you'll be the talk of the town.'

Flora stood on the steps and watched Eddie drive away.

Later, while putting on her nightgown, Flora told her mother, 'Mama, Uncle Eddie likes you a lot. He likes you more than Daddy. Not so?'

Ada picked her daughter's clothes up from the floor.

'Sometimes you're right, Flora; sometimes you're wrong. Today, you're very wrong.'

Flora looked straight at Ada, her brown eyes steady.

Ada didn't want to remonstrate. But for the first time in her life, she was relieved that tomorrow her daughter would return to the convent.

Eddie drove towards Siparia, aware of the dark immensity of the night and the glow of distant stars. He drove alongside the cane fields, flat lands, enjoying this new acceleration. The warm wind rushed by carrying the smell of fire, ruffling the ribboned leaves of the coconut trees along the last stretch. He speeded over the bridge and the black river, and glimpsed ahead the lights of the village. He swerved into Kushi estate, headlamps like two eyes, and roared down the track towards Chatterjee's house. Eddie tooted the horn and they all came to see – Long, Horatio, Gelliseau, Grace, Mercy. Their faces hot from hurrying up the hill to see what was going on. Sita appeared in her housecoat.

Horatio called out, 'Eh-eh, Mister Wade!'

Callaghan stood back with his hands on his waist and gave a low whistle. He walked around the car, bent down to look at the spokes, the orange tail lights. He shook Eddie's hand.

'She's something else.'

Eddie clapped. 'Who's clean enough to go for a spin?'

No one spoke and Eddie realised something was wrong. There was an atmosphere he hadn't caught when he first arrived. He looked around at the familiar faces. They looked downcast.

'Take Sonny for a drive,' Sita said, her voice quiet. 'Sonny need a pick-me-up.'

In the excitement, Eddie hadn't noticed that Chatterjee wasn't there.

'What happened? Where's Chatterjee?'

Earlier that day, Chatterjee was resting after lunch when something woke him. He wasn't sure what it was, a sound like the boom of a gun. Perhaps he'd dreamt it. He checked his wife and she was sleeping deeply. He rubbed his eyes, looked at the light slashing through the curtain. He got up, patted his hair, pulled on his shirt and went downstairs. He looked around – at the table, the photograph of his father and mother; the broom against the wall.

Everything was as it should be. A large moth was crashing itself against the screen door. He cupped it in his hands, stepped outside and released it into the hot afternoon. Should he go back upstairs and rest? It was only 3 pm.

Outside the sun was pouring through the leaves onto the cracked, baked ground. It had been days since rain fell. But it would come soon – the static in the air told him so. He was no longer tired. As if summoned, he left his house, walked through the shady part of the forest, where the remaining cocoa trees were dark, their branches full with bright green oval leaves. He could hear the hissing of cicadas, loud as if drilling between his ears. A white butterfly was ahead, wings like white cotton. The air was hot and stifling.

Where the land had been cleared, to the right he could see derricks pinned against the afternoon sky. He could see Horatio climbing up the tower, calling to workers below. Their days were long and exhausting; soon they'd break for a drink, some fruit. Grace would carry fruit or cake to the camp.

To the left was tall grass, some untouched trees and vines that draped green sheets over them. In the distance was the boundary line to his estate. But something was different. He felt it. The light? A low cloud was shaped like a table-top. He looked at the same spot. The edge of the field. He felt suddenly cold, a pricking up of his flesh. Sonny put his hands up to his head and prayed it wasn't so.

He started running up the field, his heart banging inside him, a feeling of dread pushing down inside his stomach. This could not be, this could not be true. He was still dreaming. He was not here; this was not so. He was imagining all of this. He ran along the field until he reached the end, out of breath, and stared at where the silk cotton tree had stood. He called out. 'Oh God! Oh God!'

He clambered over the fence and took in the full horror of what lay before him. The trees' enormous roots were sticking up; black, brown and grey and monstrous. The tree lay on its side. The pale grey trunk, too wide to wrap his arms around, was severed and stretched across the field, its long branches snapped, broken and smashed, its masses of bright bunched leaves splayed over the ground.

He shouted at the men working there, some standing around a truck marked APEX, there to drag the chopped tree away. Chatterjee's voice was sharp, screechy. 'What you did! What you did! You blasted idiots!' One of the Apex men in brown overalls, with a helmet and a sunburnt face, stared at him. He was holding a cutting tool. Its whirring, terrible sound made it hard to hear. 'Shut it off! Shut off the damn thing!' Then they were all staring at him, the intruder. Eight or ten men from England and Scotland who knew nothing.

The man with the cutting tool said, 'Sir, you're trespassing on crown land. It belongs to the king.'

Chatterjee charged at him. 'How you could do this? You know what it is to cut down this tree? You ent know what the cotton tree is?' He flung out his arms. 'This tree sacred. Sacred you hear.'

Tears were dripping down his raging, red face. He started to pick his way through the broken boughs, the young leaves, the strong branches. He saw the great roots and the earth thrown up. He fell on his knees and could see amongst the dirt the precious shells, stones, jewels, gold, bottles of rum, and all manner of devotional offerings and treasures – the prayers and wishes of hundreds of men and women.

'You know how old this tree? Three hundred years. Three hundred fockin' years.'

Chatterjee put his face in his hands, trembling and shaking. The men looked at one another. Above birds were circling, calling out. Hundreds of black African bees made dark clouds.

When Chatterjee returned, he called out to Grace who was on the track, carrying a bucket of oranges. She smiled, but he didn't smile back. He asked her where was Eddie, and when she said he was in Port of Spain, he pointed somewhere behind him. Grace didn't know what he was pointing at. But she had a strange feeling that what he was saying was the truth.

'Tell everybody. Tell all of them, trouble coming.'

THIRTY

The night air was cool through the car as they raced past St Madeleine. Trees and bush flashed by in the light of the headlamps. High grass, the occasional coconut tree, the broad lacy head of samaan. From the houses, smudges of gold light.

In San Fernando, Eddie drove slowly, tooting his horn all the way down Coffee Street, then up onto Rushworth, like a motorcade on the Fourth of July. People came outside, peered from their verandas at the car gleaming like an opal in the moonlight. Callaghan told Eddie to hurry up or the party would soon be over.

Outside the Paramount Hotel, more people came to look. The manager came outside, shook Eddie's hand. 'A showstopper,' he said. 'It belongs in the movies, like you and your friend, here. You're welcome any time.'

Young men and women came from the line of people queuing to find their way into the party. 'Can we touch it?' They slid their hands along the chassis. Fingered the silver laurel leaf. They stroked the bonnet. Eddie said yes to a couple who wanted to sit up front. 'How do you start it?' He held up the key to show them. 'It has an ignition?' 'Yes sir,' Eddie said. 'First car on the island with an ignition.'

The air was sweet with cigarette smoke, the scent of cologne and of good things to come. Eddie felt he'd arrived somewhere, a place he'd looked for all his life. What was that? Money? Success? Belonging? He thought of Ada; she was part of that good feeling. He wished that she was there.

He said, 'You ever notice, Callie, how money has a smell? You can actually smell money. I can smell it tonight.'

'We smell of money, too. We're just like them, these people. No difference; just our fingernails; the oil underneath giving us away.'

A live band was playing in the courtyard. The singer, a man in his fifties, wore a dinner suit, his hair combed back; his voice was deep and crackly. A trio of girls were sitting at a round table; their hair was curled and polished, they all wore the same style tasselled dresses. They were striking; their excitement was palpable.

Eddie and Callaghan went to the bar, and ordered whiskies.

Callaghan said, 'Do you ever think you want things?'

'Like what? Like my car?'

'More than that. Your own house with land. A boat to sail. You could do it now. Maybe go to Oklahoma, see Kathryn. You and Kathryn could get married. Have another child. Make a proper family. Make a real life for yourself.'

Since his father died, Callaghan had lived with his mother and his younger brother, who'd had polio. His life had been hard.

He said, 'It's like you and me; we're camping out. Drifting here and there. It's no way to live. You could have a life. It's there if you want it.'

'Kathryn had her chance. She took out my guts. Remember that, Callie?' Then Eddie said, 'You could have those things, too. A big house, a wife. A family of your own. It's not too late.'

'Sometimes. I look at Mercy and I'd like to fuck her. But you don't play around with that, you know. You have to mean it. She's got some growing to do. There's things I want. But I don't know if you can buy them. I don't even know what they are.'

He cast his eyes about; the bar was filling up.

'Look, you should know. Macleod saw Ada coming out of Rattans. Everyone knows you stay there. Macleod made some comment to Grace on the road about you and Tito's wife. There are rumours flying around the place.'

Eddie took a glug of whisky, slid the empty glass towards the bartender.

'Grace didn't believe him. Sour grapes and all that. But if he told Tito, he might think different. You don't want him pulling the plug on all this.'

Eddie's heart was jumping about.

'They can say what they like.'

'I figured you'd never do that to Tito. Risk losing all you've made. You're good friends.'

'There's no doubt about that.'

'Now Ada, she's been spoilt. She has everything. She might want a bit of rough with you. You should watch out for yourself.'

'Thanks for the tip. But don't worry. I wouldn't go near.'

Eddie wasn't sure if Callaghan believed him, but he needed him to know this wasn't his business.

They watched young people in the fountain splashing their feet in the water; they were laughing.

It was getting late, the music had changed, slower tunes.

'Remember those idiots in Beaumont,' Eddie said. 'If it wasn't for those crooks we'd still be looking for oil in Texas, hoping that Hopi man was wrong.' He laughed, and Callaghan laughed too.

Eddie drained his glass, called the barman over and ordered two more whiskies for the road.

Callaghan looked tired, a little drunk.

'You need to stop thinking so much. Take Mercy out. Buy her dinner. Marry her. No one really cares. I can see you all get along. Maybe you'll fall in love. You're a good man, Callie. Don't let anyone tell you different.'

That night Eddie's dreams were vivid, images of the time he lost his virginity – a girl called Rose McCann, who's skin was covered in freckles like sprinkled sand. He dreamt of the wheatfield where they lay, clouds like foam. Her breasts were small as buttons; she'd taken him into her small and tight place; she had told him that she loved him. Why was he thinking of her now?

It was as though Ada was somehow freeing inside him events he'd long forgotten. Like the day he fell out of the sky.

Tuesday March 3 1918, Carcassonne, France. He'd eaten breakfast – black pudding, hot rolls, poached eggs, a mug full of tea. One of the pilots, from Chichester, slapped his back: 'I'd rather be lucky, than good,' he said, which Eddie had thought a strange thing to say.

Then they took their bags, went outside into the cool morning. Five or six aeroplanes were parked up on the runway. When he climbed into the cockpit, a thought came to him: what if that was my last breakfast? It was possible. Thousands of men were dying every day.

He'd been up there for half an hour, hovering at 3,000 feet, circling, awaiting instructions, thinking for some reason of his dead mother, when, just like that, the engine cut. It was a problem with those planes; he'd known it.

A silence fell over the world and he fell and the right wing tipped, the aeroplane spinning now through the blue; twisting and rolling – like a canister falling through the air down towards the tiny houses, purple ribbons of lavender and green squares and it sucked him down, down, towards the pine forest. *Please God. Not now. Mother, father help me. Help me. Another chance. Not now.* And he saw the face of his corporal, his moustache twitching, dead eyes staring at Eddie, and his mother's face. He was going to die, after all that, after everything. He was not ready. I AM NOT READY. He saw the ground rising up towards him and everything was growing bigger. Please God, another chance.

Then, a miracle: a strong wind caught under the wing, lifted him up, upright, and he held the wheel steady, and the wind lifted him again. He swayed, dipped, steadier now and floated above the field like a butterfly, down and down, until everything was close enough to reach and touch and he bounced hard onto the rocky field of corn – bounced off, lifting, and then thumping down again. The plane lurched, one wheel skitted towards a line of elms straight and grey as soldiers, and the plane smashed into the gap between them. He was lobbed out through the top, and tossed like a sack of potatoes in the mud, a pool around his head and he knew it was blood and he could taste its familiar flavour in his mouth of broken teeth. A crowd of four or five quickly gathered and behind them the sun's light sprayed through. A young woman asked if he was dead, and he saw her shoes were made of light. She started to sing in a language he could not understand, in a tune he remembered from when he was a boy. He saw the crowd was dissipating like smoke, and he wanted to go with them. But when he opened his bleeding eyes they were gone. He hadn't realised how much he wanted to live until then.

Eddie woke the next morning, remembering that feeling. He was damp with sweat, his mouth dry. He wasn't sure why he'd dreamt of this. Now, even more than then, he wanted to live.

THIRTY-ONE

Two days later, a signal came from Apex that a well was coming in – the loud horn hooted across the site. Eddie looked out to see people heading towards the derrick on the other side of Chatterjee's fence, walking quickly. His own men downed tools and started in that direction. Callaghan waved at Eddie to go over and see what was happening. First strike in six months; Macleod would be in his glory. Eddie should show his face; give him that.

But as Eddie started towards it, he had a sense that something else was happening, and found himself running to get a closer look. Instinctively, he ran alongside the field, not towards the derrick. He caught sight of Macleod on the thribble board, hands on his hips, face red; he was shouting at the crew who were in a whirr. Something was going on. Something was wrong.

Macleod swung down on the guy wire to the derrick floor. Three men were standing at the mouth of the well on top of the rotary drill. By now there would usually be a sign of something happening, but it was quiet. Eddie figured on what they were doing: attempting to bypass the gas, relieve pressure, to let out the oil coming up slowly, and God knows what else. By now he would have expected to see a fountain of oil gushing out. The men had ropes around their middles, to get them out quick if the well blew.

As Eddie got closer, he saw Macleod leap backwards, spring on to the lower platform, fright on his face. There was an almighty crack. Eddie watched the liquid blast out and whoosh up over the crown block, and the wooden boards of the derrick floor flew off, pap, pap, pap – snapped off like sticks, and the entire casing shot out, curled up and twisted, taking out the men in a terrific fountain of water, oil and sand. Stuff was spraying out of the hole that looked like grey water. Where were the men? People were shouting; it was difficult to see. Eddie ran onto the field.

A different bell – a broken ring, an emergency alarm. It was so loud Eddie covered his ears; he looked for Callaghan who was now some yards away. Everyone was looking at the tower. The whole iron rig was twisted up and half gone. One driller was naked at the foot of the structure, clothes blown clean off. He was bawling, his fists in his eyes. A black man, a local man, perhaps. Then up on the bank above where the pit was dug, another man sat, some of him gone. Flung onto the other side of the platform were two more men, naked as children, their clothes taken off in the blast. And there was Macleod, scrambling over the broken frame, yelling at the first aiders to hurry, to bring help. Where was the ambulance truck?

Eddie ran to the man on the bank; he recognised him. He was sitting up now, covered in blood and water, laughing about his missing trousers. Eddie told him to wait, someone was coming. Then Eddie saw the top of his skull was missing and part of his brain was exposed. The man said, 'Who are you? You come to take me?' He was crying now. 'You come for me? You come to take me away?' He started to beg Eddie. 'Please sir. Not now. Don't take me anywhere.'

Ambulances arrived with the doctor they had on call – an English doctor, his face white as chalk. Two men were lifted on to stretchers, yelping with pain. One of them lay on his stomach, and Eddie saw a hole in his back blown out, the size of a tennis ball. Eddie's men were standing in a clump, horrified, waiting for instruction; their faces blank with shock. There was a routine drill here, an emergency plan. Macleod had enough men. Eddie felt useless, helpless. 'Oh Gawd, oh Gawd,' the man cried.

Macleod was shouting to bring the vehicles closer. He was holding a clipboard, but his hands were trembling so much he couldn't hold a pen to tick off the missing names. Grace had come down from the house; Mercy was close behind her. They were walking quickly, picking their way, and then Mercy started towards a limping man, holding his hand over his mouth from where blood was pouring. He was cupping his teeth. She had a bucket and box under her arm. She went to the man and put her arm around him. It was midday, the sun lashed down and the sky was blue; a hawk was wheeling high. God have mercy here on these men. The smell of gas was everywhere. He saw one of Macleod's men throwing up, then another. Another man lay face down on the ground. The air was filled with a smell of shit and piss and puke.

The ambulance carried some of the men away, while others were checked for injuries and wounds. Eddie and his men stood by, feeling useless. Macleod was yelling at the top of his lungs, trying to gather up his men. He had cut the side of his head, a streak of blood down his face, on his shirt.

Eddie said, 'Charles,' and he swiped at Eddie, and Eddie jumped back. Macleod was heading up to the bank where the equipment was broken up and tangled, twisted like spaghetti. Water was still fizzing out of the hole. Some of the men crowded over it, tried to stop it off. There was no platform, just the broken structure underneath which looked as if it could collapse. It was chaos, a scene from a war.

THIRTY-TWO

It was after five when Callaghan and Eddie met Chatterjee up at the main house. They sat outside in the porch on Chatterjee's new wooden chairs, in the half light. Eddie smoked a cigarette; he was longing for a drink. He felt as if he had been up all night. The light was strange, yellowish.

Chatterjee's face was troubled, his eyes downcast. Sita came and sat beside her husband, her small frame perched like a bird.

Callaghan was explaining what had happened. 'Intense gas and too much pressure. It could be part of a highly pressurised reservoir. It happens.'

Eddie said, 'But on their land, not on ours. Why?'

'Who knows why. It could be right under our feet. If we hit it, it'll make a mud pie of us, too. There's no real way of telling.'

Eddie leaned in, 'We didn't have it on the first well. We didn't have it on the second or the third. Why would we have it now? You're being pessimistic. We've no evidence so far.'

'Not to the same extent, but we had pressure. The deeper you go the higher the pressure. They must be down 2500 feet. Macleod is stubborn as hell. He should've already given up on that well weeks ago, called it a day. He kept going until he hit something. But look what he hit.'

'We've talked about this. Configurations here are random.' Eddie ran his fingers through his hair. He didn't like where this was going. 'There's no reason to think it will happen here at Kushi. I'd put my life on it. It's not going to happen.'

Sita looked at Eddie, her eyes were two nails.

'How many dead?' Chatterjee asked. 'Grace, Mercy come here crying. They say plenty hurt.'

Callaghan spoke, 'Two dead so far. But probably more. There

210

could be more. It usually looks worse than it is. But in this case, I don't know.' He shook his head.

Outside a cockerel crowed, then made its way inside. A pocket of red baggy skin under its beak. It shook itself, then wandered off.

Chatterjee looked at each of them, 'We must stop.'

'You mean quit?' Eddie said, his expression incredulous. 'How can we quit? We're not done. We quit when we're done.'

Eddie got up from his chair, walked to the edge of the porch. He could see Chatterjee's two boys out in the yard; they were rolling a wheel along the ground with a long stick. Barebacked, in shorts, and barefoot. He realised they had grown since he'd been there. They were fine-featured, gangly.

Sita got up and went inside. Eddie saw her disappear into the dark kitchen; she tugged the curtain shut behind her. She was letting them know what she thought.

Chatterjee said, shaking his head, 'I have a bad feeling. Sita have a bad feeling.'

Eddie said, 'We can't stop because of superstitions. We go by the evidence. We do our best. We test the land. Maybe Macleod was overconfident. He's been drilling too deep; we've been saying it all along.' Then Eddie said, 'Macleod cut down the tree. Not us.'

'Sita want to sell.'

'What about you, Sonny? Your father's estate. You'll give it up because of a blowout on a piece of land next door. There's no gas coming out. What happened with Apex was unlucky. Even if it had something to do with the tree, which I know you think it did, that had nothing to do with us. Trinidad is strange like that. Formations are unpredictable.'

He could see that Chatterjee was puzzled.

Eddie carried on. 'We still have two months left on the lease. Our contract has two more months. We've one more well to drill.'

Chatterjee said, his voice high, strained, 'But after that, I finish. One more. All you hear? I finish. We make an agreement for a year and no more. I sticking with that.'

Eddie said, 'I crashed a plane in the war. The plane tumbled through the sky like a tin can and I was sure I'd die. I saw angels come for me. But it wasn't my time. And I knew it wasn't my time. When it's your time, it comes. No matter how you run from it, it will come.'

Callaghan got up. His face was pinched. He put his hands in his pockets; he looked at Chatterjee and then at Eddie.

Eddie said, 'We keep looking ahead. We're not going back. We do what we can. The first whiff of gas and we get out. Macleod should have given up on that well weeks ago. I blame him entirely.'

Callaghan said, 'The next well we drill must be on the other side. Closer to the river. Away from the Apex site. It's all we can do.'

Eddie knew, for all this, it wasn't just gas they had to worry about. High flow-rates from the unconsolidated oil-sand reservoirs allowed large quantities of sand to sit with the oil. This same sand, under high pressure, was highly abrasive to control valves. It could quickly rip through metal. He'd seen it in Beaumont, he'd seen it in Houston. He'd noticed it on the last well, a high sand content. They had spare pipe; they needed as much as they could as back up. It wasn't just gas, it was sand. There were more things to worry about than gas. Callaghan had told him of sulphur leaks in Forest Reserve, where men were poisoned by gases, and how it turned their clothes yellow. He'd told Eddie that so far they'd been lucky, but many others weren't. 'We work in isolation here. It's easy to forget. But take a look,' Callaghan said; 'every week we're hearing of something.'

Eddie didn't want Chatterjee to know any of this. They would keep it to themselves. For now, they just needed to get the oil out.

That evening the men were quiet. Eddie didn't know what to tell them, only that they must be grateful. He asked Grace to say prayers. She sat at the long table, her face puffy from weeping, and prayed in a way that made everybody feel as though they were a part of something. She shut her eyes tight, raised her hands, spoke to the clouds. Eddie thought for a moment about the spirits of the dead men and where they might be now – circling the camp like nighthawks. Did they know they were dead? Were they able to comfort their loved ones? He told the men to take the night off, go home to their families, see their wives.

'Do what you need to do. Forget about this for a while. It wasn't you, and we are safe. Right now, we're all safe. Understand, what happened did not happen to you. God is good.'

While Eddie reassured the men, Sita walked up and down the yard. Chatterjee stood in the porch smoking. It was late and she was fiddling with her necklace. A sign that she was agitated.

'I feeling it in my body.'

She poked her chest, shoulders.

'Sita,' Chatterjee said. 'We can't decide now. It not just me – Eddie, Mister Fernandes.'

She threw him a look, her eyes narrow.

'Eddie say we don't have gas. He know for sure? It might have gas here, too. Callaghan say so. Callaghan tell Mercy she right to be frighten.'

Callaghan had confided in Mercy? This wasn't a surprise; he knew Callaghan and Mercy were friendly. Were they together? He didn't know for sure and he didn't care.

'Look, Macleod drill and drill. He drill where it dry so he hit gas.'

Chatterjee didn't know if this was true but it sounded right.

She wagged her bony finger.

'No, Sonny. He drill like all you drill here – only better tools, more experience men. Yuh hear what I say? Ma say it from the start. I say it. No one listen.'

'Eddie wouldn't risk his life so. He want to see his daughter.'

'Mercy say he have something with Mister Fernandes wife.'

Chatterjee looked up at her, and made a clicking noise in the side of his cheek.

'Mercy like to talk. All you women like to talk. You talk shit.'

'You cyah see? If he lie to Mister Fernandes, who's you? Who Sonny Chatterjee?' She looked straight at her husband now; the light caught her eyes and they were silver, strange, shining – as if she was someone else.

'Wake up yourself, Sonny. Wake up.'

Everything Sita said made sense to Sonny. But he was determined not to encourage her. He needed to think calmly about what he must do, for the good of his family and the estate. He felt it himself, a sense of foreboding, deep down in his belly and he couldn't shake it. He was frightened. If his father was here, his father would tell him what he must do. The tree had gone. Lives were lost. They would drill this last well and that would be that. The soul of the land had let loose its fury on the people who'd harmed it. Macleod had brought disaster upon himself. He had disturbed the spirits of the land. It was obvious to Sonny. He should warn Macleod. He would tell him to get out; there was more to come. Macleod was not safe. His men were not safe. None of them were safe. Sonny stood alone in the yard and the wind seemed to circle him; the voices of the forest were hushed, as if plotting.

Next day, Macleod came to see Eddie. He appeared on the steps of Eddie's bungalow. It was early morning, the sun just up. Bats flitted through the open veranda. Two or three small young ones. Eddie had found a baby yesterday on its back, little teeth exposed, wings thin as black silk; it looked like it was grinning. Grace said the dead bat was a sign of the blowout to come.

Surprised to see him, Eddie came outside with his cup full of coffee. Macleod looked ghostly, exhausted. He wore a bandage on his temple.

'Save your sympathy, Eddie; I don't need it.'

Then he put his hands on his waist, and Eddie saw he'd lost weight, the belt on his trousers pulled tight. Reedy and grey, Macleod had aged ten years in a few days.

'Is there anything you need? Anything we can do?'

Macleod cut him off.

'I don't need to tell you your business, Eddie. But this land, this land is full of gas. There's no room for mistakes, or hotchpotch equipment. You know that. I lost three men.'

'You were lucky, you could've lost more. I saw it. I was there.'

He looked at Eddie, his eyes glassy and small.

'Three is too many. You don't know that, Eddie? You don't know that? These men – two of them married with children and wives, and lives ahead of them.' His voice was full of pain. 'Three is too many. If you don't know that then I'm sorry for you.'

'You didn't know those trees are sacred?'

Charles looked out at the steam room, the men coming out of their barracks for breakfast. The sun was covered with cloud and the colours of the site were muted.

Charles said, 'You always struck me as a hardheaded guy. Not dumb. Hardheaded. But maybe I got that wrong.'

THIRTY-THREE

When Eddie saw Tito appear on the hill like a phantom, he felt uneasy. They had their weekly meeting in town in a couple of days. Why was he here?

Tito limped in the semi-darkness to where Eddie was standing.

'Old age is a bitch, Eddie. You'll see. Everything starts cracking up. Most men lose their hair too, but I'm lucky with that. Looks like you will be, too.'

He hoped Eddie didn't have plans. He'd come on a whim. Maybe they could get something to eat. There were things to talk about.

They drove Eddie's truck into the village. It was dark when they found themselves outside the parlour. Gloria was friendly, and Eddie was glad to see her. She was sorry to hear about the trouble over at Apex. They wouldn't talk about that now. 'Eat,' she said, putting down a plate of sweet and sour pork dumplings. 'I'll bring more. This man,' Gloria gestured to Eddie, 'he don't eat. He forget to feed himself. When he come here, I feed him up.'

The night was still; the song of crickets came from the yard. Tito lit his cigar, puffed out a long plume of smoke, and then held up the little torpedo.

'You know when they make these cigars, they use leaves from the highest part of the tobacco plant which makes them expensive; hard to get. It's why people want them.'

Smoke came out in little gusts.

'I'll keep you a carton at the store.'

'Sure,' Eddie said, 'I'd like that.'

There were mosquitoes out tonight. Eddie clapped his hands and caught one. He was feeling uncomfortable. It still wasn't clear why Tito had come.

It was quiet out here, no traffic, or noise from the city. Eddie was used to this, but he suspected it might be different for Tito.

Then Tito said, 'Do you have any kind of faith or religion, Eddie?'

'I believe we're here to fulfil a destiny of some kind, but once we've done that, who knows.' He looked out at the sky. 'I saw some things when I almost died, but I don't know if they were just playing in my mind. Things I wanted to see.'

An Indian man arrived; he was wearing a chequered shirt and shorts. He nodded at Tito and Eddie. The road was right there, but there were no cars. Beyond the road was the river, the start of Chatterjee's land.

'You think the wells are done here?' Tito put up his hands, as if holding the land within them.

'I don't know. I've never known a place like this – it's like nowhere else. Chatterjee's land is floating on oil. It seems to stop right at the land boundary. There's no reason we can't get to it. It's just the gas we have to watch for. Callaghan says we need a new blowout preventer. We'll see. He's a little overcautious.'

'Cautious is good. Look what happened to Macleod.'

'I know.'

Then Tito said, 'I was sitting in my office in Frederick Street, and I thought about those men, and I felt overwhelmed with grief. I can't explain it. I had to get up from my desk. I didn't say where I was going, just got in my car and started out of town. I felt such a heaviness, like the end of the world. I thought about their families.'

'It hit everyone hard.'

'How many died in the end, one or two?'

'Three. One from South Africa, and a guy from Scotland, same as Macleod. Then a guy from the village. Another one is holding on, but looks like he might die, too.'

'And the well was dry. The well was *dry*. How can that be? Yet right next door we find 80,000 barrels.'

'Variables in the land. Where we are there's an anticline, a big pocket of oil as far as I can tell. Macleod must've figured that if he went close to the border, he'd tap into it. It backfired.'

Tito shook his head. 'You never know. You have plans and then – boom! – everything changes in a moment. Those men had plans for their evening meals. You think Macleod made a mistake?'

'No, he was unlucky. He hit gas. There's luck here in all of this. Macleod is thorough. More than anything, safety is important to him. He had the right equipment, enough men. Who knows, maybe he lost his instinct.'

'How so?'

'We all have an instinct, usually it works okay. But you get too driven or greedy, or you want something so bad, and before you know it you've lost it. You can't see your way. Macleod lost his instinct. He was desperate.' Then Eddie said, 'He'd been watching us here, pumping oil out of the ground for months. It was sending him crazy. He should've never cut down the tree. Chatterjee said it's sacred.'

'That may well be; country people don't think like us. But there's gas there?'

'There's pockets of gas like there's pocket's of oil. He hit something and it blew. He ran out of luck.'

A breeze blew and with it came the smell of cooking meat.

'You a lucky guy, Eddie? I think you probably are.'

Eddie ran his fingers through his hair. 'Who knows. Let's hope so. So far here I've been lucky enough.'

They clinked glasses and swilled back the rum. Tito rubbed his face. He looked tired, mauve hoops under his eyes like someone had punched him.

The sky was black and the air was still. Frogs were bleeping in the bush.

'The call of love,' Tito said. 'You hear them? They're wooing their beloveds.'

Eddie recognised the high-pitched call. He filled Tito's glass.

'You know Eddie, when I was your age, my fiancée left me at the altar; it was the worst thing that ever happened to me and the best thing that happened to me. And you know why? Because if she hadn't left me, I'd have married her, and then I'd never have married Ada. You see how life works out? At the time, I was on my knees, humiliated. I spent a year cutting up my wedding cake and eating it. A little slice every afternoon with my cup of tea.'

Tito patted his stomach.

'Not so good for my waistline.'

'Where is she now, the lady?'

Tito waved his hand. 'Oh somewhere in Dominica, I hear.'

'And the guy she left you for?'

'Dead, apparently.' Then he said, 'And if I'm honest with you, I'm glad.'

Eddie puffed on the cigar, swirled the smoke around his mouth.

'I like to think Ada's been happy enough, but who knows. You can never get inside someone else's head. When I started dating Ada, people said she was too young, too pretty for me. I tried to ignore them. But I've wondered at times if maybe she was.'

Tito straightened himself in his chair and he stared out at the yard and its dark trees.

'Everybody wants money. Money is important. We can buy things; a house with a garden, a second home if we're lucky, a car or two. We buy jewellery for those we love, go out for meals, travel, see the world. But let me tell you, it's not the only thing that matters.'

Tito took a deep breath, then sighed. 'Remember we talked about it the first time you came for dinner. Well, I stand by it.'

'I remember.'

'Once we're done here, I want to take a holiday with Ada and Flora. Europe, maybe. To Paris, Amsterdam, London. I want Flora to see the world. It's only by seeing the world that you understand people. We talked about that too, remember. Ada said she wanted to travel – Nova Scotia, California, and now I'm older, I resist it. But she's right. Trinidadians live in a damn cocoon. You never notice that, Eddie? I'm guilty of it too. They don't realise there's a world out there.'

'Maybe they like their little worlds.'

'Maybe.'

Then Tito said, 'You know Eddie, there's something I need to tell you.'

Eddie caught Gloria as she passed, and signalled for another drink. He braced himself for what was coming.

'The day I met you, I had lost a lot of money, and I didn't know what I was going to do with myself.'

'But you had money, you put money in here?'

'I had a lot more money. A small fortune in America hidden in stocks. Then the market crashed. Remember what happened? Wall Street. You heard all about that. Well I had money in there.'

Eddie topped up Tito's glass. They were going through rum that night.

'Before I picked you up I'd been to Manzanilla. I drove there to figure out what I was going to do. I thought about killing myself. Can you believe it?'

Eddie was taken aback.

'What stopped you?'

'Well, I saw something. I won't say what it was because it might sound dumb. But it was enough to make me reconsider,' and he swirled his hand in the air, 'and give all this another chance.'

Eddie thought of the truck that day, the heat. His trip to see Chatterjee.

'So in a way, you saved me, Eddie. You saved me from despair. You made me see what's important here. I'll never take those risks again. I see what I have – my Ada, Flora, my friends, like you. People I love and people who love me. What more could I want? I owe you, Eddie; I'll owe you for the rest of my life. If this hadn't worked out, I might not have found the courage to keep living.'

Eddie looked down at his boots.

'Tito, I'm sorry. I had no idea.'

Men were standing inside now; the hurricane lamps hung over the bar. 'Living is an act of courage. You know that, Eddie?'

'I believe it.'

'There was a moment recently when I was thinking about it all again. I started imagining things, wondering if you and Ada might do what Matilda and Carlos did. I know she likes you. I know you like Ada. I thought that maybe there was more to your liking. But then I realised you were made of different stuff. I saw what was right and true. You're not that kind of man.'

Tito looked Eddie straight in the eyes and Eddie knew he had a choice, right there and then.

'I'm not that kind of man, Tito. I'm not.'

'I know, Eddie. I just needed to say it.'

Tito's eyes were watering; they were full of kindness and what looked to Eddie like relief. He felt a flood of warmth and tenderness for Tito; this man who had taken him into his home and his life and trusted him like a brother, and Eddie felt ashamed.

'You can be standing next to someone and not know they want to kill themselves. You probably had your fair share of gloomy thoughts. I've had them all my life. That day they came to get me. You saved me.'

Tito took out a handkerchief and wiped his face.

'I guess that's why I drove here this afternoon. When I heard about those men who died, and how they died, I realised how lucky we are. I wanted to thank you for all you've done.'

He stood up and Eddie stood up, too. Then Tito hugged Eddie, patted his back. Eddie felt shame and sadness for all he'd done. He wanted to cry and tell Tito he was sorry.

They walked together back to the estate; Eddie carried a torch and shone it ahead in the bush. Tito said he liked to hear the sound of the steam engine running and see the lights on the derrick as it reached into the sky.

'What's next Eddie? The last well? Chatterjee must be getting twitchy.'

On the roadside just outside the estate, there was a *For Sale* notice. Eddie knew then that Chatterjee was serious. Chatterjee told Eddie, yes, they were leaving. But there was no rush; it would take time to get the right price. Eddie was shocked by his appearance; ten years had been added to his demeanour, any recent trace of joy had vanished.

'You'd really sell Kushi to those vipers? You know we can't compete with big corporations. They'll hack up your land; they won't care.' He shook his head.

Sonny wanted to tell Eddie, he couldn't afford an accident on his land – for equipment to blow up, lives to be lost, for their enterprise to end badly like it had with Macleod. He wanted to say that at least if he quit now, he was quitting before his wife had the chance to tell him that here was another failure, here was more bad luck, because, despite the guru's marigold he caught in his five-year-old hands, up to now, Sita was right that everything he touched seemed to end in disaster.

Chatterjee turned and walked off up the hill, holding his tin cup, hunched over, looking defeated. When Eddie started to follow him, he put up his hand and walked away.

Eddie wanted to shout at him, but he knew it was pointless. Chatterjee could be unreasonable, stubborn. He'd seen it from the start. If he leased the land now, he'd get a good price; it came with a promise of more oil, another ten acres to drill. Perhaps a big corporation would use the wells they had and try for deeper reserves. Callaghan said there could be more oil further down. Offers would come from America. He and Tito wouldn't stand a chance. He would have to get what he could in the time remaining.

When Eddie found Callaghan, he agreed that they needed to do what he'd suggested – drill far away from the fence and Macleod. Would two hundred yards north of the river be best? The soil was already showing traces of bitumen. They'd set up in the next few days, start drilling in early December. There was no time to be lost. By Christmas they might be lucky.

THIRTY-FOUR

They would meet at the back of the Red House. It was risky, the sun's light all over them, Eddie's glittery car, people starting their day, people they might know. Perhaps they should wait until Tito was out of the country, but the option of waiting was intolerable for Ada.

Tito would be taken up all day with an audit at the store – chunks of money coming in from the wells, the store in Barbados. He'd warned Ada he wouldn't be back for lunch. If he was lucky, he'd be home in time for dinner.

'Today is a day of hell,' he said, as he put on his hat. 'Wish me luck.'

Ada waited in the shadow of the trees. She'd scraped back her hair, wore shorts, a blouse, pumps. Eddie pulled up and she quickly jumped in, stayed low in her seat. He drew up the roof.

He drove through back streets, headed out of the city towards the mountains. Roads were empty and for a while they saw no one. The dry season was coming again, the hills were crisping up, distant curls of smoke appeared in the green. The sky was a brilliant azure blue.

They were quiet. Something felt different between them, but neither spoke of it. Eddie had decided not to tell Ada about Tito's visit. He would save it for another time. It would start a bigger conversation that he didn't want to have today. He looked for the sea, the stretch of land he recognised.

Ada said, 'Do you think about being happy?'

'I think about doing what's in front of me. If it makes me happy, then that's plenty.'

It wasn't true. Eddie had been feeling anxious; it was only a matter of time before they slipped up. There was no way back.

'I think about it a lot. Every time I get close to feeling happy, it evaporates like mist. It's eluded me most of my life.'

They drove for more than an hour without speaking. The wind blew through the windows and Ada kept looking out. The winding roads could make her feel sick.

By the time they reached the beach it was almost noon. They took off their shoes, made their way down the steep bank, balancing on the warm grey stones. Eddie held out his hand to help her; he'd already stripped off to his bathing trunks.

There was a high call. A shriek.

'What's that?' she said. 'A monkey? A sad monkey. Don't you think it sounded sad?'

'Not sad at all.'

The river was clear and still as a mirror. On weekends, families came with coal pots and spent the day. During the week it was quiet. Beyond, lay the Atlantic, and its large rolling waves. The current was strong and temperamental.

'There's no one around,' Eddie said; 'you can take off your clothes. Here, let me help.'

She lifted her blouse over her head and flung it with her shorts to the rocks. Her bathing suit was ruched and white with tiny red flowers. At times she was strange to him, otherworldly, crafted from the flesh of the moon. She was nervous, her eyes darting about.

'Take your time.'

Ada sat on the riverbank, prodded the muddy sand with her toes. The water was warm.

'It's shallow here,' he said, making his way into the river.

She looked up at the canopy of dark green – large trees hung above her, their vines like trailing hair offering shade.

'Come,' he said.

She stepped down and into the water, her elbows pressed tightly to her body, her heart banging in her chest. She walked a little to where Eddie was, until the water reached her knees. She took a sharp breath. She was afraid of what lay underneath, a sudden yank of current – as gentle now as an underwater breeze, the muddy, gloopy sand. But what if she was sucked in. She remembered a girl who had been caught in a whirlpool. Up at Toco.

Eddie took her hand.

'I thought a body would float but it doesn't. The lungs fill with water and it sinks. Until it's rotten enough to come back up. Did you know that about drowning?'

She searched his face. 'It's only the poisons that push a body back up to the surface. That's what they said about my father. He didn't look like my father any more. Fish come and eat the eyes. It's not how you imagine.'

'You're not going to drown, Ada. You're going to swim.'

He lowered her gently into the water. She kept looking at him, and he wanted her to keep looking at him. He let her feel the water up to her waist, and then a little deeper.

'It's okay,' he said. 'We can stop any time you want.' Then he said, 'How about if I carry you?'

He took Ada in his arms, and lifted her through the soft current to the other side.

'How's that?'

'Better.'

For a while Ada sat on the bank. Eddie smoked a cigarette. The sun was directly over them, the middle of the day.

'I have an idea,' Eddie said, 'I'm going to lie you on the water.'

He scooped his hands under Ada's waist and held her up so she lay flat on her stomach like a tray. Ada laughed.

'I feel like a child. Put me down.'

'Use your legs like scissors,' he said, 'let them snip the water.'

She lifted her arm and dragged the water away. Then she did the same with the other arm.

'That's right. Keep going. Keep kicking.'

'Don't let me go.'

She made her way to the other side. Then they turned and came back again, with Eddie holding her, Ada carving out the water, her legs splashing and kicking.

'Again?'

She swam from one side to the other like this. Fifteen feet or so, back and forth. And Ada could remember how she once swam when she was a girl, and she was less afraid.

After twenty minutes or so, Eddie let go, and while he stayed within reach, Ada swam alone. It was astonishing to her that she could remember what to do – the same things she'd learned from Ruth in Bacolet all those years ago.

'See,' he said. 'There's nothing to be scared of, Ada Fernandes.'

Eddie built a small fire and they cooked the pieces of pork she'd brought in ice, seasoned last night – she used thyme from her garden, a little hot pepper, salt. She'd brought bread, saltfish, cucumbers shredded and mixed with mint, a little vinegar and sugar.

They sucked oranges and Ada ate the coconut cake Henrietta had made. Eddie didn't care for cake. They lay in the shade of the sapodilla tree, and she felt the warm ground under her. Eddie reached up and plucked the brown little fruits shaped like eggs, cut them open and dug out the sweet meat.

She climbed back in the water, willingly now, and she swam with Eddie a little further. They swam where rocks were large and the river opened out and she could see the Atlantic. They watched the waves. She took it all in, the fading light, the warmth of the sun, the smell of the dying fire; she looked at Eddie's boyish face, and she felt that all things were possible and impossible.

THIRTY-FIVE

Ada was sleeping when Henrietta came to tell her Ruth was downstairs. She threw water on her face and pulled on a house dress, bare feet, her hair clipped up. She wasn't expecting Ruth.

Henrietta made tea, and clattered it outside to the veranda on a little trolley. The afternoon was still hot.

'You're glowing.' Ruth gave Ada a look. 'How so?'

Ruth was wearing a floral shift dress; it made her look like a box. Her hair was freshly set.

'You look wonderful. You've lost weight. Tell me how. I need to do the same. Gerry teases me; he says I'm getting fat and one day I'll be big as a house. So I tell him he's like his father – an old man.' She rolled her eyes. 'Maybe we're all getting old.'

While Ada poured tea, and cut up almond cake, Ruth wanted to know about the oil wells.

'Gerry says the more they look for oil, the more they find.'

Ruth had heard about the explosion at Apex, the men who'd died.

'Gas,' she said, shaking her head. 'Gerry said it all along.'

Ada wanted to tell Ruth that she'd been to the river; that she'd swum for the first time in twenty-five years, gone in and out of the water. She wanted to tell her about Eddie, to say his name aloud – Eddie, Eddie, Eddie.

Then, as if she knew something, Ruth started talking about Ella Singh. She reminded Ada of the parrot who revealed Ella's affair with Arthur to his wife. Now she described how Ella had come to the Brown's house where Arthur and his wife were having dinner. It was 6.30 in the evening; the maid had just brought soup to the table.

'Next thing, somebody rattling the gate and crying for Arthur.

Ella Singh is outside. She tell the whole neighbourhood how Arthur say he love her, how Arthur make love to her every week and swear he'll leave the marriage, how the wife has a faulty heart, and she frigid as an old woman. Ella was drunk, wearing only her slip, no shoes or panty. She was bawling.'

'Poor woman.'

Ruth made her eyes big. 'Poor woman?'

'What did they do?'

'Arthur gave her a tranquilliser, then he called the madhouse.'

'They took her away?'

'Yes, she's there right now. She will die in there.'

Ada's blood drained to her feet.

'She was in love. He lied to her. Isn't that enough to send a woman mad?'

Ruth pulled a face.

'Ada! It has nothing to do with love. At least for him. She imagined he wanted her. She was deluded.' Then Ruth said, 'Men are like that. They screw you, tell you they love you, then carry on reading the newspaper. You have to be dumb to believe otherwise. Ask your husband. Ask any man. They're all the same.'

Ada pointed her toes, stretched the back of her calves. She felt like getting up and going into the garden. She didn't want to hear any more. This conversation was making her miserable.

'I hope Ella thinks it's worth it, because no one has a good word about her. The whole of San Fernando is buzzing; they'll dine out on this for months.'

Ruth sat back in her chair, and sighed. 'If we're lucky, when we die we'll be punished for our sins, but Ella Singh will be damned. On the steps of hell, she'll regret it.'

'God makes allowances.'

'For some things, yes.'

Then Ada said, 'I never knew you were so judgemental.'

'I'm not judging her; I have an opinion. In my opinion, Ella Singh should burn in hell.'

That night, Ada was kept awake by her troubled thoughts. She heard Tito come to bed around midnight. She fell asleep when a bird started singing outside her bedroom window. The bird was blue and grey and its song was dull, repetitive. She woke before lunch to find the feeling of dread still over her. Her father would have called it a malaise of the soul, a flagging loss of hope in God.

She spent most of the day in bed. By the time Tito came home in the late afternoon, Ada hadn't long been dressed.

'Are you all right, darling?'

'I'm exhausted. Does my skin look yellow?'

'Not so much.'

Had Ada forgotten, they must pick up Flora and take her to meet her new horse? Today, the mare was officially registered in Flora's name. They had special dispensation to take her out of school. It was the last thing Ada felt like doing. But she put on lipstick, comfortable shoes, and teased her hair. It wouldn't take long. She wanted to see her daughter.

Flora scrambled over her mother into the car, and squeezed in next to her father. She smelled of guavas and of outside – heat, sweat. One of her teachers had brought in a crate of guavas; all afternoon the girls made jam to send for the lepers. If Flora never saw another guava she'd be glad.

'Where we going? Somewhere far?'

'Not far at all,' Tito said, revving the engine. 'Close your eyes.'

They drove back up to the Savannah, and circled around the west side. A cool breeze came into the car, and with it the sound of a brass band playing under the trees. Tito slowed down and found a place to park.

'Why we here?'

'Stop peeking.'

Tito covered his daughter's eyes, and guided Flora across the grass. In her green gingham dress and white ankle socks, her limbs were brown and long.

'Mama, tell me! I can't bear it.'

Ada followed, enjoying her daughter's giddiness. People were walking with their children, some with their dogs. Young lovers held hands. Life was going on. It occurred to Ada that this was happening every day. The last few weeks she had been oblivious. She'd thought only of Eddie. Her life had become reduced; she'd been living in the shadows. It was starting to make her feel like an outsider.

The fenced-off area held a small ring, with jump logs; there were troughs for grain and water. A patch of longer grass for grazing.

Tito stood Flora away from where her young horse was tied. 'Now you can look.'

Flora opened her eyes.

The horse was tall, its legs gangly and awkward. Its shining coat was red; it had a red mane, a thick red shaggy tail.

Flora gasped, covered her mouth with her hand.

'Daddy! Ma-mah!'

'She's a Tennessee Walker,' Tito said. 'Look at her eyes. They're like yours; they know things.'

She reached up to stroke the top of the mare's head. Its ears were strong-looking, the bulge of its cheek firm and coppery.

Tito gave her an apple cut in two halves. 'Here, give her this.'

She put out her hand, holding the green-skinned apple, and the horse lapped it away with its huge pink tongue. Flora started to laugh, wiped the spit on her school dress.

Ada stood back, watched her daughter. Light shone on her bobbed dark hair; her neck exposed, a light brown stem. She wanted things for Flora. She wanted her to be happy, confident; to reach for great things. Things apart from love.

Tito drew Ada towards him; put his arms around his wife and daughter.

'Look at my beauties.' Then softly to Ada, 'Don't be sad, my darling. This too will pass.'

At home, that evening, Tito came upstairs early. He lay down beside Ada, tilted her face towards him. She'd been lying in her slip without a cover, trying to cool down. There was no breeze; the world was still. He nudged himself towards her, ran his finger along her cheek, running it down her neck; he traced the line of her left clavicle. He leaned in and softly kissed her lips.

Ada wanted to turn away. Everything in her recoiled. Tito's face was fattish and shining. She told herself that she must try, and when he kissed her again, she closed her eyes and remembered that she cared for him.

'Come, my Ada.'

She allowed herself to go with it, to open herself to him.

'Yes, darling,' he mumbled. 'Yes, my Ada, yes.'

On the hillside, the Abbey of Our Lady of Exile was beautiful to Ada. Eddie parked by a tree with bark like flaking skin. He walked up the stony path towards the white church and she followed. Her shoes were slippery; she should have worn flat shoes. What was she thinking? She watched Eddie, so familiar to her now: rolled-up sleeves, the tanned forearms, the triangle of his back. She hadn't told him about Ruth, and the things she'd said. She hadn't told him about Tito, and how he'd come to lie with her.

Our Lady was pale. Some of the gold of her crown had worn away. Her gown was a familiar blue, her lips the colour of roses. Her fingers tapered, nails defined and short. She had a dreamy look in her eyes as if she had glimpsed something wondrous: the face of love. Was there such a thing? From the front of the church, came the deep and comforting voices of the priests singing the liturgy. There were very few people there. Ada took her place in the pew, got on her knees and closed her eyes. She felt a little space open up inside her, and through this small space tears came.

She found Eddie outside under the flamboyant tree, its flowers like sprays of blood. He was smoking a cigarette, looking out at the central hills; the land was a patched-up sheet.

'I want you to leave Kushi,' she said. 'I don't feel good about it.'

He glanced at her, surprised.

'How much money do you need? Haven't you made enough? Is that all you men think of – how much money you can make?'

THIRTY-SIX

While Ada tried to persuade Eddie to quit, Tito was determined to keep going for as long as they were able. He'd heard talk of Trinidad Leaseholds making a generous offer to Chatterjee by the end of the year. He thought that they should have another two or three derricks operating at once. Despite what had happened to Macleod, they should increase production, not reduce it. Hire more men. Why not? If rumours were true that Macleod was closing down the Apex site, it was possible he might sell them some equipment cheap. He'd want to recoup his losses. Apex would demand it. He would talk to Eddie when he was back from Barbados.

Tito was thinking about this as he disembarked from the boat in Bridgetown harbour around 5 pm. He had been anxious since the morning. On the boat, he had felt nauseous, a fullness in his chest. He wasn't sure why; there was nothing for him to be concerned about. He had made thousands of dollars on the last well. Alfie told him Fernandes/Wade Holdings were making more money than any of the local oil companies. The stores were thriving. But that morning, as he stood on the upper deck, beneath the yellow awning and felt the breeze against his face, he felt wretched. He took a shot of rum in the Pursers bar, ate some dry bread. He was feverish, a little weak. He undid the top button of his shirt.

He was feeling better now, as he took a taxi into the shopping district. The store would be open until late. He hadn't told them he was coming, he preferred to keep them on their toes. He wondered how long he could keep this up. He was getting tired of these long trips; he preferred to stay at home.

The shop was busy. Mothers with their children, young

women wearing heels and well groomed, stood about the make-up counter. Downstairs was an ice cream bar – something Ada suggested – to keep children occupied and happy while their mother's browsed. He liked the way his wife thought of these things. Upstairs – where they sold sheets and towels, rugs, ornaments, crockery – was busy with housewives, well heeled, keen to see the new Christmas delivery from London. He checked the refrigerated fruits, the fresh produce – peaches and pears and apples, some of which were looking soft and overripe. Then he went into the office to speak to Raul.

'Mother sent you this.'

Tito threw his brother a small package – peppermint, tamarind balls, tulum.

Though handsome, tanned, Raul looked tired, battered. He wore a white suit, a white shirt.

'Irene said you took off for a few days. You don't have to say where, but next time, let her know.'

'Tito,' Raul said, opening the parcel. 'If I'm away, Irene steps in. She's capable.'

'Don't vanish without telling her. You should let her know.'

Raul had been wondering whether to tell his brother by letter, or telephone, or when he next saw him, that he'd heard Ada had been seen in Rattan's Hotel with his business partner. Irritated by Tito's remonstrations, Raul was about to counter with this news, but the moment passed as Irene came in with a tray of glasses and a jug of sorrel juice.

Tito showed Raul the latest catalogue: a collection of wooden toys arriving any day from America, train sets, porcelain dolls, building blocks. He'd ordered a selection of perfumes, soaps, cosmetics, and costume jewellery. He stayed for a while to talk through the figures, update Raul on the recent audit. He wanted to discuss Raul's plans for the upcoming holidays. Sales in the new year.

After an hour or so, Raul stood up. 'Where shall we go for dinner?' He ran his hand over his hair. He'd heard of a new restaurant/club owned by Gary Cooper, the Hollywood film star. A live band was playing later. Members only. He could get them in.

'Maybe tomorrow night. I'm not feeling up to it.'

Tito couldn't wait to leave the store and get to his hotel.

He took dinner alone. There was a party in the hotel bar and he was bothered by the noise. He sat outside where he could watch the frothy sea. This was his favourite hotel, 200 rooms, exquisitely designed by a New York interior specialist, furniture from France, and soft pastel walls, Persian rugs on marble floors, hot running water, four-poster beds. He wished that Ada was with him. In the hotel store, he found her a linen trio for her dressing table, embroidered with pineapples and tiny palm trees.

Later, that night, he felt worse. He lay on his bed and clutched his stomach. An acute ache in his abdomen. Indigestion? Or was it higher, the heart? Was his heart in trouble? He knew the signs; he thought it could be so.

He slept badly and at some late hour he threw up his creamy shrimp dinner. He felt relieved to be rid of it. He could call the hotel doctor, but decided against it. If he could sleep, then he would be okay. He kept the shutters closed, and slept until 9.30 am. By the time he was dressed, he had missed breakfast, so he drank a cup of black tea with sugar.

Rather than spend another night away, Tito decided that he would leave for Trinidad on the earlier boat. He wanted to get home. Tomorrow he would see his doctor. Instead of passing by at the store en-route, he decided to take a taxi straight to the port. He would call when he reached home. He felt a sense of urgency about getting back to Trinidad. He wondered if he should telephone Ada and let her know that he wasn't feeling well. He didn't want to worry her.

Once on the boat, he felt more like himself. The sea was calmer on the return journey. He lay down on a bench, sat up when the waves swelled and then he felt sick. A steward asked if he could help him with anything; Tito told him he had never been a good sailor.

He was relieved to arrive in Port of Spain, to see the familiar sight of the docks, the tall clock tower in the evening light. He had a sudden memory of his mother and father greeting him at the same docks, when he was a boy returning from boarding school. His mother neat as a doll, his father dressed in white, wearing a biscuit hat.

He disembarked and found his way to the taxi stand. The savannah was dark green, and its trees were full; the hills behind were washed and new. The sight of the savannah affected Tito deeply. Today its beauty was a much needed tonic. He would call in to the office in Frederick Street, before heading home to Ada. Tito felt better; he was back where he belonged in his beloved Trinidad.

THIRTY-SEVEN

They were finished. Humidity was high, the air thick with it. Ada's hair was a nest of clips and pins. She would need to put it up, do something.

She had felt as if Eddie had reached the end of her but now his cock was shrunk and purple, like something she might find in the sea, an anemone.

'When you're away from me, do you miss me?'

Eddie put his face close to hers.

'Yes.'

'You told me you never miss anyone. Remember?'

Ada looked up at the ceiling. They lay side by side. The fan was spinning, the lace drapes fluttering. She preferred it here at the Ice House Hotel. From the window she could see the square.

Eddie said, 'You could stay here tonight. He's away.'

He sat up. He fiddled with his lighter – a slick little gold lighter that Ada had given him with a semi automatic starter, his initials engraved on the side in italics. It was called a banjo, and the banjo was refusing to play. It probably needed gas. When she left, he would follow her downstairs to the bar for matches. The bartender was a pretty Venezuelan in her mid-forties called Maria, of whom Ada was jealous.

Ada pulled up the sheet. 'Sometimes when I look at you, I feel as if I see you – the real you.'

Eddie leaned on his elbow, watching her thick mouth.

'Mostly people don't see each other anymore. Years go by and we don't see one another. It's the thing that makes us die.'

A fly buzzed against the window. She was not herself. He knew it as soon as she arrived; she'd seemed agitated. But when he'd asked her, she said it was nothing.

236

Then she said, 'I look at Tito and I wonder if I'm waiting for him to die. Is that what I have to do?'

Eddie didn't answer.

She sat up and swung her legs over the side of the bed. He sat up, drew back the sheet. He slewed back a mouthful of rum. He wanted to tell Ada about Tito coming to see him. It had been playing on his mind over and over.

'In Beaumont, I had a guy I worked for called Walter. Walter's wife was sleeping with his foreman. When Walter found them together, he took a gun and shot the man.'

'Tito wouldn't shoot you, Eddie.'

'He might. Or he might kill himself.'

'Why would he do that? He wouldn't take his own life.'

Ada pulled Eddie towards her and kissed him hard on the mouth. She pushed her hand through his thick hair. She wanted to cry, she didn't know why. Perhaps she should go now. Henrietta would be expecting her. 'I can see you in the morning. He's not back until tomorrow evening.'

Eddie pulled on his trousers, buttoned his shirt. He followed Ada out of the room and into the corridor. Ada held herself steady on the mahogany bannister, carved with birds and flowers.

The bar was busy, a small group of men was playing poker, the piano was dreamy – 'If the Lady Loves'. The restaurant was famous for its Parisian chef; a pork pâté presented in a pig's head. The chandelier was huge, glittery. A far cry from Rattans.

She would usually go out the side door, but today, preoccupied by her thoughts, Ada clopped out of the front door into the street and the soft evening light. Eddie followed her, wary of meeting someone they knew. But it was Sunday; the street was quiet. She stood on the corner looking for a taxi. She was noticeable: her heels, her dress, her dark hair.

'Ada. Call Henrietta. Tell her you'll be home in the morning.'

Tears ran down her cheeks.

'It's all hard, isn't it. It's all very hard. You, me, Tito. I look for answers and there are none.' Then she said, 'You know how much I love you.'

A cab was turning into the street and she put out her hand. She didn't realise it was occupied. She didn't see Tito.

237

But Tito saw Ada talking to Eddie by the hotel entrance, and his first thought was to ask the driver to pull over next to them. They could have an early dinner together, a drink at the Queens Park Hotel. But Eddie and Ada looked as if they were having a serious discussion about something; he couldn't imagine what. His wife looked upset. Then he saw Eddie put his arm around Ada to comfort her. He realised that this was something he wasn't meant to see. Whatever they were discussing was private.

The driver said, 'Here?'

'No,' Tito said, his face burning. 'Keep going, keep on. Slowly.'

He looked back at the two people outside the hotel, and he saw Eddie take Ada's hand and pull her inside The Ice House Hotel, their bodies intimate as snakes, and he felt in that moment his whole life unravel, the floor of his stomach open like a trap door, a terrific pain to his heart like the blow from an axe. In a voice he didn't recognise, Tito told the driver to stop as soon as he turned the corner. As the car turned into Frederick Street, Tito hurled himself out, and threw up on the sidewalk.

His forehead was soaked, his complexion yellow. His whole body was trembling. He looked around at this street he had known all his life, at the shop fronts, the tram lines, the clean wooden lines of the buildings, and it all looked the same. He told the driver to give him a few minutes. He stayed on the sidewalk, his hands pressed into his waist, as if somehow holding his body together.

After a minute or two, a thought came to him. He must gather himself. This situation was not new. He had stomached it before. He had lived through something similar when he was a young man. He must find out what was true and what was not true. Then he would know what to do.

By the time Ada reached home it was evening. She didn't expect to see the lights on upstairs. Tito was sitting in the dark living room; she switched on the overhead lamp. Startled, she said, 'Tito. What are you doing?'

'You're surprised to see me?'

'Yes,' she said. 'I thought you were coming home tomorrow.'

'Where were you?'

She'd been for a walk after a long day stuck in the house. She needed to go to the bathroom. Ada quickly climbed the stairs, her heart beating quickly like a little bird's.

She didn't think to ask Tito why he had come home early.

THIRTY-EIGHT

Eddie was glad to escape down to La Brea where a tanker had arrived from Boston. The American crew were bothered by the heat, sandflies, and the sea coming in through the Bocas had been rough. Eddie brought some men from the village to help, ferried them down to the jetty. It took the whole day to shift the barrels and the men worked hard.

After a few hours, they were loaded up with 80,000 barrels of oil and headed for the return trip. The oil was destined, under a contract worth half a million dollars, to Beacon Oil who had a refinery in New Jersey. Tito had secured the deal, the first of its kind in Trinidad. There were moments like these when Eddie was astonished by his good fortune. How did it happen? How did he get here?

On the way home, Eddie stopped by at the post office. A letter from Kathryn. She thanked him for the money. Little Edith has started speaking, putting sentences together. He ought to visit, Kathryn said, before she's wearing lipstick and attending dinner dances. Or perhaps they could come there. At once, Eddie sent a return telegram telling Kathryn that he would be there in time to catch the cherry blossom he'd heard so much about. 'I want to meet my daughter more than you could know. You were right about the darkest skies. See you in the Spring.' An escape plan, perhaps, in case everything went wrong.

Back at the field, Long and King were sitting outside on the steps. The estate was quiet. Chatterjee had taken his family to Rio Claro. They wouldn't be back until tomorrow.

There were loose clouds floating and Eddie wondered if they were a sign of rain coming in. He saw the men were subdued.

Horatio had come back to the site with news of an accident in Mayaro. Two men were wounded when a derrick collapsed like a tower of sticks. Eddie already knew, he'd heard about it. He hadn't planned on mentioning it to anyone. They'd had enough bad news.

Callaghan filled him in. 'They were drilling and got stuck around 500 feet. Larry was pulling the pipe when the derrick fell. Carlos, the other driller who'd just walked onto the rig floor to take up his shift, was clunked by one of the girders.'

Eddie knew Carlos. A popular, competent driller, with twenty years in the business. He'd asked him to come and work with him when they first started out. He'd fathered a couple children in the village. It was easy to spot them by their green eyes. Carlos was good-looking; he had an effect on women.

'How'd it happen?'

'Who knows. No structural weakness, no loose or missing bolts, or missing girders. It seems like the pull on the stuck pipe, in trying to jerk it loose, was greater than the derrick could stand. A fluke'

'It's all a fluke, eh, Callaghan. What can you do. You go with it, ride it out.'

'I drove down there. It was a mess. Carlos still there, his body busted up, and waiting for the doctor. He was speaking in Spanish. Laughing one minute, then shouting.' Then Callaghan said, his eyes moist, 'You see some things in this business. You see some goddam things.'

But this wasn't the only news. In Fyzabad, a fire started when a flame jumped from a boiler into a flowing well. The fire followed the oil into the river and fried up fish and caimans.

'Vultures came from as far away as Port of Spain. You hear that, Eddie? Vultures flew from Port of Spain to peck at the cooked carcasses.'

The mood that night was muted; the men seemed unsettled. Horatio was quiet, picking his way through a hill of screws rotten with rust.

Eddie drove to the parlour in the village and bought a crate of cold beers.

It was a strange atmosphere. Grace spoke to him; she warned him of unrest.

'This last well. They frighten – what happen at Apex happen here, too.'

He told the men to get some sleep, tomorrow was another day, and it was going to be a long day. Just because this had happened to someone else, someone they knew, it didn't mean it would happen to them.

'I believe in you all,' Eddie said, 'and I believe we'll get this job done safely. We have one more well. That's it. Now tonight, say a prayer for Carlos, then let it go. Don't think about it anymore. God has his plans. And we have our plans.'

THIRTY-NINE

The sun threw a pale light around the land; it seeped through the trees, and the air was cool enough for warm clothes. A sharp cry from above, a corn bird perhaps. He'd noticed the woven nests hanging like brown bells in the mahogany trees on the way up to the house. Eddie had always liked this time of year, the Christmas breeze. The thick heat of the last few months had ended; everyone stopped complaining about the heat. In the evenings he'd been reaching for a sweater, especially here in the forest. It made him think of Texas, the start of fall. He took a cup of coffee and wandered outside, smoked a cigarette. Some of the men were sitting on the steps eating fried eggs and fried bakes.

Two derricks reached up to the morning sky, their criss-cross patterns like a tower of bones; he saw smoke coming from the steam room, puffing out, and the storage tanks, the flat roof of the mess. His truck was parked up, two dogs were sleeping in the tray. Trinket had found a friend, and Callaghan called him Twinkle because of the sheen of his coat.

Grace had been there since dawn. She brought a bag of grapefruit from her father's yard. She was wearing a jacket, rubbing her hands together.

'It cold this morning, sir. The cold wake me up. You see how cold it is, just like in New York. I hear New York real cold.'

'You've no idea, Grace. Texas was so cold the river froze over. You could walk on it. Icicles hung from the roof beams, long like me, and they hung like spears of glass. It's so cold you can't breathe. Your toes go black and fall off.'

She shuddered. 'Not me. I never want to feel cold like that. This plenty cold enough.'

He'd seen it this morning, the lilac, misty light he loved. He had come full circle, that first trip he'd made to Kushi almost a year ago now, and he was already thinking ahead to a time when he would be away from here. He thought of Ada. He thought of Tito that night in the parlour; how Tito had thanked him, and how ashamed he'd felt.

Eddie put on his work boots and made his way down the steps, across the dusty ground to the meeting house where Callaghan was fixing his braces. They needed to get moving today; he had felt things changing on well number 3. Yesterday, around 5 pm, they were at 400 feet when he thought there might be signs of oil coming through, then they'd hit rock and broken the bit. They had to pull out the string, attach a new fish-tail.

Callaghan said maybe they could wait until later in the morning when the light was up. The generator was giving trouble; it was difficult to see. But Eddie told them, 'Lower it back in now and start over. No time to lose.' The last few days, Eddie had felt a sense of urgency. He knew the others felt it, too.

Horatio had taken the part to Two-Weeks. The blacksmith shaped the broken bit on a charcoal forge and used an oilfired oven to make it like new. If it happened again, they could fix it again. The earth was full of stones and rock.

Now Callaghan looked at the mud, the thick brown clump from the core. He smelled it, licked it, and was confident. 'Right near the surface. Under the skin. We'll hit it later today, I'm sure of it. I have a good feeling.'

Eddie said, 'I trust you, Callie.'

It was a glorious day. The air was dry, the sky as blue as he'd seen it; there were no signs of cloud.

Around 10 am Horatio spotted white water starting to bubble out of the well, and he called out to Callaghan. Callaghan stood back from the drill pipe.

'Look what I told you. Look what's happening here.'

They set the conductor string; the men lifted and mounted the blowout preventer on top of the casing. Everyone was calm, and they knew what to do.

Grace said, and her voice was cheery, 'I pray last night the well come today. And when it come, all will be well.'

'If we don't see oil by the end of the day, my name's not Michael Callaghan.'

Chatterjee hovered by the steam room, close enough to the path in case of a blowout. Sita was up at the house.

Malaki kept walking around the rig, and checking the well. He didn't want to miss the first sight of oil. Mercy said he would make himself dizzy.

Eddie put in a call to Tito. If he wanted to see a well come in, this was a good a time as any.

'There's no guarantees, but I expect it will be in some time early evening.'

'Why don't I come meet you for lunch at The Paramount. Get some champagne on ice. I can be there for 3 pm.' Then Tito said, 'I'll try to persuade Ada to come. She needs cheering up.'

Ada had been feeling anxious; Tito was not himself. Since his return from Bridgetown, he was bad tempered, distant. When she asked what was wrong, he told her there were things on his mind.

'Can I do anything?'

'No.'

'Did something happen in Barbados? Do you need to see a doctor?'

That night he slept in the spare room. In the morning he took his breakfast early and left for the store. She went through his pockets, checked his small suitcase, but there was nothing unusual. She could only guess that he had heard something. But if he had, then why hadn't he confronted her?

He came home at lunchtime, something he rarely did. As if he wanted to catch her out. He asked her to sit with him at the table. But when she joined him in her usual place, Tito carried on reading his newspaper. Eventually, to make conversation, Ada asked if there was news on the well at Kushi.

'You like to hear about Kushi, Ada?'

He jumped up from the table, knocked his dinner plate on the floor. The shatter of porcelain went through her like an electric current. Henrietta brought a broom but Tito sent her away.

'You like news of Kushi, eh? That's what you want. Is that what you care about these days?'

245

'No, I don't care. I'm glad to hear good news, yes. But I don't care about it. Why would I care about it? It means nothing to me.'

Tito looked at her as if he hated her. Then he went into the hallway; she heard the front door slam. Henrietta came to Ada in the dining room, her face full of questions. She had never known Tito to raise his voice. She swept up the broken crockery, hovered by the door.

'Henrietta, you can leave now.'

Upstairs, Ada closed the shutters and lay on her bed relieved to be alone. She thought about asking Flora to come home, to see if she could lighten up her father. Flora had a way of lifting Tito. But what if Tito started to behave as he did at lunch. She decided to wait; she would try to talk to him that evening.

She had waited for Tito to arrive home from work. She waited and waited, and the sun fell away. She took up a book and sat in the drawing room watching the breeze blow out the lace curtains. She ate dinner alone. Tito didn't come home until after midnight, and by then she was in a light sleep. She had no idea where he had been. He clonked along the passageway, opened the door to their bedroom. She could feel him standing there, looking at her. She heard him kick off his shoes; she heard the creak of the boards as he walked along the passageway to the spare room.

Tomorrow was a new day, she would hope for it to be different.

The telephone rang. It was Tito calling from the store. A well was due to come in at Kushi. He was heading to San Fernando to meet Eddie for late lunch, and he wanted her to join him. He sounded more like himself. He wanted her to dress up. Look her best. They could make a day of it. Invite Ruth and her family to see the well come in, too.

'Are you sure you want me to come?'

'Why not? Why wouldn't I?'

It was 11.00 am.

Relieved, she picked out a cream silk dress. She put a little bow in her hair to keep it back from her face. She clipped on earrings, then fastened her new white shoes, a smaller heel. She took care with her make up: raspberry blush strong on her cheek bones, kohl around her eyes, dark lips. She took her shawl, just in case; sprayed her neck in the neroli scent she knew that Eddie liked.

Before she left, Ada went to the kitchen where Henrietta was peeling cassava. The fan was spinning; the door was open onto the garden. Ada wished it was an ordinary day and she could go outside and water the orchids.

'I'm sorry about yesterday. Everything will settle down.'

Henrietta tilted her head, as if looking at Ada from a different angle. She didn't believe her; she knew something bad had happened.

'Is alright, Miss Ada. Tomorrow another day.'

Tito picked up Ada and drove in silence across the park to Mrs Fernandes's house.

She had just finished eating breakfast, Alfie Mendes was visiting, and he was sipping a cup of coffee. The radio was playing and the house smelled of salted fish, doors flung open to the bright yard. Tito turned down the volume, and Ada could see that her mother-in-law was irritated.

'Come, Mother. Come and see it. Alfie, you should come, too.'

Alfie said, 'Maybe I will. I could bring my wife. Or maybe I could drive your mother in my car.'

'You know how tired you feel when you old like me, Tito? One day you will know and then you will feel bad for your old mother.'

'But how often will you see something like this? The roads are better now; it won't take so long. We have champagne in the trunk. It's your last chance. There won't be another well at Kushi.'

Mrs Fernandes looked at the ceiling; she was weighing it up in her mind. Then she got up and smoothed her dress. 'I don't want to be late back, you understand.'

A bird flew from the veranda into the dining room. Its black wings darted, flying hard towards the shutters. Mrs Fernandes threw up her arms. 'Get the bird out, Tito. I can't stand birds flying into my house. Call the damn maid.' Tito called out at the back of the house, and the housekeeper came out.

'I'll come,' Mrs Fernandes said, 'Let's all go. Anything to get out the house. We will go with you in your car, Tito.'

Ada gazed out into the vast sky as they drove south. She was glad of her shawl. The air was cool. December, her favourite month. In the back of the car, Alfie Mendes and Mrs Fernandes sat together. Alfie said it had been a long time since he'd been on an adventure. But maybe it was time he saw with his own eyes this Kushi estate.

'You proved me wrong, Tito,' he said. 'It's not often that happens.'

Ada said, 'Tito, when we get there, we'll be able to see the oil? I want to get close to it. I've never seen it up close.'

Alfie said, 'It probably looks like the pitch lake. You went there, Ada? You went to La Brea?'

While he drove, Tito thought about Ada and Eddie – the same thoughts he'd been fighting with these last few days. Things were fitting together in his mind – how long had it been going on? When did it start? How often did they see one another? Had Eddie had been to his house while he was in Barbados? Did they meet at the hotel? He must ask Henrietta. When did they meet? How often? Is it possible he was wrong? He would know today when he saw them together. The last few days had been the worst he could remember. He thought of how Eddie had come into his life – taken his money, his hospitality, his friendship. His wife. His life. All these years of loving her, his beloved Ada. Had it meant nothing to her?

'What is it, Tito, are you unwell?'

Without realising he was driving faster, barely aware of the road. It was just after Gasparillo when he saw something, twisted the wheel and swerved the car, mounted the grassy verge, throwing the frightened passengers back into their seats.

Mrs Fernandes called out, 'In the name of God.'

He reversed, and then he stopped the car. Tito got out and looked into the bush. What was it? Did he really see something? Was it a cow? Or a goat. It was bigger than a goat. A horse. Perhaps it was nothing. Perhaps he was losing his mind.

'Are you alright?' Ada called from the car.

Alfie went over to where Tito was standing, peering into the bush. He put his arm around his shoulder; Tito allowed himself to be comforted. He pressed the heels of his hands into his eyes.

'Maybe you're tired. I have some pills, take down your blood pressure. You want some? I can give you. They're easy to swallow.'

Tito shook his head, as if to shake something off. 'No,' he said, and started back to the car. 'It's nothing. I thought I saw something, but whatever it was, it's gone.'

'This was a mistake, coming all this way.' Mrs Fernandes's voice was hard. 'I should have listened to myself.'

FORTY

Eddie bathed out the back, and he was glad of the blue soap that cut through the dirt and mud. Up the hill, he could hear the men pulling in the string; they began to dismantle the lines of pipe and he knew this would take some time. He felt proud of his men, and how far they'd come. He told Callaghan to let him know if there was more news. He'd be at the Paramount; he could be back on site in 45 minutes.

Eddie drove with the roof down towards San Fernando. He passed a man with a cart filled with coconuts, pulled along by a water buffalo. The man looked familiar. Eddie waved and then overtook the cart, slowly so not to startle the beast, speeding up as he headed on towards San Fernando Hill. The road was empty and on the dial he hit 75 miles per hour.

They were already seated by the window when Eddie arrived.

Mrs Fernandes was sitting next to Alfie, fanning herself with a menu. When she saw Eddie, she primped her hair with her fingers. Though his khaki shirt was creased and marked, he looked handsome, tanned. He took up her mottled hand.

'Mrs Fernandes,' he said.

Then Eddie lightly kissed Ada's cheek. He wondered if anything showed in his eyes.

Tito got up, shook his hand.

'A movie star, eh, Eddie? My wife is like a movie star.'

There was music playing; the sounds of a small band of musicians in the lobby carried through to the restaurant. The familiar melody was catchy and cheery. Ada was glad of it.

'You see her feet,' and Tito pointed down to Ada's legs, crossed at the ankle, 'they start itching when she wants to dance. Ada missed her calling.'

'Sometimes I think I missed my whole life,' Ada said.

'Your life is exactly as it should be, darling.' Tito called over the waiter. 'Let's have some drinks.'

'So, Eddie, another well is about to pop,' Alfie said. 'You've had luck on your side. They say luck is always against a man who depends on it. Seems like you did it on your own terms. Takes some skill.'

'Something like that, sir. I have a strong team.'

On the table, anthuriums were pink and shaped like tonsils. Ada had never liked them.

Then Alfie said, 'Once Kushi is sold, where are you headed? America, Europe?'

'We'll see. There's oil showing up in Guiana.'

It was strange to hear Eddie talking like this. Ada didn't like it. She looked outside at the fruit trees, full and lush after the rains.

Tito said, 'You'll go and see your lady friend, Kathryn?'

Eddie looked surprised at the mention of Kathryn's name.

'I'll see my daughter. Her mother will no doubt be there.'

'Here's to that,' Tito said, and raised his glass.

Mrs Fernandes suggested they eat something before she passed out.

Tito ordered a large platter of seafood, crabs seasoned with garlic, sourdough rolls, bouillabaisse. Side dishes of sweet potatoes and buttered beans with pumpkin. When the champagne was finished, Tito ordered another bottle.

The waiter brought the chef's signature dish, Pompano en papillote. He plopped the little parcels onto each plate, and gave each diner a small pair of silver scissors to cut it open.

The sack burst, spilling out the seafood smells in a puff of hot smoke.

'Good Lord!' Mrs Fernandes sat back in her seat as the steam left her plate.

Tito called the waiter over and asked for pepper sauce.

'Pepper, sir?' The waiter looked surprised. 'We do not have pepper sauce with this dish. It is well seasoned in the kitchen.'

Tito said, 'I'd like pepper sauce.'

'Sir, I think if you try it you will see it needs no help with seasoning.'

Everyone looked at Tito.

Tito said, 'Why don't you call the manager?'

Eddie looked around. Over the last few months, he had come to know the general manager well.

The maître d' appeared.

'Tito,' his mother said, her voice low and clipped, 'what are you trying to do?'

'Mister Fernandes,' the maître d' said, 'I assure you, the dish does not need further seasoning.' His grinning face looked frozen. 'The dish has been seasoned fit for the gods in our kitchen. Any further seasoning would be a desecration.'

Tito said, 'I don't give a fuck if this dish suits you or it suits the waiter or it suits your cook. We are paying for our lunch, and if I want pepper sauce, then I shall have it.'

Mrs Fernandes put down her cutlery.

Guests at the next table were staring.

Alfie said, 'I'm sure they'll bring it. Let's not get upset.'

Ada excused herself and got up and went to the bathroom.

While she was gone, Eddie was called away from the table by the concierge. There was an urgent phone call at the desk. Callaghan was calling to let Eddie know that the well would likely come in within the next couple hours.

Eddie excused himself from the lunch; he must go, he said, he would see them at the field in a while. He hoped everyone would come.

'We can carry on the party,' Tito said, sounding a little drunk by now.

Ada insisted that they stop by at Ruth's house. At first Tito said no, there wasn't time. But Ada reminded him that he had suggested it. She called up to the veranda. 'Ruth! Ruth!' She left her mother-in-law, Alfie and Tito waiting outside in the car, and ran up to the first floor.

Inside the tall house, there was soft music, a gathering. Ada had always liked this house, the long wooden table, the satin drapes that hung in the large window; the heavy mahogany furniture. The wooden floors were covered with patterned rugs from Morocco, where Gerry had worked for three years. Ruth was excited to see Ada. She'd arrived just as they'd been wondering if they should play cards. Last night, Arthur, her brother-in-law – a blond and foppish-looking man, who Ada liked at once, had beaten them at every round of poker. Ruth and Gerry were drinking cocktails; the shutters were open out onto the garden where light shone through the trees.

Arthur said, 'I've never seen a well before. Can I come, too?'

'Ruth, bring a blanket, it might be cold. We can sit on the side of the bank and watch from there. We have champagne, and sandwiches in case anyone gets hungry.'

'I'll bring cake,' Ruth said, making her way to the kitchen.

The children wanted to come, but Ruth said it was too late.

Quietly in the hallway, she said to Ada, 'Are you all right? Last time I saw you, you weren't yourself and you were cross with me. Come spend a few days here and we can talk. Or I can come to you. We mustn't argue. There's so few of us left.' She took up Ada's hand and squeezed it.

Ada was glad to have Ruth. She was feeling strange, as if she was travelling with people she didn't know, people who didn't like her. Tito must know something. His eyes were stones. She had never seen him like this. Who could have told him? Had Raul heard something in Barbados? One of his cronies from Rattans? What would she say? She would deny it, just as Eddie had told her. Deny, deny, deny. Until she died. How could he prove it? When she was back in the car, she looked at him, his hands on the steering wheel, his hat pushed down on his head. Tito was not the same man.

Two cars drove slowly through the estate; lights were bright through the trees, and down the rough trail. They parked up near Chatterjee's house, and a line of people, mostly dressed in white, walked down the hill: Tito, Ada, Ruth, Gerry, Arthur and Mrs Fernandes, who held on to Alfie. Tito carried a bottle of champagne in each hand. He would send someone later for the picnic hamper.

They reached the field just in time to hear the bell ring out and see men come running – from the stores, the steam room, shouts from the truck, the top of the hill. Others were running up to the bank. Then a roar, heard as far as the village. The force was so strong under their feet that the ground trembled, and Ada clung to Ruth and Ruth clung to Ada. For a moment Tito forgot his pain, awed by the black tower of oil as it shot up, jetted high over the top of the derrick and headed for the clouds. People shouted, cheered and clapped. Everyone was looking up.

Mrs Fernandes gripped one hand on Alfie's arm, the other on her startled heart. She was sure this was a disaster. How could it not be?

Eddie yelled above the noise, stared up at the sight. He was covered in oil, his face was black. He hooked his arm around Callaghan, kissed the top of his head. 'I knew it, Callie, in my blood and in my bones. You see that feeling,' and he thumped his own chest, 'it's never wrong.'

Callaghan was red-faced and sweaty, keen to close off the well, and get it under control. He called the men to the floor, and signalled to Horatio who was standing near the top, with the derrick man above him. Callaghan twisted the drill pipe.

'Jesus, Eddie,' he yelled and skidded on the sopping floor. '320 feet. It gets better and better.'

Together, Callaghan and Eddie put the stopcock onto the drill pipe while the oil spewed out like black syrup. They tried to cut the flow. Callaghan's strong hands twisted around the slippery valve, and it was difficult to grip, the spray was blasting in their faces, making it almost impossible to turn the valve shut. Eddie called for goggles. They could barely see what they were doing but they knew the shape of the valve and they knew what it should feel like. They worked as if they were part of the same man. It was almost half an hour before they managed to get the oil under control. Relieved, unrecognisable, Eddie had a feeling about this last well. He thought about little Edith. One day he would tell her of the wells in Siparia.

'Let's get something to drink,' Eddie said.

He jumped down and looked for Tito and Ada, and he saw that Tito was looking straight at him. Eddie made his way up the bank, shook Tito's hand, apologised for his filthy palm.

'Another minute and you'd have missed it.'

Tito gave Eddie a cup of champagne, and Eddie drank a little.

He wouldn't have any more; he'd need his wits about him. There would be plenty of time for that later.

'What happens now?'

'We close it off, make sure there's no leaks. These boys know what they're doing.'

'They look so.'

Chatterjee was looking at the oil coming out, checking to see that the men appeared confident. For Chatterjee this was another miracle, and so far so good; there was nothing unusual here, nothing to worry about. He felt relieved, glad the well was coming in as it should, and as it had done before. He'd stay here and make sure it did.

'Sonny,' Eddie said, 'you sure you want to hand this over to Leaseholds?'

'You want me to be like you – with no wife. A man with no wife have no home. He's a gypsy, with half a life.'

'It depends on the wife.'

They shook hands, and Sonny hit Eddie on the back.

Eddie glanced up towards Macleod's office. He thought he saw him, the outline of his hat, as Macleod looked out at the field. He'd heard Macleod was closing down the site. He wasn't sure how true it was, but right now he couldn't see the usual line up of his men and the place had been quiet since the accident. He'd heard that Macleod was there most days, and often late into the night. A mark of respect or decline in hope; Eddie wasn't sure which and he didn't much care.

'Mister Eddie,' Grace said, and showed him her filthy dress.

'It looks like you need a new one, Grace; it looks so.' He took out $20 from his wallet and gave it to her.

Callaghan said, 'No sign of Sita or the boys.'

'They frighten,' Grace said, tucking the money down her dress. 'Frighten of the gas.' She shook her head. 'I tell she, only Apex have gas. It safe here at Kushi.'

Grace was relieved that the well had come in safely. She'd had her doubts, dark thoughts, fears of all that could go wrong. She had kept them to herself.

After a few minutes, they checked the pipe was fully locked off. Eddie told Horatio to get the men to clean up the floor. They all needed to wash off, take turns to rest or eat if they needed to. It had been a long day for some, and it wasn't over yet. Check the generator; make sure the tanks are ready. Make sure the pipes are clear.

'There's some whistling coming from the hole. We'll keep an eye.'

'It's possible there's a little gas still coming out. I can't tell right now.'

Eddie said, 'It's unlikely. But even so, not much. If it was coming, by now it would've blown off the floor.'

'It's sand we have to worry about,' Callaghan said, wiping his face with his sleeve.

Ada tried to see where Eddie was. He was talking to Callaghan by his car, parked up in front of the derrick. She wasn't sure what happened next, but she imagined they'd want to celebrate here on the bank.

The owners of the parlour arrived – Gloria and her husband; they'd heard the noise, and had come to see the oil. They'd closed up the parlour and brought food, carried on bicycles. Everyone was talking about the oil. More were coming from the village. People were standing around, some were sitting on blankets, faces Ada didn't recognise. Tito had the hamper brought from the car, and Grace and Malaki dragged the trestle table out and Mercy helped to lay sandwiches on platters and trays. Eddie came and spoke to Gloria, shook her husband's hand. He wanted to talk to Ada, standing with Ruth, and he was about to go to her when Callaghan called him over.

Apparently, pressure had broken through the steel sealing surfaces of the blowout preventer, oil was leaking out. Initially it came as a trickle. But now sand was firing through with oil and water, and the flow was increasing, gushing out from the growing crack.

It was difficult to get close enough to see exactly what was happening. The sand made a sharp fizzing noise as it was ripping through the metal. For now, they must try to contain the fluids, to stop it getting out, to somehow secure the stop once again.

By now the sky was a light blue; the sun was going quickly.

256

Darkness would soon come. They needed to fix it while there was daylight.

'It's hard to see what's going on. The generator isn't working properly; lights flickering on and off.'

Callaghan said, 'We might need help. Come take a look.'

He jumped up on the derrick floor, a lamp attached to his helmet. Eddie shouted over the noise.

'Let's not panic. There's ways around it. There's ways around everything.'

By now the oil had filled the pit below the derrick, the shallow drain; it was pouring out like a black stream, flowing over the pathway.

'My God,' Ada said, to Ruth, looking at the pit where the oil was making a small black pool. 'Imagine if it keeps on coming out like that. We could drown in it. Isn't it glorious?'

For a while Eddie found a way to turn down the pressure, to reduce the flow. If he could manage it while they found a way to fix the leak, they would be okay. Horatio could bring Two-Weeks, to see if he could do something. But he needed Horatio here. There had to be a way. He needed to think clearly. They needed help.

Chatterjee was suddenly there, his hands on his head. His face was twisted up. He didn't remember the other wells leaking like this.

'What's this, Eddie?' he nodded at the pool of oil. 'It all going to waste? We losing oil? We losing money? What to do?'

It was obvious that it wouldn't be long before the oil filled the pit and then it would need somewhere else to go.

Eddie said, 'Let's get the men to dig a trench, just in case; let the oil go in there for now.'

Chatterjee would go up to the village to pick up lamps and spades. He'd be back as soon as he could. They must start soon.

Charles Macleod had been on site for most of the day. Around midday he left for San Fernando, to pick up something to eat. He'd spoken to Apex from the telephone at the post office about shutting down the camp. He'd tried to persuade them to keep the operation running for another six months. Through the hissing line, they were emphatic; the site would shut in three weeks.

Macleod then stopped off at home where his wife was anxiously picking at her cheeks, a new unappealing habit. Her face was covered in small red marks where she had broken through the skin. She was having early labour pains. Ruby was mopping up her waters from the bedroom floor. She told him that nothing was likely to happen for a good few hours. He told Elsie he would be back in a while; there were rumours that the well had come in at Kushi and there were problems.

Back in his office on the site, he sat at his desk with a bottle of whisky, rising frequently with his binoculars to see if he could work out what was going on. When he was young on the ships, he'd been a heavy drinker. It was an easy habit to fall in to. He'd stopped when he married Elsie. For years, he didn't go near it. He told himself it was poison. But in the last couple weeks, it had calmed his nerves like nothing else.

In the mornings, he'd been waking suddenly, jolted by pictures he wanted to forget. He thought about the men who'd died. He prayed. He came here to the office for quiet; time to think. He'd written to the wives and mothers of the men, while trying to make sense of it himself. There was no sense or meaning to be found. He blamed himself. He cried. He prayed some more. He told himself that he would know what to do when the shock had subsided. But time was running out.

When Eddie arrived, Macleod wasn't surprised. He put his boots up on the table, leaned back in his chair.

'Mister Wade,' he said. 'You've some nerve.'

Eddie was filthy. His hands were black, his soggy shirt and trousers clung to his body. He took off his hat, pushed back his hair.

'We need a pump, something to help divert the oil. The pressure blew a hole; sand is making it worse.'

Macleod got up, and walked around his desk. He picked up his binoculars. It was impossible to see much, a smudge of light, some activity beyond the fence. The sky was dark, no trace of a moon.

'You can't see from here. Believe me, it's pretty bad.'

Eddie could see he'd been drinking. Macleod looked exhausted, bleary.

258

'It's a good problem to have. You have too much oil. I have too little. In fact, I have none.'

'I can't fix that for you, Charles. I never could. Right now we're in trouble. It took a lot to come here.'

'Well, I have a bulldozer, a strong pump. I have portable lights. I might even have something that could fix the tear in your blowout preventer. I have no men.'

He ran his eyes over Eddie – shiny like ball bearings.

'Even if I did, you know what I'm going to say. I'll say the same thing you said to me. Every time I asked. Every time I suggested we pull together and you came back with the same answer. And you know what that is.' He shook his head, a fake grin that showed his small teeth. With a finger he drew out the letters in the air. 'No.'

Eddie wanted to rush at him.

'What do you want? We can talk tomorrow, when this is over.' Then Eddie said, 'Don't be childish, Charles. We've had enough death round here.'

Trembling now, the blue line throbbing in his forehead, Macleod drained his glass, and pelted it at the wall above Eddie's head. It shattered, its splinters everywhere, hitting Eddie in his hair, down the back of his shirt, tiny shards were sharp on his arms.

'Get the hell out of my office, and get off my land.'

Ada looked around at the site – the visitors on the bank fifty yards or so from the well, sitting now on blankets, the lights from the generator like pearls strung around the derrick, shining down to where Callaghan was working. The flowing oil had filled the mud pit around the base of the derrick.

Ada asked Horatio, 'Where's Eddie?'

'He went by Apex. He'll be back any minute.'

She hadn't seen him go. She looked out for Tito, and he was standing with Alfie, talking intently about something.

Mrs Fernandes had a bench to sit on. A blanket was draped over her legs. She looked fraught. She wanted to go home, but apparently Tito wanted to wait.

Ruth stood with Ada. She drank the cool champagne and it was soothing to her throat. The air was dry and the breeze was chilly.

Then Ada left Ruth, and walked up towards Eddie's bungalow. Grace was there taking out dry, clean clothes for Eddie.

'Mister Chatterjee send for men in the village to help dig out the dam. My son working with them. Malaki. He love Mister Wade.'

'Your son,' Ada said. 'Yes, Eddie told me.' Then she asked, 'Is this how it usually is? Is it always like this? Is it so chaotic?'

'Not so much. Usually they does put on the stopper and the oil stop. Some of it have to come out, but not so much, not like this. This must mean the well real big. Plenty oil. Plenty money.'

There was noise from the hill. Chatterjee returned with shovels, and more men from the village. They would set about digging a dam around the site. At least the oil would have somewhere to run. They could siphon it off into barrels if they needed to. For now they needed to put it somewhere.

Chatterjee was shouting, 'We throwing away money! All of you start now. Dig! Make the trench deep as you can.' He pointed to where they must begin and the men began. Then Arthur and Gerry came, and they, too, took up spades and started to dig. Their white clothes were no longer white.

Gerry said, 'We might as well do our bit.'

Ruth said, 'Oh for a cigarette,' and Ada laughed. She caught sight of Eddie, making his way up now onto the derrick floor. She wanted to go to him.

Callaghan told everyone to stay back. Keep the area clear.

Mercy brought a tray with cups and fresh water to the bottom of the derrick. Callaghan took a drink, and Ada saw a tender look pass between them.

As far as she could tell, Eddie and Callaghan were trying to secure the pipe. Horatio was guiding the oil into the tanks and into the reservoir the men were making.

'We need more men.' Eddie shouted, 'Close off number 2 well. Just a precaution. Close the thing off.'

Tito wanted to know what he could do to help. He asked Callaghan.

'Keep the spectators back. That's the best thing you could do. There's no more shovels; they're doing all they can.'

260

Callaghan pushed his hands through his hair. 'You feel the air, the air feels thick to me. I think there's gas. By God, one single spark and we're all gone.'

A pump started up in one corner of the field to pump the oil from the ditch in the newly dug-out area. For a moment, it seemed as if there was some calm.

Ada's eyes were now used to the dark. Eddie walked along the bank, encouraging the men.

'Horatio, what's that song ? Remind me.'

Horatio started to sing and the men joined in.

Lord, I long to see that morning,
When thy gospel shall abound,
And thy grace get full possession
Of the happy promised ground
And all the borders, all the soil
All the forests, all the oil
Of the great Immanuel's land!

Grace asked Ada, 'Your daughter not here, ma'am?'

'No, Flora's in school. She's at the convent. We'll pick her up tomorrow.'

'I tell Mister Eddie he should bring his daughter here, too. She should come here and see Trinidad. He tell me, he will go see her next year, then bring she back to Trinidad.'

The air was still. Ada was feeling tired, her head thick from champagne. There was silence now; everyone had stopped talking. Ada looked at her husband, he was standing away from the derrick, his foot on the step. Eddie was a shape moving in the darkness, and she could hear his voice.

Meanwhile, men with torchlights strapped to their helmets scoped their way towards the river. They could see where they needed to dig further. Soon the oil would be running into the river.

Horatio told Eddie, the storage tanks were overflowing. The generator had stopped working – the lights were gone. This wasn't good.

Ruth put a handkerchief over her nose. 'Can you smell something. It's a funny eggy smell.' Ada could smell it now, too. She was cold. She saw Grace watching the men on the derrick. Malaki was on the derrick floor holding a torch in each hand. Grace looked worried.

Ada was shivering. She told Ruth she might go back up to the car and get her shawl. 'I was in such a hurry to come and see that I forgot it.'

Ada took a torch and she said to Tito, and it was the last thing she would say to him, 'I won't be long. You keep an eye on Ruth. We don't much like the smell. It's like gas. Maybe we should go soon.'

Ada happened to catch Eddie then, as he turned to look at her. She forgot herself and smiled. She held his eyes for a moment. Then she saw that Tito was standing on the platform watching them.

Callaghan said, 'Jesus, I'm gonna clear the people from here,' and leapt off the derrick to go and tell everyone to move away, go up near the hill. He shouted at the crowd, urged them to take their belongings and move away. The pressure was getting stronger. Gas was coming out in breathy gusts.

Callaghan's face was fraught, and Chatterjee felt suddenly afraid; his bowels wanted to open. He ordered the men to put down their shovels and head off. Sita, Sita. She was up at the house with the boys. He'd seen her when he returned from the village. He'd told them to stay there. He must make sure they were still there. He started to walk quickly now, his blood rushing in his ears, sweat pouring down his face.

'Sitaah! Sitaah!'

Callaghan called out to Tito.

'Maybe you should go up with the others. There's gas coming out like hell. I can't see a damn thing. If I could see I'd know what to do.'

The thought easily came to Tito.

'Your car lights. Throw me your keys.'

Eddie threw Tito his keys. Tito looked at Eddie, and he felt something pass between them as if a clock had stopped and the world had ceased to spin. A starter ignition. A single spark. He saw the pain in Tito's eyes; he saw his humiliation and rage, and he understood it like a fact that Tito knew. Tito had uncovered their affair. And while Tito opened up the door to Eddie's car, slotted the key into the ignition, Eddie wanted to shout, tell him he was so very sorry, that he had never intended to hurt him like this, beg Tito not to do what he was about to do. But it was too late.

The force of the explosion picked up both men and hurled them into the black sky. A brief moment of terror. Eddie was aware of its brightness and roar. He could not see his hands. He could not feel his legs, his feet, his tongue in his mouth. He saw nothing, only white. White. Then gold and green as though the world was turning inside out and he was falling and falling, like a star breaking into a trillion parts, and he said to himself, It's over, It's over. He was not afraid. There was nothing to be afraid of. He could not stop himself from falling, and he said, Help, Help me. And then like a miracle he felt himself lifted up and he was following a high white light ahead and the light feet of women he recognised. It doesn't matter he told himself, it doesn't matter at all, because nothing matters now, not oil, not money, not the car, not Chatterjee, not Tito and what he did to Tito. None of it matters now and none of it ever really mattered and all that mattered was that he go where he was going and follow the white light. While Eddie felt himself spinning away, falling into the sky, Tito saw bursts of colours coming through him, coming from inside his heart and its mighty chambers. He saw along its pathways, stretched and laid out like a highway, his father waiting; he saw there the figures of his ancestors – and he was gladdened by what he saw, and he felt no pain, not for Ada nor for Eddie nor for all he lost, and he knew that what he had done was not right and it was not wrong. He had done what he had to do. It didn't matter now. Nothing mattered. The only thing that mattered was the palomino walking away into a constellation of stars; swishing its tail of white ribbons, and he wanted to follow it. *The air of heaven is that which blows between a horse's ears...*

Horatio kept running with the force of heat behind him now, naked apart from his boots; he glanced back over his shoulder to see a huge balloon of yellow with things falling off it and he kept running. He saw Malaki bent over like a hunchback alight with flame, and Malaki was stumbling towards the river to put out the fire eating him alive. He hurled himself into the water not realising that the water too was soaked with oil and it made a funnel of gold and orange and Malaki was lost inside it. Horatio heard the new blast and he kept going and he ran until he reached Apex, and the safe barricade of their fence, over which he threw himself, and from where he could see the whole field on fire.

Four miles north, Charles Macleod was sitting in his bedroom with his wife. She paced the room, then crouched down on the floor, her head pressed against the wall. She was hot, she said, and she wanted this baby out. Macleod wished the baby would come, for her sake, for his, for all of them. He knew that she was terrified. In her eyes, he'd seen the look of an animal, and he barely recognised her. He hadn't wanted to see her like this. On all fours. Ruby was assisting her, wiping her forehead, and now grappling between his wife's legs, checking the baby's position.

The generator had blown, and they were forced to use candle-light. The shadows would frighten Elsie. He had been outside trying to fix it. Glad of something to do. It was too late to take her to hospital, the doctor would soon be here. For now it was him and Ruby. Their son was staying at a friend's house.

But the first cries of Charles's new daughter were drowned out by the terrific explosion that came from across the fields. He knew at once it was Kushi. He ran outside and stood on the top of his truck. The sky was bright with flames. A huge rolling ball of orange and yellow suspended above the estate. He stared at it in horror.

Horatio told his mother that the last time he saw Mr Wade he was standing by his car fifty feet from the derrick. Tito Fernandes was nearby. He had offered to start the car so Mr Wade could see what was going on. Malaki was trying to help. He shouldn't have been there; he should have gone with the others. His mother told him he was the luckiest man alive. God had saved him. He told her that God had saved others, too.

He'd heard Ada Fernandes was on her way to the house, talking with Sita; she was going to get a shawl from the car. Thank

God she did, Horatio said. The little things you do sometimes change your destiny. But Mr Fernandes' mother had seen it all, poor woman. Just like Grace. She stood wailing on the bank while Malaki's charred body was dragged in pieces from the river. Things a mother should never see. Plenty people were hurt. Burns, hair loss, their clothes blown off in the blast. A young man had been visiting from England. He said he never felt heat like that in his life.

A couple of mornings later, Horatio asked for his cousin to carry him back to the site. The fire was still burning through the cocoa trees. He saw men from Apex carrying away bones in their trucks. He watched them and cried. He'd heard that when Ada Fernandes came back to the site, she lay down on the ground and scratched at it with her fingers like a dog. They found Mr Wade's watch in the mud pit; beside the bones of Tito Fernandes, were two jade earrings. As Horatio walked up to the top of the road, he passed Sonny Chatterjee in his car, his wife beside him, the two boys in the back. He'd waved at Chatterjee, but Chatterjee did not wave back.

FORTY-ONE

The sea is clear sapphire. Her feet are pale and the water is warm as she walks into it. The sand below is gritty with coral and chunks of broken shell.

Ada pushes off and uses her arms to carve through the water. It is shallow here. She dips her face under the surface, feels the cool water as it licks her hair back. It feels good to break through the surface. She does it again, and again. Ahead she can see Flora practising handstands, legs sticking out, leaning, pointed toes.

It is the first time she has been in the sea with her mother. Earlier, Flora insisted on climbing the rocks; they could see the bay where waves are strong as horses.

They've been out here all morning, swimming up and down. They dry off for a while, sit in the shade of the almond trees, take a drink, eat a little coconut cake.

'They don't go anywhere,' Flora says. 'They're in another room. We can visit them at night.'

Last night she dreamed of her father.

'I believe you,' Ada says. She would like to tell her daughter, I lost not one but two. Instead she tilts her face to the sun. These days her body starts to shiver without warning, as if her blood is filled with ice. Dr Shepherd tells her it will pass.

She imagines Eddie is still travelling, looking down where cane grows tall and beautiful, clouds low like thrown cotton. Sometimes she sees him chopping through the sea, or lying beside her in the early hours. There are many things she forgot to tell him.

As if it was yesterday, she pictures her husband in the porch of Eddie's cabin, his legs stretched out, the day they talked of Texas while the sun went down, their hearts alive with new dreams.

Now, nearby, with a long stick, Flora pokes holes in the ground to force out crabs. They are not afraid; their backs are orange, their legs dark red. One large crab stops to pick at a fish scrap, raises a claw like a fork to its mouth. Its eyes are little black bubbles and they looked straight at Ada. The crab scuttles down another hole; Flora peers inside after it; her hair falls around her face.

'They have knees on the sides of their legs; it's why they run like that.'

'Like this,' Flora says, and shimmies along the sand. Her wide smile shows her teeth.

The Bacolet house is exactly as she remembers it – same blue walls, the moonflower vine trailing the veranda. It is impossible to see the trellis for purple flowers. It is calm in the big rooms.

Aunt Bessie and Ruth arrive tomorrow, and Ruth will bring her boys. They will play here on the sand, dash in and out of the water. In the evenings, they will search the beach for chipchips. Sit around the mahogany table and play cards in the golden light of the hurricane lamps.

Last night Ada and Flora went outside to look at the stars. They are especially bright here – Orion, the Plough, Sirius. Ada has explained to Flora, it is not the star you see but the light left behind when a star has gone.

Aunt Bessie tells Ada she can stay here as long as she wants. The summer stretches out before them.

When she returns to Trinidad, Ada has agreed with Horatio and Grace to go to Siparia. Apparently the field is still black and nothing has grown there. Together they will plant heliconia, hibiscus, jasmine, elephant grass, a silk cotton tree.

NOTE FROM THE AUTHOR

FORTUNE was inspired by the real-life events of the tragic Dome Fire in 1928 in which 17 people lost their lives. In writing this novel, I drew on Father Anthony De Verteuil's excellent essay about the Dome Fire from his book, *Eight East Indian Immigrants*; I also read the novel, *Creole Magic* by Yseult Bridges (aka Tristram Hill), and *Tales from the Derrick Floor* by Mody C. Boatright and William A. Owens. Ultimately, of course, *Fortune* is a work of fiction, and the characters who appear in it are the creations of my imagination.

Acknowledgements

I am extremely grateful for input, especially in the early days of research, to Marlene Soodeen and Frances Mendonca. Also, Angelo Bissessarsingh, who spoke to me at great length about this time in history, and who took me to the site where the tragedy took place. Gratitude also to Reg Potter, Bridget Brereton, John Frampton, Gerry Besson and Adrian Camps-Campins who filled in many gaps about oil and Trinidad society in 1920s. Thank you Lorraine Nero and Dr Glenroy Taitt for providing me with a desk in the quiet, peaceful air-conditioned Special Collections at UWI.

Thanks to Arts Council England for funding the writing of this book, and support from Hosking Housing Trust. Thank you Gary Hesketh for your commitment and talent in the artwork cover design. Thanks to superstars Geoff Duffield, Shona Abhyankar and Emma Dawson. Thanks to Tindal Street Fiction Group, Jonathan Davidson and Saskia Watkins. Thank you, Judy Raymond for your support in the press; Chris Cleave for your wonderful encouragement.

Huge thanks to those who patiently read various drafts of the manuscript: Jane Harris, Neel Mukherjee, Mez Packer, Natasha Carlish, Andrew Palmer, Carol Barnes, Mick Lawson, Gaynor Williams, John Williams, Kerry O Grady, Luke Brown, Alan Mahar, Alan Beard, Dr Kenneth Ramchand and Keith Jardim.

Special thanks to those who were there when the road was

hard: Alanah Julius, Ira Mathur, Brigitte Jacquillard, Norma Roche, Helen Tachos. Thank you Lucy Luck, my agent, who has supported me all these years. And Maria Alvarez, literary angel, I can't thank you enough.

I want to express my gratitude to my mother who has always nurtured my love of stories, and who planted the seed of *Fortune*. Also, Barrie Fernandez, Stan Soodeen, Lisa Fernandez.

I also want to remember Wayne Brown, my dear teacher and mentor.

Enormous thanks to Peepal Tree Press – Jeremy Poynting, who helped to make this a bigger and better book and Hannah Bannister for her great support, along with Adam Lowe, for the energy and commitment in getting *Fortune* out there.

Finally, heartfelt gratitude to my husband, Lee Thomas, for your love and support throughout this journey. I couldn't have done it without you. And also to my daughter, Amelie Smyth Thomas, light of my life, thank you for being you.

Investors visiting the Dome site

Close-up of a derrick c. 1920s

A photograph of a man, probably
Bobby Wade, covered in oil

The Apex site c. 1920s

Press photograph of the car that triggered the Dome fire

Aftermath of the Dome fire

ABOUT THE AUTHOR

Amanda Smyth is Irish Trinidadian, and author of three novels. Her first novel, *Black Rock*, won the Prix du Premier Roman Etranger, was nominated for an NAACP award, short listed for McKitterick Prize, and selected as an Oprah Winfrey Summer Read. *Black Rock* was chosen as one of Waterstones New Voices, and translated into five languages. Her second novel, *A Kind of Eden*, set in contemporary Trinidad, was published in 2013 and optioned as a TV series. Her fiction and poetry have appeared in *New Writing*, *London Magazine*, *The Times Literary Supplement*, *Harvard Review* and broadcast on BBC Radio 4. Fortune, her third novel, is based on the tragic Dome fire in Trinidad, 1928. Amanda teaches creative writing at Arvon, Skyros, Greece, and Coventry University. She lives in Leamington Spa with her husband and daughter.